Season of The Ruiner Book II: Sojourn

Abigail Linhardt

SpaceDragon Creations

Season of the Runer Book II: Sojourn

A SpaceDragon Creations book

This book is a work of fiction. Names, characters, places, and incidents either are the product of the author's imagination or are used fictitiously. Any resemblance to actual persons, living or dead, events, cultures, or locales is entirely coincidental.

Cover art by Andrei Bat. Edited by JH Fleming. Formatted by SpaceDragon Creations. Chapter font by Walter Velez.

ACKNOWLEDGMENTS

Once again, special thanks to my beta readers Kate Seger and KN Nguyen. This year has been rough and I owe you a black oath of my own: thanks for reading the drafts and making it better!

Also thanks to my editor JH Fleming for reading through the first book in order to edit this one. Your input, comments, and edits are invaluable! I'll see you soon for the third one!

For Mum. For caring that I'm trying. And, yes, moms count. :)

Season of the Runer Book II

Sojourn

Abigail Linhardt

SpaceDragon Creations

CONTENTS

Chapter 1
The Monk

THE EYES OF THE XIAN CAPTAIN BORED INTO THE BACK OF Tzarik's head while his lithe fingers tied one of the many knots that held the sweeping, triangular yellow sail still. The sails, unlike any he had ever seen, folded like a dragon's wing when not in use. The early morning wind picked up, sending him and many other men into the yardarms and rigging to unfurl them and catch the breeze. The wind had vanished two days ago. The Xians didn't hide their distrust of the dark foreigners on the ship, eyeing them before saying prayers to gods Tzarik had never heard of. He made himself part of the crew in the hopes of getting the suspicious glares off him. Nothing quelled them.

"Al'Myrah!" the captain barked to Tzarik, calling him after his place of origin. "Get up that mast and release that last knot. You forgot one. Or do they not count past ten on your sandy continent?"

Biting his tongue, Tzarik scampered back up the mast on the narrow rope ladder. He checked the top every few steps to make sure the crew above him did not loose the ladder. One man had fallen from the slanted yardarm and broken every limb. He had no intention of doing the same, especially out of spite.

"Don't touch it!" he growled when one crewman jokingly reached towards the swinging ladder.

The man elbowed his fellow Xian in the ribs, speaking in their fast, staccato language and laughing. Unabashedly, he pointed to Tzarik. He ended his joke by braying like a goat then winking at Tzarik before vanishing into the spiny sails.

Reaching up, Tzarik pulled the flapping end of the rope, releasing the last bit holding the sail. With a deep snapping flap, the sail dropped. The accordion-like creases smoothed out. The sail caught the wind, instantly drifting portside. Tzarik gripped the yardarm as the ladder swung violently with the un-tethered sail. Wrapping one leg around the rope ladder, he gripped it until the sail hit the mast, stopping with a jolt. The impact whipped the Runer so hard, his leg slipped out from the rungs, flinging him wide over the choppy waters below. Grunting, he held on with both hands to save himself from a fall that would surely kill him.

Catching his breath, he slid down the ladder, landing hard on the deck. His heart pounded so hard in his ears, he almost missed the captain laughing.

"Ignorant sand rat!" he chortled in Al'Myrahn. "Fasten the sail first." He turned to his crew and no doubt repeated in Xian what he'd said, but added a few choice jokes at the end. The crew snickered, eyes on the fallen Runer.

A silver-haired and gray-furred Masahk with monkeylike features approached Tzarik. He pulled his hands out from his orange and yellow robes and hoisted him to his feet. A wide, rawhide belt encircled his narrow waist, laden with marble-sized jade beads, mini scrolls, and other religious trinkets.

Tzarik clenched his jaw to reply to the insufferable sailors, the Masahk whispered, "Wait, Runer. Do not lash out here."

Leading Tzarik to the upper deck of the small vessel, his long-fingered hand pressed into Tzarik's back to force him to walk away, the Masahk smiled out at the ocean.

"Do not let them see you angry," he said calmly. He closed his eyes and inhaled the ocean breeze. "Breathe with me, Runer."

"I was never one for meditation and breathing," Tzarik said dryly, gripping the rail.

The Masahk smiled knowingly. "Of course. What kind of man are you?"

Tzarik eyed the Masahk sideways. "My apprentice and I hail from Al'Myrah."

"I gathered that from the way they speak of you." The Masahk's long mouth still smiled gently. "Why did you leave?"

Turning in to the breeze to cool his temper enough to answer without hostility, he said, "We tangled with the wrong man. A scholar. We tricked him when we found out his dark motives. Destroyed an entire city hunting a..." He stopped. How would someone like a monk react to hearing they'd hunted a necromancer?

The monk didn't press him. "I do apologize for my people."

"The Xians?"

"Of course! I am Xian. There are Masahk tribes all over the map. My mother is an immortal Alikan Masahk and my human father was born and raised here." Swinging his legs up onto the rail, his long silver monkey tail whipping out from under the robes to balance him, the Masahk sat cross-legged. He gently placed his open hands onto his knees, palms up.

"You a monk of some kind?" Tzarik asked, glancing again at the string of jade beads and a thick, silver cylinder with ornate patterns hanging from the monastic robes.

"I thought Runers were mind readers," the Masahk said, smiling again.

Tzarik shook his head. "Just observant."

"Of course I am a monk. We try to make it obvious with the orange and yellow robes. Keeps us safe when we travel."

"Why?"

The round ear sticking out from the monk's long silver hair twitched. "Holy men and women are harassed far less than, say, a Runer." He opened his left eye to catch Tzarik's reaction. "Not all on Xia are as these sailors," he added when Tzarik didn't reply. "They are closer to pirates than good, Xian men. I am sorry. Don't judge all of us by them."

The Runer nodded, chancing a look at the monk. "Every people has its asses. I may be one of them. I'm not as forgiving as my companion."

The monk pressed his palms together in front of his chest, raised them on an inhale, and brought them back down, exhaling. "I noticed her kindness. I believe they are fascinated by her. Tall, yellow hair, Al'Myrahn skin. And she speaks their language. They like that."

"I cannot learn every continent's language," Tzarik snapped.

"Xia has three," the monk said proudly. "Some might call them regional dialects, but they are different enough. With so many dynasties, houses, and the fact that Xia is one of the oldest continents, we cannot help but be diverse."

"Great." Tzarik pushed away from the rail and turned around.

Sybal had taken to the Xians since they'd taken to her. The first day on the ship, she'd quibbled with the captain in his own tongue. That had earned them his good graces so far. Tzarik had had no idea she spoke more than one language and dared not ask her what else she spoke for fear she'd make him feel inferior. He couldn't even read his own language. He'd tried to make himself useful with the crew, but all that had earned him was mockery in tongues he couldn't understand.

"Where is she?" he asked, realizing he had not seen Sybal since the night before.

Standing up on the dipping and rising railing, his balance perfect, the monk turned and pointed towards the front. "She looks to the east. Ah!" he exclaimed in delight. "My ship."

Tzarik followed the Masahk's gaze through the masts and crowd of crewmen. Near the low prow of the ship, Sybal stood with a brass telescope held to her eye. Squinting, he caught what she looked at. Another ship, far more colorful and in the shape of some sort of lizard-like animal, slowly drifted towards them. He followed the monk down the steps, across the deck, and up to where Sybal stood.

"Tell me, Sybal-kim, what do you see?" the Xian Masahk asked, clasping his hands behind his back.

Coming up beside her, Tzarik looked out over the sunlit waters. The rising orb lit up the approaching ship in flashes of gold and blue. He pulled out his own telescope and joined her. The ship was shaped in the likeness of a red dragon. Jade and gold trim covered every rail and the swooping sides of the prow. More orange-robed figures milled about the deck.

"Are they coming aboard us?" Sybal asked.

"Most likely," the monk answered. "They pray to the north, keeping the darkness of The Frozen Nation at bay."

"Prayer alone will keep monsters behind icy walls," Tzarik mumbled.

"Stop it," Sybal snapped, lowering the glass to glare at her mentor.

The monk, however, smiled and gave a monkeylike chuckle. "So far, it has, Runer. The monks go out to the northernmost isle of Xia for a time of prayer. This ship must have been blown off course. The weather has been somewhat unpredictable of late."

The Xian captain, overhearing them, laughed darkly. Behind

his lips, gaps showed three missing teeth. "Or you could plow the monsters."

Tzarik arched his brow, curious. Only once had he run into someone who thought Runers fornicated with monsters—but at that time, he'd learned that many believed that of his kind.

"That's barbaric," Sybal interjected.

"It's what royalty does," the captain said, shrugging and leering still. "Rumors say our Di-Huan slept with the Great White Snake."

An intrusive image sprang into Tzarik's mind, vivid and terrifying. He winced and glanced sideways at the monk for an explanation.

"It's not what you think," he offered evenly. "And the Di-Huan has many children and many wives."

"Ha!" the captain laughed. He turned away from them and moved to the railing again to shout at the oncoming ship.

Sybal blanched at the rude remarks. "How can he speak so of his own king?"

"Because it's probably true," Tzarik cut in. "The great rulers of our continents think they can do whatever they please."

The monk shook his head, lowering it sadly. "I believe you say things you don't mean, Runer."

"He does," Sybal said, smiling wryly, pushing against the railing to arch her back into a stretch. "But Runers can say things with contempt because we are protected."

"Oh?" the monk inquired while Tzarik also inclined his head curiously.

Sybal smiled, biting her bottom lip and sinking her head into her shoulders shyly. "I feel stronger as a Runer than I ever did as an heiress."

"How long have you hunted?" the monk asked kindly.

Tzarik noted the way his tone lilted up, humoring Sybal's

musings. She might be a Runer, but he still saw her as a rash apprentice.

She went on. "I've felt the stigma of being a Runer, but commoners don't understand the power we hold." She pulled her runes out from her leather armor. "It may be penance for a crime, but it's also a blessing. I've learned so much in the last year and think I could take on stronger monsters if I had to."

The Masahk took a deep breath, rising with a wave that pushed against the ship. "You have a pride I rarely see in Runers, lady Runer. Are you proud of your sulfates, master Runer?"

The direct question took Tzarik by surprise. Deciding against thinking too deeply about it and unearthing any suppressed convictions, he quipped, "It's a punishment. And young Runers should not boast about it. You don't understand fully yet."

"Don't chide me," Sybal gibed back just as quickly. "I've experienced more in this last year than probably any other Runer. I've lost everything and started completely new. And I've done well, thank you very much." She raised her chin proudly and faced the other ship.

In his heart, Tzarik knew she meant well. Still, she was impetuous and envisioned herself as some kind of hero. He'd never seen himself that way and didn't know how to talk her down.

"Ah, young warriors," the monk mused. "Eager to prove themselves. You should be proud of how far you've come. But, as the Great White Dragon says, 'The man who leaps in pride once he reaches the summit of the mountain does so at the edge.'"

Sybal sighed, shoulders dropping. "Yes, yes, of course. Very wise, sira monk. But I look forward to staying on Xia. Proving my power. I need to feel my own strength after all that's happened. I... I don't want to suffer weakness anymore."

"You will be a unique addition to our continent," he replied kindly. He glanced again at Tzarik without moving his head.

Behind them, the Xian captain shouted commands to his crew. The men immediately snapped into action, scurrying like disturbed ants.

"What? Why?" Sybal cried.

The monk dropped his hands from where they rested clasped at his back, his ears twitching.

"What did he say?" Tzarik asked, glaring angrily at the Xians and their foreign chatter.

"He will not let the others board," Sybal translated.

"Exactly!" the captain snapped, passing them at the front, glaring at the monk's ship. "The monks from Hikomi are not welcome aboard my vessel. They can wait until the fishermen from their village come out."

"But something could be wrong," the Masahk pleaded. "They should not be this far west. We need to take them in, hear what has happened."

The captain spat over the side, cursing. "No, we do not. They have a sickness. I can see the ill ones even now as they bring them up from below. We will not risk a frozen plague. Let Hikomi deal with their own."

Confused, Tzarik asked, "What's wrong with the lowlands?"

The captain spat again. "Loyalists."

Sybal pulled Tzarik aside. Leaning down towards him, she whispered, "Xia has been on the brink of civil war for a decade. Their monarchy comes and goes with each season of a different house's power."

The shifting monarchy and houses of power sounded like a nightmare to Tzarik. "Never knowing who is in power or who you stand against sounds exhausting," he mused.

Sybal frowned slightly. "I thought you'd been to Wu-Tang before."

The Runer nodded. "Once. For a day. Long ago."

Behind the dragon ship, the continent of Xia rose up out of the ocean like a great mountain peak. The continent, shaped like a cone with the royal city at the top, was made up entirely of mountains, valleys, and layers of grassy prairies. Filled with crevices of villages, once among the hills and valleys, it would be impossible to see the next village over. Each civilization was cut off from the next unless one resided farther up the continent. Looking down from somewhere higher up, like the province of Shiuki, every village would come into view. Those above saw all. When the continent had first come into view days ago, it had looked like a silver spike covered in moss. Then, as they drew closer, it almost flattened out, expanding over miles, until it took over the horizon.

Sybal looked up, shading her eyes. "The Royal City, as far as I know, has never been named since the monarch changes so often, sitting atop the mountain continent, everything in its range of vision."

Suddenly feeling like he was being watched, Tzarik eyed the shores and how they climbed up into the sky. "It's bigger than I thought. It looked small three days ago."

"It's an entire country," Sybal reminded him.

"I am begging you," the monk cut in, speaking to the captain. "I will pay you to take my brothers abroad and bring them inland."

The captain swore. "Our Di-Huan is mad to finance the temple monks as it is. He wastes time and gold with the useless monks. The Wushito would never waste Xia's wealth like this!"

Tzarik began to see the division already, and they had not docked yet. The way the captain had spat the word "loyalist" made him think perhaps he was not fond of the emperor, the Di-Huan. He didn't want to get involved. They were there to hide.

"I will pay you as well," Sybal interjected. "I will tend to the sick men so you need not get near them."

Closing his eyes, Tzarik willed himself to be patient with Sybal.

Before the captain could reply, a cry went out from a watchman high above them. Whatever he shouted put the men into a frenzy again. This time, blackpowder guns came out and cannons were pulled up to the rail.

"What happened?" Tzarik barked to Sybal.

"Pirates!" she shouted over the ruckus.

The silver-furred monk drew a circle over his heart and shot a quick prayer from his lips.

The captain shouted at him, pointing to the deck. Tzarik guessed he'd ordered the monk below deck as his prayers were not looked upon with favor above.

"Don't just stand there, desert rat!" the captain shouted to Tzarik. "Help the men load the cannons. Or do you want to sink to the bottom of the Shezai Ocean?"

Unsure how many more insults he could take from the Xian captain, he clenched his jaw. Sybal caught his eye over the black-haired heads of the scrambling sailors. Pleading with her large, blue eyes, she begged him to do as the captain said. The monks—innocent in her eyes—were worthy of saving from the likes of Xian pirates.

"The eastern pirates are cruel," she said when the captain ran down to the main deck. "These are holy men, peaceful. They don't deserve to be attacked and flayed by the likes of them."

"We can't save everyone," Tzarik growled back. "This isn't our fight."

Sybal whipped her head to the tall continent in the distance and then back to him. "It is if you want to reach Xia. The pirates are between us and the docks. We can't run. They have the wind."

Pretending he had any idea what she meant, Tzarik raised his chin, his hair catching the breeze. He glared into the sun where the monks unfurled the sails, desperate to move again. Even from here among the commotion on the deck, he could hear their prayers wailed to the skies. The pirates, two ships visible around the bend of the continent, gained on them. The ocean waves broke up, frothing, around their prows. Ugly masks with glaring, mad-eyed demons topped the front. The pirates ignored the monks, coming straight for them instead.

The captain screamed something to his men.

"They're going to board us!" Sybal shouted to Tzarik. "He wants you to fire a cannon."

Giving in, the Runer gripped his leather string of stones around his neck and followed the motions of the sailors, loading a cannon. The mouths of the blackpowder guns were shaped like roaring dragons, the pricker sticking out of the end of a long, tasseled tale. He figured out quickly how to load and aim the cannon; his work with other war machines influenced his instincts. He quickly learned the countdown in Xian and which word meant to fire.

They unloaded two broadsides into the pirates in a matter of minutes, but it didn't do enough damage.

"Here they come," Sybal said, gasping and gripping Tzarik's shoulder.

The pirates were visible now. They prepared ropes and grappling hooks, the dragon ship full of monks completely forgotten. Tzarik weighed them like any other monster he'd hunted: some were leaner, faster. Others flexed their brutish arms.

"Sybal, listen," he ordered, turning to face her. "Do not play the hero. Watch out for yourself above all else."

She nodded. "I'll have your back, don't worry."

He didn't worry about himself. He worried about her, constantly throwing herself in harm's way to save people and creatures she didn't even know. One day, that would get her killed if she weren't careful. He had no idea how to bear the loss of her, especially by her own hand.

The smoke from the black-mouthed, roaring cannons blinded him. His ears rang by the time the pirate ships straddled each side of the traveling vessel. He caught flashes of Sybal's bright hair through the smoke but could not lock on to her location as she darted among the sailors. The pirates tossed their ropes and pulled the ship steady. Somewhere, the captain shouted an order and the slithering of swords being drawn hissed around him. He unsheathed his scimitar and waited. A few crewmen aimed the cannons down, blowing holes in the pirates' ships below the waterline.

Like ghosts, the pirates leapt on board, appearing through the smoke with shouts and roars. Immediate chaos erupted on the small deck. The strange, straight, single-edged swords of the Xians flashed in the smokey sun. Some pulled tiny black bombs from their silken shirts, lighting them and tossing them below deck. Screams and more explosions deafened the Runer.

One pirate approached him, stopping and locking eyes with him. He realized his icy stare unnerved the Xian. Smirking, he rapidly drew halat for a quick barrier of protection, then spun in to attack the pirate. When their blades crossed, the straight sword of the pirate slid up and down the curved scimitar. This threw both men off and each retreated to get their bearings. The pirate reached into his robe and threw something so quickly, Tzarik hardly had time to register his enemy's movements. A thin, triangular dagger of some kind hissed through the air and nicked his shoulder. The thing was so sharp he didn't feel the pain until after the blood dampened his tunic sleeve.

Seeing him curiously, look for the blade, the pirate attacked again. With quick, leaping spins, he disoriented the Runer. Trying to keep up with the fast fighting style of the Xian scrambled

Tzarik's brain until he was forced into a retreat. Backing up, he kept his eye on the quick pirate. Blinded by the smoke, he didn't see the one behind him. He backed right into the sea dog. The pirate whipped his dirty hand over Tzarik's mouth, pulling his head back to expose his throat. A cold blade pressed to his flesh, angled to slice.

Before he could raise his scimitar to attempt an escape, the unmissable scream of a monkey cracked through the smoke. The orange-clad Masahk leapt down from the rigging. While he fell, he unleashed the silver cylinder at his side. It sprang open into a long, metal staff, which the monk spun around his head in a deadly arc. He bent backwards to clear a larger space, cracking a half dozen pirate skulls in the process.

Tzarik leapt off the deck, flipping over his assailant's head and landing on the railing. Kicking, he disarmed the pirate. The Masahk advanced on three limbs, one hand holding his staff out ready to strike. The pirate fled.

"Thank you," Tzarik gasped, quickly drawing artiah over the small wounds on his neck and shoulder.

"We are not safe yet," the Masahk sighed. "We're trapped between the ships. In a matter of minutes, they will no doubt shoot our hull."

The captain ran past them, screaming. "We are doomed. Over the sides!"

Fending off a few more attackers, Tzarik scanned the deck for Sybal. She should have been easy to see: taller, her hair catching the sun.

"Sybal!" he shouted when he didn't find her right away.

"No time!" the captain wailed. "We are done for!"

"Look!" the monk cried, pointing southeast. "Three ships. Jade sails. It is Wushito!"

CHAPTER 2
WUSHITO

HAVING NO IDEA WHAT IT MEANT THAT GOLDEN SHIPS WITH jade sails approached with rapid speed, Tzarik whipped his head around, hunting for Sybal.

"Keep calm." The monk's face broke into a gleeful smile. "The Wushito will save us!"

"Damn the Di-Huan and bless the Wushito!" the captain called over the railings.

The monk glared at the captain with his yellow eyes. To Tzarik he said, "Men like him keep the civil unrest alive. The Wushito love and protect Xia just as much as the one on the Sun Throne."

Tzarik growled. "I don't care. Where is Sybal?"

The monk smiled. "Your care for her is endearing."

Tzarik corrected, "I am bound to her. That is all."

Nodding as he cracked another pirate skull, the monk said, "Of course, Runer," before leaping away into the rigging to keep the pirates at bay while the mysterious ships made their way closer. Firing another barrage, one of the pirate ships tilted, sinking below the salt waves.

The scuttled ship sank so fast, Tzarik almost didn't see the crest on the sails as they sank. Old and faded, he still made out the serpent and the lion-maned dragon entwined before it vanished beneath the rippling waves. No doubt one of the many houses vying for the Xian Sun Throne once upon a time. If he could help it, he'd stay out of the continent's politics while they hid for a time.

Once the first ship's demonic figurehead touched the water, the pirates sounded their retreat. Stabbing and shooting wildly on their way out, a few souls left with them. Tzarik snapped his wrist to draw buhkar to avoid another attack only to frighten the pirate as his form vanished into black mist.

Faster than they arrived, the last pirate ship skirted out of sight, taking a wide turn around the northern top of the continent. The other three new arrivals dropped their golden anchors. A long, red boat, also shaped like a roaring dragon, with a team of perfectly in sync rowers, glided to their ship. A man in silky blue robes with silver trim climbed up onto their ship. He held his hands together beneath wide sleeves, like the monk, but no other adornments gave him away. Tzarik read by his quality of clothing that he was wealthy. A silver comb perched at the base of his high ponytail almost looked like a badge of office. Xia and its ways were foreign to him, anything else about the man hidden in a strange culture.

The man bowed to the captain, smiling pleasantly. They exchanged words in a rapid back and forth. Tzarik clenched his jaw in annoyance when Sybal's voice translated for him as she appeared right beside him, catching her breath.

"He is a leader of something called the Wushito," she supplied quickly, catching Tzarik's impatience.

Two others climbed up behind the savior. One was a lithe, distinctly Masahk female with a snake's lower half. Her white skin and violet, slitted eyes scanned the crew. The second, less Masahk with thick, defined arms, had the hair of a fox and small tufted ears where a human's would be. His human traits for more prevalent; he had very little red fur over his flesh. They flanked the boarding man closely, hands on their bow and sword.

"They watch over Xia, it sounds like. He is honored, and pleased to offer services. The captain called him Wu-ShanBao—"

At the mention of his name, the gilded Xian turned to face her. With his direct attention, Tzarik saw he was older than he'd first thought. A few smile wrinkles and frown lines showed in the now risen sun. The viper Masahk's eyes snapped to Sybal.

"I am Wu-ShanBao." The older man bowed politely to Sybal. "No one mentioned Runers were coming to Xia."

Sybal stammered for a reply, awkwardly half-bowing to the man as she searched for an answer.

"We didn't know we needed to send word," Tzarik said over his apprentice's babbling. He gripped her arm and pulled her up out of her embarrassing bow, training his gaze on the old man before them. The way Wu-ShanBao watched them closely almost made him feel exposed. Like the man was waiting for him to make the wrong move. "We won't be any trouble."

"Al'Myrahns on Xia?" the viperous Masahk hissed. Her snake body allowed her to uncoil, towering over the others. "Sounds like spies, Master ShanBao." A purple, forked tongue slipped out and back between her black lips.

"Peace, please, Wu-Zhiang," the man said calmly. "She is right, Runer. There are no Runers on Xia. Wushito has sanctuaries, but none have an Al'Myrahn majority. Why are you here?"

"We seek sanctuary, actually," Sybal offered.

Unsure if she should share the business or not, Tzarik locked on to Wu-ShanBao's person, scanning for a reaction. The man gave nothing away apart from turning back to look to his foxlike Masahk.

He replied, "We are pleased to be of service to you. And glad our friends," he clapped the captain on his shoulders, "have arrived back safe and sound. To business?" He motioned his Masahk guards to disembark and followed them over the rail, the captain shouting a thanks to them again. Pushing past the Runers, he grinned darkly and mumbled, "Best of luck to you on Xia, foreigners."

⌇⌇

"HE TURNED SOUR QUICKLY," Sybal mumbled. She flipped the reins over her white steed and led it down the gangplank onto the golden stone streets of a fishing village in the province of Wu-Tang.

"I never liked him," Tzarik grumbled, hitting the side of his horse to get it to exhale so he could tighten his saddle.

"Did it ever occur to you that you not liking someone makes them not like you?" Sybal offered kindly.

The jab stung, but Tzarik's mind was too occupied with scanning the streets, the sloping roofs of the homes, the ornate gables of a small, three-layered temple near the outskirts. The one day he'd spent in the cities of Wu-Tang as a younger man had taught him a lot about ducking and hiding among the masses, but nothing about the people. Based on his experience with the captain and the words that had sounded like a warning from the Wushito man, his danger senses heightened. Everything looked like a threat.

"Put your hood up," he warned Sybal when two Xians did a double take at them passing.

"Tzarik." She put her hand on his overly-tense shoulder. "Calm down. No one here knows us. They won't attack us just because we're foreigners. They do trade with Singad; they've seen Al'Myrahns before."

Her hand didn't leave his shoulder, gripping it like a disapproving mother until he rolled it, trying to relax.

Making their way through the fishing village, they walked out through marshy prairies, following a dirt path up the hill. Everywhere in Xia lead uphill to the top of the conical continent, unless one traveled towards the sea. They walked for hours, passing small homesteads, villages, a small shrine at a crossroads, a man with a cart and ox, before the city of Wu-Tang came into view.

Perched among hills, towering trees, and valleys lush and green, seeing far was nearly impossible. The horizon rose and fell, all mountains, pink trees with fragrant petals, blue rivers and rolling green hills. Sybal stopped and looked at the stone city from the hill they'd just crested. Below them, the structures looked like a tiny model and the moving people like black ants, hurrying about their tasks. Red and golden roofs peaked out from the landscape, topped with terrifying creatures of jade and stone, open maws roaring to the north. She panted, gasping for breath.

"Never have I scaled so many hills," she breathed, clutching her chest. "This entire continent must be a mountain."

Tzarik nodded. "Looked like it from the ship." He squinted up into the now setting sun. "Disappears into the clouds."

Above them, a single, thick line of clouds circled what they could see of the very top. The longer he looked, the more Tzarik swore they were not clouds, but a glittery, pearl-encrusted dragon. He'd never played the game other children did of spotting creatures in the stars or clouds, but this one came to him easily. The circle rotated. If it actually had been a dragon, the creature might have looked like it guarded the top of the mountains. As it moved over him, he swore a face with teeth, a mane, and long tendrils elegantly flowing from its monstrous lips came into view. He gasped as the monster form came more into focus.

"Oh," Sybal breathed despondently, breaking his vision.

Curious, but too out of breath to ask, Tzarik instead followed her gaze. She took out a glass and glared down at a palace-like structure, half obscured in trees with long, sweeping branches. The large red front gate was locked with a plank. Behind it, a crest with an entwined serpent and lion-maned dragon stood out in gold.

"I saw that crest," Tzarik said, squinting through his own glass. "On the sail of the pirate ship." Reading the layout of the home the crest was attached to, he guessed it was a wealthy family. Sweeping walls surrounded it and a few other smaller homes. "You know it?"

Sybal nodded. "House Xiaoh. The man I killed."

Tzarik couldn't stop the surprise from raising his brows as he turned to look at Sybal. "You killed a man from House Xiaoh? I heard of their warlord's exile and crusade. Bloody."

"I did not kill just any man from House Xiaoh." Sybal sighed. "Whoang Xiaoh himself. Twice, in fact."

If he'd been a religious man, Tzarik would have sworn and drawn a holy symbol over his heart. Instead, a new respect for his apprentice rose in him. "They tried you for killing an evil man? And you chose runing?"

"Better this life than death." She looked meaningfully at Tzarik.

Ignoring her jibe, he slung himself up onto his horse. "We'll ride through the night. To another province. I know the city is not fond of its exile, but I'd rather not bring the murderer of the monarch of House Xiaoh into his city."

Sybal followed suit, glad to be off her feet for once, climbing onto her horse. "Do you know Xia well enough to find the next province?" she asked.

He shook his head. "We'll head up."

⤶

THE SHIUKI PROVINCE spanned most of the middle-north of the mountainous realm. Wooden signs, painted red, announced how near a traveler was several miles out. Once the sun went down, Tzarik did his best to stay the course north and up.

"I need to rest," Sybal panted on the sixth day, wiping sweat from her brow. "No matter how much I dab away at my face, the sweat always comes back stronger."

"It's the humidity," Tzarik explained, his tone rising, glad to know something she didn't for once. "The dense trees, the rain... Xia is a wet place."

Sybal stopped, gagging audibly and covering her nose. "What is that smell?"

He'd ignored the new feelings, smells, and flavors of the air, overcome by the myriad of new senses to learn. When she stopped, he noticed it: musty, thick, black. The smell of a rotting corpse in hot, humid air.

"What are you doing?" he barked.

Sybal dropped her reins and left the dirt path, following the rancid smell. "I want to see," she hissed, going into a crouch and flipping her hood up.

Giving is horse a sign to stay, he followed her away from their destination. The long leaves of the strange ferns dripped with condensation from a waterfall ahead of them. The foliage grew so thick, they didn't hear it as they approached.

"The valleys and hills make it near impossible to see or hear," Sybal mused.

They broke through the border and beheld the roaring white and blue waterfall. It spilled down from silvery rocks covered in patches of bright green moss. The basin, lined with similar silver pebbles, glittered in the moonlight. The full moon hung above, just peeking over the frothing spill of the water.

"Beautiful!" Sybal said, gasping.

Tzarik looked for the source of the smell. To their right, several yards away, a clearing surrounded a huge, white-barked tree with more pink blossoms than leaves. The petals fell gently onto the soft grass below. He nudged Sybal, pointing.

Hanging from the highest branches, at least a dozen eviscerated men and woman swung in the gentle breeze. On the trunk of the tree, a crude sign, painted in black, crisscrossing characters spelled out a vicious-looking message.

Sybal followed his gaze and gasped, covering her mouth again. The bodies rotted in various states of decay.

"What does it say?" he asked, pointing to the sign.

Clearing her throat and stepping closer, Sybal squinted at it. "It's old Xian, I think. It's not typical wording. There are some I understand, though. I think it says, 'Spies of House Xioah, you shall not enter the Hallow City.'"

"Your warlord was greatly hated," Tzarik mused. The longer he looked up at the gray-fleshed bodies, the more his stomach squirmed with unease. "We need to keep a low profile, Sybal. Tensions are tighter than I imagined on Xia. We don't want to get involved in their civil disputes."

She came abreast with him, drawing a holy symbol over her heart for the dead. They might've been innocent. "We have the power to help turn a tide. Shouldn't we, if the opportunity comes?"

Gathering his patience, forcing himself to not sigh in exasperation, he said, "No."

"Then what do we do?"

"We hunt. Stay busy. Out of sight."

Sybal unsheathed her orichalcum scimitar. "Let's cut them down. Save some of their dignity. Not all from Wu-Tang are as guilty as Xiaoh."

Behind them, thick stalks of bamboo clicked together as a body quickly rushed through them. Tzarik grabbed Sybal, staying her.

Signaling her to be quiet, he flicked his head behind them. The watcher rushed clumsily through the ferns, coming behind the left side of the Runers.

"Do you see him?" Tzarik asked, unsheathing his own scimitar, not turning around to look.

"No," Sybal hissed, glaring into the moon-lit darkness. "I heard a sword coming out of a leather sheath, though."

Pricking his ears, Tzarik heard a gasp. Too late, he realized it was an inhale.

"Gah!" Sybal clutched her shoulder, dropping her sword. A dart with a jade shaft and red feathers protruded from her arm. "I can't feel my arm!" she gasped, pinching it.

Throwing himself in front of her, Tzarik drew halat slowly, watching the shadows. "Show yourself, coward!" he roared into the night. To Sybal he asked, "Is the sensation spreading?"

"Yes," she panted. "I feel it in my lungs. I can't breathe!" Pressing her left hand to her chest, she strained for breath, falling to her knees.

"Runers, leave!" an accented, rasping voice roared from behind them. The assailant spoke Al'Myrahn, but badly. "I see your rainbow swords. No hide from me!"

Sybal, turning blue, lurched forward as another dart hit her in the back. She fell onto her side now, clawing at her throat for air.

Torn between pursuing the shadow, which he now saw perched in the flowery tree, and saving Sybal, Tzarik hesitated.

"Bad move!" the shadow cackled.

Tzarik saw it reloading a tube with another dart. Whipping out his small black bow, he fired sloppily at the shadow. Despite the lack of aim, the arrow buzzed past the shadow's head, frightening it enough to drop the dart and vanish behind the trunk of the tree.

Checking Sybal, he begged her, "Stay awake. I'll be back."

"Wait...!" she gasped feebly. She reached out to snag his fleeing cloak but missed.

Tzarik flipped his black cloak over his head and walked low, hiding under the ferns. He found the smeared dirt at the base of the tree, showing the shadow had run northwest. He took three quick steps before he almost ran into the dart-wielding assassin. Shaken that he had not seen him before, Tzarik dropped below the ferns. The shadow didn't move. Training his eyes on it, he saw that it was actually a *real* shadow. He could make out the forest through the standing form. Standing up, he passed his hand through the middle. No distinct details gave away the form. It wore a cloak and had a sword at its side. Tilting his head, he glanced around.

"Foreigners are so easy to trick!"

With a smokey snap, the real assassin appeared behind him. Gripping Tzarik over his mouth to stop his cry, he shoved a narrow blade between his lower ribs. The man's hand clamped over his mouth and nose, suffocating him as his muscles contracted around the narrow blade.

A rippling whir whizzed past his and the shadow's head. With a thunk, a star-shaped weapon he'd never seen before in his life wedged into a tree before them. Clearly taken off guard, the assassin dropped Tzarik and turned, asking a question in Xian.

Tzarik bent over his wound. Behind him, the shadow assassin rapidly pleaded in Xian before his voice was cut off with a hiss of metal from the other arrival.

"You have gotten yourself into quite a deep rice field, Runer."

His rescuer gripped his arm, stopping him from collapsing. The older man who'd fought off the pirates days ago came into Tzarik's view. He pocketed the throwing star after pulling it from the tree.

"You?" Tzarik asked, gripping the knife in his side.

"Don't pull it out!" The man stayed Tzarik's hand, pulling him up and walking him back to Sybal. "If you do, you'll bleed out. It needs to be tended to quickly once the blade is removed. I will take you to my home. Your lady is in dire need as well."

Not arguing, Tzarik mumbled a thanks to the man. "I can take care of myself, though," he added.

Seeing Sybal lying still, he yanked the knife from his side. His blood quickly flowed, and a stinging pain that should not have accompanied the removal of the small blade seared his flesh. He pulled the runes out from his tunic and slowly drew artiah over the wound.

"I told you not to!" the older man said.

"This is the healing rune," Tzarik explained. "It will mend me well enough to travel."

Eyes wide, the old man watched as Tzarik's skin knit together just enough to stop the bleeding. "Impressive. But your lady friend is not so lucky. That poison will stop her heart if we do not get her an antidote."

"Do you have one?" he asked. Seeing Sybal's blue lips and whitening eyes, he fell to his knees and drew artiah over her chest.

Tears dribbled from the corners of her eyes into her hair. Feebly, she reached up and gripped the front of Tzarik's armor.

"Why isn't it working?" he shouted, drawing the rune again.

"Please, let me help you!" the Wushito man begged.

"I don't understand!" Tzarik roared, frantically drawing artiah one more time.

"Stop being a mule, Runer!" The man shoved Tzarik out of the way and lifted Sybal, helping her back to the horses. "Come with me if you want her saved and if you want to be kept safe!"

CHAPTER 3
HOUSE SHIKIRUMI

THE OLD MAN—TZARIK REMEMBERED HIS NAME TO BE Wu-ShanBao—led them up more rocky hills to the outskirts of the Shiuki province. He took long, steady strides, administering a draft to Sybal every minute or so. He explained to Tzarik it would keep her blood flowing, keep her alive, but they had to hurry before permanent damage set in to her internal organs.

Knowing interrogation would slow the man down, Tzarik let him take them into the beginnings of the city. Wu-ShanBao led them up one last green hill to a tall manor. Red walls with golden latticework in round windows surrounded the layered manor and dozens of smaller homes around it.

"My estate," the old man offered when he saw Tzarik taking in the royal structures before them.

The guards at the gate opened the doors when they saw their master approach with guests in tow. Some yelled to others to make way for the master of the estate. Wu-ShanBao shouted orders to a young white-haired young man of about fifteen who dashed to greet them. The young man nodded, turned, and sprinted back down the dirt path.

"The doctor is on her way, Runer." Wu-ShanBao guided them into the large, center home. "But we cannot wait."

Tzarik gripped Sybal's hand, flexing his fingers to relieve the tension. His jaw ached from clenching it the entire journey.

Reminding himself that snapping at their savior would only slow him down more, he kept his tongue and rage behind his bared teeth. He focused on Sybal. She hadn't turned any bluer and her breathing no longer came in gasping rasps. She was steady, but he didn't want to waste any more time. It was almost like this man wanted to test Tzarik's patience.

Finally, Wu-ShanBao lifted Sybal onto a bed in a room off to the side behind a sliding canvas door. The bed lay flush with the wooden floor. Colorful flat cushions and a low table waited nearby. Every move the man made—laying Sybal down, retrieving a blanket, checking out the window for the doctor—snapped a barrier in Tzarik's mind.

"Kneel beside her, Runer," Wu-ShanBao said kindly. "Breathe. I can hear your heart thumping like a horse's hooves down a mountain."

Glaring at their host, Tzarik knelt beside Sybal and placed his hand over her heart. To his surprise, her heart beat strong and steady. The rise and fall of her chest harnessed his panicked gasping, slowing it until they breathed in unison. Immediately, the tension in his head lessened and the hard muscles in his shoulders relaxed. Behind him, Wu-ShanBao smiled and hummed pleasantly.

The door to the manor burst open and two sets of feet hurried to the side room. When the door was pushed aside, an older woman with a long white braid and carrying a trunk clinking with bottles bowed quickly to Wu-ShanBao and presented it to him. The younger man from before stood behind her.

"Jin, you are not needed," Wu-ShanBao said sternly to the boy. He threw open the case and took out a thin silver knife.

"What about extra hands?" Jin asked.

"The Runer will supply." Wu-ShanBao waved his hand to Tzarik. "This woman is his apprentice, Jin. He will do well."

The young man Jin, hesitated. "Master ShanBao, I have never seen the viper poison stopped before. Let me stay and watch."

The older man ripped open Sybal's tunic and touched the knife to her flesh, poising to cut.

Quick to preserve her modesty, Tzarik covered her again. "Is this necessary?" he barked.

Wu-ShanBao stayed his hand. "I need to get to her heart, the center of the cycle."

Not convinced, Tzarik glanced between the gawking Jin and the stern face of Wu-ShanBao.

"Jin, out!" ShanBao snapped at the younger warrior. "Give the woman some privacy."

Grateful, Tzarik watched the boy file out without a fight. "Thank you," he mumbled to the Wushito man as an incision was made. Tzarik turned away, looking out a window.

"Don't look away!" Wu-ShanBao shouted. "I need your help."

When he turned back, the man held the knife out to him. He took it, setting it back into the chest of medical instruments.

"Now the cloth and the red vial," he instructed, keeping his eyes trained on the opening in Sybal's chest. "This is ruby sulfate. It will negate the poison, but we have to get it into her heart to circulate it, dispelling the rest of the poison."

"What was she poisoned with?" Tzarik asked, handing him the items.

The older man scanned Sybal quickly before looking back to his work and slowly injecting the ruby liquid. "Masahk venom. Very common on Xia. The viper tribe—House Liu—was a prominent house before House Xiaoh nearly wiped them out. Their poison does what viperous venom does: stiffens the blood, hardens the muscles—but there is an element science cannot explain that creates a different reaction every time. Purple vial." He held out his hand.

Tzarik found the purple liquid quickly and handed it to Wu-ShanBao. He filled the crystal syringe and administered it to another area.

"Why would someone from this House Liu attack us?" Tzarik asked.

Dabbing at his forehead, Wu-ShanBao replied, "Not any malevolent motive. Some simply fear foreigners. I myself have a Masahk general as my most trusted right hand. She is of House Liu. But we cannot be responsible for our kin, can we, Runer?" Wu-ShanBao gently touched Sybal's sweating chest. "This was weak venom," he mused. "Very weak. If it were stronger, there would be nothing I could do." He glanced up at Tzarik. "She was very lucky, Runer." Wiping some of Sybal's white blood away, he rubbed it between his fingers. He frowned, thoughtful. "This Runer blood might have helped save her."

Wu-ShanBao stilled, frowning down at Sybal's blood, feeling the sensation as he continued to rub his fingers together. He touched his tips together, slowly parting them, watching Sybal's blood string between his fingers. He hummed in deep thought.

"What are you doing?" Tzarik snapped.

"Having a thought," the man said apologetically. He handed Tzarik the syringe. "Needle and thread," he ordered, pressing down onto the open incision to stop the bleeding. As he stitched Sybal closed, he said, "We do not have Runers on Xia. Any chance you would let me study your blood?"

The familiar request turned Tzarik's stomach. "Do you not have monsters? Ghosts?" he asked instead of giving him an answer.

"Many," he said, nodding. "The likes of which you have probably never seen. Xian monsters will no doubt provide good training for your apprentice?"

Tzarik noted the question. "We are not here to train."

Cutting him off, Wu-ShanBao shouted, "You may enter, Jin."

Quickly dressing Sybal and lacing up her tunic, Tzarik covered her.

"Why are you here, Runer?" Wu-ShanBao asked, wiping his hands and repacking the instruments.

Jin brought in a tray of tea and a plate of food.

"I was curious when I saw you on the ship," Wu-ShanBao reiterated, handing Tzarik a cup with green tea inside. "We do not get Runers in Xia often."

"Why not?" Tzarik asked, once again deflecting the question away from him. He noticed the boy, Jin, gazing down at Sybal, eyes wide with awe.

Wu-ShanBao shrugged gently. "I supposed we've never had need of them."

"They avoid Xia," Jin offered.

"Most avoid Xia," Wu-ShanBao cut in quickly, glaring at the boy. "Unless you are a silk merchant."

"Why?" Tzarik asked. He took a drink of the green tea. The taste made his hair stand on end. The powder that made the tea clung to the roof of his mouth. He grimaced but tried to hide his disgust by taking another drink, only to wince worse at a second taste.

"Is the tea not to your liking, Runer?" Wu-ShanBao said with a smile. Something in his smile wrinkled his face a little too much.

Tzarik set the cup down. The food, a large bowl of rice and a savory-smelling brown meat, looked far more appealing.

"Where can I find lodging for my apprentice and myself?" he asked, preparing to leave.

"I'd be honored if you stayed with me," Wu-ShanBao offered, waving his silk-clad arms wide. "I have walls to protect you, guards at the gate, and am thought well of all across Xia."

"We have the ear of the Di-Huan," Jin said proudly. This earned him another sideways glance from Wu-ShanBao.

The older man approached Tzarik, helping him rise. "We cannot pretend foreigners are not looked upon with suspicion on our beautiful continent," he informed the Runer sadly. "But it has been a season of fear for some time. The unrest of the houses is growing more than it has in a generation. Our time of peace draws to a close."

"Is there anywhere to hide?" Tzarik asked. "I don't want to get caught up in a civil war."

Jin and Wu-ShanBao shared a look. The older man replied, "This is the safest place. Out among the people will be where the violence starts. And with your complexion, it is best to be seen with a dignitary like myself. The people, the lower peasants, do not understand Runers. They will fear you. Attack you, perhaps."

This weighed down Tzarik. He'd hoped Xia would be safe, far enough away from where they'd started that no harm would come to them. To Sybal. He knew what Wu-ShanBao said to be true: they'd been attacked once already.

Wu-ShanBao led him out of the room, instructing the others to leave so Sybal could sleep. "I see you were unaware of Xia's perception of Runers. Why did you come here?"

Tzarik thought carefully before he replied. "I don't mean to seem ungrateful, Wu-ShanBao—"

"Call me ShanBao, master Runer. Wu is a title for those learning the ways of Wushito."

Unsure if this was a generosity or a slight, Tzarik went on, ignoring the custom. "I am in your debt for saving my apprentice. I can pay you once we find a job here. But our business is our own."

"No payment is necessary." ShanBao smiled.

"I insist." Tzarik stopped walking and faced the man. "I cannot be in debt to anyone."

At this, ShanBao turned to face his garden, leading the Runer there as they spoke. "This is an Al'Myrahn custom?" He chuckled.

"This garden is open to all who work my estate, Runer. They pay rent to live on my land, safe behind my walls. In turn, they work my land, produce the silks that have blessed me—House Shikirumi —and my family for generations. House Shikirumi has prospered longer than most on Xia. We are older than almost all. We hold some say in important matters. But I give freely from my over-flowing cup to those in need. I expect nothing in return. That is the way of Wushito."

Chancing a glance around the expansive garden, Tzarik saw trees laden with fruit he'd never seen before. Melons crawled over the ground, and ample herbs scented the air.

ShanBao inhaled deeply of the aroma. "Young Jin is my apprentice. I took him in when House Xiaoh fell. War orphans clog our streets to this day. But I wanted to help him. Aid is what I do."

Confused, Tzarik sighed. ShanBao seemed like a good man, but this boasting grated on Tzarik's nerves. "I understand. I will stay until Sybal is strong again. But we must move on once she can fight."

"Why?"

Fighting to hide an angry smirk, Tzarik replied, "It is the way of the Runer. We do not stay in one place very long. It's safer that way."

ShanBao nodded. "I will give you a room on the top floor. I think you will like the view."

☙

A SMALL SHRINE smoked with dozens of incense sticks against the center wall of the room—a mini version of the temples they'd seen on their travels. The smoke soothed and stifled Tzarik's breathing. Outside, the moon hung whiter and larger than Tzarik had ever seen before, whether from the height of the house or the conical shape of Xia, he couldn't tell. The ground loomed below him, the tall grass moving in rippling waves from the gentle night breeze. Each side of the room opened onto a wide balcony with a low railing. He dared not move closer to it, content to look out from the round doorway leading onto the dangerous precipice. He'd never thought of heights before...

The balcony behind him looked out onto the rising mountain of Xia. From this distance, he saw small lanterns slowly meandering up and down the dirt paths, bobbing with the steps of the late-night travelers. The city below glowed with warm yellow light. The strange, sweeping branches of the trees arched out and up in graceful bows, some a deep green, others white or pink. When the wind came through them, he smelled the various kinds distinctly. Looking as high up as he could see, the shape of a palace the size of a city came into view, silhouetted against the moon.

"Everything is sore."

Tzarik whipped around, his hand going to his scimitar. He relaxed when he saw it was Sybal. "One day you are going to creep up on me and not live to regret it," he mumbled.

He turned back to the window, stopped, and looked back at her. She'd shed her Runer gear and donned a white, silken robe with wide sleeves. The embroidered hem showed petals, like on the pink trees outside. More silk thread designs crawled up the full length of the robe, depicting a dragon with golden orbs clutched in its talons. Her hair hung over one shoulder and the robe hung off the other. He noticed her bare feet slipping into view beneath the hem as she walked towards him.

She sighed in wonder as she joined him, taking in the moon and the mountainous horizon. "You can see so much from up here." She moved to the railing. "Tzarik, come look. You can see the blue rivers." She gasped. "Snow! I see snow higher up! That must be the island those monks talked about." Playfully pouting, she turned back to look at him. She raised her hand and gestured with one finger for him to join her at the railing. "I promise I won't let you fall," she said with a smile.

Not ready to allow her to mock him yet, he scoffed and marched out to join her. The moment he touched the railing, his knees tingled and weakened. He clutched the railing before he dipped. He'd never forgive himself if she saw him weak at the sight of heights.

She smiled down at him. "Your white hair glows in the moonlight. I think I see some new ones along your temple."

"I wouldn't have white strands if it weren't for you," he answered.

Nodding and looking out into the city, she sighed. "Thank you for saving me. I know it would have been simpler to allow me to perish. You could go home."

"Not true." He went back into the room to grab a clay jug next to the miniature shrine. Taking a drink, he returned to the balcony. He swallowed, pleased. Inside was some type of alcohol. It tickled his nose and tasted almost sweet. He poured her a cup of it and saw it came out clear. He went on, "I would still have to leave. We let a necromancer walk free. Al'Myrah may never forgive us."

Sybal smiled at the clay cup after swallowing almost all Tzarik poured her. "This is good. But I'm sure Tarkan left. He wouldn't stay on Al'Myrah, either."

"Sybal," he said. From the corner of his eye, he saw her look at him. "We can't go back. We've talked about this. We'll do here what we should: hunt monsters, acquire coin, find a place to sleep. Xia will be a great learning opportunity for us. There will be creatures here I've never encountered before. Different customs and beliefs about death. It will be a good challenge. You will no doubt finish your training here."

He didn't have to look at her to feel her body tense, see her knuckles turn white as she gripped the cup harder.

"I am going to offer my services if Wu-Tang attacks, igniting the civil war," she said suddenly.

Now he looked at her. Glaring, he said, "And what of your crime, woman? Does that mean nothing to you? The runes will take you if you kill another man."

She faced him squarely. "You know what Xioah has done to the people of Xia."

"We don't know anything about the tensions here. We can't get involved in someone else's politics. That's not what Runers do. We clean up the aftermath, the angry spirits, the monsters drawn to something as dark and bloody as a civil war." He took a long, sloppy drink from the clay pitcher then wiped his chin with the back of his hand. "We came here to hide."

Sybal set her cup down, pulling the robe up over her bare shoulder. "These people—the Wushito—saved me. I owe them my life. If you cared about me at all, you would owe them, too. I do not have to kill to help. The protective and healing runes are enough aid to offer should the need arise. I know you cannot stand my desire to help those around me, but we are trapped here now. Someone doesn't want us here; that's evident." Her hand went to the stitches on her chest. "But not everyone here hates us. You don't..." Her voice trailed off as she locked eyes with him.

Her hand vibrated slightly as she half raised it towards him. Thinking better, she dropped it, shook her head, and walked back into the room to leave.

"Let's go into the city tomorrow," she called back before leaving his room. "Find something to hunt. With any luck, we can placate your lust for monster blood."

Rubbing his tired eyes, Tzarik turned back to the deadly drop over the edge of the balcony. The clear fizzy drink entered his skull, releasing a swarm of bees around his brain. The sensation reminded him he hadn't eaten in days. More willing to starve than ask someone in the house to bring him food, he flopped onto the bed. Outside, a low gong of what could only be an enormous bell sounded through the rising mist. Cocking his head to catch the reverberation, he realized it didn't come from the city on top of the mountain.

Too tired to get back up from the floor-level bed, he closed his eyes and slept.

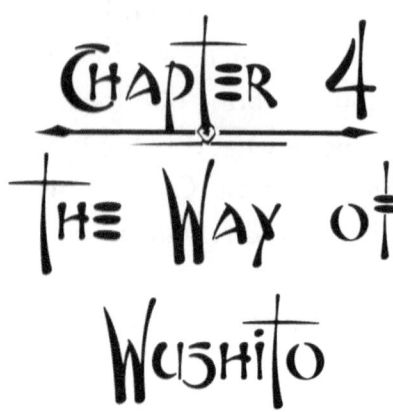

CHAPTER 4
THE WAY OF WUSHITO

SYBAL ROSE BEFORE THE SUN IN AN ATTEMPT TO LOOK around before Tzarik woke. A darkness hung over the home, the torches still unlit when she dressed and left her room on the ground floor. It took her a moment to remember to slide the parchment door to open it. Out in the wide-open area beyond, a woman in a tightly wrapped skirt shuffled quickly to the lamps. Sybal heard her long before she saw her: she wore a kind of sandal with wooden pegs on the bottom, clacking along the equally wooden floor. The servant carried a clay pot with oil and a long pole with a flame on the end, lighting the red lanterns as she went through the house.

Curious, Sybal watched her work and leave through a large, half circle door. She spied a myriad of colors and plants before the door slid closed.

"So green!" she said with a gasp, following the servant out. Unable to take in the beauty before due to the hurried anxiety they'd been forced to endure, she rushed out to take in the Xian flora and fauna.

Outside, a pink stone path lead through soft cut grass. Tiny fountains with decorative rocks and bright flowers ran along the paths. In the midst of a larger pond, filled with golden fish, a dock rose up, snaking its way down a slight hill.

"This puts my greenhouse to shame," she breathed. "Oh!" She dashed to the edge of the pond to get a better look. Floating on top of the softly rippling water were dozens of pink and white lotuses. The lily pads, thick and green, bobbed like little boats.

Just as her heart filled with a longing for a life she could never have, a shout cracked through the fresh morning air. She stood, hand on her scimitar. Another shout echoed up from the mist, farther down the hill. Hunching over and keeping to the thicker ferns and plants, she slinked down the hill, leaving the pink stone path. The walls around the lavish estate curved and broke off, sectioning off an area within.

A strange sloping post and lintel framed a gate made of round golden sticks. The red gate reached out, squaring off a portion of the yard, topped with a jade eve. The gate wasn't locked so she gently pushed it open. Inside, much of the same greeted her prying eye. Racks of staves, targets with varying sizes of arrows sticking out of them at all angles, and hanging dummies for practice littered the yard. In the center was a smaller, single-level structure on a raised wooden deck. Through the canvas doors, she saw someone inside moving with quick, strong strikes.

Snaking her fingers into the doors, she slid them open. The one inside leapt, kicking his legs over his head and thrusting a straight, single-edged sword towards her. Her instincts pulling her along, she flicked halat to deflect the blow and slid sideways, taking out her scimitar.

"That's cheating." The boy, Jin, stepped back, sheathing his sword with a playful smile. He slapped his arms together over his chest—forearms together—and bowed to her.

Awkwardly, Sybal did the same.

"Don't look down," Jin piped quickly. He used two fingers to point to his eyes. "Always keep your eyes on your opponent. Except in death. Do not let them see the light leave your eyes."

Trying again, a small smile pulling at her lips, she bowed with her eyes locked on him. "Don't Xians believe in fighting with honor?" she asked, sheathing her scimitar. "I read a story once about a Di-Huan who was given a gift by a dragon for fighting with so much honor that he died, basically not defending himself from his enemy."

Jin smiled again, his teeth glinting in the rising sun. He pulled his long white hair up and tied it with a thick blue string. "The first Di-Huan, ShunYen Siko he was called."

Sybal nodded. "I have a mighty education. I know things about other places." She returned the youth's smile.

"Do you? And yet you are invading my dojo." Jin walked to a wall of the matted room. Scrolls and hangings depicted colorful images of men and women wearing armor, fighting, and praying. Strange letters splashed across them in inky brush strokes. "Do Runers attend scholastic academies? Are you taught the ways of the world so you may fight off the things that go bump in the night?"

Taken in by his cheeky remark, Sybal followed him to a table laden with tiny weapons. "You have the wit of your wealthy father," she mused, taking up a sharp blade in the shape of a star. It greatly resembled the one stuck in the tree in the clearing where she'd nearly died.

"Master ShanBao is not my father. I am his ward." Jin took the star from her, pointing it to a thick board at the opposite end of the room. "And your husband is truly a barbarian of a man."

"Oh, no," Sybal said quickly, watching him aim the star. "Tzarik is my mentor."

Hissing an exhale, Jin threw the star. With a loud thunk, it lodged itself into the board. "And ShanBao is mine. He is the head of the Wushito and trains me in their ways."

"He was very helpful out at sea," she said with a nod. "Saved us. The captain seemed to like the Wushito. Are they your government? I thought Xia still acknowledged the Di-Huan?"

Jin turned his dark, almost black eyes, up to her. "That is an age-old discussion, one that may soon erupt. But we are ready."

"We?" She turned away as he placed his ankle on a bar and stretched over it. She picked up one of the odd, straight swords. The handle was wrapped in crisscrossing leather grips. "How do you slice an enemy with this?" She swung it a few times. It weighed less than a date in her hands, which were used to the wide, curved blade of her scimitar.

"With the sharp edge." He arched his brow at her, waiting to see if she was teasing him.

Laughing, she faced him, tilting her head in confusion. "A stab usually works, you're right. I suppose Runers do more slicing than stabbing. The curve of the scimitar is excellent at chopping heads and disemboweling."

"Must be why we have no Runers." Jin sighed, done stretching. He turned to a tiny shrine in the corner, smoking with a dozen sticks of incense. He bowed, and led Sybal out of the training space.

"I didn't mean it like that," she said, following him out. "I don't crave violence."

"How else can you stand to make your living by killing?" the boy asked. Something in him stopped his steps. He turned to face her so quickly, she almost ran into him. His age showed in his wide, sad eyes. "Is it right?"

The urge to comfort the boy took Sybal hostage like the tentacles of a sea monster. But these feelings were just the remnants of her previous life. "Killing monsters?" she asked, feeling more mature in her vocation than she actually was.

"Spirits left behind," the boy said, expanding on his statement. "Locking them away."

She frowned and shook her head. "They die when we kill them. I don't know about their afterlife. That part isn't my business."

A hardness took over her heart, one she'd never felt before. Maybe this was what she should strive for. Would this sentiment of removing herself from the situation help her embrace the runic ways?

She adjusted her stance, feeling sure. "Jin, what I do is better for so many people. These monsters are here to feed on fear. To take what is no longer theirs."

"All creatures of that ilk?"

She stammered around her answer, mind spinning. She couldn't look at him. It was too early for this kind of philosophical conversation. But she loved it. Instead, she gripped his upper arm. "I feel we have more in common than we know." She tried to smile reassuringly. "I think we will become fast friends if we continue to have discussions like this."

Jin bowed his head slightly in thanks. "I'd appreciate it, Sybal-kim. Master ShanBao says I have more convictions than is healthy. But I cannot help but question what we do."

The boy guarded his fear well. Better than she did.

Pushing past the tense moment, she turned back to the tall, many-towered house and led the boy back. "No Runers on Xia? Not one? Do you not have hauntings and monsters? Do ghouls not stalk your children?"

Outside, the house came fully awake. Servants and businessmen came to trade with the land workers who milled around the property.

"We do," Jin said.

She noticed he kept his eyes on the path and his throat tightened, straining his words. "Good. We need work. Anyone willing to pay for it?"

The boy bit his lip, turning his face away to hide his struggle. Sybal stopped, lightly touching his shoulder.

"What is it?"

His eyes narrowed and he clenched his fists.

"I've never had a sister. Or a mother," he said stiltedly. "You're nice to talk to." He finally met her eyes, locking her in.

Sybal's heart melted. The conflict roiling in his eyes amplified the sympathy that filled her. "You are much better at conversation than Tzarik. Would you mind helping me find a job? We owe Master ShanBao so much."

Jin smiled, tucking his white hair behind one ear. "He and I are going into town to get supplies for the Festival of the White Dragon, to celebrate the new harvest season. I'd love it if you came. Don't mention the coin or a hunt to him, though. I will point you in the right direction."

Recently, Sybal had been able to read the physical cues of sentient beings better. Jin's eyes gave him away more than any other feature. When discomfort drew them away, they twitched and snapped quickly back with a fleeting, apologetic smile.

"If you see the generals," he went on, "Wu-Yasuke and Wu-Zhiang, tell them you are staying with Master ShanBao and they won't bother you."

Cautiously, she furrowed her brow. "*Will* they bother us?"

"They are Wushito, very high ranks. While Master ShanBao and I are open to foreigners, they may not be. It is not personal," he added smiling up at her. "Respect our ways and you should be fine."

Pressing his lips together tight, Jin bowed to Sybal and hurried into the house. Her heart reached out to the young man as she watched him go. Not long ago, she had been a fifteen-year-old girl, dreaming of all that her life could be. She'd had a mother, father, and brother. Jin had none of that.

Ahead of her, Tzarik came out of the great doors, his eyes sweeping the magnificent landscaping. "Never have I seen so much green. Even the jungles of Bahratt are not so bright."

Sybal nodded, reaching down to touch the lotus in the pond. "The sun is so yellow here. The mountains are blue and white. There is more color than just green."

Tzarik shifted his booted feet. "That boy took a liking to you quickly."

She smiled, standing up and wiping her hands on her black tunic. "I may be the first person who's spoken kindly to him. He's lonely. And I believe he's scared, Tzarik." She made sure he met her eyes before she went on. "I believe we have fallen in with a powerful man with strong convictions about the war brewing. I know you don't want to get involved, but we may not have a choice."

He clenched and unclenched his jaw rapidly, crossing his arms. "I brought us here to save us. Not to get swept up in circumstances we have no control or business getting into."

Why could he not understand? "We have a power none here do," she tried. "Tzarik, they have no Runers. They don't have our magic."

Her mentor tensed at this. "What are you saying, Sybal? That because you don't understand what magic might lie in wait on Xia that you are stronger than they? That your runes are an excuse for you to rush into their fights? That kind of pride will get you killed."

She groaned loudly. "Pride is your vice, not mine. This man saved my life. Will you stand by and let them get hurt?"

"They hurt themselves," he cut in. "That's what a civil war is."

"Master Runers!" ShanBao called from the deck of the entry-way. "Jin has informed me you wish to see the city. Care to join us on our pilgrimage?"

Sybal bit her tongue and raised her brows. "Don't do anything to draw attention to us. Be respectful."

Tzarik blanched, insulted. "It's not me you have to worry about."

⁓

Wu-ShanBao led the small entourage down the hill into the loud, clanging city. On the way down, Jin regaled them with legends of the White Dragon and the richness of Xia.

Sybal smiled at his patriotism for his country. "I have noticed one thing we have on Al'Myrah that I have yet to see in Xia," she boasted as ShanBao waited for them at the city gates.

She noted Tzarik's eyes twitching to every eve and shadow, on the lookout. He pulled his large hood over his head.

"We have everything Al'Myrah does," Jin countered, falling back to playfully punch Sybal in the arm.

She shook her head, smiling. "We have glass."

Jin rolled his eyes. "Not in buildings like the cathedrals of Caerwren. Just to drink out of. And only your wealthy do. The common people still use clay, as we do. Though not the burnished kind we use." He glanced sidelong at Sybal. "Were you the daughter of a sheikh, lady Runer?"

He asked it simply, with a smirk, expecting her to say no. Unexpected guilt furrowed her brow and she couldn't reply.

"We all come from a variety of paths, Jin," ShanBao cut in, saving her the need to tell her own tragic story. "You above all else should know this."

"Oh?" Sybal asked, cocking her brow towards the boy. She instantly regretted it. He had not pressed her and she had not returned the favor. "Never mind. My mentor and I would like to see some of the streets on our own, if that's all right?"

ShanBao raised his head in thought. "You are under my roof, Runers. What you do reflects upon my name. Remember that."

When Tzarik didn't reply, Sybal said, "Of course, Master ShanBao. I owe you my life. I wouldn't stir trouble out of spite."

The old man smiled at her, the understanding flickering when his eyes moved to Tzarik. "Thank you. This is a good time to see the city. The festival is fast approaching, the seeds will be planted, and you will see the province of Shiuki in all its glory. It is much needed at this time."

"We understand." Sybal bowed as Jin had showed her—forearms clasped in front of her chest—and they parted ways. She turned to her mentor, his small black form motionless in the street. "Could you be more quiet next time? I could hardly think over all your chatter," she said with a sigh.

His blue eyes crackled under his hood. "How can I, when you're rambling in that foreign tongue?"

"Oh, Krishvu," Sybal swore, smacking her face. "I didn't realize. I suppose I forgot."

"Try to not let your enormous education get in the way while we look for a job," he mumbled, taking the lead and sliding in between the crowded streets.

Angry more than hurt at his ignorant remark, Sybal followed him less gracefully down the dusty, golden street. He slid between the slight Xians with ease, quickly making his way around carts pulled by hurrying farmers with wide, pointed hats, rich women carried on palanquins, and other merchants and citizens. Tall, fierce statues of Di-Huans and brave warriors past stood in almost every open square. Their arms were posed above their heads and holding long spears. Pointed helmets with vicious, monstrous masks covered their faces in roaring grimaces. All of them faced north.

He soon found his way out of the brightly lit streets of the city and led her into an area with older, leaning buildings, streets wet with mystery fluid and with fewer painted faces. Stepping over the puddles, Sybal looked up to see him move towards a house leaning too far forward. In the round windows above, three women lounged topless, fanning themselves.

"No," she snapped, freezing in the middle of the street. "What makes you think you'll find a job in here?"

To her relief, Tzarik turned and gave her an answer. "Your Master ShanBao is high society."

"So?"

"His Wushito appear to have no need for Runers and no love for those not of their caste. This is where we will find people desperate enough to pay us." He slipped inside the swinging doors before she could reply.

Aggravated, she pulled her cloak closer around her shoulders. Taking her runes out, bored while she waited, she slowly drew halat and atan in the air before her, held in the same hand. The shield bloomed into view, glowing with a white light.

"Amazing!" she mused to herself. The light-giving shield wavered. Behind it, a short figure in a blush pink cloak watched her. Remembering that—no matter how much she hoped it to be false—Runers were frowned upon on Xia, she quickly wiped the runic spells away. She froze, but the figure didn't flinch. It moved towards her.

"Runer?" a high, childlike voice asked.

Slowly, Sybal pulled her hood off. "Yes."

"A girl Runer!" The figure hurried to her now, unafraid. Pulling the pink hood down, the figured revealed herself to be a young girl. Jade and gold jewelry dripped from her headdress and neck. Her white face was painted over in blush pink and cherry red lips. "No one told me there were girl Runers," she said happily.

Confused, intrigued, and flattered, Sybal smiled. "As far as I know, I'm the first." Taking in the girl's obvious status from her dress, she glanced behind her nervously. "Should you be in this side of the city?"

"Of course not! I shouldn't even be in this province," the girl hissed, pulling her hood back up. "But I needed you to know I can pay you."

"You have a job for me?" she asked, curious. "Xia doesn't have Runers. Did you know we were here?"

"Our spies are everywhere," the girl said. She began to hop on the balls of her feet, anxious. "When we heard there were hunters among us not from the Hallow City of the Wushito, I knew I had to find you."

"I see you're worried," Sybal said soothingly. "I won't waste your time. What is it?"

The small, pink hood looked down each side of the dark street quickly before answering. "Those who say their prayers to the Di-Huan are not opposed to your kind, Runer. We have no love for the Wushito."

Sybal frowned. "If you knew Runers were in your province, you have to know where we are staying," she interjected. "ShanBao has only been kind to us."

"Please!" The girl thrust her hands out towards Sybal, clasped, begging. "I will pay you whatever you wish. There is a nu-gui that haunts an abandoned temple higher up the mountains. You can find it easily; the path the pilgrims used to take is still visible. Search for a path with old wayfinders in the shape of lions. Some may still have golden flakes on them. These lead to the temple."

"It's abandoned?" Sybal asked.

"Yes, but I need it cleared." The girl's hand snapped to her thick, silken belt. She pulled a pouch of shiny make from it and handed it to Sybal. "I will pay you now." Her head snapped around again like she'd heard something. "As a woman, please!"

Shaken by the girl's begging, she took the bag. "Of course."

Before she could say more, the girl dashed away, vanishing into the sunlight like she was made of it. "As a woman?" she questioned, weighing the bag in her hands. Wondering what the girl meant, she slid the pouch into her satchel and leaned against the wall opposite of the house where Tzarik had vanished.

Several minutes later, he reemerged with purpose in his step. "Good news."

"A job?" she asked, pushing herself up.

"Not quite." He fell into stride with her as they made their way back up out of the slums. "The Wushito are the ones who keep the monsters and hauntings in check."

She nodded.

"But not all love them as much as your Master ShanBao would have us believe," he went on.

Our spies are everywhere, the girl had said. *We have no love for the Wushito.*

"So I've heard," Sybal replied. "I have no quarrel with him."

Tzarik ignored her. "There is an underground network that looks for outside help. Some of the houses, though I couldn't find out which, are in favor of replacing the work the Wushito do. For a steep price, I was given a tip where to find someone who could give us a lead on a hunt."

Pleased with herself, Sybal smiled. "I have something better. A job."

Tzarik stopped. "How?"

Sybal cast her eyes up and down the street, but not so much as a silk slipper showed where the girl had vanished to. "I was approached. There is a haunting at an old temple. And I was paid in advance." She took out the silk pouch and tossed it up, catching it to make the gold inside clink.

Tzarik took the pouch, pried it open, and looked inside.

His eyes widened.

"Well done, Sybal," he mused.

❧

GLAD TO BE out of the dreary side of the city, Sybal took in the sights and unusual smells Xia offered. While there was a dedicated square to merchants, sellers lined almost every street, accompanied by forgers, farmers, fishermen, and other trade workers. Everyone rushed about as if there weren't enough time in the day. More than once, she found herself dodging around a hurrying citizen.

Every other doorway was adorned with a red lantern, a white dragon painted over the thin paper. Other decorations popped out of windows, on red arches, and groups of performers dressed in red and white costumes practiced in the streets. Music lilted over the wind and a salty smell she couldn't identify made her mouth water.

She was about to comment when a rush of a dozen or so people fled around a corner, away from shouts of terror. Gripping her scimitar handle, she bounded forward.

"Sybal, don't," Tzarik called after her, more weary and annoyed than worried.

Around the bend, a large, round clearing spread out in front of a five-layer structure atop wide, sprawling steps. It looked to be a town hall or another kind of political house. A group of men and women in judicial robes and odd, flat hats mumbled together on the steps. A group of onlookers gathered in the yawning square at the base of the hall as two prisoners were brought forward. The ones bringing the prisoners forward were the generals they had seen on the Wushito ship alongside Wu-ShanBao, one, the half Masahk with the foxlike ears, and the other, the serpentine woman with the lower half of a man-sized white snake. Her slitted purple eyes flashed as she spit venom at those who dared get too close.

"Is this the way of Wushito?" a wealthy man cried, trying to break from the onlookers.

"Your sons are traitors!" the viperous general hissed, rearing up to a great height like she might strike.

"Lies!" the man screamed back. "There is nothing traitorous about speaking with Oceanya! Our own Di-Huan has a treaty with them."

"Trust Wushito!" the general spat, tossing her prisoner to the ground. "We see what our Di-Huan does, not from his Sun Throne."

The second general came forward, pressing down on his prisoner until he knelt. "Wu-Zhiang means to say we are sorry for your loss, shino. The Hallow City will repay you for your loss."

"Silence, Wu-Yasuke!" the viper hissed, her white tail twitching. "You do not speak for the Hallow City."

"Nor you," Wu-Yasuke cut in, his fox ear turning to hear her. "Shino," he addressed the man by the continent's honorific sadly, "your sons have been caught with papers asking for aid for a war that has not begun yet. Warmongering is punishable by Wushito law and Xian justice. We do not want this stirring to erupt. If this civil unrest escalates, this war will be fought on Xian soil, among our mountains—not far away where it can be ignored."

Sybal swallowed. "Are they going to execute them in the street?"

Tzarik grabbed her right arm. "Don't interfere."

But she had already stepped forward, detaching from the

circle of onlookers. Unsure if the offense was justified, she knew every man had the right to beg or bargain for his life.

Wu-Zhiang's slitted, purple eyes snapped to Sybal. "Care to make a statement, foreigner?" She coiled her body around one prisoner and squeezed. The man gasped.

She opened her mouth but couldn't find the words. All eyes turned to her. Behind her, she could all but hear Tzarik groan.

"Have you sympathies with traitors to Xia?" Wu-Zhiang whispered, squeezing so hard the man's eyes turned red with blood.

"This is why we must not bend a knee to the Wushito!" the father of the prisoners cried out. "Does the Di-Huan not hear our calls?"

"Enough!"

The circle parted and ShanBao and Jin came forward. Shan-Bao's salt and pepper brows angled down into such a deep scowl, his eyes were nearly hidden. "I expect this from you, Zhiang. But Yasuke?" He sighed sadly, his shoulders falling. "I thought your empathy was stronger than this."

Relief filled Sybal and she allowed Tzarik to pull her back, out of sight.

"You are right, shino." ShanBao faced the pleading man. "This is not the way of Wushito. But you may not like my offer."

"Please, Master ShanBao!" the man begged softly. "They are my only sons. House Shang will be devastated without them."

"Thus should be all houses who oppose Wushito," Wu-Zhiang murmured, her forked tongue gliding between her lips.

"What are they saying?" Tzarik asked softly.

Sybal relayed the situation. While she did, ShanBao spoke too softly to his generals to hear. Suddenly, Wu-Zhiang constricted her entire body with such force, her captor's head fractured from the pressure. Blood and white chunks from within smattered her snake-like visage. The father screamed, covering his face. The other prisoner—the dead man's brother—turned his face away.

"What have you done?" Sybal screamed.

"The way of Wushito does not concern you, foreigner," Wu-Zhiang hissed, releasing the corpse and slithering a good distance away. "Yasuke, come. We take this one with us."

With a solemn face, the other general pulled the prisoner up and led him away.

ShanBao and a stone-faced Jin joined the Runers at the edge of the dissipating onlookers. In Al'Myrahn—for Tzarik's benefit—ShanBao said, "It is unwise to intervene, Runer. This is Xian justice."

"That was barbaric," Sybal gasped. "Public executions should be outlawed."

"It was all I could do," ShanBao interjected. "There was evidence of House Shang asking aid of Oceanya should civil war come upon us. House Shang sided with House Xiaoh when they first rose against us. Oceanya is neutral, but if a good enough offer was made... Well, we cannot be too careful."

"And the other prisoner?" Sybal asked.

"He will be a ward of Wushito, like me," Jin offered. "It is a steep price to pay, but it is better than death."

Sybal's mouth dried up. Jin had told her he was ShanBao's ward. Of course that must mean he was Wushito. What did he mean, better than death?

She wasn't unfamiliar with the concept of a dire fate better than death. Were she and Jin more alike than she'd thought?

ShanBao nodded. "He will be trained in Wushito. If he cannot be broken from his traitorous ways, then he will be executed. Most come around to our ways."

"Trained?" Sybal repeated. "What exactly does Wushito do? You are separate from the Di-Haun and his royal guard?"

Again, ShanBao nodded. "We adhere to the people. A private order. You might consider us a monastery; we take in children of families who cannot afford them. Orphans. Wayward pilgrims. Turn them into civil servants."

To Sybal's surprise, Tzarik spoke up. "You, your Hallow City and army of warriors, have an opinion on the civil war? A side you support?"

The old warrior smiled. "Never, Runer. We have the people's interest at heart."

CHAPTER 5

Hunting

PLAYING THE PART OF A GOOD GUEST, TZARIK PUT IN GREAT effort to look as if he enjoyed the hospitality of their host. For Sybal, it didn't take as much pretending. He watched her enjoy the trappings of wealth and all the ointments, fragrances, sweet fruits, and comfort that came with ShanBao's status as leader of the Wushito. She soaked for hours in hot baths, brushing her yellow hair until it shone like the sun. She'd adapted quickly to the life of a Runer and trials—this pleased him. Seeing her revert to her lavish ways tarnished the pride he'd felt. Then there was Jin. The young man was taken with her, his eyes always on her face when she spoke or told him myths from Al'Myrah. She openly boasted about her victory over a ghoul and the edimmu.

A few days after the public execution display, Tzarik found Jin and Sybal sparring in the dojo in the garden. He'd waited as long as he could to avoid any suspicion, but grew restless in the house. ShanBao had left days ago and hadn't returned. Now was the time to move and find the haunt.

"Jin," he called as he whipped the sliding canvas door open. "I need you to guide me to an abandoned temple."

Sybal sighed, coming out of a defensive pose. Jin had been

teaching her to spar with the bo staff. "If you'd be so kind," she added to the young warrior. "There is a haunting and we'd like to dispel it."

Jin tied up his white hair, wiping sweat from his brow. "What temple?"

"Supposedly it's abandoned," Sybal supplied. "Wayfinders in the shape of wooden lions guide the way. But we don't know where to start."

Tzarik didn't miss the spark that lit up Jin's dark eyes, though he quickly snuffed it.

"If ShanBao finds out you are hunting..." He glanced over his shoulder, half expecting his mentor to appear. He whispered, "I know the place very well. I've tried before to rid it of the nu-gui, but I can't."

Tzarik forced the smirk away, his brow twitching in amusement. "How do the Wushito hunt if they don't use runes?"

Jin held his head high, glaring into the Runer's eyes. "The way of Wushito is only known to those who take the vow. Not even those who live within a day's walk of the Hallow City know."

Intrigued by his conviction, Tzarik let the taunt go. "Take us to the temple."

⚬⚬⚬

Jin led them the long way out of ShanBao's estate. Tzarik realized the boy didn't want to be seen leaving with the Runers in tow. They wound their way around the city and down back streets until they hit the edge, trading the sloping red roofs for the colorful canopy of the trees. He'd advised them to bring water and gear in case they got stuck away overnight.

Sybal chatted with Jin about combat and her life back on Al'Myrah before her runing.

"Are all Runers criminals?" Jin asked, leading them off the main path into tall ferns.

"Yes," Tzarik answered when Sybal looked over her shoulder at him. "It is the price we pay for our misdeeds: a life of fighting that which others cannot."

"Why can they not?" Jin inquired.

"The runic oath is bound by the sulfates in our veins. It's magic and not meant to be understood."

Jin glanced back, his eyes tracking the runes hanging on the outside of Tzarik's black armor. "Can you not use the runes without that white poison?"

"No," he said shortly.

"Where do you train?"

Sybal snorted, laughing. "Wherever we are. Under the stars while you scratch at sand fleas, mostly."

Jin frowned in thought. "There is no academy for Runers? No training for this wretched life you must live?"

"If there was, it wouldn't be a punishment," Tzarik grumbled.

"And you are the first woman Runer?" Jin asked Sybal, eyes sparkling as he beheld her.

Again, Sybal glanced at Tzarik. When he didn't reply, she took a guess. "So it seems. But Tzarik didn't hesitate. The quadi didn't want a woman to be runed. Tradition, I suppose. The current sultana is the first of her kind as well." Sybal's eyes studied the path in front of them a little too hard. "Did you have reservations about runing me, a woman?"

Tzarik stopped, spotting the first of their wayfinders. One day he might be able to open up to Sybal about everything that had gone through his head and heart that day. Not now. Especially with Jin's eager eyes boring into him.

Hardly visible, the wayfinder stuck out of a thicket: an old, cracked wooden statue of a lion. Behind it, an old notice board hovered just above the greenery. Faded parchments, splotched paint, and a few canvas banners hung on it. One canvas showed a stylized painting of a well-dressed Xian on a throne that resembled the sun, bursts of light shooting out from behind him. He cradled a round white swaddle in his arms with a baby's face atop it. Though the paint had faded from years of exposure, he saw the man on the throne had white hair under his flat, beaded headdress. The baby's hair was also white.

Seeing his studious gaze, Jin said, "An announcement from the last Di-Huan when his son—the current Di-Huan—was born, the first in a long time for a Di-Huan to receive a dragon-touched as a son. This canvas is older than me." He smiled.

None of the citizens Tzarik had seen in the city had the same white hair. He glanced sideways at Jin, at how the sun glowed between his colorless strands.

"Let's continue," he said, striding away from the other two. "I don't want to fight this thing in the dark if I can help it."

As they walked, Sybal teased Jin with questions about the Wushito for each one about Runers he asked. Just as before, he didn't let much information slip. Sybal didn't mind as she seemed to be captivated by the joy of the conversation with the boy. Finally, she asked about his parentage.

"How did you come to be in ShanBao's care?"

Tzarik heard her voice take on a tone he'd never heard before. She spoke softly, sympathetically. Her brow furrowed and she watched his face as she asked, looking for any sign of discomfort. What would it be like to have someone so invested like that? To gaze into his eyes, honest and loyal?

"You don't have to talk about it," Sybal offered gently.

"I am happy with ShanBao," Jin said instead. "He taught me everything I know. He saved me."

Sybal cocked her head but Jin didn't elaborate. "You haven't had an easy life?" she guessed.

Jin scoffed, smiling. "That is an understatement. But I wouldn't trade my upbringing for anything. My father wasn't very fond of me anyway, so I think I have a better life with ShanBao. Even with all the secrets and training," he added when her face wrinkled in worry. "And I have ways of finding pockets of happiness. Even love."

"Oh?" Sybal droned mischievously, her face lighting up.

Raising his brows and pressing his grinning lips together, Jin shook his head.

"Ugh, so many secrets!" she said, giggling.

Hearing the conversation go into territory he'd rather steer clear of, Tzarik watched their steps on the path. Sybal's much larger feet overtook and covered another set of prints. He followed their hypnotic stride until Jin's foot went into one of the prints, matching it perfectly. He'd been up this way before. Recently. Probably the time he'd tried to kill the nu-gui.

If Tzarik were honest with himself, he didn't know what a nu-gui was. He assumed it would be like any other haunt on Al'Myrah. The creatures of the afterlife and other monsters all reacted to orichalcum, wielded in the hands of a white blood, the same way. The runes worked on any creature with ill intent.

After passing a few more lion statues and one empty pillar where one used to sit, they eventually found the temple in question. Overgrown with trees, creeping vines, and thick foliage, its dark windows looked exactly like the place to find a ghost. Statues of guardians in armor with terrifying masks and helmets over their faces guarded the remains of the temple.

"Why was it abandoned?" Sybal asked as they scanned the front for the best entrance.

Jin took the lead, his stride confident, winding through the brush and dodging around a door well hidden by a rotting board. "A lady killed herself here. I'll show you."

"Ah," Tzarik mused. "A vengeful spirit, perhaps."

Sybal half-smiled. "You don't know what a nu-gui is?"

"I don't have your wealth of knowledge," he growled. Immediately, his face paled and he wanted to take the words back. Sybal pulled away, following Jin more closely. Could he never learn to curb his anger?

Inside the small temple was just one room. A short railing blocked off a shelf that spanned the entire length, making an alter elevated above the rail. Small statues, favors left years ago, red envelopes, and other sacrifices littered the altar. Hanging just above the rail, dead center, was the corpse of a woman. The smell coming from the corpse was faint as the temple was mostly open on all sides.

The Runers approached, scanning the corpse.

"A few years old," Tzarik mused. "She still has an unusual amount of flesh left on her." He took out his scimitar and turned the body. Her face spun to greet them.

Sybal covered her mouth after a quick glance.

"Her eyelids have been cut." Tzarik stood on his toes to see better. "See the jagged line?"

Sybal nodded, not looking.

"Yes," Jin offered from a safe distance away. "We Xians believe that if someone kills you, you must close your eyes. This stops your enemy from seeing your life go out, takes away their pleasure in your demise."

Sybal hummed in thought, finally inspecting the corpse. "That makes sense, I suppose. Most believe only cowards die with their eyes closed."

Tzarik stopped his inspection. "Someone was here when she died? She wouldn't have cut her own eyelids off."

"Or she was forced," Sybal said.

"We may need to find the one who killed her, then," Tzarik mused, sheathing the scimitar, "if she is out for vengeance. Who was she?" he asked Jin.

The young warrior shrugged. "I don't know. She appeared one day. I came here and—"

A shriek from the rafters above split the air. All three below shouted in shock and pain, covering their ears against the siren wail. Recovering first, Tzarik snapped his head up and spotted the haunt in the shadows above them. Her eyes, perpetually open from their lack of lids, glared down at him as white, ghostly orbs. She lay horizontal with the roof, her dress and black hair defying her hanging posture.

"Move!" Tzarik pulled Jin up and pushed him a few paces away. "Sybal, get your runes." Angry that he had to command her to act, he unsheathed his scimitar violently and roared at the spirit above. He took a few steps back when it didn't move.

Panting, Sybal fumbled with her runes, finally drawing halat.

A bright light blinded Tzarik in his left eye. Squinting at it, Sybal stood behind a white glowing protective circle. She clutched halat and atan in the same hand. Before he asked how she'd drawn two at once, she screamed, backing away as the spirit appeared before them. Through cracked, bloodied lips the ghost spoke harsh, rage-filled words.

"What's she saying?" Tzarik asked Sybal, holding up his own runes and the blade to ward her off if she attacked.

Shaking, but looking the specter in her wide eyes, Sybal translated. "She says the Wushito have tried to banish her." She swallowed, listening. "I think... I think she wants to be at peace."

The specter howled, dashing towards Sybal. It hit Tzarik's protective circle, knocking him back. He fell hard, winded, against the wooden temple floor.

"Help!" Sybal choked. The specter had her rotting hand around Sybal's throat.

Tzarik leapt to his feet, brandishing a freshly drawn halat to push against the spirit. To Jin he shouted, "Tell her she need not feel my blade if she lets Sybal go."

Clutching his own sword, Jin called out to the specter in their own tongue. This got her attention. Slowly, her lidless eyes turned to Tzarik. She asked him something he couldn't understand in a slow, measured tone. Almost curious, her gaze drifted over the runes. With a gasp, she lurched down on Sybal, mouth wide like a snake.

Sybal screamed, clenching her eyes tight. Tzarik didn't move, smirking.

"You can't possess her. Not with these." He held up the runes when the specter realized she could not take Sybal's body.

Enraged, the dead woman gripped Sybal with both hands and slowly ascended back towards her dark rafters.

"Release her!" Tzarik shouted, going for his bow.

"She wants to speak," Jin called, already nocking an arrow.

"Your arrows won't harm her at all," Tzarik informed him, nocking his own orichalcum-tipped shaft to his short black bow. He aimed at the specter, the bow creaking as he heaved the string back. "This won't send you on to the next life, but it will make this one far more painful. Drop her!" He aimed.

Sybal gasped, her legs weakly kicking as she reached behind her to assault the specter. Her hands meeting nothing, she looked at Tzarik, begging him to save her.

Without waiting another second, Tzarik released the arrow. It passed through the specter, who screamed in pain, and Sybal tumbled to the ground. Her runes slipped over her head in her fall, clattering just inches from her. Seeing the wards gone, the specter took her chance.

"No!" Tzarik shouted, diving to grab the runes. Before he could slip them over Sybal's head, the dead women vanished into her body.

Like a tiger, the now possessed Sybal leapt up onto all fours and glared at Tzarik through her sweaty strands. He locked eyes with hers, now pure black and wide. A growling emitted from her throat, deeper and more terrifying than anything he'd ever heard from her lips. The moment passed in a flash. The possessed woman launched herself at her mentor, flattening him against the floor. All the wind knocked out of him as her long, heavy body smashed against his.

Coughing, he hardly got his breath back before she grabbed a handful of his hair and smashed the back of his head against the floor. White light flashed before his eyes, blinding him. Something in his skull cracked and instant nausea filled his gut.

"Listen, stranger!" Sybal hissed through a throat that had been broken, the rasping voice of someone hung by their neck for years.

"Sybal?" he gasped. He reached up to push her off, but the strength of vengeance surged through Sybal's arms from the specter. She gripped his wrists and pinned them down hard over his head.

"I need her tongue," Sybal's lips said. "You are not like the Wushito. They put me in the dark, but I come back again and again!" She winced, tears forming in her eyes. "I never stay gone. The agony!"

Gathering his breath and focusing on calming his roiling stomach, he looked up into her manic face. "What do you want?"

Sybal leaned down too close to his face. The tip of her nose trailed over the vein pulsing on his exposed neck; she inhaled the stench of his sweaty skin. "To feel hot flesh again is more than I could hope," she hissed. "These young ones come and make love bellow me, hidden from the prying eyes of their families."

He'd rarely had the opportunity to speak to a vengeful spirit. Always assuming they were stupid, mindless creatures, the speech of the dead woman stopped his fight. Relaxing into the floor, he held still beneath her.

"You can leave," he offered. "What holds you here?"

Her lips touched his neck, making him flinch. "I see this girl's mind. You know I cannot leave. You are hunters. Why do you tease me so!"

With a shriek, she headbutt him hard, once again sending the bright white flash into his eyes. This time, his nose bled. He coughed on the blood trickling down the back of his throat.

"Tell me what you want!" he spat. His blood speckled Sybal's face but she didn't so much as wince.

She reared up like a snake about to strike. "He who sent me to my death must die. I will take his spirit with me."

"That could be anyone!" Jin said with a gasp.

Tzarik had forgotten the boy stood by and thanked any god that would listen that he'd wisely stayed his bow, not harming Sybal or enraging the nu-gui. But this drew her attention to him. She snapped her head, growling at the young warrior.

"Wushito slave!" she spat at him. "You who locks me in the crypt again and again." Turning her gaze back to Tzarik she whispered, "The man is of the same ilk. Bring him here to be killed."

"I don't know how to find him."

"Stupid foreigner!" she screamed, lowering herself just a fragment above his face, Sybal's spit flying into his eyes. "You are wise, crafty, cunning. This woman says so. Find him!"

Wincing, Tzarik turned his face away. "I'll make you a deal. I will bring you this man if you leave the lovers alone. And leave Sybal."

Sybal arched her brow and sat up, intrigued, though her grip on his wrists did not lesson. "She tells me you can be trusted...

Runer?" She looked down at him inquisitively, testing the word on her tongue. "You have until the last harvest to bring he who killed me to this temple."

Feeling emboldened by her willingness to negotiate, he commanded her, "Tell me his name. I'll drag him here today."

Sadly, she shook her head. "In death, I am under oath to not make known his name. If he knows you hunt him, he will take you." She tilted her head. "This woman thinks she is stronger than he and his kind. She is proud, stupid. If he knows you hunt, he will send me back." She shook her head. "I will not say his name."

The strangeness of this worked its way through anything Tzarik knew about death oaths. It took merely seconds for him to scan everything he knew, which wasn't much.

"If we made him pay—brought justice to him—would that suffice?" he asked, wondering if he could trick his way out of the deal.

"Revenge only," she whispered. She let go of him and stood up. "She doesn't like it when I hurt you." Drawing her own blade, she gripped it tight in her hand. She gasped as white sulfates leaked between her fingers.

"Don't harm her!" He moved to leap up.

"No," she hissed. Sybal yanked the sword from her grip, crying out in pain. Then she held the poisonous blade to her own throat. Pressing down, she drew more white blood from the bulging vein on Sybal's neck. "So promise me." She laid the blade over Sybal's wrist now. "Kill him. Then I can be banished."

Worried she might take it as an attack if he stood up, Tzarik stayed down and nodded. "You have my word. On my own, black oath, I swear to bring your justice to this man. Don't hurt her." He raised his hand in surrender and slowly stood up.

To his left, Jin moved like a shadow and lightning. Something in his hand sparked as he pressed his palm to the back of Sybal's neck. The woman screamed, arching into the touch.

"What are you doing?" Tzarik shouted, struggling to keep his ground lest the spirit harm her more.

Sybal's black eyes widened then, swirling like a maelstrom, the blackness pulled out, leaving her eyes clear and blue. Sighing, Sybal hung her head and her arms went limp, dropping the sword. With a gasp, she went ridged and then collapsed. Tzarik lunged forward and caught her before she hit her head on the floor. Jin, almost weeping in relief, joined them on the ground.

"I've never in my life seen anything like that!" he sniffled. He picked up her runes.

Grunting, Tzarik snatched them from him. "Don't touch those." He glared at the boy. "What did you do?"

"The runes saved her from being possessed!" he cried, avoiding the question. "Many a Wushito has died from possession. These are amazing."

Tzarik scoffed and checked Sybal's vitals. She stirred while his hand pressed against her wounds. Immediately, she quaked with shivers.

"I'm so cold," she gasped, her lips turning blue.

He pulled her cloak tight around her shoulders. "We'll give you sulfates when we get back. You've lost too much over these last few weeks."

"Is she gone?" Sybal asked, looking around. "That was horrible."

He slipped her runes back over her head and sighed. "Good thing you got paid in advance."

Jin recovered, not rattled by Tzarik's harshness. "Who paid you?"

"We don't know," Tzarik said over Sybal opening her mouth to reply. "Someone approached us in the street."

A cautious, playful smile slowly spread Jin's thin lips. "A woman?"

"Hardly," Sybal scoffed, sitting up and straightening her armor.

Jin nodded. "Then perhaps you could help me with something."

CHAPTER 6
A Letter of Love

THE JOURNEY BACK TO THE CITY PASSED IN SILENCE WHILE Jin fiddled with the sleeves of his layered tunic, planning how to ask the Runers whatever ailed his mind. Sybal thought they'd be back in ShanBao's estate before he finally opened his mouth. She took the silence and the walk to focus on the icy sensation the ghost had left inside her. Once the runes had left her neck, terror had filled her for the one second it had taken the ghost to thrust itself inside her. She'd watched it dive onto her. While being possessed, she could hear the woman's thoughts. The ghost's feelings filled her until they shared the rage. She even saw a dark outline of the man the woman wanted revenge on. He stood stiff and proud, his hand gripping his thin, straight sword at his side as he looked over cities from a rocky perch.

Shivering, she came back to the present, the moonlight lighting their way. Wondering if Tzarik had ever been possessed, she stopped herself from asking. He wouldn't tell her anyway. Just before they embarked for Xia, she'd thought they'd made a connection and he'd be more open. He hadn't. Instead of prying into her mentor's past, she pushed the chill and fear behind her and strode to fall in step with Jin.

As warmly as she could, she asked him, "What is it you wanted to tell us? We want to help." *I want to help*, she corrected herself in her mind. She glanced sideways at her mentor to find him inclining his head towards them. Encouraged, she went on. "It's that girl, isn't it? Do you know her?"

"What girl?" Jin said, turning his face away.

Sybal smiled. Young love was not something she'd gotten to experience. The love she did have showed her how giddy it could make someone. She missed that. Longed for it. Her eyes flitted to Tzarik only for a split second before she refocused on Jin. "Tell me about her. She gave us this job. You knew where it was. You two have been meeting here, haven't you? Is love forbidden in Wushito?"

Jin shook his head. "Not at all. It's complicated."

"Always is," Tzarik mumbled, keeping his eyes on the path ahead.

Sybal nodded, urging him on. The lights of the city flickered warm and bright before them; they were running out of time.

"Her name is Yui. She lives in the palace of the Di-Huan," Jin said, letting out the answer on a defeated sigh.

"Oh." Sybal couldn't stop the smile and excitement in her tone. From the corner of her eye, she caught Tzarik turn a disapproving head towards her. "So this lady. What do you want us to do?"

The light that brightened Jin's eyes warmed Sybal's heart. She couldn't help but reply with a huge grin.

"I just need to get her a letter," he said excitedly. "But I cannot take it to her."

Tzarik finally spoke to the boy. "What makes you think a couple of foreigners can get into the palace and not one of the Wushito, like yourself?"

"I could," Jin said simply, but guarded. "But Runers will be allowed in quicker. I'd have to wait—probably days!—to see her. The Di-Huan will be eager to see you. Fascinated, if nothing else."

In the back of her mind, something pulled at Sybal's brain. It reminded her of being stalked by a wild beast: no danger yet, but something wasn't right. Looking at the motherless boy before her, the feelings of fun and care far outweighed the tingling her instincts gave her. The girl—Yui—had said almost the same thing as Jin. The Di-Huan might be interested in Runers.

"No reason we couldn't," she said.

"Why not have ShanBao take you or deliver this letter?" Tzarik asked. "Sounds like he spends enough time in the presence of your rulers anyway."

The young warrior didn't audibly reply. His lips stretched thin and his eyes danced as he tried to come up with an answer. "It would behoove you to meet the Di-Huan. How often do you get to meet the eyes of such great rulers?"

Tzarik understood: ShanBao didn't know about Yui and Jin, and for whatever contrived reason, Jin didn't want him to know. "You could accompany us," he suggested.

Jin shook his head. "I cannot be gone when ShanBao returns. No one can see me climb the mountain of the Di-Huan."

At this, both Runers glanced towards each other. Sensing his burning desire to not get involved, Sybal quickly confirmed.

"We'll do it. Give us the letter. Tell ShanBao, when he returns, that we have gone out to hunt. Tell him we went down towards the marshy lowlands."

Jin turned and engulfed Sybal in a huge hug, smiling wildly. "Thank you, Sybal! When we return, I'll get you the letter. When will you leave?"

"At first light," Sybal promised.

SYBAL ROSE EARLY the next day, thinking to get up and meet with Jin before Tzarik woke. She should have known she'd never out-rise her mentor. When she couldn't find either of them in the house or the dojo, she went out to the front gate to find Tzarik waiting there with their horses.

"I have it," he said, handing her the reins. "We'll need to take breaks often and probably walk the horses. They're not used to these hills and hard ground."

A little annoyed, she snatched the reins and checked her saddlebag. He had filled it with some jars of cooked rice and the strange, salted fish she'd smelled around the market. "How long do you think this journey will be?" she asked, stepping up into the stirrup.

"I'm not sure we won't have to take a long way back, or hide for days," he replied.

"Why would we?"

Looking into her face before he kicked his horse to move, he said, "You are too open, Sybal. You don't see how different this place is and how they may turn on us. We were fortunate to be found by a man of such standing as ShanBao. But I don't trust even him."

"You don't trust anyone, Tzarik." They wound their way down the path out of the city before turning up towards the marked mountain path to the royal palace. "I choose to see the good in people. To believe in helping my fellow sentients."

He didn't reply. She sensed she'd defeated him. He had no desire to argue with her. A little hurt that he didn't reply, she let it go, internalizing the wound. She thought he'd bring up the inci-dents on Al'Myrah, the devastation she'd suffered by forcing herself into the lives of people who didn't want her around. She was guilty; perhaps it came as part of her punishment as a murderer.

A few hours later, the landscaped changed from lush green hills to rocky silver mountains covered in roaring blue waterfalls. They heard the rushing of one river for hours before they finally came upon it. Small, sloped roofed houses lined a cavernous gorge. Tiny docks with fishing lines, nets, and bamboo cages hung off them. The people of the river village meandered up and down the bank, checking traps and hauling in nets. The waterfall, hundreds of feet tall, stood guard half a mile away. The white froth lathered so thick, it bobbed all the way down the river.

Sybal's heart thudded against her chest as she gasped in the humid air. "Never have I seen so much fresh water!"

Beside her, even Tzarik's eyes trailed over the sight, his mouth slightly parted in awe. He coughed. "This damn air is like breathing under the ocean."

His comments didn't dry up her awe. "The silver mountains. The pink trees. This is a magical land. So many colors!"

A family on the docks of the nearest tiny home stopped their work to look at the foreigners gaping at their waterfall. Wrapped in their black eastern clothes, Sybal realized they must have looked strange, black folds of billowy pants and cloaks against the vibrant colorful background. She smiled at them and timidly waved. A mother, father, young boy, and elderly woman gazed back at them.

Deciding they were lost, the family went back to their work. The Runers had just begun their march when the older woman cried out, clutching her chest. Stopping, Sybal watched as she tumbled from her seat and rolled towards the edge.

"She'll fall!" she cried out.

Before she could take action herself, Tzarik leapt from his horse and ran towards the dock. He didn't reach her in time. With a gasp, she rolled over the edge into the river. Shaken, the Runers looked to the family. The father shrugged, tears dripping down his cheeks, saying, "We cannot stop it if it is her time."

Sybal relayed the dark message to Tzarik.

Glaring at the father, Tzarik leapt into the rushing river after the woman.

"What are you doing?" Sybal screamed, throwing her leg over her saddle and dashing to the side. Terror filled her chest, constricting her breathing in the already heavy air.

Tzarik's black head disappeared under the rushing blue and white river. Panicking, she screamed his name before seeing a rope nearby.

"Foolish foreigner," the father said, sighing and shaking his head. "He will be damned for taking her from Tiang."

"He's trying to save her!" Sybal spat.

Flabbergasted, the father his shook head again. "If it is her time, she must be left to die."

"That's shit!" She grabbed the rope and ran down the bank, tracking Tzarik's black form.

The river took his body like a leaf, tossing it and turning it over and over until she was sure he'd pass out. His arms flailed towards the limp form of the older woman.

"Tzarik!" she screamed. "There's a branch!"

His arm shot out of the water, reaching for it but missing by a good foot. She'd misjudged how far above the river the branch hung. Panic surging through her, she dashed down the bank with the coil of rope in her hand, the father screaming at her the entire time to let them go.

Finally getting ahead of the two in the river, she tossed the rope. "Watch out!" she shrieked. They careened towards a jagged rock in the middle of the river she hadn't seen.

Getting his arm around the woman, Tzarik drew halat in a flurry, bouncing them away from the rock with a jolt. The impact, despite the shield, rocked him. She saw his head snap back. Desperate, she flung the rope around a dock post and grabbed the two ends, rushing out into the river. With a desperate cry, her hand seized the back of Tzarik's cloak. Being taller helped a little. The river was deep, but she could fight against it with long legs and powerful strokes. Using her other arm, she pulled all three of them to safety.

Tzarik coughed, spewing water onto Sybal, but she didn't care. Once she saw him breathing, ragged but gulping air, she turned to the old woman. Her chest heaved but her eyes had already glazed over. Pressing her ear against the woman's chest, she heard the faint fluttering sigh of a heart giving out.

"You foolish foreigner!" the father shouted, running down, followed by his family. "Her heart was to give out at any moment. When it is time to die, you cannot save them. It's not permitted. You will stop her soul from entering Tiang and she will go to Diyu instead. Forever separated from the Dragon!"

"That's bullshit." Sybal shook, her own breath rattling. She rubbed Tzarik's back where he lay hunched over, shivering from the cold water. "If you had grabbed her before she fell, you might have been able to save her. The river killed her. It was not her time."

The father shook his head. "You do not understand our ways. You do not belong here." He gripped his son's shoulder and forced his family back up the steep bank.

Clutching Tzarik's shoulders, she took his cloak off and gave him hers. The longer hem engulfed him. "Why did you do that?"

He crossed his arms and marched to the horses. "Seemed like something you would do."

"So let me," she shot back.

"Can you swim?" He glared at her.

"Can *you*?" Her eyes bulged, enraged at his thoughtless dive.

Pulling her hood over his head, he growled. "Thought that wouldn't matter to you."

Shaking her head, confused and mad at his careless attempt to save someone, she went to the horses. Once they'd both mounted and caught their breaths, they started back up the mountain. Sybal couldn't wait in silence very long, however.

"That wasn't like you," she said softly, not wanting to ward him off with a harsh tone.

"Hmm," he hummed thoughtfully. "I wanted to know what it felt like to be like you. To help someone."

The thought made her smile sadly. "I've never thought about it. I think about how it annoys you." Her smile broadened. "It was brave. I wish they didn't see it as a spiritual attack."

Tzarik nodded. "I told you this place was different. We need to keep our heads down."

Of course he'd change the subject. "I don't always feel good when I try to help people. I want to be free of such feelings. Like Vicdan." Thinking of their old companion made her heart twinge a little. He'd briefly entered their lives only to make her life more complicated. Then he'd turned into an invaluable ally.

She didn't want to press her mentor to elaborate on why he'd leapt to his death. They walked in silence until long after the sun set and set up camp facing a dense thicket behind a rocky hill, blocking the light of the fire from the main road. Once they dismounted, the horses sighed in exhaustion.

"Take the saddles off and give them a rest," Tzarik ordered. He removed the bridle and pushed his horse towards the creek, encouraging it to drink.

Excited to sleep on grass, Sybal quickly smoothed out her bedroll and lay on it. She had not spent much time on Bahratt or in the jungle, so she had rarely seen the stars through a canopy of thick trees. It pulled a genuine, aching smile over her face. A lone, floating red lantern passed over her view. Giggling, she wondered if one had gotten away from a family setting up for the festival.

"Make a fire," Tzarik barked from where he sat, opening the jars of rice he'd packed.

Sighing, she got up, gathered some wood, and built a triangular stack of timber. She went back under the trees to gather some dead moss for kindling. She wandered farther and farther into the woods until she couldn't see Tzarik anymore.

A white shadow above her moved.

She froze, her breath gone. When it shifted, it reminded her of the assassin in Porsh. She swallowed a dry lump in her throat and deafened herself in the stillness. Her body screamed at her to turn and shout for Tzarik, but she didn't want to give away that she'd heard something. Realizing her frozen frame already gave it away, she scanned the branches above her. The white bark and light-colored flowers and leaves were the perfect place for someone in a mottled white cloak to hide. The white moonlight and gray shadows covered it well.

Having enough, her legs stiffening, she turned and sprinted back towards the camp. A rushing of movement followed above her in the branches. It overtook her, getting ahead. Suddenly, a white explosion lit up the trunks of the trees, thick white smoke exploding up from the ground. It instantly blinded her and burned her eyes. Gasping, she sucked it into her lungs and coughed violently. A hissing accompanied the smoke. It entered her brain, turning her around. Waving her arms wildly, she charged off in the direction she thought the camp lay.

Over her hacking, she caught the sound of swords clashing through the thick trees. "Tzarik!" she screamed, her throat burning.

She heard some grunts and then silence. It took her an agonizing three minutes to finally make it back to the camp. Tzarik spun around near the unlit fire, scimitar in hand, looking for the assailant.

"Are you hurt?" she coughed, tears streaming from her eyes. "That bomb must have been made with curry." She sniffled, realizing her nose was running, too.

"He came from the trees. I thought he'd killed you." Tzarik fought to control his wild gasps. "He came so quick." He stopped and turned his eyes to the saddles. "The letter!" He threw open his saddle bags and pulled the items out. "I know what you're going to ask: 'why would they steal the letter?' "

"Yes, why?" She stood over him as he scattered his belongings over the forest floor. "It's a love letter."

He grunted, not replying.

"Don't start an evil theory about a love letter," she mumbled.

He sat back on his heels, arms falling to his side. "It's gone. It's the only thing missing. My sulfates, the black box, the codex— everything else is here."

"Why?" Sybal cried, her hopes of delivering Jin's love letter crumbling. "Maybe they mistook it for something else. Secrets or something."

Tzarik stood up, placing everything back. "So they chose to attack us because we were alone? Why?"

She didn't have an answer. She opened and closed her mouth, desperate to find one. She wanted to complete a sweet mission for a starry-eyed boy, and now it had turned sinister. Defeated, she said, "I don't know why I always hope things are innocent."

Nodding in agreement, Tzarik said, "Let's make the fire, get some rest, and we'll go to the palace."

"Why?"

"I think we may find what we're looking for anyway." When he saw this didn't placate her, he added, "At least we can tell Yui that Jin meant to send word."

Satisfied, she went to work making the fire.

BY MIDDAY, the city of the Di-Huan finally came into view. Sprawled over the hills, valleys, and layered prairies that made up the highlands of Xia were small villages and homes made of lavish materials. Spikes of jade and gold twinkled amongst the clouds. A teal-colored river ran still around the golden city, crossed by wide, arching bridges with gate houses on each end. Every piece of lumber glittered with gold leaf, burned bright red, and was topped with a lion-like creature, roaring to the north. Up here, the grass and flowers grew plentiful but short. One great tree reached up and out over half the city. Above the timberline, shade was constructed out of towering gazebos and pavilions on single spiraling posts. Every eve and lintel dripped in lavish decoration. On the eastern side, facing the sun, the river turned to gold. The white ring of clouds now drifted at eye level.

The air grew thin. Coupled with the mysterious humidity, this made Tzarik short tempered. The horses gasped as much as he and Sybal did, so he eventually gave in to walking the last leg of the journey. Sybal expected the palace to rise to meet them, but instead caught herself glancing up with one eye squinted against the sun. From where they stood, the sun peeked over the great, stacked, sloping roofs like it was perched there, looking down on the ruler of the continent. It stood at attention, surrounded by glittering emerald waters, tall statues of warriors in monstrous helmets, and hundreds of statues in the likeness of lion-like creatures. The splendor took the last of her breath away.

"I suppose it's easy to govern from here," she mused, catching her breath. "Perhaps our sultana would like a throne in the clouds to watch over the whole continent."

Turning to look out, they finally broke the tree line. Carefully skirting the edge, she could look down and see everything. "It's huge," she whispered. "And so round. I bet from the top of the palace you can see for miles."

Before they moved into the Royal City walls, Sybal cut off the path to find a hidden place to relieve herself. When Tzarik didn't complain, stop her, or urge her on, she knew how exhausted he must be. Leaving him on the road, she ducked into a field of jagged boulders and rocks. Ditches twelve feet deep dropped all around here. Carefully, she found one to crawl into that she'd be able to squat in and safely exit.

As she climbed down, she noticed pink and green veins in the rock. The green she recognized as the jade that decorated most everything on Xia. The pink looked like quartz. She began to wonder if she could make runes out of any stone when she hit the bottom. Turning, she gasped.

Smeared over the rock, bloodied, cut, and his neck snapped, was a man in a white robe with a hood. Hidden knives on his wrists, the empty sheath at his side, and the white, round bombs on his belt told her this was the assassin who'd attacked them last night.

His eyelids had been removed. This had been an execution.

Suddenly unable to relieve herself, she scrambled back up to Tzarik.

"I saw his body," she whispered quickly. "The assassin."

This perked Tzarik up. "Show me."

She took him back through the crags and pointed into the drop off. He knelt down, rubbing his chin, examining the body from afar. "That looks like the one from Porsh."

"Or very similar," she breathed. "Would a Reaver follow us all the way here? And how did they know where we went? We covered our tracks so well. Took the long way."

Standing up, Tzarik murmured, "Unless he never left the back of us. Or knew where we were going. Or knew where we might hide."

"Why would anyone, even Sharar, suspect we'd come to Xia?"

Her mentor chewed the inside of his cheek, frowning deeply. "I'm not sure. Unless he suspects we'd come here for a reason."

"Would he think we've gone to Caerwren? Runers are more understood there," she offered.

Tzarik shrugged, tired. "He might've known that and decided we wouldn't go there, thinking that we knew he might think we went there."

"Oof." Sybal rubbed her brows. "That was confusing. And I'm tired. And hungry. And I smell."

Tzarik nodded. "Very much."

Sybal's jaw dropped and she smacked his shoulder, turning back to the horses.

⸙

"A shibboleth won't get you inside the palace, Runer," the guard said to Sybal when they finally made it to the gate of the Di-Huan. "Those passes are for the west only."

"I told you, we have a letter to give to someone in the palace," she pleaded. "Her name is Yui."

The guard took a step back. "A letter from who?"

"Uh," Sybal touched the buckle of her belt nervously. "I am just the courier," she fibbed strongly. Close enough, she thought. "It must be given to Yui by my hand. She is expecting it," she added quickly.

Squinting, the guard motioned for them to wait and went inside the palace gates.

"I suppose not just anyone can get in to see the palace," she said with a sigh. "Is it true that Xians believe the Di-Huan was a god once?"

Tzarik shook his head. "I have no idea. They believe that in Alika. Their pharaohs are gods incarnate. According to them." He smirked sarcastically.

Affronted, she turned back to the gate. "I say my prayers and read the mihal, you know? Do you think so little of me?"

He didn't reply. She carefully glanced at him from under her black hood and saw him lower his head. His left foot kicked at a pebble.

The guard reappeared. "Come in," he said hurriedly. With quick movements, he pulled them through the gate. "The Di-Huan wants to meet the Runers from Al'Myrah."

A little concerned at being a roadside attraction, Sybal readied herself to read Tzarik's cues when it came to answering questions. Gods, please let him speak Al'Myrahn, she begged for the sake of Tzarik.

The stone path to the palace door cut across a wide, open stone courtyard. She'd expected it to be empty, but dozens of soldiers packed the area, all in perfect lines. Outfitted in light armor with odd, peaked helmets, they all moved in step to a man calling movements at the front. Each was armed with a yari, red tassels hanging down, fluttering with each quick movement. At first terrified of the shouts, the synchronicity calmed her. They passed with not one man or woman breaking the furrowed concentration on their faces.

The inside of the palace yawned open and spacious. Concubines, servants, and scribes hurried about their tasks. One scribe carried a small table on tiny legs with an ink pot and bamboo pen out of one room and into another. They didn't have much time to look before the guard ushered them into the throne room.

Sybal gasped when they entered. She'd never been inside the

palace in Hatal, but she bet it was not as elegant as the throne room of the Di-Huan of Xia. Only red pillars lined the sides, open to the colorful gardens outside. A gazebo filled with loud children could be seen over an ornamental shrine and pond to the left. Stacked near the front of the room were rows of bamboo and canvas painted walls for putting up against the pillars should the weather get bad.

Around the room, many knelt or stood, chatting in gold, jade, and silk garments. Women fanned their painted faces, their eyes glued to the strange, tall blonde woman who passed by them. Men in dark-colored robes, armed to the teeth and with long, sweeping braids, made way for them. The guard took them to the foot of a raised platform where a small man sat on a throne made of gold, sun beams fashioned behind it, bursting out from where he sat at the center.

The guard bowed onto his knees before the Di-Huan. "May the sun never set on your majesty. The Runers." He stood up and moved aside, waving to them.

Watching Tzarik stiffly come forward and nod, she did the same, but with a whole bow.

"Gloriousness," she stammered in Xian. "May the sun never set on your majesty."

The Di-Huan smiled down at her so tightly his eyes almost vanished into his round face and wrinkles. He stood—coming no taller than when he sat on the throne—and waved for her to rise.

"Runers, is it?" He beamed. "How marvelous. You are here with a message for my daughter Yui?"

Sybal heard Tzarik audibly choke. She stifled a gasp. "Daughter?"

"Well," the Di-Huan waved his hands dismissively, making his long, silky sleeves flap. "Her mother is not a wife or concubine, so not really my daughter, some would tell you. But I love my little monkey." He pointed to the left where a parade of children came around to join the others.

At the head, a beautiful young woman of about fifteen glided along. She had large, round eyes and carried bundles of silks in her arms. She broke from the group and went down a set of stone steps to a large, round, green pond. Two long stalks of some sort of wooded plant crisscrossed the pond. The princess stepped out onto the stalks.

"Ah!" the Di-Huan sighed, with a beaming smile. "A bamboo dance. She has practiced for years."

With the utmost ease, the princess glided out onto the bamboo and held her head high. With a flourish, she tossed the bundles of silk out before her. They cascaded away, attached to her sleeves. The water rippled and the slim bamboo she stood upon moved but she never lost her footing, moving into a slow and elegant dance.

"And my first son." The Di-Huan drew their attention back inside and motioned for a young man off the side to join him. "Hiro, first prince of Xia."

The man, close to Sybal in age, joined his father at the arm of the throne. His stoic face didn't change as he bowed stiffly. The soft pad of shoes from farther behind the throne made Hiro freeze halfway up from his bow and grimace. Glancing from the Di-Huan to the Runers, he mumbled something inaudible and left.

"The desert man before you does not speak Xian, your gloriousness," a smooth voice rumbled from behind the throne where Hiro had just vanished. ShanBao stepped out, his hands hidden inside the opposite sleeves of his robe.

"Oh, pardon me!" the Di-Huan said quickly in Al'Myrahn.

"Nothing to worry about," Tzarik said softly. Sybal noticed his eyes were locked on ShanBao.

"So," the Di-Huan sat back on his throne. "A message for Yui? From whom?"

Sybal and Tzarik both glanced at each other. She looked to ask for permission to speak but his eyes crackled with lightning. Confused, she deflated, the magic of the love letter lost.

"It is to be delivered to her," Tzarik tried.

ShanBao almost smirked. "We have important business to discuss anyway, your gloriousness. The Runers are staying at my estate should you want to speak with them. Later." He emphasized the last word.

The Di-Huan didn't face ShanBao as he spoke, forcing himself to look into Sybal's eyes. "I'd love to have a conversation with you and your man someday. Soon."

She smiled at his attempt to use Al'Mayrahn words to describe her and Tzarik's relationship. "Another time, then."

"See Yui on your way out," he commanded them.

Tzarik and Sybal bowed and exited into the garden. The Di-Huan's eyes sadly watched them go.

"Go," Tzarik murmured to Sybal, ducking behind some ferns and backtracking to the throne room.

"Don't!" she hissed, but he didn't stop. Stamping her foot, she moaned and turned to find the princess now engaged in painting near the water's edge.

"Your highness?" she asked in Xian.

Turning so her dripping golden adornments clinked, Yui smiled when she saw Sybal. "Runer!" she gasped, leaping up and clapping her hands. "You found me!"

"With help. Jin told us where to find you, but he left out a few details. As did you." She scrutinized the young princess. "Are you seeing him in the old temple?"

Yui's face fell and her hand clapping slowed. "What...? No. Why?"

"He gave us a letter to give to you. After you asked us to clear the temple of the haunt. The ghost told us young lovers met there."

She raised her brows. "Princess, I care about Jin. This secrecy has me concerned, is all."

Yui's young face broke into a glowing grin. "Don't mind us." She leaned in and whispered, "It's so fun. Sneaking around. Chancing a glance. Steeling a kiss. Meeting in the dark of night..."

A longing for something missing in her life pierced Sybal. Her chest ached. She'd been young and in love only just over a year ago. She'd told herself over and over, she didn't need that. That didn't stop the desire. The loneliness.

"Jin asked us to give you a message," she said with a sigh. Behind her, Tzarik approached. "But we lost it."

"Lost?" The smallest hint of caution darkened Yui's eyes. "What did it say?"

Sybal shook her head. "I'm sorry, I don't know."

The princess pressed her bright red lips together and craned her neck to get a glance back inside the distant throne room. Hiro slowly walked towards them with a careful gait. "Wushito has come to see my father more and more as the spring comes to its apex," she said casually, eyes boring into Sybal.

"It must be nice to see Jin more, then," Sybal replied, trying to read the girl. "But I supposed you cannot spend time with him."

Yui's lower lip trembled. "Ours is a hope for a peaceful future. We make the most out of our time."

Again, Sybal felt the princess tried to impart a hidden message, but she couldn't find it.

"I must go." Yui smiled to Hiro and turned. To a servant, she asked in Xian for a courier pigeon to be brought to her. She didn't follow the parade of children into the royal gardens, instead doubling back towards the palace.

Defeated, Sybal watched the princess go.

"Might I take a moment of your time?" Hiro asked the Runers in their native tongue as the three of them converged.

"Is it a crime to say no?" Tzarik asked gruffly.

Hiro's lips parted in shock and he stammered softly before Sybal cut in.

"Of course," she said gently, leading the way down a gravel path away from the densely populated areas. She didn't know where the path led, but Hiro followed between the two of them.

The prince stood a head shorter than Sybal but taller than Tzarik. His somber face never cracked, and his eyes stayed honed on the path before them. His long black hair wafted in the breeze and Sybal smelled cherry blossoms coming from its glossy strands. Draped in royal silken robes with a ceremonious sword at his side, she saw just how he dressed the part of the symbolic prince. Based on what she'd heard, he'd never sit on the throne.

He unclenched his tight jaw. "I am a mere decoration for the palace," he said. "But I am not stupid nor a coward."

Sybal and Tzarik looked at each other, slightly confused.

"I know my father hopes for Yui or some child of hers to take the throne after him," Hiro went on. "In other cultures, it would be me. I don't hate her, Runers, but I do fear for my country."

Tzarik looked away, sighing and fighting to not roll his eyes. Sybal glared at him before she answered.

"Is there a reason you have chosen to speak to us, your highness?" They seemed to be an item of interest to all in the royal household and she couldn't think why.

"You are outsiders," Hiro quipped, his eyes scanning the area for any prying ears or eyes. "You do what Wushito does, but do not threaten us."

Tzarik lifted his head at this. "How do they threaten you?"

"They saved us," Sybal reminded him. "ShanBao saved my life."

Hiro's breath came faster and his head snapped around to look for something neither of them could see. They stopped outside a pavilion-like shrine, guarded by statues of two strange creatures. "I can't tell you because I don't know," Hiro said, almost pleading. "The generals have flexed their authority more recently, and ShanBao comes to the palace more than usual. I am afraid for my father and my people."

When Tzarik crossed his arms, interested, Sybal couldn't help but scoff.

"Tensions are high, that's all. Why won't the next Di-Huan be selected as before?" she asked.

Hiro looked down, despondent, to the guardians outside the pavilion. "No one is coming forward from any house save House Xiaoh. They fear Wushito's power too much."

Sybal grimaced. "I wouldn't want them on the throne, either. But how do you know anything bad might happen?"

Tapping one of the statues, Hiro said, "This is a Phi-she and a Mong Sho. They appear when the balance of the continent is in jeopardy. One heralds the end of a great ruler and the other will attack those they believe are the threat."

Finally something he understood coming up in the conversation, Tzarik asked, "And you saw them?"

"Not I." Hiro shook his head. "Yui."

"Omens?" Tzarik asked, his voice taking on the skeptical lilt Sybal had come to hate. "You want us to get between two ruling powers on a foreign continent because of omens?"

The shock that shot from Hiro's eyes made even Sybal doubt her loyalty to ShanBao.

"Xia is unlike other countries," the prince tried. "Our land stays erect simply because the Dragon wills it. His messengers must be heeded."

"Perhaps by you." Tzarik shook his head and turned to leave.

"I'm sorry," Sybal said on her mentor's behalf, sighing. "He has not taken to the new land well. I know you must feel genuine fear for your father and your people, but..." She shrugged helplessly. "ShanBao saved me. Twice. I understand the work they do. I don't believe you have anything to fear from ShanBao, and as he sits at the head of Wushito, I don't believe you have to fear them, either."

Apologetically, she bowed to Hiro and followed her mentor back.

⁓

"You were suspicious of ShanBao from the start," Sybal pointed out from under her cloak while they trotted down the woodland paths to the Shiuki province and their host's home. "Why not now?"

"Perhaps I don't care enough," he said loudly over the rain. He shook out his long hair before pulling up his own hood even though the rain drenched through it already. "Why do you?"

She held her head a little higher before replying. "I care about Jin. And Yui. What they have is special. And dangerous."

He cocked a repulsed brow towards her. "The boy, I understand. Why do you care about them together?"

Taking a steadying breath, she said, "Love is powerful, Tzarik. It can mend nations, bring great kings to their knees, make a woman queen, and humble the proudest man. If anything happened to Jin, I'd hunt down the sands of time for Yui so she could turn back the sun."

Tzarik turned towards their path. "I don't understand you, Sybal."

CHAPTER 7
HOUSE XIAOH

THE LAST TWO HOURS OF THE JOURNEY TO THE SHIUKI province had passed in torrents of cold, heavy rain. The Runers were soaked through by the time they crossed the threshold into ShanBao's blessedly cozy home. Tzarik was hyperaware of the mud he tracked over the clean, glimmering floors. ShanBao came around a corner followed by a stone-faced scribe.

"Runers," he said placidly, eyeing them up and down. "You should not be out in this weather. The rain fever should not be taken lightly."

Dripping onto the stone floors, Tzarik saw a flash of steal in ShanBao's eyes. "How did you get back here before us?"

ShanBao smiled, steepling his long fingers. "I know this continent in and out. I was in a hurry and I did not dally with Hiro. I am sorry to tell you, Runers, but things might get ugly."

"What do you mean?" Tzarik asked. "Is this why you were at the palace?"

"I was at the palace because I frequently meet with the Di-Huan," ShanBao offered calmly. "The Wushito only want what's best for Xia. Sometimes, since sentient kind are naturally evil, that requires a little more tact than I'd like to use."

Tzarik agreed with the philosophy, but speaking with ShanBao at that moment reminded him of speaking to Sharar during their negotiation: something dangerous lurked beneath.

"What's happening?" Sybal asked, handing her drenched cloak to a servant woman who approached them, hands out.

ShanBao ushered them into a side room. A sunken area filled with round cushions and small bamboo tables filled most of the room. Tzarik hesitated; his soaked clothes would leave a terrible watermark. The Wushito master called for tea and a hot bath to be drawn for Sybal. Once the tea arrived, he asked them to sit.

"Don't worry, they are replaceable." He floated down onto a cushion, picking up a pair of narrow sticks and snapping at a tray of seafood and rice with them. "We have received intelligence recently that House Xioah is rallying and on the move. I had to warn the Di-Huan."

Tzarik caught Sybal sitting up straighter. "I cannot imagine a people who would attack their own," she said sternly. "Al'Myrahns still hold on to their tribal nature. We are a close continent, always protecting what is ours."

Nodding slowly, ShanBao chewed and swallowed what Tzarik was fairly certain was a rolled up raw eel. "Xia is not Al'Myrah. I'd like to invite you to get to know my country through the Dragon Festival in a fortnight. If House Xiaoh has not attacked by then, it will be a splendid opportunity for you."

Sybal deflated. "It would be magnificent to experience it."

"I pray you do." ShanBao waved in a waiting servant. "Your bath is ready, Sybal-kim. Tzarik, stay a moment, will you?"

Tired, with her back bent, Sybal followed the servant out, not looking back at him once.

Alone with ShanBao, Tzarik pricked up his instincts and attention. "Intelligence, huh?" he asked, fighting to keep the suspicion out of his tone. "I'm curious about Wushito and your relationship with the Di-Huan. His army didn't look like it needed any external help. The discourse on Xia looks to be between those who follow you and those who follow the Di-Huan."

Pouring more tea and avoiding Tzarik's eyes, ShanBao said, "You are astute, Runer. I underestimated you because of Sybal. I see how you watch her. And I see how she watches Jin. She's quite fond of him, and I wouldn't have believed it, but he is of her as well. Jin has longed for a woman in his life, ever since I took him from his deranged father. His father killed his mother, of course, when he made it clear he wanted their dragon-touched son to rule the land. Jin is so talented. He has made an excellent Wushito warrior, though his philosophy has strayed some in recent years."

"He doesn't believe all sentient beings are naturally evil?"

ShanBao tapped his temple. "There is more to it than that, Runer. Xian philosophers have spent millennia studying sentient kind. We really are just black and white. There is good and there is evil. Knowing what the two are, however, that is the point to your existence."

The rain permeated his skin and a shiver that started far below the surface of his flesh set in. His legs shook first. "I'm not a philosopher, ShanBao. Sorry to disappoint you. I know civil war is never the thing to bring a country together, but I don't have to be a scholar to know that. I'm here to find a moment of peace. I don't like that you're threatening that. I don't like to be used."

"Used?" Sitting up and dropping the sticks, ShanBao said, "I think you don't like that Sybal sees it differently than you. I think you came here to be with her. I think you lie even to yourself to keep her with you."

That wasn't true. It didn't stop Tzarik from shifting on the cushion, though. ShanBao thought he was clever and could get inside his head.

"So you are going to attack Wu-Tang even though they have not made a move yet?" he asked, clarifying.

The Wushito master chewed and nodded with indifference. "We know they are. A missive was on its way to certain parties, detailing their plans. Tzarik." He leaned forward, capturing the Runer's glance. "Hiro wants to be Di-Huan after his father. He will crush any uprising and call on Wushito for aid. Let us eradicate the threat before they reach us."

"There are innocent people in Wu-Tang," Tzarik said, his voice becoming unexpectedly soft.

ShanBao swallowed, eyes never leaving Tzarik's face. "I have tried for decades to tame the province of House Xiaoh. The peace must be kept until a dragon-touched worthy of Wushito law and Xian justice can sit on the throne."

Tzarik leaned forward to meet the older warrior's gaze. "People don't like to be used, Wu-ShanBao."

Standing up, bowing stiffly, he excused himself and went to find Sybal. He asked a few servants and they pointed him to the back left side of the house. Without thinking, he slid open the canvas doors to the bath house.

"Ra'hala!" Sybal gasped, using one of the gods of Al'Myrah as a curse and dropping under the foggy, steaming water. "Knock before you enter a lady's room!"

She submerged herself, but not before he caught the gentle, dark curve of her back leading to her round backside. She'd been standing with her hair over one shoulder, brushing it with oils and scented rubs. Now she sat with just her eyes and forehead peeking over the surface, glowering at him.

His throat constricted, forcing him to cough to clear it. "I'm going to Wu-Tang," he said stiffly. The heat from the bath made his face pale with rushing sulfates. His heart would not listen to him and pounded against his ribs.

"Tzarik, no," she pleaded. "They don't deserve to be warned. Let Wushito descend on them."

He could explain to her, but she'd argue. She always argued. "It's not for them, it's for Xia," he said steadily. "Civil war is not the way." He knew how to convince her. "If they fight, Jin fights. He's young and inexperienced."

Sybal's blue eyes widened. "I can't see him fighting, bloodied on a battlefield. Not now that I know he's secretly in love with the daughter of the Di-Huan." She sighed, pushing a path in the steam with her breath. She smiled shyly. "I know you don't care for such things, but it's romantic." With heavy lidded eyes, she looked up at him. "Are you leaving now? Or do you want to rest and clean up first?"

The water rippled, showing her breath had picked up. Slowly raising her hand above the surface, she patted it like a chair, inviting him. The heat, the gentle trickling of the fountain that fed the bath, the pink flowers around it, and the delicious scent of whatever she'd rubbed in her hair almost weakened him.

She's my apprentice, he hissed to himself.

"I have no time to lose," he said stiffly. "ShanBao must have spies everywhere, or he wouldn't know Wu-Tang is organizing. If they know that Wushito knows they are coming, they may wait."

She nodded. "Safe travels."

He turned on his muddy boot and marched to the exit.

"Tzarik!" she called.

He stopped.

"I'm glad you decided to do this."

The pride in her voice swelled his ego just enough to get him through the rainy, cold night. Her words warmed him and gave him the energy he so desperately needed to leave the gates.

THIS TIME, his stalker was not near as careful as the now dead one. It didn't have the same breathing patterns or white shimmer. Not being a Reaver, he feared it far less, but being followed had lost its thrill several miles back. The rain allowed him to hear the clumsy squelching of his follower's steps. The only time he couldn't track exactly where they were was when he made camp.

Tzarik shivered in the cold Xian rain, huddled close to his fire. It had been a year since he'd traveled the road alone. Never had it been so wet. He'd spent most of his life on Al'Myrah, Bahratt, and even some time on Alika. Rhostrana was reserved for desperate hunts. As one of the wealthiest continents, even peasants paid his prices to have a ghoul slaughtered. Rarely meeting another Runer made it so he never had to compete for the coin, either. Since Azar had left him, he'd been alone.

Taking a long stick, he jabbed at the fire, forcing the cinders to collapse before adding fresh logs he'd been drying next to the embers. If it hadn't been for the leftover kindling and firewood on his saddle, this one wouldn't have sprung into life.

Tired of the thoughts of loneliness that edged slowly into his mind, reminding him of how he used to be not long ago, he took a quick drink of arac—the liquor from his home that he kept a small supply of—leaned against a tree, and tried to sleep. Not worried about his shadow, sleep took him.

Two days later, the rain mercifully stopping, he arrived above Wu-Tang. He recognized the road now in the setting sun and spotted the tall manor that had made Sybal want to avoid the city. Made of stone, but still in the shape of most Xian architecture, Wu-Tang cut a far more ominous image. Surrounded by tall, steal-colored crags and mountains, the trees with the sweeping branches fought for their lives, cutting through rock and stone to reach towards the sky.

Not sure who he should talk to, he easily passed the city wall:

no gates bared the way and the black- and gray-clad guards eyed him only slightly curiously. Instead of the crisp, gold-inlaid silk of Shiuki, most guards and citizens wore dark colors and grungy, fur-lined garments. Since the city was made of stone, every drip from the rooftop and step in a puddle could be heard. To blend in, he pulled his hood over his bright blue eyes and started to weave his way through the streets. Behind him, his shadow tried to keep up. Glad the city provided some cover, he started quick movements and sudden turns to lose it.

It took less time than he'd thought. In a matter of minutes, the follower vanished, and he doubled back, climbing up the easily scalable side of a stone structure. Hiding behind a roaring stone dragon where water sputtered out into a gutter, he scanned the street behind where he'd just been. He spotted his shadow. A short, slight male figure in a dark cloak. He had a sword strapped to his hip, and several tiny star-shaped knives around his boot. Tzarik recognized those.

Curious, he followed the shadow. This couldn't have been the one that had attacked them when they'd first gone deeper into Xia, could it? That assassin had been far clumsier than either Reaver they'd encountered. So was this one, but he had a little more grace about him. Tzarik followed as he looked for him. The shadow cut through an alley. Tzarik only had to glance around to see the alley lay empty of any other passerby. This was his chance.

Like a falcon, he leapt from the roof, landing with his feet against the shadow's back, knocking all the wind out of him and thrusting him to the ground. Pinning him with his legs, Tzarik spun him around, pointing his hand-held crossbow at the stalker's face.

"Tzarik, don't!" Jin cried, holding his hands up by his head.

Shocked, he almost lowered his weapon. He remembered the knife on his boot and held fast. "Are you the attacker from before?"

he hissed, holding a handful of Jin's hair so he couldn't look around for aid.

"I don't know what you're talking about, so I doubt it," the boy replied quickly. He didn't shake or cower. "I followed you because I want you to help me."

Tzarik never liked being confused or to have riddles thrown in his face. Nothing about Jin in the moment gave away any harmful intent. Annoyed, he let go and stood up, but didn't offer him a hand. "I suggest you tell me what you want, and in the plainest way you know."

Smiling and adjusting his cloak, Jin said, "I'd never want to be on your bad side, Runer, which is why I am going to confess to you. But not here. Somewhere safe." Seeing the lightning snap in the Runer's eyes, he added, "It's not far. I swear it's safe."

If he hadn't known how much Sybal liked the boy, he'd have left then. The image of her asking him to be safe, surrounded by soft steam, held his temper for him.

Grudgingly, he motioned for Jin to lead the way.

Like a pair of shadows, they kept to the darker parts of the city and eventually wound up outside the estate with the lion-maned dragon and serpent crest.

"House Xiaoh?" Tzarik asked. Suspicion rose but his sulfates did not tingle and his instinctual guard did not go up.

Jin nodded, going inside. The stonework almost reminded Tzarik of a cathedral he'd seen on Rhostrana, with its soft echoes and dark coldness. It had none of the warmth and glowing lights ShanBao's home did. Racks of spears and other weapons lined the walls. Somewhere out back, a man shouted and a mixed chorus replied in kind as they trained. Jin led him up a set of stone steps into what Tzarik understood immediately to be a war room. A mix of human and Masahk mingled there, discussing tactics over maps and armor.

When Jin passed them, they bowed low and addressed him with an honorific Tzarik didn't know.

"What is that they keep saying to you?" he asked. "*Xai-long?*"

"It means white dragon," Jin offered, stopping at a large, round stone table.

Trying to put the riddle together before he was told, Tzarik cycled through all he'd heard up till this point. Unwilling to get involved, he had a hard time remembering everything. When Jin let his hood down and his white hair shone in the nearly set sun, he remembered.

"Touched by the dragon," he thought out loud. "The sign of one who can rule."

Jin nodded. "Xia believes those born with the mark of the dragon," he grabbed a strand of his white locks, "are to be the next Di-Huan. Xia used to thrive on its traditions. It was always that way. But now, our Di-Huan wants to change that—have his first son sit on the sun throne. That cannot be. A dragon-touched *must* rule."

Tzarik rubbed his chin. He didn't speak his thoughts out loud, but recalled Hiro making it seem like the Di-Huan spoke of Yui or her children as being the next ruler. Everyone wanted to sit on Xia's throne; despite that, they all knew or believed they were not the right ones for the task. The traditions didn't seem to be stopping them. Would one of them stand up above the rest, possibly destroying the ancient kingdom?

Before he could go on, an entourage of guards in dark Wu-Tang armor led in a single weather-beaten woman in purple robes with gold trim. She clutched a scroll in her hands and bowed quickly to Jin.

"Jin Xiaoh," she addressed him before launching into a long, trickling speech in a lowland dialect of Xian. She spoke differently enough from those in Shiuki that Tzarik guessed she came from another province. But that wasn't what had piqued his interest.

After a quick back and forth, Jin thanking the woman and commanding she be given accommodations, Tzarik turned to Jin, his hand resting on the hilt of his scimitar.

"Jin Xiaoh?" he asked measuredly. Secretly, he thanked any gods he hadn't let Sybal join him.

Drawing himself up, Jin nodded. "It's what I wanted to tell you. My father, Whoang Xiaoh, attacked Shiuki and went on a crusade to bring the dragon-touched back to the throne after I was born. The Di-Huan's son does not have the mark of the dragon."

Remembering back to his quick visit to the quiet ruler, he remembered the sullen young man he'd introduced as the crowned prince. His black hair had stood out against his gold silks.

"You're right," Tzarik admitted. "But most would just accept him. He is the legitimate son of the Di-Huan."

"That is how you westerners do things," Jin said with authority. "Not here."

He bit his tongue; it wasn't the first time he'd been called that. He didn't like being called a westerner. That was reserved for the savage lands of Caerwren.

"If you only put those touched by the dragon—"

He couldn't keep the sarcasm out of his voice and noticed Jin's eyes narrow at the insult.

"Sorry." He controlled his prejudice thoughts. "Then anyone could claim to be ruler."

"Yes!" Jin said excitedly. "It keeps Xia honest. We believe the dragon will touch anyone. That way, you cannot favor one house over another. You are more careful who you stab in the back and who you show kindness to."

"Sounds overly confusing," Tzarik mumbled. "You should know, Sybal hates your house."

Jin cocked a brow.

Before he spoke, Tzarik stopped to consider what telling Jin who'd killed his father might do to their relationship. She was practically in love with the boy. He decided it was not his place. He couldn't ruin what she had.

"Whoang Xiaoh is widely hated," he said quickly. "Many only know of his conquest over Xia. It was bloody and dark. He left the continent and tried to gather off-shore allies."

"And that was his greatest sin," Jin confirmed. "He left me behind, abandoned. But I am not convinced he was wrong. I am touched by the White Dragon. Ze'oul has offered me their support. That woman was a messenger from a powerful house. We in the lowlands want our Di-Huan to remain on the throne, and those with the mark to be his successor. It has to be that way, Tzarik. Hiro is not what Xia needs."

Guessing the answer, Tzarik asked, "And who thinks otherwise?"

Smiling because Tzarik had caught on, Jin pointed to an empty spot on the map of Xia before them. "Wushito. The Hallow City is hidden here. No one on Xia can find it except those who know where it is. ShanBao and his generals rule with fear. I admire the work they do for Xia—they call themselves patriots—but Wushito wants to rule Xia in place of a Di-Huan. Again, that's not right."

Tzarik rubbed his chin, looking at the empty spot on the map. It lay north and higher up the continent than Shiuki. He knew where it was; he'd heard a bell ring from there on his first morning in Xia.

"ShanBao is not evil, Jin," he tried. There was something about him he didn't like, though. But the boy didn't need to know that.

"You don't know, Tzarik." Jin looked up with large, earnest brown eyes. "The Wushito may seem like quiet philosophers and benevolent warriors, but you've seen a taste of their ways."

The public execution floated to the front of his mind. The

Masahk generals put the fear of the gods into the citizens of Shiuki.

The boy went on cautiously, "ShanBao will support the Di-Huan's desire to put the prince on the throne because it serves him. I cannot break my oath of silence, but there are other weapons at Wushito's disposal. If Wushito is somehow subjugated, they may use it."

Defeated, Tzarik sighed. "There are forces moving in the world greater than a dispute here on Xia," he said cautiously. "A war is the last thing you'll want right now."

A stern determination bent Jin's brows. "This is my continent, Runer. I have been marked by the dragon. It is my duty to not let ShanBao and his thugs take it from me or the people, or to let him manipulate the Di-Huan."

Jin was young, hot-headed, and ambitious. Unsure how to make him understand, Tzarik offered information instead. "I came to warn Wu-Tang. ShanBao said he had intelligence on the city rallying. I see that's true. He wants to strike before you're ready."

The boy drew himself up and smiled. "Thank you, Runer. You have set things in motion for me." He clasped Tzarik's shoulder, grateful. "I know you will help me. Don't tell Sybal. She would not think as well of me if she knew what I was doing."

Tzarik looked away. "You may be wrong. I came to warn Wu-Tang in the hopes of stopping an attack that will tear your country apart. You *say* you want peace, but your actions show me other-wise, Jin."

Jin firmly planted his hands on the war room table before him. In a shadowy corner, a man covered in warpaint looked up from a spear he was sharpening, eyeing Tzarik to make sure he did not attack their young master.

"Tzarik," the boy started again, "making a stand is what we do. But my cause is greater: to save my home from the growing authority of Wushito and the foolish want of our Di-Huan to let Hiro rule after him. They are not meant to rule. ShanBao raised me for a reason. Early on, I sensed his desire to control me. I won't let him. I will not be his king on a game board. I have a plan to unite the people. My conquest will not be as my father's."

"You won't tell me that plan," Tzarik mumbled, defeated. He didn't need to ask.

Jin shook his head. "To protect someone I love, I cannot."

The boy before him suddenly changed to a man. A dangerous, incautious man. Realizing he'd put himself into the situation by trying to maintain the peace—now trapped— Tzarik nodded.

"Very well, Jin Xiaoh."

CHAPTER 8
MONG 3HO

THE DAYS IT TOOK TZARIK TO REACH SHIUKI AGAIN ALLOWED him (tortured him) with time to think. He couldn't stop it now. He'd—as his mentor would have said—let the djinn out of the lamp.

"Why did I go to Wu-Tang?" he asked his frothing horse. He slid off the saddle to give it a rest. Wiping the condensation off his brow, he growled. "Why is the air so damn wet and hot here?!"

The humidity seeped under his armor, chafing. His thighs were rubbed raw from walking and riding. Everything stung and he couldn't get a proper breath from the muggy air. Maybe the climate made him short tempered and rash? He shouldn't have gone to Wu-Tang. The city, lorded over by House Xiaoh, should not be on the throne. He'd heard of Whoang Xiaoh when the warlord had crusaded for what he'd thought was his right. Tzarik assumed he'd just been a bloodthirsty man, bent on ruling the continent. Now he wondered if Whoang Xiaoh had genuinely believed his son should be Di-Huan. Jin had aspirations for good. Would it be so bad if he ascended the throne?

Now that he knew ShanBao's concern, the old warrior didn't seem to be in the wrong. Still, something about him made Tzarik's sulfates run cold. Conflicted, he eased his mind by asking merchants on his way through the city about sulfate ingredients as best he could. Most didn't know what he asked for and others pointed out of town, babbling quickly. He spotted one of the generals, the one called Yasuke with the foxlike attributes, leading a set of guards around the inner walls. A couple of street urchins, spotting the general, ran and vanished under a barred grate in the stone street. The one day he'd spent on Xia as a younger man came back in flashing light.

He remembered running from Azar and trying to join the street urchins. He couldn't understand a word they said, but knew it would be better than the fate that awaited him. Trying to blend in, learning quickly from the others how to duck and meld with a crowd, he hoped when Azar came back from the northern island, he'd be so well assimilated, his master would leave without him.

Laughing dryly at his younger self, he lazily saluted the guard who opened the gate to ShanBao's home. He'd just taken two steps inside, desperate for a cold drink of water and maybe one of those baths Sybal liked so much, when her scream cut through the house walls. Dropping everything but his scimitar and runes, Tzarik dashed through the front doors, his weariness vaporizing. He blamed the humidity again for clouding his judgment.

"The other one ran down the stairs!" Sybal's voice shouted from above.

"Behind you!" ShanBao cried.

A bone-chilling roar rumbled through the rafters. Sounding like the roar of a lion and the scream of some unknown creature, the roar was accompanied by the clacking of heavy, sharp hooves.

"Where are you?" Tzarik shouted, whipping around and looking above.

A yowling like a jaguar tore through the air, followed by a rabid stomping.

"Tzarik!" Sybal shouted. "One ran down the stairs! Watch out!"

"What is—?" He stopped. Turning to face the back entrance, he froze. Every drip of sweat trickling down his back turned to ice.

Facing him at eye level, a massive beast blocked the back double doors. The creature locked eyes with him. Too afraid to break the connection, Tzarik scanned the beast with his peripheral vision. It's sandy-colored coat rippled with equine muscle and form. Its long legs ended in sharp, cloven hooves. The coat reminded him of a lion, as did the mane surrounding the dragon head on its long neck. The eastern dragons did not have the reptilian features of Al'Myrah or the far west. Covered in pearly scales with soft, flowing whiskers, its short face demanded respect, not fear.

Unable to move his feet, his hand hovered over his scimitar handle. The sulfates rushed in his veins, his heart pounding. Looking into this beast's eyes was not like looking into the eyes of other monsters he'd vanquished. Though he shook, he didn't sense a threat. The longer he looked, the more he felt a whispering in his mind.

I see you, it said.

His eyes dried from not blinking. Taking a chance, he licked his lips, suddenly dry, and mumbled, "What do you see?" He didn't expect a reply.

You, the deep, rich-timbered voice replied.

Above him, Sybal screamed. Without hesitating, leaving the monster that had trained its eyes on him, he turned to look up. Another, exactly the same creature, pounced upon her. Its dragon face snapped its maw towards hers. ShanBao appeared behind it, raising a yari to stab the creature. With a jaguar scream, the one behind Tzarik leapt all the way up to the second floor, tackling ShanBao and saving its comrade.

Panting again, Tzarik dashed up the stairs, wishing he'd seized his bow from his horse. As he ascended the stairs, guards from outside came in, yelling at the sight of the monster inside. Without waiting a beat, he swiped at the beast that pinned Sybal down. Hitting it hard on its flank, the monster roared and reared up like a horse, clawing the air with its hooves. Sybal rolled to the side to get up. The monster turned on Tzarik, baring its fangs. With a leap, it snapped at him, stopping just inches from his chest. Confused and relieved, he spun around it to cover Sybal, swinging wildly at it. It backed away, yowling as it did so.

"Help ShanBao!" Sybal called, shoving Tzarik down the hallway the other monster had leapt down.

Trusting she could take care of herself, Tzarik sprinted down the hallway past rooms to the balcony hanging over the garden. ShanBao crouched there, the yari posed before him like a jungle hunter fending off a tiger. He took slow steps to match the beast's and together they circled the balcony.

"Have you ever encountered a mong sho, Runer?" ShanBao called, flicking the yari to taunt the beast.

"No," Tzarik admitted, regripping his scimitar.

"I am glad to give you your first Xian lesson, then." ShanBao lunged at the mong sho, but it leapt lightly to the side, snapping at the spear tip.

Tzarik came around behind it, knowing surrounding the prey was always a good bet.

"They never randomly attack," ShanBao informed him, jabbing and then leaping back as the mong sho snapped and swiped at him. "It is said they cannot hurt the innocent. I've never seen one invade a home before."

The mong sho roared and spun, pouncing on Tzarik. Its dragon face bit at his chest, unable to get close. Drawing buhkar, he slipped from under the beast in a black mist. Re-materializing, he ran a few steps away, gasping for air. Unsure why the beast hadn't torn his heart out, he counted it a blessing.

"Astounding!" ShanBao mused, smiling as Tzarik joined him. "You Runers are worth your weight in emeralds. If the Wushito had your abilities, there would be no contest."

"To what?" Tzarik asked.

ShanBao couldn't reply. The mong sho ran at them, leaping over them. As it did, ShanBao raised the yari, stabbing it in its middle. The creature roared but seemed more inconvenienced than hurt. ShanBao held the spear tight, pulling the creature towards them.

"Use your blade, Runer!" he grunted in the effort to keep the yari impaled inside the creature.

Conflicted but wanting to bring safety to Sybal, Tzarik spun, slicing the mong sho's elegant face. As expected, the orichalcum cut deep, spewing red blood over the jade floor. The mong sho roared in pain and jerked the yari from ShanBao's hand. Turning to face Tzarik, it locked eyes with him. Again, he felt a message from the creature, staying his hand.

"Finish it!" ShanBao shouted.

The mong sho turned and leapt over the railing. Tzarik ran to watch it lope away, but no sign of it showed on the ground below but four bloody hoof prints. ShanBao joined him, looking down. They both took a moment to gather their breath. Behind them, Sybal's hurried steps announced her arrival.

"It vanished," she said, panting.

When Tzarik turned, he saw her clutching her side. Rushing over to her, he pulled her hand away.

"It bit me," she moaned, moving her hands from the leather armor for him to see the jaw marks on her side.

"Are they venomous?" Tzarik shot to ShanBao.

ShanBao shook his head. "No. They shouldn't be in my home! What is happening?"

"Are they an omen?" Tzarik asked, pressing his hand to Sybal's side.

Frowning in thought, ShanBao said softly, "Sometimes." He sighed. "I should tell you, I suppose. These two mong sho have been stalking me for some time. I cannot shake them. I would be grateful for your protection while you are here, since they have broken the boundaries of my home."

"We owe you, anyway." Sybal hissed, her wound stinging. "At least I do."

"Your debts are mine," Tzarik confirmed in a soft mumble.

Sybal glared at him for his tone. "Do you know anything about a mong sho?" she asked him.

Shaking his head, he glanced sideways at ShanBao discreetly. They didn't attack the innocent. Twice the creature had tried to clamp him in its maw, but hadn't been able to reach him. Or something had stopped it. Looking at Sybal's wound, he wondered why it had been able to bite her.

"I suggest you two clean up." ShanBao sighed, slipping his hands into his sleeves and drawing himself up. "Perhaps relax from all your travel..." His eyes rested too long on Tzarik. "Perhaps think about partaking in the festival. We have many traditions you may enjoy."

"A festival. Really? Is that what we should focus on?" Tzarik asked before he could stop himself. The exhaustion ate away at his sensibilities.

ShanBao didn't turn to face him, but he heard him smiling as he replied. "Oh, yes, it is."

BACK IN HIS ROOM, Tzarik peeled his sweat-soaked pants and tunic off. The rooms were equipped with almost an entire wall of mirror so he couldn't help but see himself. Blisters covered the insides of his feet and his legs glowed red and raw. Taking off the layers of grimy clothes felt like being reborn. A silk robe waited, folded into a perfect square by the bed. Deciding it looked soft enough, he donned it and prepared to lie down to sleep when someone tapped on the canvas door.

Without waiting, Sybal slid it open and peeked in. "I can smell you downstairs. Come to the bath house with me." She smiled.

Something he'd never felt before stirred just below his navel and he didn't like it. "I'm fine," he grunted.

Raising her brows and grimacing, Sybal laughed lightly. "Like hell you are. Stop being gloomy for once and come. I want to take your mind off things."

Sighing in defeat, too tired to fight much harder, he followed her out. He became extremely aware of his legs in the robe and tried to discreetly hold the front closed. Sybal walked unabashedly before him, her long legs flitting in and out of the opening up to her thigh, leading him to the bath house. She'd let her hair down and it hung to her backside in waves of thick, swaying white gold.

Inside the bath house, steam rose up from the deep pool in the ground. Lotuses, fruits, and other colorful foliage surrounded it. Somehow, the steam was scented with amber and cherry blossoms, wafting up from the water and immediately penetrating his mind. His limbs screamed to be floating in the hot water, weightless.

"Turn around," Sybal said.

Without asking why, he turned away from her. The sound of the robe slithering to the ground made him tense up. Then a soft plink of a delicate foot stepping into water made him turn around, glancing over his shoulder. Her naked form slowly, carefully, stepped down the stones into the steam. He watched as the foggy water rose up her calves, thighs, and then enveloped her buttocks. She dipped under the water then stood up, face up to the ceiling to get her hair out of the way. Bending her knees, she floated to the side, only her head above the water.

"Now you," she called.

He turned around, waiting for her to avert her eyes. When she didn't, an uneasy feeling of being trapped made him shift his weight. "Look away," he barked.

She sucked her cheeks in, trying to hide a smile, and turned around. Her hair arched around her, floating on top of the water. He dropped the robe and froze, one foot on the stones. She didn't peek.

On the last step, the floor dropped from under him. The pool was much deeper than he'd thought and he sank. Forcing himself to not sputter as he kicked off the bottom to come back up, he gripped the side and found a shallow spot. His face burned from the steam and embarrassment. Hearing the water slosh, Sybal turned back around and shimmied over next to him.

She reached behind them to a plate of soaps and a strange sponge. A few other colored bottles filled with mystery oils waited, too. He sank until the water touched his nose. Allowing him his privacy, she pushed the plate to him after lathering one of the sponges in scented soap. She scrubbed herself below the surface for a few minutes before looking at him. She raised her brows expectantly.

"You know how to wash yourself, right?" She tapped the plate. "You smell. Get clean. I want to go to the festival with you, but you won't embarrass me with your offensive hygiene."

"It's in a week," he mumbled. "I'll be filthy with sweat from this damned continent by then."

"Yes, but you can bathe more than once a month." She turned away and stood up so most of her torso rose above the water. Her long hair covered her. She gingerly used the sponge over her bite wound. She scrubbed it so the wounds opened in the opposite direction of the way the flesh needed to lay.

"Don't do that," he said quickly, grabbing her hand. "If you push it the wrong way like that, it will take longer to re-attached and heal. You'll give yourself a scar and open it to infection."

She let go of the sponge, leaving it in his hand. "Show me," she whispered, looking down at him.

Taking his other hand, he trailed his fingers over the marks, laying her torn flesh down flat. Gently, patting the bite, he slowly ran the soapy sponge over it. Under his rough fingers, her skin glided like silk. He stood up to get a better angle. She turned, gathering her hair over her shoulder, and bared her back to him.

His mouth went dry and that feeling in his lower gut came back. He still didn't like it. It made his head swim with imagining what she looked like out of the water. He didn't mean to insult her with his thoughts, but he couldn't stop it before it happened. Slowly, he scrubbed the grime and sweat from her back.

When she'd had enough, she motioned with an elegant hand for him to turn around. He did and she went to work on his back. The sensation of being touched drove his mind wild, made his heart hammer against his ribs, and also eased every knot and tense muscle. The hot water soaked into his bones as he fell into her touch. She gently pushed his long hair over one shoulder and traced her finger over a scar leading from his neck down to his left shoulder blade.

"So many scars," she whispered close to his ear. "I've thought about them ever since that time at the farmer's home on Bahratt."

He caught her voice hitching, no doubt remembering the first time she'd almost killed him. Unconsciously, his hand went to the wound on his side where she had hit him, his own blade biting into him. That was the closest he'd come to death in some time, and it had terrified him. He'd not expected that.

"Twenty-one years of monsters and wars," he said. His voice felt heavy in his throat, like he shouldn't be speaking at a time like this. But her hands on his marred flesh coaxed the words out of him.

He shivered. Her fingers touched his scalp lightly, running through his hair before she dragged a comb through his tangled locks.

Was this what that time should have felt like? He'd heard his whole life what being with a woman would be like. But the one time he had been with one, it hadn't been for her love. A desire to ask her to not stop, to run her hands over the back of his neck and his arms, consumed him. His breath shuddered and she heard it, stopping. The burning inside him screamed for her hands to come back.

"Sometimes I wish you hadn't had to live like that," she said suddenly, turning back to her own grooming. "Other times, I wish I could catch up. So I'd understand you."

All the warmth and tingling sensations that had built up inside seeped out. "I don't wish it on anyone. It's a punishment, not a blessing."

Sybal's blue eyes unfocused. "Yes. One I deserve. Even if it was an accident."

"Both?"

Her eyes snapped to him over the water and through the steam, glaring at first. Then sadness slackened her visage. "No. But I still don't think what I did was wrong. ShanBao says all sentient kind are born evil, so it's no wonder my instinct was to kill."

A chill shot down Tzarik's spine despite the hot water around him. "You told ShanBao your crime?" he shouted.

Taken off guard, Sybal shook, freezing in mid brush. "Oh,

gods, I did. I didn't mean to, Tzarik. It just came out. I'm not used to guarding my life's secrets. Besides, there is no reason I shouldn't let our host know that I, too, despise House Xiaoh."

He dropped the sponge back onto the plate and rinsed himself of the soap. He sensed the turn the conversation was about to take. "He can use you now, Sybal. He knows our weakness."

"He won't," she shot back. "Did you warn Wu-Tang?" she asked quickly when he moved to the side.

"I did." He stopped, not wanting to get out with her eyes on him. "I couldn't stop them." Looking over his shoulder at her, he remembered that she was his purpose. The uncomfortable feeling in his gut told him that was beginning to take on a whole other meaning.

"I hope they burn," she hissed, cutting off his comforting thoughts. "Every last one of them. For what they did to others and to me."

If she knew about Jin, he couldn't calculate how she'd react, or what the boy would do if he understood that she'd killed his father. It was more complicated than he cared to understand. He wondered if he'd ever understand the culture of Xia and its people. The hate seemed like such a waste. But the last thing she'd said cut through his emotional armor. If she'd not killed Whoang Xiaoh, they'd not be together now.

They allowed each other a private exit and went to their separate rooms. Tzarik craved a rest on the soft mattress. Reminding himself to not get used to it, he lay down on his left side, scimitar clutched in his right hand, and closed his eyes.

"Runers!" ShanBao's voice cut through the entire estate. "The city guards have sent a runner. Wu-Tang comes!"

Tzarik's eye snapped open. Would he ever be allowed to sleep?

Chapter 9
Civil War

Two days later, Tzarik stood on the balcony, watching the dancing torch lights of the minuscule army marching up from Wu-Tang. With nowhere to hide from the elevated eyes of Shiuki, the ragtag warriors marched out in the open. He tracked them, lacing up the side of his light armor. His fingers slipped on the leather strands, hesitant to join ShanBao and his generals.

"The Di-Huan's guards from the city are coming," Sybal said, joining him on the balcony. "This will be a slaughter."

He nodded. His hands slipped, dropping the leather thong. Grunting in aggravation, he finally pulled his eyes away from the coming army.

"Here." Sybal came to his side, placing his forearm on her shoulder and lacing the armor for him. "You've done this a million times without my help," she said, smiling.

"I've never taken it off so much," he replied solemnly. "And I don't want to put it on now."

Switching sides, she asked, "You are going to stand with Shiuki? The province's warriors will be there, risking their lives. Even if the Xiaoh army is small, people will die today."

He looked up at her. "It's not our fight. It's not what we're here for."

Her eyes danced between his. She narrowed them to blue slits, weighing something in her mind. He saw her contemplating: he'd gone to Wu-Tang to warn them. She'd be a fool to not know this was his doing, his intent irrelevant. Fortunately, she didn't mention it now.

"They are bold," she said, sighing and handing him his scimitar. "Marching in plain sight like that."

"They have no choice," Tzarik reminded her. "Everything they do can be seen by Shiuki."

She walked away but stopped when he said this. Turning on her heel, she said slowly, "You do not sympathize with them, do you?"

Bracing himself, he faced her square on. "I do not intend to fight today, or any other day, for Xia. I brought you here for protection, to hide. For once, can you not rush in to someone else's affairs? Stop trying to be the hero. It's only hurting us."

For a moment, Sybal's face slackened as she took in his words. Then she shook her head in disbelief. "I always think you're different than when I met you. But then I remember how you manipulated me. I get conflicted thinking about the night before we rescued Zeva, how you were open and honest. Selfless. But maybe that was just a tactic. You want me to stop using this curse. Why? So I can be just as miserable and angry as you? As alone as you are?"

"I left my home, too, Sybal!" he snapped, taking a step forward. "I took a great chance on you. I made a choice."

"Because you were lonely," she shot back. "Ra'hala!" Her face fell into her hands and she clutched her head. "Why can't you be more like you were the other day? Why can't you just..." She couldn't go on.

Seeing her angry hurt. Should he go to her? Apologize? Put his convictions aside and fight with her in a brewing war that had nothing to do with him?

Nothing has anything to do with me, he thought while the conflicting urges wrestled in him. Why could she not show the same compassion to him that she showered on others? *What did I do wrong?*

She drew herself up. "I'm going. Come or not."

Panic shot through his veins and he called out before he could stop himself. "Sybal!"

She turned, shocked. When he didn't say anything, fighting for words, she smiled gently. "Tzarik?"

His heart pounded. "Be careful," he managed to get through his tight throat. "I'll be close by."

Her face fell. She nodded stoically. "I will."

❧

Sybal's heart sank as she ran down the steps two at a time. She chided herself for expecting anything else but an order to be careful from her mentor. Why she'd expected more at that moment, she didn't know. The odd rush that now accompanied seeing him annoyed and confused her. It annoyed her because it often led to disappointment. It confused her because she'd not had those feelings in some time. The last time she'd felt them, she'd taken her betrothed in her arms, almost begging him to cross a line. A line she'd never crossed.

"Sybal." ShanBao fell into step beside her, outfitted in scale-like armor with his house's crest beveled into it. "Where is Tzarik?"

"Not coming," she quipped.

"Just as well."

She almost missed ShanBao's eyes flit to the upper levels where Tzarik stood before he went on.

"My generals will meet us farther out where there are fewer residents, along with the Di-Huan's present guards. It's not much, but I don't expect Wu-Tang's meager march to put up much of a fight. This is almost a formality. We will show them they cannot rise against us and no doubt quell the fire of insurrection. We are glad to have you and your powers on our side."

She was about to ask when ShanBao stopped and turned to face the back exit. "Jin!" he shouted.

Thinking the boy hadn't heard, she expected ShanBao to call again. In the wide-open doorway, the boy appeared, slowly walking towards them, taking his time. Even from this distance, she noticed his tight shoulders and stilted gait.

"I was hoping you were home," ShanBao said softly, his eyes tracking the boy. "Follow us out."

"Is it safe?" Sybal asked, stopping herself from protectively keeping Jin from leaving.

"I am a warrior, Sybal," he said solemnly. "I appreciate your concern, but I'd rather fight beside you."

Outside, they mounted their horses and rode down a dirt path outside the city walls. Up a small incline, they came to a rocky edge surrounding a grassy plain. About fifty men and women in the red and gold armor of the Di-Huan and the two Masahk generals waited there. A royal commander named Zhen, near ShanBao in age, approached them. He bowed.

"Wu-ShanBao," he began, "they are just below the Hallow City. Call down the Wushito upon them. It will be a slaughter they will not soon forget."

ShanBao's ever passive face slackened even more as he watched the approaching enemy. "This trite march and show of weakness does not warrant the Wushito," he answered. "Besides, the Di-Huan," his eyes flitted to the royal insignia on the comman-der's armor, "has not signed an accord with the Hallow City. We do nothing. You are lucky I am here."

At this, the serpentine general, Wu-Zhiang, laughed and shared a knowing glance with her fellow Masahk general.

"Zhiang," ShanBao said after a moment of silence passed, during which he scanned the surrounding mountains and valleys. "Take Sybal-kim with you and come around for a flank." He pointed to an open area with a small pond and a steep drop off. "Their current path will lead them through there. If not, follow them and attack when I signal you with a fiery arrow."

Wu-Zhiang bowed. "Of course, Wu-ShanBao." Her slitted eyes landed on Sybal and a forked tongue slid out and back between her lips.

"Jin, Wu-Yasuke," ShanBao went on, "take the right side of the army. The royal guard and I will come head on. You know what to do."

"Strike first," Jin whispered like a prayer.

"Witnesses?" Wu-Zhiang asked with a long hiss.

ShanBao folded his arms inside his sleeves, contemplating. The corner of his lip twitched wickedly. "One. And it will be a blessing if he cannot describe what he witnessed here today."

Cackling venomously, Wu-Zhiang dove onto her snake belly and slithered away like lightning, hardly giving Sybal time to catch up. Kicking her horse's sides, she trotted after the Masahk.

She turned around. "Jin!"

The boy's face brightened when she called his name.

"Be careful!"

Smiling genuinely, he waved as she departed.

"LEAVE THE HORSE," Wu-Zhiang whispered. Her tongue again flicked out between her lips. "Loud animals will alert House Xiaoh."

Sybal hopped off, tossing the reins over a low branch. She took four or five steps towards the open area ShanBao had mentioned when the huge snake body of her companion shot across her path and circled around her. Shaken, Sybal stopped, laying her hand on the hilt of her scimitar. Wu-Zhiang's swaying human body slinked up before her, coming so close Sybal could see the flecks of yellow in her purple slitted eyes.

"What are you doing?" she asked. Her chest constricted as her Runer instincts tingled. This time, she felt the sulfates in her veins. They fizzled in anticipation of an oncoming attack. Shivering, she accepted the sensation.

"You Runers taste so different," Wu-Zhiang hissed. Her tongue flicked out, tickling Sybal's cheek.

Sybal winced, cringing away from the close encounter.

"I've wanted a moment alone with you since your intrusive display in the city square." Wu-Zhiang coiled closer to Sybal, starting to cut off any easy escape. Her lips parted to show her venomous fangs. A purple poison secreted from one, dripping onto her lip where she licked it off. "That's not blood under your flesh."

"Correct," Sybal whispered as if facing off with a real snake. She leaned back only to hit the snake body behind her.

Wu-Zhiang bit her bottom lip. "I want to wring it out of you like a wet rag." She giggled in a deep, throaty laugh. Lightly running her hand over Sybal's shoulder, her eyelids grew heavy, imagining something horrifying Sybal didn't want to contemplate.

"We need to get to our post," she said, gasping. Her palm sweated against the hilt now.

The snake eyes flicked up to hers. "Do you obey your dark,

handsome mentor with this same ferocity?" She smirked. "I'd like to get my coils around him, too."

"Don't you touch him!"

The scimitar screamed as she drew it. With the flash of the rainbow blade, Wu-Zhiang skirted away on her belly, shooting towards their post. Glaring back at Sybal, she snatched up a viper she'd disturbed in the bush, bit its head off with one strike, and swallowed it whole.

"I like the feisty ones," she hissed. Wiping the venom from her lips, Wu-Zhiang slithered up to the overlook. "Come, Sybal."

The sulfates calming inside her, Sybal gathered all that remained of her patience and followed the general. Not wanting to ever be that close to the general again, she chose a perch a few yards away behind a boulder. Just as she ducked down, the small army came into view. She'd expected them to be outfitted in matching regalia, gleaming armor, and spears. The troupe that emerged was a ragtag team in mismatched pieces of armor. Some wore furs patched together with black leather. These had black paint on their faces and over their eyes. They looked harder and fiercer than the others. The placards they carried were the only uniform item; it bore the familiar crest of House Xhiaoh.

"They're peasants," she whispered. "People."

Wu-Zhiang scoffed. "What did you expect of a people who want to overthrow Wushito? Ignorant rats."

Touching her runes under her tunic, Sybal said, "I will not kill them. I will stop them."

The Masahk narrowed her eyes suspiciously. "As you wish. I have no qualms with killing those who seek to overthrow my creed. On my signal..."

Swallowing hard, Sybal prepared herself. For the first time, her crime floated to the front of her mind. She could not cut down another sentient being. She didn't know what would happen. All she knew was that the recompense was said to be horrifying to witness and painful for the oath breaker. A long, grueling death, no doubt.

Rearing up, Wu-Zhiang held her yari aloft and struck down into the army. Without hesitation, Sybal jumped after her, drawing halat as she landed. She opted for her bow, kiting away from on-coming attacks. Drawing buhkar, she misted away and was able to stay back from the attackers. Wu-Zhiang was not as merciful nor inhibited by a magical oath that would take her life. Her fangs flashing in the moonlight, she bit the enemy with quick, deadly strikes. Arching her spine, she turned upside down to fire a fatal arrow into a man who threw a spear at her.

Sybal thought they'd gotten the upper hand too quickly. She'd released a half dozen arrows into shins and feet when the invading army turned and ran forward into the trees.

"Follow them!" Wu-Zhiang hissed, wiping blood from her lips. "They are heading right to Yasuke!" A wicked grin warped her face into demonic joy. "To the bluffs."

Chasing after the serpentine woman took all Sybal's speed and strength. When the Masahk went down onto her belly and shot off, she moved with the speed of a hunting viper. A whipping, hissing sound alerted her to ShanBao's arrow going up from where the others waited. This should have been their signal, but Wu-Zhiang had preemptively struck. Now it signaled Yasuke and Jin to move in. Sybal saw how well ShanBao knew his generals when she heard Yasuke give a wild, canine cry.

The two women came over the rocky outcropping and stopped.

"A trap!" Wu-Zhiang shouted.

Below, another horde of Wu-Tang warriors waited, unleashing arrows towards Jin and Yasuke. Sybal prepared to scream for the boy to duck, but he easily dodged the arrows with elegant flips, scaling a tree before hopping across to another, shooting his own arrows down at the same time. Yasuke leapt into the frey for melee attacks, using his claws. His fur stood on end as he roared. A fiery fox shadow appeared behind him as his attacks grew in rage.

From behind Jin and Yasuke, the Shiuki warriors emerged, spears and staves in hand. Sybal skirted around the edge, the blood from the Wushito general's savage attacks painting the vibrant green grass red. She met with ShanBao and the royal commander.

"I will lose my rank for this," Commander Zhen stuttered, his face white. "We are involved in a civil dispute. A battle! The Di-Huan will have my head."

"This was unexpected, Zhen." ShanBao watched, horrified at the bloodletting. "They played us for the peaceful fools we are."

Below, Sybal watched a royal warrior brought to his knees by a man welding the banner of House Xiaoh. The royal warrior begged for his life before the Xiaoh fighter stabbed him with the placard, standing it up in his corpse. Unable to bear the sight, she leased an arrow into the Xiaoh warrior's knee.

"Careful, Sybal!" ShanBao cried. "Your oath."

Glaring at the evil sigil, she spat. "It is far worse a punishment that I cannot take my revenge." In truth, she had killed Whoang Xiaoh twice. She had tasted her revenge. But the opportunity to fell more of his kinsmen and followers loomed before her in insatiable temptation.

"Guard your anger," ShanBao whispered, touching her shoulder gently from behind. "I do this to protect Xia. House Xiaoh wants one of their own on the throne."

"Why are they striking now?" Zhen cried as he watched his men fall. "I thought we were close to an accord."

"Hardly," ShanBao replied. "The Di-Huan is ignorant and indecisive. His son has no desire to rule."

Zhen swallowed hard before he spoke. "He is not touched by

the dragon. They must be frightened their rule will be challenged."

ShanBao scoffed. "An outdated tradition. There are many dragon-touched in Shiuki alone. My Jin is one of them."

Sybal watched the boy fight. He moved like silk in the wind. Though he didn't have runes like her, he moved like mist, spun to defend himself without a shield, and inflicted a wound with every movement. The Xiaoh warriors were getting the upper hand as the royal warriors started to cower, lose their nerve.

"Wu-Zhiang!" ShanBao shouted. "Turn them to stone!"

With that command, the serpentine Masahk unhinged her jaw. With lighting strikes, she sank her now dripping fangs into warrior after warrior while Yasuke covered her back. She wrapped her body around those who fought back, constricting until blood burst from their eyes. The ones she did bite and then squeezed didn't scream, their blood solidifying in their veins. Sybal watched it seep out their eyes like jelly. Horrified, she forced herself to watch.

Shouting a praise for the Wushito, the royal warriors wrangled up the stragglers. Faster than it had started, the fighting stopped and cries of pain, death, and mercy went up to the stars.

ShanBao led Sybal and Zhen down to the kneeling Xiaoh warriors. His face placid and his hands in his sleeves, he faced them.

"House Xiaoh," he called loudly so they all could heard over the gurgling, dying, poisoned fallen. "This is not the time for a fight. You have been decimated this day. Why you insist on creating civil unrest is beyond my wisdom."

"Wushito moved first!" a panting warrior spat, clutching his wounded chest. His blood blossomed over the house sigil.

"No, we did not," ShanBao said softly. "We intercepted word

from House Xiaoh. It spoke of rallying the other provinces. It mentioned treason to our Di-Huan and his son."

"He is not touched by the dragon," the dying warrior retorted.

ShanBao sighed sadly. "I am a man of tradition. But Xia cannot live in the past. The changing of authority is no way to live."

The warrior looked up, confused.

"But your house is not the one to rule," the old warrior said softly.

Sybal saw at least one other fallen warrior with the tell-tale white hair. He lay dead amongst the others. Her eyes flitted to Jin where he stood impassive, his young face smattered with blood. Did he think about the symbol? On the one hand, ShanBao might be right. Changing which house or family had power based on a birth defect might sound foolish to an outsider. But she also knew the power of being touched by a magic outside the regular realm of comprehension.

She'd never tested it, not even today. The fear kept her in check.

Sudden doubt ticked inside her. She could ask Tzarik if a Runer really had ever died from breaking their oath, committing the crime for which they were runed. Of course he'd tell her yes.

Realizing now was not the time for a conflict of faith, she came back to the battlefield. ShanBao instructed the generals to help the invading warriors out of the boarders of the province and onto the main road. Jin moved to follow but ShanBao called him back.

"Sybal will go," the old master interjected when the boy opened his mouth to argue.

"I'll see to it," she promised him reassuringly.

The Wushito generals barked orders to the living remnants to gather their dead and carry them themselves. Sybal watched in horror as the wounded lifted the dead, as many as one man could carry, and formed a line to march out. Weeping, gasping mumbles of pain filled the air.

Guarded by the generals, scared of Sybal, the decimated army marched for an hour to a main, flatter road lined with trees.

"Halt here," Wu-Zhiang called. "Drop the dead."

Confused, some whipping their heads around for a quick exit, the hostages did as they were told.

"One witness," Wu-Zhinag said, smiling darkly. "Wu-Yasuke." She snapped her fingers and the other general flew through the remaining living, slashing their throats with his single-edged sword, clawing those who needed just one push over the edge. As he blinked from one dying warrior to the next, the fiery outline of a demonic fox followed him in wafts of white smoke. Sybal froze, watching the Masahk zoom in fire and blood, nine fox tales waving behind him as he did. This petrified her so much she didn't notice him taking their eyelids with a savage swipe of his claws, so they could not hide their death stares from him.

"What are you doing?" Sybal screamed.

"One witness," Wu-Zhiang repeated, turning over a stiff, stone-like corpse. "It will be a blessing that he cannot describe what he sees here today."

The viper struck a warrior close to her who dared run, coiling tightly around him. With two long, claw-like nails, she dug her fingers into his eyes.

The screaming ripped Sybal's heart. She hated Whoang Xiaoh and what he'd done to his country and hers, but this man might not have been part of that. Unable to bear his cries, she covered her ears and turned away. But the man did not stop. His cries went on and on, each gasping wail a fresh wave of pain through Sybal.

"Stop cowering," Wu-Zhiang called to her. Handing her several coils of rope from the Xiaoh warriors' own horses, she instructed, "Toss these over the branches."

Her mind going blank at the horror, Sybal mindlessly did as instructed. An hour or so later, the main road was lined with trees dripping with mutilated warriors bearing the sigil of House Xiaoh. The eyeless man stopped wailing, lying unconscious nearby. Finally, Sybal blinked and beheld the carnage.

Satisfied, Wu-Zhiang turned and slithered back up the road, heading towards Shiuki. Sybal was left alone with Wu-Yasuke.

"Why?" Sybal croaked. She turned to look at the other general. The sadness that twisted his face relieved her.

"I may be a master of Wushito and its martial ways," he said, sighing, "but I do not pretend to understand the philosophy yet, nor its path of blood. It preaches honorable death and reconciliation through penitence."

Turning back to the horrid road, Sybal said, "I do not see that here."

"Nor I." Wu-Yasuke moved closer to her. "I am sorry you and your mentor came to Xia. It is unfortunate. You seem like a good woman."

"Don't be sorry," she said. The conversation helped her regain her composure. "Our choices led us here. Looking back, there are many things we should have done differently. It would have been easier for us, but not for those around us." She sighed and looked down. "I am no good at avoiding getting tangled up in other people's affairs. Tzarik, on the other hand..."

Wu-Yasuke smiled warmly, scratching behind one ear. "You have a good heart."

She shrugged. "Thank you, Master Yasuke."

"Just Yasuke," he offered. "Sybal-kim, might I suggest something?"

She looked up at him. "Of course." As she said this, his body tensed.

His left foxlike ear twitched and he didn't look her in the eye. "Wushito are trained to kill monsters."

Confused, she half-frowned. "Jin said as much. He seemed to have a problem with a spirit, though. How do you do it without runes and the orichalcum blade?" she asked, suddenly curious.

"Do what?" Yasuke asked, tapping the back of his neck and turning away from her. He marched away quickly.

"You just said...?" She watched him go. Not wanting to be alone with the corpses, she hurried after him, taking the hint and not questioning his secrecy.

As she clambered up the boulders out of the main road, she reached up to touch her own neck where a burn had appeared the day of her possession. What had been shapeless, raised skin now felt like a distinct brand. Lightly running her hand over the mark, it felt like Xian letters. She stopped her trek to examine it more closely. Tracing up and down, eyes closed and holding her breath, she almost made out words, but it was old Xian. Unsure where the mark had come from, she couldn't begin to guess what it meant.

CHAPTER 10
Foreigner

PACING SHANBAO'S HOME DID NOTHING TO SETTLE TZARIK'S mind. The humidity mingled with the anxious sweat beading on his brow. The hot bath from the other night still stewed under his flesh. Even now, his skin smelled the same as Sybal's.

She was out there, fighting for a cause that had nothing to do with her. Risking her life and her oath. He went to the dojo and kicked around Jin's practice dummies only to grow more annoyed at the wet heat. Not knowing if she was alive or not spun his brain. It wasn't until the smell of salted fish rose up from the kitchens below that he realized how famished he was. Deciding to not walk into the kitchen and awkwardly ask for something to eat, he took his horse into the center of the main city and hitched it to a post near a public barn.

An anxiety he'd never experienced before made him pull his hood far over his face, close his cloak over his front and walk quickly through the streets. This made finding food difficult. He wished fleetingly that he knew more about hunting. As a Runer, he spent most of his time near civilization. He'd never had a reason to hunt. Stopping to look into a small cafe, he spun out of sight when the lady behind the bar turned to glance in his direction.

What am I doing? he thought angrily. He couldn't find within himself what made him feel this odd fear. He pushed through the crowded streets until a loud, screaming trumpet made him freeze.

Down towards the road that led to the lower regions, a colossal gray beast with glittery white tusks blasted the musical note to the sky, flapping its giant, leathery ears. A huge yoke attached the creature to a small three-masted ship, rolling along on log-like wheels. Slowly, it pulled the ship along, up the hills towards the inner city. Gold and red banners and silks adorned the sides while lithe aerialists clung to the ropes in colorful costumes. Intrigued, Tzarik trotted down the path to get a closer look at the creature.

A few monks in orange and jade robes gave orders to workers on the ship. Behind it came a parade of wagons and rickshaws filled with red and gold materials and dignitaries.

"Runer!" a familiar voice called out. "How do you like my elephant?"

Shading his eyes, Tzarik looked up to see the silver-furred, monkeylike Masahk swinging from a yard arm covered in garlands and bells. He spun like his primal brothers, his tail wrapped around the wooden post, flipping and landing on the railing before bounding down. He stood up and straightened his monastic robes, his wide lips parting in a gleeful grin.

"I did not suspect you'd come into the Shiuki province," he said jovially. "Ze'oul or Wu-Tang would offer a better hiding place."

"So I'm beginning to think," Tzarik replied, allowing the monk to sling his soft, furry arm over his shoulders. "What is all this?"

"Dragon Festival!" the monk said, throwing his arms wide. "Three days of celebrating the White Dragon and his gifts to us. It marks the start of our new year and reminds us to give thanks for the year that has gone."

His eyes glued to the elephant, Tzarik couldn't help but hear the monk's words through a veil of fear. "Xia no longer follows the White Dragon." He meant it as a question, but after what he'd witnessed, he wasn't so sure.

"Mmm," the monk hummed, scratching his round ear. "Xia is a big place. They say it took the first Di-Huan one hundred and twenty-five days to walk around it before being taken to the top by the White Dragon, where he was given the knowledge to rule."

"I suppose you believe in the White Dragon?" Tzarik asked, curious.

"Ha! I was born under the sun of the pharaohs." He closed his eyes and drank in the air as it filled with a cacophony of scents. Food preparation for the festival was underway. "My god is Exrhamia and my goddess Sep'thet—may they give us light." He made a holy sign over his head as he spoke the blessing. "But I am fond of the White Dragon and follow his teachings. I came to defend the border against The Frozen Nation as a small child and never left."

Seeing Tzarik captivated by the elephant, he asked, "Would you like to ride it?"

Taken by a wave of uncertainty, Tzarik stammered, "No. I've just never seen one this close. As a slayer of monsters, great beasts fascinate me."

"Come, Runer, there are ropes to hold on to. Do you think these hands are not familiar with climbing?" The monk signaled the man atop the elephant's head to stop and drop down a silken rope ladder.

Feeling refusal would not be heeded, Tzarik gripped the side of the ladder and swallowed hard.

"I never introduced myself to you, did I?" the monk asked,

easily scaling the wrapping decorations coming down the elephant's side. "I am called TaoShin. And this is Jade." He patted the elephant's side. "She is quite experienced with timid riders."

"Tzarik," the Runer replied, haltingly climbing the ladder. He gripped it hard, but the sweat and humidity made the silky fabric slippery in his hands.

"Well done, Tzarik," TaoShin called down to him when he'd perched on top. "I believe in you."

Embarrassed, the eyes of other monks and the aerialists watching, he bit down and climbed the ladder. To his surprise, he made it fairly easily. TaoShin grabbed his arms and pulled him into the box-like saddle.

"I deduce I need not tell you to not look down," TaoShin smiled. "So look outward! The world is magnificent from the back of an elephant."

Fixing his eyes on the horizon, he gripped the front of the saddle. The elephant started her long, swaying gait again, pulling the elaborate ship up the hill.

"We monks take the parade very seriously," TaoShin said over the ringing of the thousands of decorative bells. "Would you help me in decorating the rest of the ship?"

Tzarik's mouth watered as they passed tents and other temporary structures going up, with makeshift fire pits cooking savory dishes.

"I have food," TaoShin bargained.

Fighting to find the right words, Tzarik explained, "I'm no good at that kind of thing."

"Then sit with me while I braid."

Realizing the Masahk was not going to let him leave without paying him his time, he nodded. He glanced over the edge. A gray halo instantly appeared at the edge of his vision, slowly sinking in. His head weighed down and his neck weakened.

Painfully, his head lolled to the side; he could no longer hold it up.

"Ho, there, Runer!" TaoShin said, gripping him to steady him. "We're nearly there."

Tzarik felt the monk help him down and onto the boat several minutes later. His senses blurred together, making time rush by until he felt the firm deck of the ship under his boots. TaoShin set him down on a throne made of barrels filled with something liquid and held up a hot bowl of rice topped with tiny, round, pink-fleshed sea creatures.

"Eat now and get your bearings." The monk squatted next to him while he offered a few bites. "When was the last time you ate?"

Tzarik shrugged, reminding himself not to seize the bowl and swallow all the contents in one mouthful. He forced himself to eat slowly, allowing TaoShin to feed him small bites. A few minutes later, the world came back into focus and the tingling in his head stopped. TaoShin handed him the food.

"I've been busy," Tzarik said after swallowing. "Traveling. Spying, probably."

"I appreciate your candor," TaoShin mused, sitting cross-legged. He picked up a bundle of ribbons and began a complicated weave. "You worry about things out of your control, I think. Why?"

Before he replied, Tzarik tried to use the two thin sticks to pick up the pink sea creature and scoop rice into his mouth, as TaoShin had done. The tiny utensils wouldn't obey him. Frustrated, he dropped them and contemplated using his fingers to grab handfuls of the stuff.

"Thusly, Runer." TaoShin produced another set and placed the sticks in his hands: one in the corner of his thumb, and the other supported by his thumb and fingers. "Like a crab," he said, smiling and clicking his tongue while pretending his long, wrinkled fingers were pincers.

Unwilling to try, he grabbed the meat with his thumb and forefinger and used it like a spoon. TaoShin smiled and shook his head.

"This place is foreign to me," Tzarik said over the rice.

"You are the foreigner, Tzarik," TaoShin reminded him. "But each city is unique with its own history, myths, and pride."

The Runer grunted. "It all looks the same to me."

"Ah, Runer, don't be unkind." TaoShin laid his tail down around his saddled feet. "It must look like that from an outsider's point of view. But if you really looked, met some of the people, you'd change your mind if you had any desire to experience another culture. Like talismans, dumplings, and drums. Oh, the drums, Runer!" he crowed joyously. When Tzarik didn't react, the monk shrugged. "When I was a boy, some four hundred years ago now, I couldn't tell Bahratt and Al'Myrah apart."

"The gods will help with that. Have you seen a Bahratt temple?" Tzarik grimaced, remembering the skull belts, red tongues in onyx faces, and the circle of arms around some of the gods Bahratt worshiped. "Sometimes the maharajas make up new gods."

TaoShin smiled. "When I was on Alika, in the very presence of one of the pharaohs—at the time a distant relative—I thought it was Al'Myrah. 'It's all sand,' I told my father. 'How are these places different?' "

A blow to his homeland's pride pulled his attention away from the food. "Al'Myrah is a great land. We have governments not seen anywhere else. Our sultana was one of the first women to rule."

"Outside Alika?" TaoShin asked. "Ancient pictures show women pharaohs."

Tzarik shrugged, aggravated. "I don't know history. We were the first to mine and use black powder."

"And now have some of the greatest pirates roaming the five seas!"

Why was the monk attacking Al'Myrah? He couldn't defend his home. He didn't know the histories, the legends, the greats who came from its sandy prairies.

"Look around. How many Xians do you see?" ToaShin asked.

The brain fog gone, his feet safely on the ground, Tzarik allowed himself to observe. He swept the boat and made note of the aerialists, the workers, a few cooks, and some excited onlookers.

"Dozens," he replied.

"And others? From anywhere."

He looked again. Al'Myrah boasted a diverse populace. Any market would have a Xian craftsman, a blacksmith from Alika, or a rambunctious bard defecting from Caerwren. With how close it was to Bahratt, the people often intermingled. The only ones rarely seen were Porshains. The ones they did see were nomadic, traveling in tribes, never staying long due to their history. Still, Al'Myrah teemed with foreigners. From where he sat, he spotted one: a dark-skinned beauty with long, frizzy black hair. She had the stocky build of those from Oceanya. She spun fire for a group of children on the upper deck of the ship.

"One," he said finally.

"Does that bother you?" the monk asked.

Tzarik scoffed. "I see what you are trying to do, monk, and it won't work on me."

"It bothers me," TaoShin confessed.

This statement shocked Tzarik. He stopped chewing and looked over at the Masahk.

"Xia is too closed off." He tied off one weave and started another one. "They do not like foreigners. When someone leaves, they don't..." He swallowed. "They don't come back. Life is too long to spend it hiding and keeping foreigners out."

Tzarik heard the hurt in the monk's voice and noticed his quicker, more aggravated movements. He'd expected him to be peaceful, pious, and calm. This change interested him. "Who didn't come back?"

"My son. And his fiancé." TaoShin sighed. "I am old, even for a Masahk. As a monk, we are trained in birthing and healing, and I suppose seeing all those little souls enter the world made me want my own. I wanted grandchildren. My family."

"Where did he go?"

TaoShin met his eyes and smiled sadly. "Al'Myrah. The hub of progress, as you make it out to be. The center of the world. That's why I know your language. He met a woman there and fell in love, as young men do. He fought in the wars and I received a black letter."

Frowning, Tzarik racked his brain to think of what war. There had not been a war on Al'Myrah's sands since before his time. They often sent armies out into other wars, but blood had not been spilled on Al'Myrahn shores in a generation. Battles, perhaps, but not a war. But that might change soon...

"I forget you Masahk live longer," he said.

TaoShin nodded. "Doesn't lessen the pain." He touched a jade bracelet on his wrist. He wore an identical one on the other wrist. "Black envelopes are a Xian tradition, signifying bad news. She sent me one, knowing I would understand. I didn't open it for weeks. I'd never met her, the mortal woman who'd chained my son to foreign shores. But I trusted his heart. She's long dead now. I wish I knew where her children might be, so I could see them." He sighed heavily, still smiling. "There is a sadness knowing my grandchildren will not live long and that my son would have outlived her. Had they been Masahk, they would have gone on forever until an arrow or poison took their lives. But a mortal baby?" He closed his eyes and touched his chest. "They are so precious. So fragile. I often begged the mortals I aided in birth to love their children, since they have maybe thirty years with them. Such a short time. Here." He took the bracelets off his wrists and handed them to Tzarik.

Gently, the Runer took them in his hand, setting aside the now empty bowl. The bracelets clinked delicately in his fingers, like colored glass. Shaped like Xian dragons, their mouths opened wide and he saw the bracelets were hollow.

"I am not a man who appreciates decorative craftsmanship," he confessed. "I prefer the curve of a blade and the lightness of good armor."

"Then take them as a lesson," TaoShin offered. "You have your companion with you, yes?"

"Sybal," he replied. He'd stopped worrying about her for about an hour and now his stomach knotted again. "She's off fighting a battle she has no business adding her sword to."

"Oh, dear," TaoShin mumbled. "So I'd heard. I prayed it wasn't true. Poor, torn Xia. This will not end well. But," he said, facing Tzarik, "you care for her."

"No," he said quickly. "Of course I do," he added when the monk raised his brows. "She's my apprentice. I am bound to her until she parishes or chooses to leave. From the first moment I set eyes on her in that courthouse in Ala'Nar..." His throat closed. Coughing, he finished, "The runes bind me to her."

"Ah, the runes," TaoShin sang, examining the string hanging around Tzarik's neck. "Very mysterious things. But Sybal is more than your apprentice."

Tzarik didn't reply.

"She's quite something, isn't she?" TaoShin prompted.

"She's on a path of pride and revenge," he said. A feeling of comfort rose when he spoke his fear aloud. He turned the bracelets in his hand. "She's rash. Foolish. I don't know how to stop her."

"Why not go with her?"

Tzarik shook his head. "It's not my place."

"It never is." The monk went back to his weaving. "Unless it is."

Sighing in frustration, Tzarik shot back, "There are a lot of things I hate about Xia, monk. One of them is the cryptic, eastern philosophies that have a never-ending string of mantras and no answers. Another is your damn, wet heat. And these stupid sticks." He tossed the utensils into the bowl and stood up. He thrust the bracelets back towards the monk. "I'm not the one you want to give these to."

TaoShin didn't reach out to take back the proffered jade bracelets. "You may like this, Runer, man of black magic and dark oaths. These bracelets are meant to hold that which is most precious. Take a tiny piece of canvas. Write down that which you love on it and feed it to the dragon." He pointed to the open maw of both. "The dragon will protect the written word. If the bracelet breaks, you know the thing inside is lost."

"So much for the dragon's protection," Tzarik grumbled.

"Runer!" TaoShin laughed, standing his staff up on its narrow end. He climbed it like a tree, not tilting in the slightest. He wrapped his feet around it and hung on with one arm.

Tzarik admired the balance. He almost asked how the Masahk did the trick, but stopped himself, sensing the monk had more to say.

"Some of us may be dragon-touched," the monk went on. "This is not always a gift." He flipped up and stood atop the narrow end of the staff, squatting as if he stood on solid ground. "However, other times, you must take on the courage of a dragon.

Becoming the dragon, taking advantage of its strength, and bringing gifts to others."

"What?" he spat, wincing up at the monk in the sunlight.

"Exactly." TaoShin stroked his furry chin. "What, indeed."

Frustrated, Tzarik said, "You know your country is about to be torn by civil war? I'm not your concern."

TaoShin leapt down and went back to his weaving. "Of course I know. That's why I ask you, white blood, to consider the dragon."

Tzarik took two steps away from the monk before he stopped. Turning, he made an awkward bow to the monk, a feeble attempt at an apology. "Thank you for the food."

Once his feet were back on ground not attached to a monstrous creature, he examined the bracelets. He swore they'd been smaller when the Masahk handed them to him, since his thin wrist was so much narrower than Tzarik's own. Now it easily slipped over his hand. The other was slimmer.

While he walked back up the path to fetch his horse, he heard astonished whispering start to ripple through the busy people preparing for the festival. The only word he caught that he understood was "Wu-Tang."

Without waiting another second, he picked up his step and hurried to gallop back to the estate, hoping word would be waiting for him.

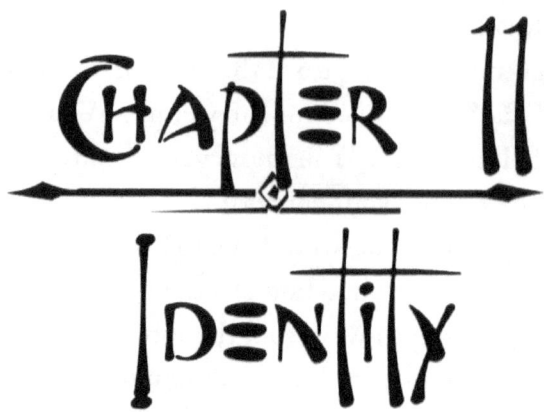

CHAPTER 11

Identity

EVERY TIME SYBAL BLINKED, SHE SAW THE HORRIFYING TREE-lined path in the darkness, the warriors hanging, blood dripping from their corpses onto the sunlit path below. She clutched her string of runes. Praying they understood she hadn't killed, she checked in with her body. The veins didn't burn. No foreign feelings came over her. She did this at night when the war party stopped, taking longer to get back into a hub of civilization. During the day march, she walked behind the rest of the group, bringing up the rear.

"Murder, was it?" General Zhiang whispered, appearing beside her. The Masahk towered over her in swaying motions as they slowly walked back to the main city. "Not one of your arrows found its way into a treasonous chest."

The confidence she'd felt only days ago vaporized under the serpent's stare. Attempting to push past her insecurity, she stammered for words, showing her weakness.

"Interesting," Wu-Zhiang replied over her mumbling sputters. "So if I came at you—"

With a spitting hiss, the general struck at Sybal, fangs flashing.

Sybal gasped and leapt back, tripping over her own feet. Tired from the days of marching and haunted by the slaughter, she didn't have the strength to fight back. Wu-Zhiang loomed over her, cackling.

Ashamed at her lack of comeback, she stayed on the ground to not encourage the Masahk further. Her placidity excited the general, though. Slowly slithering around her, Wu-Zhiang examined Sybal like a scared rabbit. Her eyes traced a white vein on Sybal's neck, down into her tunic.

"If I wasn't exhausted, you'd not stand a chance," Sybal boasted.

The viper's purple eyes widened in mock shock. "So proud. You think you're stronger than me, Runer?"

Sybal scoffed, smirking. "We have powers you don't. I am stronger."

Wu-Zhiang licked her lips, looming closer to Sybal's neck.

"Enough, general," a stern voice commanded.

Behind the snake, Jin appeared on his horse, eyes of fire boring into the Masahk. Wu-Zhiang drew herself back up.

She bowed her head to Jin. "Excuse me, master Jin." Winking darkly to Sybal, she slithered towards the front where Yasuke and ShanBao rode.

Jin slid off his horse and rushed to help her up. "Apologies for ShanBao's generals. Wu-Zhiang is something of a ruthless leader. She never got over Yasuke being promoted above her. But he's better with the people than she is. ShanBao believes in public image when it comes to the people."

Her face burning, Sybal dusted her black pants off. "I couldn't thwart her intentions. I feel so weighed down. And she guessed my crime. Tzarik said no one should know."

"Why is that?" Jin asked, falling into step beside her.

Choosing her words carefully, Sybal replied, "It gives an individual power over a Runer, knowing the one thing they cannot do. Mine is the worst. Defending myself is nearly impossible. If someone comes at me, how can I fight back? An accident could spell their death. And my broken oath." Just as the words left her mouth, she sucked in her breath. *How careless am I?* she chided herself. The one rule Tzarik insisted she follow was to never reveal her crime.

"Oath sworn," Jin mumbled, seeing her sudden regret. "Are there no oath breakers among Runers?"

Sybal shrugged and shook her head. "I'm not sure. I doubt it. Tzarik said going against the runes would kill me. I've...experienced a little bit of it. Something as simple as laying them aside nearly killed me in the beginning." She touched the runes around her neck. "It's a cruel and mysterious pact."

"Why did you take it?"

Sybal chanced a glance at him. Jin walked with his eyes forcibly trained on the ground before him.

"I was tried for murder," she explained before she stopped herself. Closing her eyes in annoyance, she sighed. "What does it matter?"

Jin took her hand in his. "I'd never use that against you. I'm glad you told me. I like knowing." He smiled sweetly at her, his boyish face honest. "I can defend you, now that I know."

Warmth trickled through Sybal's heart. "I'm glad for the company. The road is usually lonely."

"You have Tzarik," Jin said. The light in his eyes dimmed. "Can you trust him with your life?"

The question surprised Sybal. "It's complicated. I can, yes. But he's..." She winced, trying to find a respectful way to explain to the boy just how frustrating her mentor was to her.

"Do you like him?" Jin asked helpfully.

Sybal pulled at a thread on her saddle, unraveling a pedal of the lotus embroidered there.

"I know what it's like," he went on, taking her hand away from the thread to prevent her damaging the design. "Liking someone you cannot say it to, or show it to."

A weight fell on her shoulders with these words. "It's more difficult than that."

"Is it?"

"I hate him," she lied quickly. "He's used me, lied to me. I was just coin to him once."

"But can you trust him with your life?"

The answer waited in her mouth. "Yes," she finally said. "More than anyone in the world, I can trust him."

Jin looked up into the trees as the city appeared before them. "That trust—knowing someone is there for you—is invaluable."

"I trust *you*," she tried cautiously. "You know my darkest secret now."

"Am I to give you one in exchange now?"

They'd made it back to the city. Jin led them through the streets, breaking off from the royal guard, towards ShanBao's estate. ShanBao and his generals trailed away in a different direction, leaving them alone.

"What secrets could you have?" Sybal teased, gently pushing his shoulder.

Jin glanced around them before he answered. "Sybal..." He froze, facing her.

Looking into his dark eyes, she saw a dozen things he wanted to say pass behind them, each one shoved aside from the next, more important one.

Sensing his agony mounting, she gripped his shoulder. "You

don't have to tell me anything. I was teasing. I admire you, Jin. I had a brother once. You remind me of him. He wanted to a be a big strong man like our father. It took me leaving for him to find his stride. I wonder if strong men are born out of trial. I see you being a great man—a warrior. Have some faith in yourself."

They reached the stables near the dojo and Jin lifted the saddle and bridle from his horse. A servant took the horses from them and hurried them off for a washing down. His hands now empty, Jin fidgeted with the handle of his sword.

"I do have trust in myself," he said steadily. "It's those around me I don't trust. There's so much at stake."

The sulfates in her veins rushed as the tiny hairs on the back of her neck stood up. Almost like she sensed danger. "Did the attack bother you?" she asked.

Jin whipped his head up, mouth open to reply, but stopped the words before speaking them.

The agony of the fight going on in his head tore Sybal's heart. His young face twisted in anguish. Unable to stop herself, she pulled him to her chest, wrapping her arms around his shoulders. Hugging him tight, she hoped he understood: she'd not press him, she'd just be there with him.

Slowly, he replied to her embrace, wrapping his arms around her middle. Comforted, she closed her eyes and pressed her cheek against his white head. Whatever battle was going on inside him, she wanted to be part of it, to lift some of the burden, to help him like no one had helped her when she lay dying in that slaughterhouse. She never wanted to run out on someone the way Tzarik had on her.

"I'm afraid what you might think of me," Jin whispered. He shivered in her arms.

Sighing, she replied softly, "I don't think I could ever hate you. I see a sadness in you I recognize all too well. A loneliness. You're surrounded by splendor here. ShanBao brought you in, educated you. He is like your father. But still you feel alone." She took a shuddering breath. "Nothing is worse than being surrounded by people who should guide you and still feeling alone."

Jin pulled away. Tepid determination replaced the indecision on his face. "I've done something wrong," he began, "but not out of malice."

"Sybal."

Tzarik's deep, gruff voice shot through her, ruining the moment. He appeared a few yards away outside the house.

"Are you hurt?" he asked, keeping his distance when he saw Jin.

"No," she said quickly, keeping her tone even. "We stopped the invasion."

Jin and Tzarik exchanged a glance so fleeting, Sybal thought she imagined it.

Bowing and offering Sybal a warm grin, Jin excused himself. The setting sun blinded Sybal as she tried to watch him leave.

"They had an ambush set up," she began, continuing back towards the main house. "It was lucky ShanBao and Wushito responded. The royal guard couldn't have quelled them on their own." She checked Tzarik's face to see his reply, but he remained silent. "They attacked Shiuki; the Di-Huan should be told. This was an act of war. Tzarik!" She grabbed him by his arm and spun him to face her. "Why did you warn them? Why did you go there? I should have stopped you." She gripped her hair in frustration, marching a small, agitated circle. "What if something had happened to me or Jin during that fight?"

Whipping himself out of her grip, he shot back, "Perhaps we should leave. Go back to Al'Myrah and face an entire continent that wants us dead. It'd be simpler than this."

"I will not leave Jin, not now," she hissed back, towering over him. "You started this by going to Wu-Tang; I will see it through. It may be more complicated, but it's the right thing to do. Xia is fighting to find its own identity. I want to be part of that."

She hated to see Tzarik give up so easily, but didn't want the tension to mount any more than it had. She wanted him to stay with her, to help her. She had to smooth things over at least a little.

"I'm tired," she said, sighing and backing down. "I want to wash and sleep. I've seen gruesome things and I need to rest."

"Of course," he relented, stepping out of her way. They were both exhausted. If they fought now, they'd say things they didn't mean.

⌇

LET HER GO, Tzarik thought as she disappeared into the house. *She's not running away.* No, that's what he did: ran from everything that asked him to do more than just slay a monster. Even after a year, he'd not gotten used to having an apprentice. And Sybal was a difficult one.

"I hope you two find reconciliation," ShanBao offered. Now out of his armor, he looked just as weary as they.

Tzarik almost jumped, unaware the older master had appeared behind him.

"Come inside and have tea with me." ShanBao walked around Tzarik, placing his hand at the base of the Runer's neck and forcibly guiding him inside to a low, square table. A steaming pot with a bamboo handle and several tiny clay cups waited for them. He sat Tzarik down and joined him, pouring the dark tea ceremoniously.

His hand shaking slightly, Tzarik picked up the proffered clay cup and drank slowly. The black tea smelled strongly of earth and something almost foul, but tasted sweet. When it hit his gut, an enormous wave of calm washed over him. His head lolled forward and his spine bent with relaxation.

"Does the trick every time," ShanBao said, smiling. "They call it a soldier's respite. During war, many warriors find it hard to sleep at night—always on guard, waiting, wondering when they will die. You've not slept in days. Neither have I, but I have new information after my little jaunt towards our enemies. I've met someone who has reignited my interest in you. Tell me what you're really doing on Xia, Runer."

Afraid he'd drop the cup, Tzarik set it back down. He felt compelled to tell ShanBao the truth after all they'd put him through. "We're on the run. We came to Xia to hide from those who'd sooner see our heads on posts than hire us to dispel a demon. But Sybal never wants to hide." He swayed, his eyes getting heavy.

ShanBao nodded sympathetically. "The young ones always become a little zealous once you hand them power. All the young warriors in the Hallow City go through this phase. They learn a few techniques, slay a jiangshi, drive away a mogwai, and think they are ready to save the world." He looked at Tzarik over his teacup. "I don't get that sense from you, though, Runer."

His brain slowed to a walk. Like a horse in a sandstorm, he couldn't make it move forward with what he wanted to say. He tried to answer the question and ask his own. His words stumbled over his lips until he stopped, pounding the table in frustration.

ShanBao tried again. "You do not use your gifts for the greater good, Runer?"

"It's a curse," he spat out. "Why doesn't she know that?" The words came out as if pushed by over-drinking, his inhibitions gone.

"She's still new to this," ShanBao said, pouring him more tea.

"She feels unstoppable. She's trying to find what she can do and what she cannot, testing her strength. And she has a good heart. She thinks she can use your black magic for good. Surely you remember what it was like?"

Shaking his head, Tzarik replied in slurred speech. "Azar used me for his own curse. He runed me to keep me alive."

Through his ever-drooping eyelids, Tzarik noticed ShanBao perk up.

"Azar? That name. I know that name. Drink, Runer." He slid the cup back into Tzarik's hands. Forcing it to his lips, he tipped a little more tea down Tzarik's throat. "How likely is it that more than one man has that very name?" ShanBao spoke more to himself than Tzarik.

Tzarik's white blood rushed, warning him of danger. He stood up, but tripped over his own feet. He fell and hit the table, destroying the clay teacup. His head slammed against the wood and his vision blurred until he went blind. A familiar feeling of knowing he'd not remember any of this when he woke warned him to not answer another question.

"What have you done?" he slurred. He couldn't push himself up, his limbs not listening to him.

"Forcing you to rest." ShanBao appeared behind him again, towering over where he lay crumpled on the table. "You've been very passive and easy to handle, Runer. I hope you stay that way. When you wake in two days' time, you will not remember this, understood?"

Compelled to agree, he nodded. "What was in that tea?"

"There are only three substances in the world that can affect your cursed white blood. I thought you'd know. Maybe no one has hated you enough." He leaned down. "You will take your meddling whore to the festival and feel no threat from me or my men. Do you understand?"

Rage surged through him, allowing him to get one foot on the ground and almost rise. ShanBao spun, kicking him back down. Tzarik slid onto the table on his back. He'd never guessed the old man possessed the strength. His mannerisms were deceiving.

"She's not...a whore," he coughed. Now that he lay on his back, sleep enveloped him.

"Of course she's not." ShanBao's voice echoed in the darkness as his eyes closed. "Runer, what happened to Azar?"

Tzarik heard him but could not answer. He wanted to dream. Wanted to sleep. He hadn't closed his eyes in days. Nothing worried him right now.

"Runer!" ShanBao shouted, but his voice was muffled. "Damn it."

❧

THE NEXT MORNING, Sybal wandered out back into the dojo, hoping to find Jin, but he wasn't there. Tzarik still lay in his room, perfectly silent. She didn't disturb him. In the middle of the hot day, she took her horse and road out to clear her head. The slaughter still fresh in her mind, she sought out one of the pink groves Xia abounded with. Every few miles, a luscious grove calmed by a stream or waterfall appeared in the shadow of the dense forests. Once outside the city limits, travelers became fewer. Wayfinders and notice boards carried more and more calls to arms the farther out she went.

Finally coming to a grove she liked, she dismounted and trudged to the pool at the base of a clear stream tipping over the blue rocks. She hadn't splashed into the shallows yet when a loud, roaring moan made her freeze. To her left, a thicket of wide bamboo obscured a cavern opening into the mountainside behind it. Something moved behind the bamboo. Wrapping her fingers around her scimitar, she prepared for whatever might come jumping out. The old bamboo clacked together, some of the tops broken off at varying lengths. A deep growl rumbled out to her.

The thing inside had bright green eyes. They glowed out of the darkness at her. Round pupils peeked out, questioning.

Something by her foot moved, smacking her ankle. Panicking, she kicked at whatever it was. It cried out, rolling to the water in a perfect round, black and white ball.

Two things happened at once: the thing in the cave moaned loudly and charged her, and behind her, Jin's voice shouted for her to stop.

Conflicted, Sybal rooted herself to the spot, flinging her head back and forth. Bursting from the bamboo came a bear.

"Shit!" she shrieked, holding the knife up to stab the thing as it tackled her to the ground.

"Don't hurt her!" Jin shouted.

Thinking he was addressing the bear, she pulled the knife from its shoulder and made to stab it again as its claws pressed down onto her face.

"Sybal, she's protecting her cub!" Jin called.

Drawing halat, the barrier defended Sybal against the long sharp claws and she rolled away towards Jin. Once away from the bear, it lumbered into the shallow water and went after the thing that had rolled away from Sybal's foot. Turning it over, the black and white bear showed Sybal it was indeed a large, fat cub. It had reached out to touch her shiny buckle and she'd kicked it away, angering the mother bear.

"I didn't know," she panted, almost laughing now. "I've never seen such bears."

The round cub rolled away into the water, reading its mother's worried swipes of her paws as playing.

"They don't normally attack," Jin explained, pulling Sybal

away from the creatures, "but when you kicked her cub, she had to defend it. I think we should ascend to avoid her wrath."

He led her into the bamboo stalks and began to shimmy up one like a monkey using the balls of his feet and hands.

"Will she come after me?" Sybal asked, unsure how the black and white bear reacted to threats. Gripping the bamboo, she looked up. How had Jin done that?

"She might," the boy called down, standing atop the broken stalks of bamboo now and walking over them as if they were a bridge.

Reaching up, she grabbed the wooden pole and wrapped her legs around it, trying to climb. Not surprised, she slid back down and the skin of her palms screamed.

"How did you do that?" she called up, smiling. "Did you follow me out here?"

Jin nodded, squatting to look down at her. "This is one of the first lessons Wushito are taught. Children can do this, Sybal." He winked mischievously at her.

She tried again to no avail, earning her palms another bolt of pain. Behind her, the mother bear watched with round eyes. It didn't look near as frightening now. Its round body and face were almost cute.

"What is that?" she grunted, jumping up to try once again to join Jin.

"Panda," he replied. "They eat bamboo and sleep, mostly."

Grunting, she stepped back. "I give up."

"Are you a Runer or aren't you?" he crowed down to her, standing up and leaping from one stalk to the next. He took out one of his two swords and twirled it, stopping to pose. Standing on one leg, he pulled the other into his belly and bent like he might kick out.

"I'm a great Runer," she called to him. "First of my kind!"

With that, she leapt up, pressing her foot into the stalk and catching it with her hands. Using the opposing tension, she suddenly shot up the stalk to join Jin. "Yes!" she shrieked, frightening the pandas below. Sweat beaded under her thick hair.

"Now..." Jin set his foot down and touched his blade to his forehead before holding it out to her. "We spar."

Unwilling to let him win, she stood up. Shaking, the entire stalk wobbled under her. "There are a lot of strange things you Wushito do that Runers do not," she whispered, begging the bamboo to stop moving. Once up, she took out her scimitar. "If I fall and break an arm, I blame you."

Jin bowed, steady as a mast on a ship. "I'll go easy on you. Spare you my Wushito tricks."

Allowing herself an evil grin, she nodded.

She waited for him to come to her, knowing she couldn't dance on the tops of the stalks like he could. He advanced. Jin leapt, spinning off to the side, his robes flapping and snapping. When she didn't move, he stopped, back in front of her again.

"Sybal, you have to at least—"

Drawing buhkar, she vanished into black mist and appeared behind him. When she disappeared, Jin spun to look for her, so she came up on his right side. Appearing softly, she whispered, "Watch your back," before pushing him hard.

The shove knocked her off her feet and she had to pirouette to land with both on two different stalks. Jin tumbled backwards, turned the fall into a backflip, and caught the wooden pole with grace.

"Runer tricks," he mused. "You fight with dishonor, Sybal-kim."

She shrugged. "Criminals don't play fair, I suppose."

At this, Jin's face fell and he slowly climbed back up. "Did the slaughter bother you?"

Taken off guard at the sudden mood shift, she dropped her defense. "A little. I try to be strong. My runing was...devastating. Tzarik can't understand. Then I lost everything and had to help save the man who had a hand in my misery. I've always felt weak. I don't want to feel that anymore. I don't want anyone to be able to threaten me again."

"Who threatened you?"

She readjusted her foot on the top of the stalk. "A man from Xia."

Jin's left foot lost its grip but he quickly got it back.

Sybal went on. "Because of him, I am what I am today."

"What do you mean?"

Shaking her head, she looked away. "The slaughter reminded me that this is my life now. That I must overcome my own weaknesses. I want to test my strength. Ever since we left Al'Myrah, I've wondered if now is the time to try my prowess. Leave Tzarik for a time. Prove I am powerful."

"You don't have to prove that to anyone," the boy replied softly.

Something in his demeanor had changed, but she couldn't quite place it.

She *did* need to prove it. "I need to know that all the loss, the trials—it was worth something," she said.

"It is," Jin said earnestly. "I lost my childhood to Wushito. I was made a man too soon. But I don't regret it."

"I never said regret," she interrupted. "Maybe I did regret it, once. But this is now. I have a power no woman has had before, and I don't want to waste it."

"Nor do I." Jin slid down the stalk. The pandas had wandered off. "We have more in common than you think, Sybal. We could be good allies."

Sliding down far less gracefully and landing hard on her back-side, Sybal grunted. "We *are* allies, Jin."

Chapter 12
Dragon Festival

Tzarik's head pounded mercilessly when the sun hit his eyelids through the wooden slats. Inflating his lungs with a gulp of the sweet, smoky air, he woke more fully. He drank in the oxygen, having thought that he'd never wake again, and savoring the feeling of life in his chest. It felt like a big stretch after a hard workout and a moment of sedentary rest.

It took him some time to pry his lips apart, stuck with thirst. He reached for his waterskin only to remember he'd slept in a bed under a roof, not out among the beasts and stars. Groaning, he rolled over to push himself up. His arms shook with hunger again, the rice and strange seafood the Masahk monk had given him long gone. He rubbed his dirty, stubbly face. It was covered in impressions from the silken sheets.

The sleep and need for food and water hung so low over him, he didn't jump to alertness when a maid came shuffling in, bringing a basin of hot water and a tray of tea. Slumped on the mattress, he watched her place the items on a vanity and leave.

Grumbling internally, he realized he'd let his guard down too often while sleeping indoors. Comfort was the enemy of the prepared.

A soft tap preceded the canvas door sliding open again.

"I thought you'd been poisoned," Jin said from the doorway, looking in cautiously. "You've slept for days."

The longer Tzarik sat on the bed unmoving, the more he wanted to turn right back around, lie down, and sleep again. He winced, trying to remember what had happened that had prompted the long sleep. The time before he blacked out was trapped behind a gray barrier he couldn't wrap his mind around.

"I don't know. Feels like it," he mumbled, stumbling to his feet.

"It could be the journeys you took without pause," Jin added, helping Tzarik to the basin. "I've only seen warriors show such drive. And..." He glanced back to the door, listening before he went on. "I wanted to thank you. The last thing Wu-Tang needs is the armies of Wushito and the Di-Huan descending upon it. We'd have been devastated."

"Don't thank me," Tzarik said, sighing and plunging his face into his cupped hands, splashing water over himself. He clenched his eyes; the water was scented and the oils burned. "I did it to save myself and Sybal. We came here for sanctuary."

"You couldn't have chosen a worse place." Jin met Tzarik's eyes in the mirror. "Whatever your reasoning, it saved me and my people."

Tzarik picked up the fluffy towel and dabbed at his face. It got caught on his rugged chin and he had to pluck the small fibers out of his sharp stubble. He looked around for a blade.

"If you are Wushito," he asked, "why don't you just stop the feud?"

Jin smiled sadly. "I wish I saw things the way you did, Tzarik. So simple. When something annoys you, you get rid of it; when you don't want to do something, you don't. Do you practice this in all aspects of your life?"

The boy made it sound easy. It must've looked simple to an outsider.

"I fight every day for the will to live," he replied. "Staying out of other people's affairs helps."

Jin opened the drawers to the vanity, pointing out the grooming items Tzarik was looking for. "Sentient life is a great driving force behind all we do." Seeing he'd offended Tzarik, he continued. "I stay hidden in Wushito for myself and for Xia. Even for my father. After what he did, and with the mark, I could have been killed if ShanBao had not taken me. But I must not forget I sleep with wolves. Wushito is more than just a sect of warriors high in the mountains. ShanBao has elevated its reach and influence beyond what any Wushito master ever has. Wushito must rule in balance with the Di-Huan as was instructed by the Dragon when he pulled the continent from the ocean's depths. That's all I want."

Taking the fine-toothed comb to his long, ratted hair, Tzarik didn't reply at first. Pulling at the knots made his eyes water. "Sounds like chaos: a different house or group on the throne because of a birth defect."

"Xia was ruled thusly for millennia, Runer. Start at the ends," Jin added when Tzarik moved to hack at the tangles again. "It is our way. Those who seek to destroy tradition risk our wrath and the disappointment of the Dragon. But they also wish to stir up insurrection, strife, and vanquish those who stand against them with violence. Did Sybal tell you what the generals did to the Wu-Tang warriors?"

He shook his head. "We haven't spoken." He tossed the comb, tired of trying. This was stupid anyway. Never had he cared what he looked like. What was this place doing to him? "Are you sure this isn't just you wanting to sit on that damned high throne?"

Jin averted his eyes and took a step back. "That's too simple, Tzarik. I'd love to be on the throne. It is my right, as one touched by the White Dragon. But I know I couldn't stand it forever. There are others, better than me, who should rule."

"How do you decide who really does become Di-Huan?" he

asked. "I've seen more than one white-hair in the city alone. And Wu-Tang is filled with them."

"My father was not dragon-touched," Jin explained. "We believe that those not descended of a king are better suited. Those with my birth defect, as you call it, are far rarer. But it is easier to convince Xia that we are chosen by the White Dragon because it is less likely that the 'defect' was caused by our blood. We compete, or vote, and a white-hair is set upon the throne."

"Still sounds like it would lead to bloodshed."

Jin nodded. "Sometimes it does. But it is the lesser of two evils. Wushito tells us that sentient kind is evil and must be taught to be good. Trying to bring peace in this way ensures we maintain the balance and strive for goodness through repeated intention . Xia believes this and so does not rise against the dragon-touched. It is our way."

Rubbing his stiff neck, Tzarik looked back in the mirror. He couldn't believe that an entire continent strove for the good of everyone living on it. He'd never believed in striving for goodness. Good people died, were lost, were punished. That's what he knew.

"But I came to bring you this." Jin held up a wad of canvas wrapped in a pink ribbon. "It is traditional clothing. During the festival, we tend to dress well. For our partners." He smiled coyly. "I thought Sybal would like it."

Knowing she would, he took it from the boy. Cautiously, he said, "You are very fond of her."

Blushing, Jin clasped his hands behind his back. "I was an only child. Very rare for a Xian. My father was not affectionate after mother died. Sybal is very kind. Very generous with herself."

Tzarik couldn't stop the judgmental scoff. "She's foolish and inexperienced. It will kill her if she doesn't take her experiences to heart."

Quickly jumping to her defense, Jin said, "She's not a natural-born killer, like us."

Tzarik raised his brows, clamping his mouth shut. The room darkened as a cloud rushed across the sun.

"Please don't try to ruin her." Jin gestured to the package. "There are garments in there for you as well." The boy turned on his heel and left the room, sliding the door closed gently with amazing self-control.

Seeing the young warrior get offended on Sybal's behalf gave Tzarik a strange feeling. Something in his chest warmed. He rubbed his sternum hard, trying to dispel the feeling. He set the clothes down and glared at himself in the mirror. The haggard face that stared back at him was almost a stranger. He rarely examined himself in a mirror.

The scent of a luxurious bath wafted into the room as he wondered what to do. Somewhere, Sybal was preparing herself, no doubt eager to partake in the festivities and enjoy herself. This was the kind of life she used to lead, and she no doubt craved the normalcy. They'd had twelve months of running, fighting, and hunting. She hadn't fought against the new life, but she didn't accept it as easily as he did, though she tried.

Touching the pink ribbon, he decided to try for her as well.

He opened the canvas, took out his red robe, white silken pants, and golden shoes. He called for a servant to take the rest—pink and jade garments—to Sybal's room. He tore a bit of the canvas off and stowed it in his hip satchel. The jade dragon bracelets were still there.

⌒⦚⦚

AN HOUR LATER, he stared hard at himself in a full-length mirror he'd had the servant bring in. The runes showed under the thin

Xian silk, but the rest hung smooth over his hips and legs. The wide sleeves made his arms look even shorter. He'd managed to get every last knot out of his hair. He hadn't realized his hair hung down to between his shoulders because it had not been smooth and combed in years. White locks painted vibrant, glowing streaks from his temples. They showed bright amidst his midnight hair. He couldn't stop touching his face, now smooth and clean. The garments smelled like incense and soap.

Before he went out into the torch-lit hall to meet Sybal, he slipped a jade bracelet over his wrist. Checking himself one last time, his gut clenched just like it did before a hunt. Confused, he took the last swallow of tea. Why was he nervous?

Before the bravery left him, he pushed open the door. Sybal already stood in the hallway, her back to him. The back of her pink robe was covered in jade and golden embroidery depicting a lotus. She had piled her blonde hair up onto her head in elegant waves and adorned it with tiny flowers. She turned to face him, smiling broadly. When she met his eyes, her smile slid off her face like a sandy avalanche.

Her eyes roamed slowly over his entire frame until dread stopped his heart.

"What?" he asked, his mind racing to figure out what he'd done wrong. Suddenly, he felt foolish and bare without the grime to hide behind.

She walked to him, her hand outstretched to feel the soft fabric of his garments. The heat from her hand melted through it, seeping into his chest where she touched him.

"You look amazing in red," she said. Lightly, she touched the soft ends of his hair. Her grin turned softly sarcastic. "I don't think I've ever seen your hair so straight and clean."

Her scrutiny of the details made him hyper aware of every bit of his body under her gaze. It wasn't unlike being stalked as prey by a monster. Just below the surface, he wished he'd get caught.

"Someone seemed to think I needed to try something new," he said gruffly.

"I'm so glad!" She giggled. "Shall we?"

Together they left the manor, meeting ShanBao and Jin outside. ShanBao hailed down two rickshaws, allowing them to enter the main part of the festivities alone.

"How are they celebrating after what happened?" Tzarik mused.

Sybal shrugged with one shoulder. "Always amuses me how quickly a mass desires to return to normalcy after something like that. But they weren't there. As far as they know, it was a small scuffle. Nothing to worry about." Her face darkened. "I suppose keeping them unaware was the right thing to do."

"With this lot, probably." Tzarik kept his eyes on the buildings, the ruckus, music, and shouting hammering against his senses. "Xians seem volatile. Combustive."

"Don't be rude," she said lightly. "They hold different values."

"They're certainly not holding their food with those sticks," he grumbled.

Sybal smiled but shook her head sadly. "Getting off Al'Myrah might be good for you." She stood up when the rickshaw stopped. "Let's find something you like about Xia."

Together they disembarked and took in the festival. Red and gold bedizened the entirety of every building, citizen, animal, display, dancer, and merchant. The air hung heavy with the salty smell of fish and rice and was filled with the high plucking of strange instruments and the deep bass booms of giant drums on a dais. The raised area held three round stages, each with a different performance on it. Acrobats flew through the air and dancers moved in slow, rhythmic steps in glitzy costumes with sharp head-dresses.

Street performers moved between patrons as well, crowding the pathways. Plays, the actors putting on shows in front of simple canvases, dotted the corners. These mostly consisted of some kind of warrior fighting off a lion-maned creature. People dressed as white dragons could be easily spotted among the red and gold crowd. Monster faces flashed out of the mass, orange eyes glowing.

An entertainer dressed in a rickety costume bedazzled in white and red beads hurried past, antlers bobbing. A throng of children and teenagers rushed after it, shouting.

"They're following something called a qilin," Sybal translated. "If you catch it, you get a blessing."

A woman, chasing after her son, stopped and panted, clutching her chest. She spoke to Sybal in rapid Xian, smiling. Sybal replied with a polite laugh. They went back and forth until Sybal turned bright white with a sudden rush of sulfates.

"What is she saying?" Tzarik asked.

The Runer shook her head. "Nothing. Just that traditionally, when a white qilin is spotted, most will rush to meet it in the hopes of good luck and a blessing." She tugged at the collar of her silken dress and fanned herself. "We should catch it!" she piped suddenly.

"If you run in this crowd, you'll trample someone," he mumbled stiffly, crossing his arms.

Her ears turned pale from another sudden rush. She pressed her lips together tightly.

The closeness pressed in on Tzarik, stifling his breath. The deeper they went, the harder it became to breathe. A flash of a white robe threw his heart into a wild beat when he tried to track it. A woman approached them, trying to sell Sybal perfume. The foreign chatter rattled his brain. Just when he thought he couldn't handle the crowd anymore, Sybal took his hand in hers and smiled down at him. Attached to her, they moved through the thickest part and out into a standing cafe. She ordered some tea and something he didn't understand that turned out to be sweet rice, molded into a ball a little smaller than his fist.

"Times like these, I am grateful for your education," he said, catching his breath, hoping to repair the damage from before.

She rested her hand in her palm, looking over the steaming tea pot at him. "I speak other languages too, you know? We traded with Volograd and of course Northica, where my mother was from."

Realizing he didn't know much about her, he closed his mouth and let her speak. When she saw him watching her, she half-smiled, blushing.

"My brother Abdul and I competed on things like language learning, myths and legends, history, and combat."

She tapped the table with a polished nail. Tzarik noticed her long, clean fingers. He remembered them on his scalp.

"Father always said competition bred advancement and growth. He was fair in dealing with competitors." She sighed. "Like Sheik Ahmoud. Xiaoh wanted to pit them against each other. He threatened to kill one of Sheik Ahmoud's house to start a feud and put the city in the middle."

"And so you leapt into action," he said, keeping his voice low and even.

"Just like I do now." She took a bite of the sweet rice and chewed, watching his face. "Why does it bother you so? I ask because I cannot sit by and watch House Xiaoh destroy this country. I'd like to know why you think I should."

Because it's not our fight, he wanted to say. *Because if you killed, the runes would take you. If one of them took your life, I'm afraid of the kind of Runer I'd turn into.*

Realizing he hadn't kept the conflict from settling on his face, he turned away.

"Don't do that," she pleaded. "Don't look away from me when you feel weak. Tzarik, you do not have to be strong and angry all the time. I know better. You think you hide everything from me, but you are my constant subject. You taught me to look, to see what people are thinking when they won't say it. I practice on you all the time."

Grudgingly, he glared back at her.

"That is your annoyed frown," she said, smiling. "It's different than your thinking frown, where your eyes are softer. Angrier than your guarded glower. I see when you hide your smile." Her hand rose towards his face.

His neck stiffened when he instinctually wanted to pull away. Fighting against that, he held himself still. Gently, she placed her hand on his clean-shaven cheek. Her thumb caressed his sharp jawline.

"I feel your pulse quicken," she said.

"I don't like crowds," he quipped.

Biting her top lip, she tried to stop the smile. "When you lie to me, you quickly look from my left eye to my right. Like that." She almost laughed. "When you lie to others, your shoulders slacken. It comforts you."

She had him trapped like a rabbit in a snare. Every twitch of his eyes, every breath he took, he was aware of now. He'd had no idea she watched him so closely. Why couldn't this be his life? Soft banter among cheerful people and ruckus celebration. Her hand on his face.

"We haven't hunted in a while." His throat went dry, making his voice crack. He took a drink of the tea, taking her hand away from his face with his other. "We need to hunt."

"What's this?" She took his hand in both of hers, smiling down at the jade dragon bracelet on his wrist.

As she lightly touched the intricate carvings, his heart skipped a beat. "That monk we met gave it to me." He reached into his hip satchel when her prying eyes latched onto his face to read him. There was no use in hiding from her.

He set the matching one down on the wooden table and slid it across to her. Relief flooded him when she let go of him and picked up the bracelet, gasping in delight. Lightly tracing the open maw, she examined it closely.

"It's inscribed," she said loudly as the crowd began to scream and applaud the performers.

He hadn't realized it had writing on it. The Xian language often looked like woven sticks and designs to him. "What does it say?" he asked.

She pressed her lips to one side. "It's old Xian. I'm not sure. Something about the dragon in me sees the dragon in you." She shrugged, holding it back out to him.

"For you," he said before he could stop himself.

Her face lit up like an Al'Myrahn sunrise. Her white teeth glowed in the darkness. "A gift for me? Thank you, Tzarik!" She slipped it over her elegant wrist and leaned over the table to embrace him. "The Di-Huan!" she shouted as the cheering reached its peak.

Pulling away from the hug, he turned to watch the parade behind them. A line of wagons decorated as dragons and other beasts filed past with loud music and whooping cries. The ship pulled by the elephant appeared first. The monks, dressed in their orange and jade, waved to the people, tossing gold coins with a hole in the center to them. Cheers rose up with each toss. A few other dignitaries paraded past on displays just as lavish until one in the shape of a giant gold mountain wheeled by. A line of huge drums lined the base of the display. Shirtless men chiseled with knotted muscle banged the drums in rhythm. The thunderous cracks and booms reverberated in Tzarik's chest.

Atop, on a throne shaped like a beaming sun, sat the Di-Huan. His round face glowed as he waved to his people. Servants tossed petals, gold, and jade marbles. Then a yawning brass basin tipped from either side of the mountain, showering jade envelopes onto the people. The children rushed forward to grab as many as they could hold, squealing with glee.

The Di-Huan spotted the Runers and waved energetically to them. His white hair glinted with red and gold adornments. His stoic son stood behind him, solemn faced, eyes darting to the building tops and street corners. On the Di-Huan's right stood Yui in bright colors, waving energetically as well. When their eyes met, she bowed to them.

"The prince is worried for his father's safety," Tzarik said to Sybal. "He senses the unrest."

"The royal guard reported the attack," Sybal said, her face finally taking on a serious, but small, furrow. "They know. A commander from the palace called Zhen fought with us."

Lastly, a herd of cages rolled past.

"Gods," Sybal breathed, tracking them.

The Wushito generals led the line of prisoners. Wu-Zhiang hissed and spat in venomous glee as she poked and prodded them along. Bound in heavy chains, some walked and others wept miserably in the cages. The onlookers shouted at the prisoners but didn't show any other animosity.

"What are they saying?" Tzarik asked. The pit of his stomach dropped out. Every prisoner was a foreigner, none a Xian.

"They are praising Wushito," Sybal translated. "These prisoners are going to the Hallow City. Convicted of crimes, it sounds like."

"Why to the Hallow City?"

Shrugging sadly, she said, "I don't know."

Tzarik noticed her eyes tracking Wu-Zhiang, darkening.

Sybal gasped, gripping Tzarik hard.

"What is it?" he asked, wincing under her monstrous strength.

"I knew it," she stammered, eyes darting around. "I lost him. But I swear...!"

"Who?"

Eyes still sweeping the parade and then the streets, Sybal gasped again and said, "Tzarik, I swear I saw Sharar!"

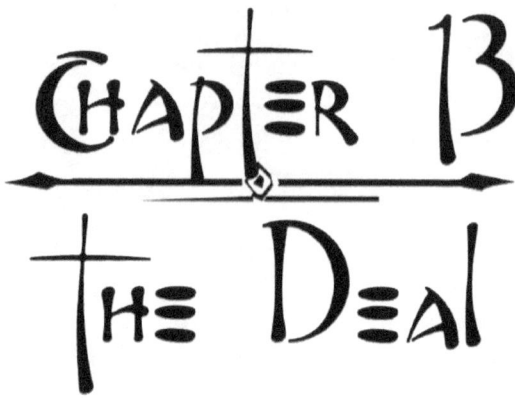

CHAPTER 13
THE DEAL

TZARIK SCALED THE CITY BUILDINGS EASILY, GRASPING ONTO their many monstrous guardians, which were perched on every corner of the sloping roofs. Pulling himself up onto the third of a five-story building, he scanned the street. The golden slippers he'd put on had no traction and he slipped. His heart hammered in his ears while his legs tingled. After steadying himself, he swept the glowing alleys. Looking across at Sybal where she perched on the spire of a shorter building, he shrugged.

She glared down, eyes narrow. "I know I saw him, Tzarik," she called. "He wore a green Xian robe and a pointed straw hat to cover his face."

"If you're right, he's probably watching us now," he called back.

"Are you sure?"

No, but she didn't need to know that. Ever since parting ways with the scholar on Al'Myrah, he'd had nightmares about him. His ever-watching eyes followed Tzarik everywhere he went, glowing like lightning in the sky, tracking his every move. Sometimes he met him face-to-face in dreams: the shadow of the demon behind him, reaching for Tzarik.

Signaling for her to climb down, they met up back in the crowded street. "I could be paranoid," he said, sighing and still checking over his shoulder.

Sybal put her hand bracingly on his shoulder, leading him out of the middle of the street as a drunk rickshaw runner bolted past them laughing, pulling a gaggle of giggling girls.

"I'm sorry. Perhaps it wasn't him," she suggested. "How could he know we're here? Wouldn't he think we'd go to Bahratt? Or even Caerwren?"

Rolling his shoulders to release the tension, Tzarik half-shrugged. "Bahratt, maybe, if he knew you had connections there. He might even think we'd hide out in the wreckage of your estate if it hasn't been seized by the government yet. No, he has no reason to track us here."

They sat down in a circle around a stage show where a street magician performed some basic illusions. Sybal watched for a moment before asking, "This is far for him. Would he come here?" When Tzarik didn't answer right away, she laid her hand on his, their matching bracelets clinking together.

"I don't know," he said haltingly. "I'm sorry."

She gently rubbed the back of his hand with her thumb, looking down at their clasped hands. "You don't have to apologize. This is *our* fight. You're not alone."

A lump appeared suddenly and painfully in this throat. He tore his eyes away from her hands to meet her eyes. She smiled, sighed, and pulled her hands away, pressing them against the table. The swelling in his chest burst.

"Lanterns!" she cried. She leapt up and ran to a huge red wagon with golden spokes on the wheels. A man with a broad grin handed out paper lanterns of varying sizes in exchange for a few gold coins.

He watched her pick through the lanterns, all of different

colors and paintings. She stood at least a head over most of the Xians, her golden hair glowing in all the torch light. Asking a question of the merchant, she shuffled through a few more. Finally, she looked up at Tzarik, smiling slyly. She paid the merchant and ran back, hiding one lantern behind her back.

She sat down, slapping a round pink lantern on the table. A dragon painted in gold leaf wrapped around its middle. It clutched orbs in its taloned fore claws. Her playful grin caused a sensation he was unfamiliar with.

"This one is for you." Beaming, she produced a second lantern with a flourish. Unlike the other lanterns, which were red, white, pink, or gold, this one was black.

Confused, he picked it up and unfolded it. It depicted a white horse-like creature with cloven hooves and what appeared to be antlers sprouting from its head. Frowning, he looked up for an explanation. "That wish-granting creature?" he asked, unsure he understood her from before.

She sighed, looking up to the sky and closing her eyes. "At last! I know about a creature the great Runer of Al'Myrah does not!" Looking down, she went on. "Yes, the qilin. In addition to that, the merchant said it appears only in the presence of a great man. Or at the passing of a monarch, but who cares about that part? The one people flock to see?" she reminded him when his face didn't change.

Something akin to embarrassment, honor, and nervousness replaced the sensation from before. Or maybe all the rice and fish just didn't sit well in his stomach.

"No great men here," he mumbled, taking the lantern and unfolding it the rest of the way despite his comment.

Smiling knowingly at him, Sybal stood up. "Let's light them."

They followed a huge throng of people down to an open field outside the main city. Sybal translated that the man shouting was saying something about the first night of the festival ending and that the White Dragon would bless them if they sent their lanterns up to meet him in the clouds.

Feeling foolish, Tzarik let Sybal light his lantern. She lit her own and closed her eyes, holding her breath while she mouthed a prayer. He'd never been a man of prayer or gods, let alone a beastly one like a dragon. Still, a prayer-like wish formed itself in his mind. He didn't utter it like the others surrounding him. He'd been told once that if a man wished for something, he prayed to any god on hand to make his wish more than a fantasy. Real men made their own wishes come true.

"Do you have something to ask for?" Sybal asked, lifting her lantern up.

"Yes," he whispered gruffly.

She let her lantern go. When he didn't release his at the same time, she gently placed her hands over his, lifted it up, and released it with him.

Their lanterns were not a yard above them before something louder and closer than thunder cracked across the sky, followed by bright, colored sparks. They both jumped, grabbing each other in terror. The loud explosions and thunderous reports did not stop, the sky shattering into multiple colors and flashes. Clinging to each other, they looked up. Blossoms of color peppered the sky in showering sparks.

"Fireworks!" Sybal cried, easing her death grip on Tzarik's hands.

Confused and still shaken, he asked, "What?"

"They are for celebrating," she said, sighing and shaking the fight out of her hands. "I thought it was something else."

Realizing how on edge they both had been, Tzarik followed her lead and calmed his nerves with a few choice inhales and a rolling of his shoulders. The fire brought up fearful memories and the sounds shook him to his core. "So did I," he confessed.

Once the initial jump had eased out of them, they stood close together and watched the night sky erupt in a beautiful display. Their lanterns drifted together, joining the others as they flew towards the stars.

※

THE NEXT TWO days of the festival drifted by in a haze for Tzarik. Relief flooded him when he woke up to a cloudy sky in the Xian highlands, knowing he wouldn't be forced to try a foreign drink, eat food with sticks, or wonder if he should hold Sybal's hand. The strain of the new emotions took a toll on him. His shoulders were stiff as he rolled over on the soft bed. Trying to get some feeling into his toes, he flexed his legs and stretched. Normally, a morning stretch enlivened him. This time, it shot a surge a hot pain through his veins. It vanished before he gasped from it.

Sitting up, he held his hand out to examine the white veins under his dark skin. Normally he could see them entwining around his wrist bones and over the center finger bone. This morning, they sank just enough to notice. Confused, he clenched and unclenched his fists. A slight buzzing hummed under his skin.

He didn't have time to contemplate. Sybal's door slid open and he heard her long, booted strides make their way down the wooden landing to the kitchens below. A jolt helped him leap up and throw his shirt, pants, and boots on to follow her before she got too far away.

When he made his way down the stairs, he instantly regretted his quick rush. In one of the great rooms he passed heading towards the dining area, he spotted a cluster of armor-clad people around a table laden with maps and tomes. He would have passed on except he spotted Sybal's long golden braid among them. Ducking behind the wall where the door stood, he tucked in his shirt and smoothed his hair. Reclaiming his emotionless facade, he walked in to join them.

"Ah, excellent," ShanBao said, looking up from some odd instruments he'd been walking across the maps.

Tzarik noted the maps showed the lowlands.

"What's going on?" he asked cautiously. Sybal stood with her arms crossed and brow furrowed.

Jin stood apart from the crowd, but still alert. Around the table were a few guards and a messenger with the Di-Huan's royal symbol on their ornate pauldrons; the other two were the Masahk generals, Wu-Zhiang and Wu-Yasuke.

"They want to answer Wu-Tang's threat," Sybal supplied in their Al'Myrahn tongue to remind the others that Tzarik couldn't understand them in their local language.

ShanBao held his hands palms up before steepling them before his chest. "You seemed ready to aid us before, Sybal-kim. What has changed?"

"I still do," she defended herself gently.

Tzarik noted her hands. They fidgeted with a leather cord hanging off her shapely armor. Almost like a nervous tick. She held her shoulders stiffer than the days before.

"I need someone to accompany Wu-Zhiang," ShanBao said in a tone that told Tzarik he was repeating himself, albeit apologetically.

Without waiting, he cut in. "I will. Where are you going?"

The serpentine general unabashedly let her thin purple lip curl in pleasure. "We're having a meeting of allies outside the Hallow City. Since you are foreign, allow me to explain." She slithered closer to Tzarik, her hands waving at her sides.

"He understands, Zhiang," Wu-Yasuke cut in, his fox ear

twitching. "We are meeting with someone who could be or could provide potential allies," he added.

"That sounds like war," Tzarik mused, forcing himself to not take a step back from the imposing snake.

"Yes," ShanBao said sadly. He motioned to the royal guard.

"I have come to fetch master ShanBao to the Di-Huan to discuss," Commander Zhen confirmed.

"So I cannot go to meet the ally," ShanBao supplied. "Time is of the essence. Jin will accompany me."

Tzarik heard the force on the boy's name. He locked his eyes on ShanBao, not even allowing a quick look back at the young warrior.

"And Wu-Yasuke will as well," the Wushito master continued.

Wu-Zhiang hissed a laugh. "Because he's soft."

ShanBao dropped his instrument. "Because Yasuke understands tact, Zhiang." He glowered unexpectedly at his general.

Deflating a little, Wu-Zhiang scoffed. "Why have this Runer chaperone me? Don't you trust me anymore, master?"

To the Runers' surprise, the old master half-heartedly smirked in reply. "Don't force my hand, Zhiang. You know I feel you have been out of control recently." He shook his head sadly. "Without Yasuke to watch over you, someone has to keep you in check."

Her tongue flicked out and back between her teeth as she scowled. Sighing in a deep almost growl, she faced Tzarik, looking down at him. "Fine. But it gives me no honor."

Tzarik stepped forward. "And Sybal—"

"Will come with us to the Royal City," Jin interjected.

ShanBao didn't turn to look at his ward. He dropped his hands onto the table and hummed. "Yes, a good plan."

A small fear of being separated so easily ticked at the back of Tzarik's mind. Casting a glance at Sybal, he saw she didn't mind. She nodded, but the concerned bend to her brows did not leave.

"Please wait until we reconvene to discuss," ShanBao ordered his generals with pointed glares. "And Zhiang. We will all return in good health. You will not make any deal until you've spoken to me."

Sighing and hissing, Wu-Zhiang rolled her eyes and slithered out.

Sybal stepped to Tzarik's side quickly. "Watch her," she whispered. "I'm not just saying it because she's a snake. Be careful." She clasped his wrist where the jade bracelet still hung. "See you in a few days."

❦

"Are we going to the Hallow City?" Tzarik asked the Masahk general. His black horse had laid its ears back ever since hers had trotted close to it. He'd patted it a dozen times trying to calm it, but its wide eyes kept darting to her long coils hanging from her odd saddle.

Wu-Zhiang made her cackling, hissing laugh. "Foreigners," she said, smiling and shaking her head. "Not even those in Shiuki go into the Hallow City. By law, it is not part of the province, same as the Royal City. They are forbidden to commoners. Only under the direst of circumstances would one not pledging themselves to Wushito be able to enter the city."

Tzarik realized now how Wushito had gained its notoriety. The citizens of Xia knew nothing, everything shrouded in mystery. All they saw were benevolent warriors sweeping down from the mountains to save them.

Bracing himself, he asked, "What about the man you didn't execute? The one who sought an alliance from Oceanya?"

He looked her straight in the eye even as the path they trotted over sloped steeper up. Her eyes' narrow slits contracted in the sunlight.

"House Xioah broke the peace when they attacked us," she informed him with less venom in her voice than he'd yet to hear. "When those ignorant houses corresponded with Oceanya, we were not yet at war. They were no different than the warriors from Wu-Tang now. Except now, the one who escaped execution will fight for Wushito, no doubt slaughtering his once-comrades. What we do in meeting this ally is to strengthen all Xia, not tear it apart." Her eyes detached from his face and slowly slithered over his torso, then his legs. Her tongue flicked out and in.

He didn't reply to her and focused his energy on keeping his face placid and emotionless. That foolish, unprepared attack had been his fault. He'd acted like Sybal: running out to try to stop something he had no power nor business meddling with. In the process, he'd discovered Jin's secret. It couldn't have been that much of a mystery. ShanBao had raised Jin, taken him in. He'd no doubt done so to quell the rising of House Xiaoh once its leader left to conquer other people. There was also no stopping Jin. He believed in the tradition that the dragon-touched should sit on the throne. The current Di-Huan had the tell-tale white hair. Was Jin waiting, biding his time since the right man was on the throne?

Thinking made his skull hurt. The buzzing under his skin started again and his vision blurred a little. His left shoulder suddenly ached like an old wound. The feeling spread to his chest where his heart rate increased. He almost groaned out loud but stopped himself.

Not long later, Wu-Zhiang turned her horse towards a path that split off into a valley of the highlands. Before them sprawled a town. Some of the homes rose up on tall pieces of timber to keep the structures out of deep, watery swaths of land. Workers walked among the rows of plants, harvesting the tiny grains, their faces hidden under wide-brimmed straw hats.

"We go into the— I believe you call it a tavern on Al'Myrah," Wu-Zhiang instructed. "Finest rice wine on Xia." She smiled—for the first time—unmaliciously.

The idea of rice wine turned Tzarik's already nauseated belly. The aches and ill feelings started to annoy him more than puzzle him. He assumed the heat and lack of air this high up had finally gotten to him.

This small town had slightly different architecture than the cities he'd seen in Shiuki. More were made of stone—no doubt to protect from the constant water—the grooves still sloped and tiered up into the sky, but were more elegant. Golden arches made of thin, entwining branches crawled along the edges of the roofs. The sloping trees with pink blossoms, which were fully open now that spring had passed, grew right out of the rock and were one with some of the homes. The walls were all painted white. Wooden bridges over the rice swamps made up every road inside the village, stretched and erected between wide decks making up the town's square. The gentle trickling of water and the song of the herons made the town glow with serenity.

As they made their way down the gently winding streets, those who saw Wu-Zhiang bowed and mumbled something in Xian. She stopped outside what Tzarik recognized as a public house with its circular, doorless opening and tiny, smoking shrine outside. A few people filed in and out. As he hitched his horse, he noticed several people wearing blue and white robes like a uniform. Catching a couple of them walking away, he saw the Wushito insignia on their back.

"Students of Wushito?" he asked.

Wu-Zhiang smiled sideways at him, elegantly slithering off her horse. "We are close, Runer. The Hallow City lies just above us."

Tzarik tried to look up but the sun blinded him. He remembered the air in the Royal City and had no desire to go higher up than he was now. Despite the odd ache, his heart started to yearn for Al'Myrah. The dry air. The hot desert sun.

"Coming, Runer?" Wu-Zhiang called from just inside the doorless archway that led inside.

Tzarik pulled his gaze away from the mountains and took a step towards the entryway. A man on his right moved at the same time and they collided just outside the door.

The man apologized in accented Xian, dropping a satchel that spilled quills, ink, and blank rolls of parchment onto the street. Tzarik caught the leather bag before it hit the ground, despite the contents tipping.

"Apologies," he mumbled, handing the bag to the man. He looked up to meet the man's eyes.

"Gods!" the man gasped in Al'Myrahn, his step faltering.

Tzarik froze, looking into the dark brown eyes of Sharar. He didn't move. It was like looking into the eyes of a hunting jaguar. Sharar didn't move, either, both suspended in an awkward squat. Tzarik tried to remind himself that Sharar didn't know about their plan to free Tarkan. At least, he hoped the scholar had not come to that conclusion. As far as Sharar knew, they were just Runers down on their luck.

"Runer!" Sharar cheered, breaking the silence first.

His jovial salutation did not placate Tzarik's fear. Sharar had not moved just as he had not, both cautious of what the other would do.

"Scholar," he replied, handing him back the leather satchel.

"Far from home, aren't you?" they both commented at the same time.

Sharar smiled charmingly, his straight white teeth still clean and shining from behind his well-manicured black beard. "We both have reasons for traveling, do we not? Let's go inside. I have been meeting someone you might find fascinating."

Sharar placed his hand in the center of Tzarik's back and gently, but forcibly, pushed him forward into the house. Inside this Xian tavern, the lattice work still decorated every corner and open window, but was elegant and curved, not square and cubic like the ones in the larger city.

The scholar moved his hand to Tzarik's upper arm, just below his aching shoulder, and gripped him hard, steering him toward Wu-Zhiang. Wincing, Tzarik didn't fight Sharar's grasp. Standing taller than Tzarik by a good head and shoulders, he felt like a child being pulled along for a scolding.

"This is really is something astounding," Sharar muttered softly a little too close to Tzarik's ear. "I never would have imagined Runers coming to Xia. You have to tell me what you two have been up to. When you vanished after the unfortunate incident, I thought Tarkan had taken you."

"Nothing so sinister," Tzarik mumbled back in reply. "We took your advice and got off the continent. Can't help but think you had something to do with our exile."

Sharar gave him a sidelong glance. "I was more concerned about the rogue necromancer than you two. I do apologize."

The Wushito general sat on the floor at a long, rectangular table, already enjoying the clear, aforementioned rice wine. When she saw Tzarik with Sharar, she couldn't hide the anticipating smile on her face.

"So you found our man," she said to Tzarik, signaling for two more clay cups to be brought out.

Sharar let go of the Runer and bowed to Wu-Zhiang. "It is an honor, general, to meet you in a more civilized fashion." He sat, motioning for Tzarik to join them. "Thank you for taking up my offer."

"Do you drink, Tzarik?" Wu-Zhiang asked coldly.

"You know each other?" Sharar asked, delighted. "That should make things easier."

The Masahk used her snake body to push herself up and pour the two men a drink. "Indeed. Tzarik and his woman washed up on our shores a few months ago. He's been very busy ever since." She laid overt emphasis on the words.

"Oh, dear, Runer," Sharar said, sighing dramatically. "You should know not to get involved in affairs that don't concern you or offer you significant coin."

"I'll try to remember that," he growled back.

"But it can be hard when someone close to you pressures you." Sharar asked for food to be brought over in Xian.

Unlike when Sybal spoke it, Sharar's Al'Myrahn accent looped and distorted the words. This gave Tzarik a small, proud smile.

"I want to get right to it, general," Sharar said, shooting back the rice wine. "We've had enough dancing around the square. I am a man of progress and wholly believe in your cause. The dragon-touched tradition is far outdated and has no place in the modern world. Xia is being rapidly left behind in that respect. Plus, as a man of science, I am here to tell you that it's simply a mutation of the bloodline. It has no heavenly powers. In fact, history tells us more ancient Xians had the white hair. Of course, an entire continent won't listen to science, let alone from a foreigner. I know how Xians feel about foreigners."

Tzarik noted Sharar sniff nervously after that. While the scholar spoke, Tzarik scanned him. Just like last time, he saw nothing on him that might be a container for the djinn he harbored. Sharar traveled light, giving nothing away.

"What makes you think you can empower Wushito to settle

this war?" Wu-Zhiang asked, spinning the sticks between her long, lethal fingers.

"He can," Tzarik put in, daring to prod at Sharar.

The scholar smiled. "Glad to have you on my side, Runer." He turned back to the general. "I am going to need something more in return, however. You see, my ability to wage and win wars is a guarantee. I can give you anything you wish. If..." Here he stopped and genuine devising pulled his lips together and made his eyes squint. "There is something else I'd like to add to the docket."

Wu-Zhiang's eyes flashed to Tzarik and back. "Do you want to speak of this in front of the Runer?"

Sharar turned his lips down and half-shrugged with one shoulder, eyeing Tzarik. "He's been in my employ before. I do not fear him."

The truth, though laced with a threat, landed. Tzarik leaned his elbow onto his knee, leaning towards Sharar, and waited for Wu-Zhiang to go on.

"The crypt," Sharar quipped, taking a drink.

Familiarity twinged in Tzarik's head. Had he heard of this before?

The snake-like general's eyes twitched in her skull. "I don't know what you're talking about."

Sharar laughed, open mouthed with his teeth glinting. "Runer, do I like to have my intelligence insulted?"

Doing his best to play along, Tzarik shook his head slowly, eyes trained on Wu-Zhiang. "I assume it was expensive to acquire."

"General," Sharar said sharply, placing both palms against his knee. "I know you are working behind your master's back. He, too, has met with me. I am not foolish—I play both parties just to be safe. Pretending you don't know about the crypt in the Hallow City is stupid. Are you sentient or animal, Zhiang? Has your inferior blood caught up to you?"

"Masahk are not animals!" the general spat, purple venom flying from her now protruding teeth.

"Then stop acting like one!" Sharar roared.

His tone even made Tzarik lay a hand on his scimitar and lean away. The tip of Wu-Zhiang's tail twitched in sequestered rage. Her thin lips moved in soundless curses.

"I could kill you both," she hissed. "No one would care if Al'Myrahns died in cold blood in a public space. Scholar, do you know what Masahk venom does to a mortal?"

Tzarik watched in awe and horror as Sharar's heavily lidded eyes showed no fear. No hesitation. He was so sure of himself and his power. The scholar smirked gently, tossing part of his traditional head scarf over one shoulder to lean forward and pick up his cup again.

"I do," he said genially. "I studied for five years on Alika, among the magi of the pharaohs. I think you are losing sight of what I can do for you, General Zhiang. There are ways to expand this venture for us both. Now, I care not for Xia or whose ass sits on your golden throne. But I get the feeling you do."

The viper nodded carefully. "I want Xia to prosper."

"You just want it to do so how you see fit," Sharar added, taking a bite of a sweet black bean paste. "I can make that happen. If you *wish*."

This piqued Tzarik's interest. Sharar had wishes left. Had he made one? Two? Whatever he asked for from Wushito in exchange for a wish would be a steep price, if that was indeed what he offered.

Not missing Sharar's stony grin, the Wushito general tapped the edge of her cup and asked, "Did you have something in mind?"

"You are astute! Just like our Runer here." He slapped Tzarik's shoulder.

When he did, the tingling and pain shot through Tzarik again.

He couldn't stop the moan this time. Fortunately, the other two pretended to not hear.

"Are you familiar with the stories of the great white snake?" Sharar asked simply. He picked up the sticks and gingerly grasped a bit of meat, using it to dish rice up into his mouth and chew while the general thought over his question.

"The demon?" Wu-Zhiang asked. "It was a scandal when the people learned it had enchanted our Di-Huan. Wushito vanquished it nearly sixteen years ago. I was there. We killed her and spilled her blood over the Hallow City for protection."

At this, Tzarik almost cut in. How did the Wushito kill monsters—demons—without the runes or the orichalcum blades? He'd seen it but didn't understand it.

"Yes, well," Sharar went on, cutting into Tzarik's curious thoughts. "On Al'Myrah, we call them djinn."

Forcing his face to remain placid, Tzarik caught Sharar looking towards him. So he was here for another djinn?

"We killed it," Wu-Zhiang supplied again. "It wasn't easy, but the damn thing was so in love it may as well have offered itself on an altar. I was there."

"Mmm," Sharar hummed.

Tzarik had heard him do this false, thoughtful sound before. The scholar was playing the general.

"If only there were something else to garner my interest," Sharar sighed. "Something I could learn from. I am famished for knowledge, you see? Tomes and great *books* alike."

A light went on behind Wu-Zhiang's eyes. "No," she whispered. "Never. It is forbidden. The knowledge inside was scribed by the White Dragon himself."

"It's not here, is it, general?" Sharar glanced sideways at Tzarik. "She may be lying. Can you tell?"

Stammering, his body going dumb, Tzarik looked in the slitted eyes of the Masahk. Something hid behind her purple irises, but he couldn't tell what. His sulfates had slowed to a slugging flow under his skin and everything hurt. "I can't tell," he said truthfully.

At this, Sharar sighed dramatically and stood up. "Think about it, general. Runer, always a pleasure. Glad to see you took my advice and left Al'Myrah. We should catch up while I'm still on the continent. I have had many conversations in my meditations with you and would love to have real discourse. General." He bowed stiffly and turned, leaving.

Wu-Zhiang started to speak, but Tzarik suddenly went deaf. His ears rang and his head spun. Unable to get a breath deep into his lungs, his vision blurred. An ache shot down his spine. Gasping in anguish, he folded over the table in utter agony.

It had been too long since he'd hunted and the runes were reminding him.

CHAPTER 14
THE ROYAL CITY

THE ROYAL CITY TWINKLED WITH MORE GOLD THAN SHIUKI or any of the other smaller towns they'd passed on their long journey up the continent. Sybal remembered to breathe deeply and with intention, but this time a slight dizziness overtook her. Her hips ached by the time they dismounted just outside the palace gates. A twinge in her side like a muscle cramp made her wonder if maybe she hadn't been drinking enough water.

"We all go in together," ShanBao instructed, moving to walk beside Jin. "We are here on serious business."

At first Sybal didn't understand what ShanBao had said, then realized he'd returned to speaking Xian. With Tzarik gone, she wouldn't have to translate. Still, her mind moved slowly, and keeping up with the chatter made her feel exhausted.

"How can I help?" Sybal asked.

"I think the Di-Huan will be pleased to see you again. He was a little taken with you last time, but didn't get to enjoy your presence," ShanBao said easily. "You were focused on Yui."

She moved to walk on Jin's other side when she noticed his stiff march and forcedly placid face. "You've not been around much," she mused as kindly as she could. "I've missed sparring in your dojo."

Jin laughed heartily. "No need to worry, Sybal. I've been

honing my skills outside the Hallow City, is all." He turned to face her so ShanBao could not see. He shook his head so slightly she almost missed it.

Catching on, she nodded and stopped her inquiry. He'd let her know if she needed to.

The palace guards must have been informed of Wushito's coming because they were swiftly ushered into the inner rooms of the palace without much to deter them. Sybal marveled again at the statues of gold in the shapes of various monsters. She recognized a couple: one was the thing ShanBao called a pi xiu, and then there was the qilin she'd learned about during the festival. Seeing the creatures, a tingling ran through her entire body, just beneath the surface. She'd felt this before. A slight panic rose in her: could it be the Runer's death already? How long had it been since their last hunt?

A servant motioned for the group to go outside into a garden surrounded by high red walls.

"His majesty is outside?" ShanBao asked, confused.

The servant nodded. "He spends a lot of time in the garden."

Outside, amongst the koi ponds, wooden pathways, and tall, lush foliage sprawled a small lounge on a rug. The Di-Huan lay on it. Beside it on a tiny chair sat Princess Yui, reading out of a white book with gold lettering.

"And here is Wushito to ask to spill the blood of my people," the Di-Huan said, sighing and sitting up.

ShanBao offered a deep bow, going to his knees. Jin and Wu-Yasuke offered the same. Confused, Sybal quickly caught up, falling onto her knees too hard. She heard Yui giggle lightly before they all stood up again.

"May the sun never set on your majesty," ShanBao said respectfully. "I won't remind you, my king, all the good Wushito has done for your realm. I do not wish to slaughter your people. Wu-Tang and House Xiaoh are not your people."

The Di-Huan stood up and stretched lightly. "They are my people. They are on Xia. Once they were your people, Wu-Shan-Bao. Or have you forgotten where the book was written and who started Wushito?"

"Times change," ShanBao said sternly.

Curious, Sybal asked, "Wushito was founded in Wu-Tang?"

"Hardly matters," ShanBao cut in. "We have elevated ourselves out of the lowlands. Only our Di-Huan sits higher than us. Where our teachings come from does not matter."

Sybal didn't miss the Di-Huan's changed exterior. The last time she'd seen him, he'd nearly exploded into stardust and butterflies at seeing her. Now he hardly looked at them and started to pace away.

"Are you well, majesty?" she asked cautiously. Her eyes flitted to Yui.

The princess spoke up as her father walked apart from them, towards a pond brimming with lilies.

"He is sad that his people are at war with each other," she said in the sweetest, saddest voice Sybal had ever heard.

"Also that his son has no traditional claim to the throne," ShanBao put in. "The prince is not dragon-touched. Perhaps it's time to move away from such archaic traditions."

The Di-Huan turned around and walked back towards them. "Yes, poor Hiro."

"Wushito fully supports this, your eminence," ShanBao reiterated. "You know you can depend on us."

Sybal put in, "Many monarchies simply put the descendants on the thrones. Most in a province—even a continent—will go along with it for the sake of peace. When our sultana took the throne, there were a few riots. They thought a woman could not rule. But she quelled the uprising and has been a good ruler."

"The uprisings hardly concern me," the Di-Huan admitted. His eyes landed on Jin. "I am not fond of quelling riots, as you say. It is the will of the Dragon that I fear. I appreciate your support, Wu-ShanBao, but can you protect us from gods?"

"A leader must know when to remind his subjects who is lord of the land," ShanBao offered. "I am not really here to ask your permission, majesty."

"Oh?" The Di-Huan moved to a table full of tiny potted trees. He picked up little golden sheers and gently trimmed the branches. "Wu-ShanBao, sometimes I wonder about your loyalty to the Royal City."

ShanBao drew himself up, quickly glancing at Yasuke. His general stood close. "I am loyal to Xia, Di-Huan. And above all to Wushito. Without us, the continent would return to its ghastly dark days like the barbarian kingdoms of Caerwren. The age of the sun outshines any other continent. Wushito has blessed Xia."

"Of course," the Di-Huan said, sighing. He picked up a tree and turned it in the sun. "Yui, my pearl, come inspect this tree. The branches are brittle and I am afraid I cannot see the problem."

Sybal caught ShanBao shifting angrily. This movement was out of character for the slow, usually calm man. He hadn't even partaken in the battle when Wu-Tang first attacked. She'd never seen him withdraw, let alone be annoyed.

"Sometimes," ShanBao went on, "a re-evaluation is necessary. Start over. Like this tree. If it is dead, throw it out before it infects the others. This is very serious, majesty," ShanBao tried more earnestly.

"It is," the Di-Huan agreed.

Yui took the plant in her hands, which were covered in her

long, silky sleeves. She examined it closely, turning it this way then that, then peering between the branches.

"Ah!" she exclaimed. "A single beetle has bored a tiny whole into the trunk. Oh, she has an egg sack."

Smiling sadly, the Di-Huan took the tree and placed it apart from the others. "She can have that tree, then. But she must be separated from the others to not infect them. Once the sack is ready to hatch, we will move her outside the walls. To protect the others." He inclined his head towards ShanBao. "And to save the tree."

"Di-Huan—" ShanBao started again.

"Master ShanBao," the ruler cut in forcibly. "Would you care to stay for a feast? Yui's sixteenth birthday is this very day. It will just be family." He chuckled. "But my family is very large. It may sooth you to watch the dancing and gifts the children have prepared for their sister."

ShanBao bit the inside of his cheek. Sybal was beginning to see that patience—despite the facade he put on—might not be one of ShanBao's virtues. She tried to deduce what had instilled this rush in him. They'd had no word of Wu-Tang moving. As far as she knew, the lowland city would cower after the beating they'd received.

"Of course," ShanBao finally said with forced pleasantry.

"And lady Runer." The Di-Huan acknowledged her. "I did not mean to snub you. I am divinely pleased you have come back to see me. Thrilled. I'd love to speak with you before you leave."

"Sybal is here to observe," ShanBao said.

Something inside clicked. Her gut told her to reply to this. Following her instincts, she said, "I cannot deny a king who is pleased to see me. People rarely are pleased to see Runers."

At this, Yui giggled and clutched her book tightly. "This is going to be wonderful!" she cried.

ShanBao turned on his heel and marched out. Wanting to dissipate his rage, Sybal followed him.

"That fool doesn't understand," the Wushito master growled between gnashed teeth. "He cannot stop us."

"What are you planning?" Sybal asked hurriedly. "Isn't this just a war between the people, not Wushito and the Di-Huan? ShanBao!" she shouted when he didn't stop. He marched on without her.

"It is my duty as Wushito to keep the country safe, so long as the will of the Dragon is upheld, Runer!" he shouted back.

Confused, she stammered after him. "But you said...?" Her brain oscillated dangerously in her skull, stopping her words and reasoning.

"Leave it!" ShanBao snapped before cutting a corner out of earshot.

$$\backsim$$

Sybal looked in the gilded mirror that stood from the floor to ceiling in the private quarters that Princess Yui had insisted she have. Far apart from the main palace, a good stretch of trees, walking paths, and gardens separated her from the rest, giving her ample privacy. She had no feast-worthy garments with her, so she made do with brushing her hair and bathing. She put her leather armor on, then took it off again, judging each piece with a scrutiny she had not applied in the time she'd been with Tzarik.

She had started to braid the hair on the side of her head like her mother's people did when a knock jolted her tender nerves. She called for the person to enter, thinking it must be a servant.

Jin appeared in the mirror behind her. Turning to greet him, she stopped, taken in by his clean, neat attire. His long white hair had been plated down his back, standing out against the dark blue of his formal robe and yellow belt.

"You look so handsome," she said, smiling. "I'm just...trying."

Jin joined her at the mirror, taking her hair in his lithe fingers and tightening the braid. "You're always beautiful, Sybal. You have a good soul."

"Hah," she scoffed audibly. "Not according to Al'Myrahn law." She didn't go on, sensing Jin's tenseness. "Want to tell me what's bothering you?"

The young warrior sighed, switching sides. "More than anything. But for now, I have a request."

"Anything," she offered gently.

He slowed his braiding. "I want to see Yui tonight."

"We will," she said, trying to follow what he implied.

"No." He met her eyes in the mirror. "Time's running out. I need to see her. We love each other and we can't help ourselves. Sybal, invite her to your room tonight, after the celebration."

"Jin!" she gasped, realizing what he was asking.

"It's not wrong!" he pleaded, coming before her and gripping her shoulders. "She loves me and I love her, desperately. There is so much that wants to keep us apart, but we can't allow it anymore. If we do this and if..." He stopped, fighting to find a way to tell her what weighed on his spirit.

An ache in her heart added to the burning of her veins. She'd never been young and in love. Seeing this boy so desperate and honest hurt. "Does she really love you?" she asked, just to make sure before she said what was next on her tongue.

Jin nodded. "She's proved it time and again. Sybal, please, there is so much at stake."

Catching her face in her hands and rubbing her temples, she groaned. Yes, there was a lot at stake. The future of a continent, a people, a dynasty.

Tzarik always told her to not get involved with things that had nothing to do with her. At this rate, she hadn't found anything that had to do with her. They hid like rats in the mountains. Except when he'd gone to Wu-Tang against her wishes.

"Of course, Jin. I'll do what I can."

⌒⌲

THE DI-HUAN INVITED Sybal to sit on his right during the feast. She'd expected the feast hall to be filled with dignitaries and other house leaders, maybe even foreign diplomats, to celebrate the birthday of the Di-Huan's favorite princess. But as mentioned, only the royal family, a few Wushito in uniform, and some she couldn't place in rank milled about the long, rectangular table. She didn't have her gilded Xian costume and thus relied on the braids and some scented oil. Amongst the glittering gold and many colors of the royal children and wives, she knew her black stood out.

"I'm sorry I don't have proper attire," she whispered to the Di-Huan as he took her arm and brought her to her seat at the head of the table. "None of the princess's or wives' clothes would fit me."

"No one will mind your dress, Runer. This is a private affair," he said, smiling. "My children cannot even be bothered to put on their slippers."

Looking at the children running back and forth playing games, some of them small and some teenagers, she noted several were barefoot. One girl stopped to stare at her, entranced by the golden-haired stranger. As they sat down and conversation turned to polite murmurings, the little girl slipped to Sybal's side and unabashedly touched her hair.

"Your eyes are big," the girl said.

"Yours are beautiful," Sybal replied, her heart melting at the brave child.

"Don't be rude, Princess Mi," the Di-Huan said, leaning over. To Sybal he said, "We do not have foreigners on Xia. I apologize."

Sybal smiled. The way the Di-Huan spoke put her at ease. She'd have never felt this way in the presence of her sultana. "It's all right. That's the least rude thing I'm sure a Runer has ever heard."

The king nodded. "I have heard that Runers are not well loved, except maybe on Caerwren."

Curious, Sybal asked, "I haven't seen Runers here. I have heard you do not have them?"

Servants filed out of a wide-open doorway, carrying trays of fruit, seafood, and that clear alcohol she'd tried a few times. As they served them, they bowed their heads to not look the royals in the eye. Before them, a makeshift stage was filled with dozens of royal children. They wore badly made costumes and set up props for a theatrical production. A set of them sat on the side, strange instruments in hand.

"No. No Runers," the Di-Huan explained, serving Sybal himself. On his left sat the prince, Hiro, still sullen and silent. The Di-Huan served him as well. "When Wushito rose from the valleys thousands of years ago, Xia had no need for the black oath you have taken, and I mean no offense. I have read accounts of runings. It was a brave choice to make."

Sybal eagerly took a shot of the rice wine. It didn't burn until after it hit her stomach, going down smooth. She liked it. "I think it was cowardly of me. I am guilty. I did it to avoid death and to stay with my betrothed."

At this, the Di-Huan raised his cup to her. "For love," he said and threw back the wine.

"Yes," Sybal mused. She looked down the table and saw Jin next to ShanBao, far away from Yui, who sat at the opposite head of the table.

The princess looked up and caught Sybal's eye, smiling sweetly and raising a cup to her before applauding her younger half-siblings, whose entertainment had begun. Sybal tried to follow the tiny narrator on the side, but couldn't catch her words at this end of the table.

"I don't mean to pry," Sybal said, "and it's none of my business." She felt the ruler of Xia might not mind a personal question. He made her feel so at ease. "Princess Yui is not recognized by the people?"

At this, Hiro took a quick drink and poured himself another.

The Di-Huan smiled, his eyes drifting far away. A scandalous grin pulled at his wrinkled cheeks. "A forbidden coupling, lady Runer."

Looking around at the myriad of beautiful wives and offspring around the table, she asked, "Are you not permitted to have more than one wife?"

His cheeks reddened. "Xia has changed a lot in the past one hundred years. These women are my doing." He raised his hand as if to embrace all who sat around the table. "Growing my odds. Surely one would be dragon-touched, continuing my dynasty. Our longest run is two. My father and I tie the longest. I'd like to see mine go on."

Sybal scanned the royal family before her. Jin's white head stuck out like a sunbeam in a dark room. No others had the mark of the Dragon. She began to understand the Di-Huan's worry.

He went on. "The world says we need to catch up with them. Use black powder for warfare, not nighttime tricks. We need to have one wife and one heir. But that has never been our way. We go where the White Dragon guides us."

"Old, outdated tradition," Hiro mumbled.

Sybal choked on her mouthful of seafood and rice, shocked

Hiro was taking part in a conversation. "Highness?" she asked, respectfully acknowledging him.

"We need stability," Hiro added.

"Hiro is sad the Dragon did not bless him," the Di-Huan explained. "And perhaps I have been wrong to say he will not rule when I am gone. I often wished Yui's children would take my place. But I also think Hiro should watch over our continent." A great, unseen weight crushed the old man and he sank down. "I fear that may be wrong, though."

The prince looked away.

The king went on, "But I have assured him that does not mean he will not sit upon the sun throne for a time once I am gone. If we can manage it."

Curious, Sybal asked, "Can you promise that?"

At this, the king sighed sadly. "No. Xia is split. And the Dragon says if the balance is not held then the continent will crack, sundering us into two people. Like long ago."

"Oh!" Sybal cried, recalling a story from her childhood. "The great continent! What did they call it...?" She rubbed her chin. "All people lived on the continent and then a beast from Jannah came down and cut it asunder when the sentients began to fight, to protect them. All kinds on one mass of land."

The Di-Huan smiled, shaking his head. "No, the White Dragon came and split the continents, choosing Xia as best above all."

"One story must be true," Sybal said, defending her home and what she'd been taught. "They can't all be true."

The Di-Huan smiled pleasantly. "Maybe the gods each chose a continent. One for Xia, one for Al'Myrah."

Sybal tapped the table, thinking. "Why would so many gods choose Bahratt and Alika? They have more than one god. Some are very unpleasant."

The Di-Huan shrugged, quickly chewing the food he'd just popped into his mouth. "Hardly matters. Xia is best!"

Sybal blanched playfully, laughing. "What makes you think the Dragon chose Xia as best?"

"We are a lighthouse in Ocean Sky, closest to The Frozen Nation," the Di-Huan cried jovially. "Once the continent split from the others, the White Dragon raised it up, higher than the rest, as a sentinel."

"True, the altitude is different," she admitted. "Makes it hard to breathe."

"Then the Dragon walked with the man he chose to be the first Di-Huan, touching him, giving him the blessing."

"The white hair."

The Di-Huan nodded. "He walked with him around the continent for one hundred and twenty-five days. He gave him all the knowledge he would need to rule and to slay the beasts that came up from the darkness of the split continents. That man was the first Di-Huan. But he could not rule alone, for he could not read the Dragon tome. He had to seek out one man to become a warrior, to protect against the monsters that haunted the night. The dragon-touched chose the first leader, who would study the book he filled with the White Dragon's knowledge. That chosen one went below to protect Xia's base—the lowlands—and founded Wu-Tang where Wushito first trained." The Di-Huan smiled when Sybal didn't reply. "See? Perfect balance. Xia is best and was chosen by the gods."

Her eyes watched the children perform. One inside the long dragon costume tripped and the entire beast tumbled onto the stage with loud thuds and despondent cries. "So the first dragon-touched found the man who could read the Dragon's book?"

"Well," the Di-Huan said, shrugging innocently. "Maybe it was a woman."

"Was it?" Sybal asked, looking up at the king.

The Di-Huan nodded. "That's probably why it took him so long to find this oh-so-blessed *man*. The poor fool was looking in all the wrong places."

She clapped politely as the now simpering children disentangled themselves and made awkward bows to their enraptured audience. "What happens if that balance is broken?" she asked. "I respect your need to have a dragon-touched on the throne and for Wushito to support you, but what if—now that times are different—you let Hiro rule?"

The prince blinked uncomfortably and cut his already tiny bites into smaller ones.

"It almost happened once," the Di-Huan explained. "My great-great-grandfather was second born, dragon-touched. His elder brother, may the Dragon guide him, was to be Di-Huan, breaking tradition." He stopped, his joyful face slackening darkly as his eyes watched a long-gone story told to him by his ancestors. "The continent shook. He came from the Hikomi province. As punishment, most of that province broke free, sinking and drifting from Xia."

Sybal's mouth popped open in understanding. "The northern isle!"

The Di-Huan nodded. "Let go from Xia, it was cursed, filled with monsters from The Frozen Nation. Wushito was almost wiped clean keeping them at bay. They had to take terrible measures to quell the hordes. The monks joined them and have not yet left their post."

Sybal emptied her cup again, lavishing in the warm buzzing and the Di-Huan's story. "Every continent has a story like that," she said in defense of her home once again. "I love Al'Myrah. I miss it every day. I believe it has just as grand a history."

"As well you should." The Di-Huan patted her hand on the

table. "I do not mean to say your home is lesser. Xia has allowed itself to be left behind, I think. But some things are hard to let go of."

Sybal took more fried fruit and dumped it onto her plate. "Enough of myths. Go back to telling me about Yui's mother. Forbidden love?"

Gazing up into the black and gold arched ceiling, the Di-Huan sighed longingly. "A legendary story of love and..." he looked down, meeting her eyes, "...taboo."

"Father," Hiro mumbled, embarrassed.

"I'm sorry?" Sybal asked, dreading the answer.

"Nothing like you might expect," the Di-Huan said, waving his hand. "Her mother was...from far away. My love got her killed."

"Oh, I didn't know," Sybal breathed. "Who would dare take the life of a love of the Di-Huan?"

"Wushito protects us," Hiro hissed, barely moving his lips.

"They killed her?" Sybal couldn't believe what she heard. "Why?"

The Di-Huan brought his cup to his lips, fixing his eyes on ShanBao down the table. "You are clever, lady Runer. I am sure you can deduce why a monster hunter might want to kill something."

She wasn't human or Masahk, Sybal thought. *It's none of your business, Sybal!* she added to herself.

"Sira?" she chanced. "What would happen if someone touched by the Dragon were to rise up and try to claim the throne now?"

A second group of royal children filed in from the garden and started to perform a dance for their older sister. Yui smiled and clapped joyfully as she watched.

"Sybal," the Di-Huan replied gravely, "I am torn. So long as I live, it is my privilege to do what is best for Xia. What am I to do? I want to change the way things are here. I want Hiro to replace me when the time comes—just as he does. He is a good man, so wise and fair. He is a patriot as well. But he would be the first without the white blessing on the throne." He closed his eyes, mumbling a silent prayer. "I often ask the gods why this happened in my time. It was simple for my father; he was touched and so was I. If only there was a way to join the two sides. Keep the balance."

Sybal's eyes shot to Jin and then to Yui.

"Maybe the Dragon would understand, then," she agreed.

Chapter 15
The Great White Snake

Tiny torches lined the golden halls of the royal palace, warming and dimly lighting the way Sybal knew either Jin or Yui would take. Who would come first, she wasn't sure. She kept poking her head out from her private quarters to check, listening for the soft padding of feet or slippers. A trickle of guilt slowly slid down her back the longer she waited. The Di-Huan had become less of a distant king and more of a regular man the longer she'd spoken to him at dinner. Perhaps a bit childish, but she wondered if that was a facade he put on to hide the struggle he really felt.

It had to be well past midnight when the hairs on the back of her neck stood up. Eyes touched her back.

Whipping around, hand on her scimitar, she turned to find Jin rising up from a crouched position where he'd dropped onto her balcony.

"Krishvu! Just come in through the door like a normal person," she hissed, pulling him inside the room. She quickly pulled the gauzy drapes shut.

"And walk past a dozen palace guards and gossipy servant women?" he said, smiling in reply. "Thank you for doing this."

She returned the smile. "I don't feel good about it. Going behind the Di-Huan's back has got to be breaking some sort of law."

"I believe they call it treason," Jin offered boyishly.

"Jin!"

Before she could go on, a gentle knock on the door cut her off. "Lady Sybal?" Yui's high, smooth voice called. She spoke loud enough to penetrate the door. "I brought those books you wanted," she added louder.

Realizing she was covering her tracks and creating a narrative, Sybal opened the door. "Princess, thank you! Come in." She pulled the girl in. "Clever," she whispered once they were both inside. Planting her hands on her hips, she surveyed the young lovers before her. "I'll put up protection. It won't muffle anything, but it will stop anyone from coming in who means harm."

She slid her leather cord out from under her black armor and picked up halat between her first two fingers. Standing with her back against the door, she held her hand up, drawing the shape of the rune agonizingly slowly before her and walking the parameter of the room. Jin blew out most of the oil lamps and candles in the room so that prying eyes would not be able to see in past the curtains.

Sybal drew atan for a bit of temporary light, intending to leave the lovers alone and going into the small library off to the side of her quarters. Her back was to the couple when a gasp cut through the silence. She spun around.

"Don't look!" Yui shrieked.

But it was too late. When Sybal turned, the fading light from atan touched the girl. Underneath her pretty flesh, a white, curving shadow appeared. Her instincts ignoring the plea, Sybal drew atan again and held it up, casting the light farther.

"Stop!" Jin begged, shielding Yui from the rune light.

Sybal saw her before he moved to protect her. Underneath the princess's royal appearance, a ghostly, great white snake recoiled in fear. The pink slitted eyes turned back into the large, afraid brown ones before Sybal's horrified gaze.

"What is that?" Jin snapped, now glaring at Sybal and her rune. "Make it stop."

Quickly closing her hand around the white light, she snuffed out atan, plunging the room back into orange darkness from the two lamps left burning. Sybal breathed steadily, unsure what she had uncovered or seen.

Hunting for any answer, she asked, "Are you Masahk?"

Yui cringed behind Jin, shaking. "No. I can't tell you. It would put you in danger. Or you'd..." She couldn't go on. "I trust you, Sybal. But I can't say."

"Sybal, please," Jin begged. "It's not what you think. The monks and Wushito would descend upon us if they knew."

"Your father knows?" she asked, keeping her voice measured.

At this, Yui smiled and laughed nervously. "Of course."

She recalled what he said about her mother. Taboo?

"I am still me," Yui whispered. "It's just a part of who I am."

"And I love her," Jin added. He gripped her arms, pulling her close to himself. She leaned her head into his chest, gazing up at him longingly.

Sybal nodded. "Take your time. I'll be in the next room."

She tore herself away from the lovers and quietly shut the door to the library. Leaning up against it, catching her breath, she heard them giggle as they flopped together onto her bed. Her mind raced with what she'd uncovered. She didn't have the slightest guess as to what it meant. Tzarik might.

Noticing the scroll-lined walls, she slowly walked among the shelves, reading the wooden handles of the scrolls. Some were so old, she couldn't read the titles due to them being worn down. Others were written in old Xian that she could only partially make out. She collapsed onto a lounge near a wide window and tracked familiar constellations in the sky. At least the sky was the same no matter the continent. A sudden homesickness soaked her insides. She alighted on one constellation: it was supposed to be the shape of a man—warrior—slaying some beast. Like a Runer.

She imagined it was Tzarik, hunting a monster among the stars. Studying the stars around it, she held her hand up and drew in another hunter. Deciding it was her, she realized she missed hunting. With him. As if prompted by the fantasy, her fingers tingled familiarly.

"We need to hunt," she whispered to herself. How long could drawing runes and keeping their swords close stave off the inevitable? The aches and pains came on as if the runes knew they hadn't done their duty. One could not take up the runes and not comply with their purpose.

Through the wall, Yui gasped and then giggled.

Despite being happy for the pair, a new feeling cultivated itself in Sybal's mind the more she thought about how happy they must be. It started off with wanting to roll her eyes at their glee. Maybe go in and break them up. Then bitterness sank in. Sadness quickly overtook that sour taste.

I'm jealous, she realized. Sighing sadly, allowing herself to sink into the sensation, she laid her head down on the lounge. Her fingers traced the floral designs of the fabric. It had been over a year since she'd lost Rahul. Lost everything. But his loss hit differently than the others. He would have been someone she could trust completely. He'd never have abandoned her. Betrayed her.

She missed Tzarik.

Her chest pulled painfully tight and her eyes burned. After this long and all she'd done, she'd expected the need for love to dwindle. Go out like a candle's flame. Now it hurt more than ever.

The jade bracelet slid down her wrist as she traced the pattern. Taking it off, she held it up to the moon so the white light made the dragon glow, almost like glass. Knowing he had the exact same one gave her a smile. Maybe it was time for her to move on. Either tell him of her feelings or leave him for good. He'd all but said she was ready to go out on her own, be a lone Runer, forever chasing down monsters to kill, curses to lift.

I don't know about lifting curses, she reasoned with herself. *So I should stay with him.* But staying and not telling him how she felt would be torture. But if she said something and he didn't feel the same way…

"I don't really love him," she said to the dragon bracelet. "I'm just lonely. He's horrid, anyway." She sat up on her elbows. There had to be another way to alleviate the loneliness.

A friend from before, Vicdan, floated before her eyes. She remembered how he'd always looked her in the eye, made her feel like the only person in existence when they spoke. Once he'd even tried to get her into bed. But Tzarik had interfered. She wondered if—now that things were different—if she ever saw him again, she'd let him bed her. Biting her lip, she wondered what it would be like. Would she know what to do?

"Ugh, Sybal!" she moaned, falling back onto the lounge. "You old spinster."

Her mind wandered and she ended up counting the wooden slats in the floor over and over as she waited. She stood up and sat back down, dozing in and out of anxious sleep. Finally, she relinquished herself to a lounge in the corner and closed her eyes.

"Sybal?"

She sat up as orange light cut across the dark floor. Yui stood in the doorway wrapped in a long silky robe. "Can I join you?" she asked timidly.

Nodding, the Runer pushed herself to one side of the lounge so the princess could sit next to her. Yui fell onto the seat with a sigh, pushing her now disheveled black hair behind one ear.

Glancing sideways up at Sybal, she said, "Thank you. We have only been able to meet like this a few times. Last time, we were almost caught in that abandoned temple and Jin was too scared to try again."

A strange urge to chastise the young lovers boiled up in Sybal. Forcing herself to not ruin the moment, she nodded instead. "Of course. I'd do a lot of things for love. Even if I think it's wrong."

"Surely you understand," Yui said gently, laying her hand on Sybal's arm, her fingers lightly touching the jade bracelet. "Who wears the other one? He must have your heart."

Sybal couldn't stop the scoff. "I'm not sure what he was thinking when he gave me this, but it wasn't that. He sees me as a child. A fool. Someone he must tether to a post to stop from running away. Displeased with all I do."

The princess pressed her lips together to stop from grinning. "He doesn't know how to show affection. When one is out of love for so long, it's hard to show it. Just like hunting."

Sybal finally met the princess's eyes, frowning in question.

"Like hunting," the princess said again. "If you gave it up for years and years, you'd struggle to aim a bow, be slow in combat. Out of practice."

"I see," Sybal said generously. "I don't think love is like that. I think when you feel it, you know."

"He knows." Yui turned to watch Jin on the other side of the doorway, tucking in his shirt. "He just doesn't know how to say it. You might have to help him. And be ready for any terrible thing he does while trying to swim in the new waters you've put him in."

Help him? Sybal mused. She'd never helped Tzarik do anything. Only gotten in the way. Made him angry.

"How do I know?" she asked.

"You don't," Yui offered. "You have to take a chance."

Would it be worth the hurt and damage to their relationship? What if he was repulsed by her attempts? Or it enraged him to run again? She wasn't the weak, new Runer she had been then, but thinking of him leaving still frightened her. She didn't want to be alone.

"Are you going to tell me what I saw in there?" she asked suddenly. "In the rune light. It shows hidden magic, true forms."

"Ah." Yui adjusted her seat next to Sybal. "My mother's blood. She was...not human. Nor Masahk. My father loved her, though. It's not like some will tell you—that she enchanted him to trick him. He was in love." A far-off, whimsical smile overtook the girl's face. "She could grant wishes. Father wished for me." Pride swelled the girl's chest. "I don't have her powers, though. A monk once told father that I may have one wish in me to grant. But just one. It would consume me to grant it." She held her hand out as if asking Sybal to read her palm. "See, I am too human. What you saw was my spirit. I cannot change form like her. This is who I am."

A lump formed un Sybal's throat. "Your father must love you mightily."

Yui nodded. "And her, too. He didn't take her last wish. He wanted to free her. But..."

Without warning, Sybal's left shoulder locked up in a spasm of pain so great, she doubled over, crying out.

"What is it?" Jin shouted, joining the women in the study. "Sybal?"

The two knelt beside her, supporting her.

The pain eased just enough for her to mumble, "I have to get back to Tzarik. We have to hunt."

"Leave now?" Yui cried, not wanting to let go of the moment they were having.

"If I don't, we may die," she grunted. She immediately thought of Tzarik. He had to be feeling it, too. "Gods, please don't let him be hurt."

CHAPTER 16

Gini

Tzarik paced back and forth in front of the estate, gripping the reins of his horse in frustration and for support in case another agonizing seizure took him. The servant had said ShanBao and his entourage should be returning from the palace today. He'd been waiting for three hours. He was just thinking of leaving to find them a hunt when the clamor and chatter of the group came around the last bend. Sybal and Wu-Yasuke brought up the rear, chatting.

"Where are you off to, Runer?" ShanBao asked, sliding off his horse. "Outfitted for battle?"

"No, Master ShanBao, a hunt. It's what we Runers do." He pulled his big black horse over to Sybal. "Can you ride out now?"

Glad to see his urgency matched in her face when she nodded, he led his horse away to mount.

"Where's Jin?" he asked, noticing the boy was missing.

"Wushito business up north," ShanBao cut in.

Tzarik realized the old man had not taken his eyes off them since he'd come hurrying down the path to greet them. Unwilling to give him any explanation, he mounted and clicked his tongue, jerking his head to signal Sybal to follow. They trotted away from the prying eyes of the Wushito master and out of earshot. Tzarik pushed his horse down the paths that led into the forest areas rather than taking the main roads.

"Are you sure you're not too tired?" he asked Sybal. "We've traveled for days. I'd understand if you wanted to rest before a hunt."

"I'm exhausted and I smell," she replied in good humor. "But I feel it so strongly. I didn't know it would set in so quickly."

Tzarik appreciated her candor. "Ever since Moshav, I have decided to never doubt the swiftness of the runes' punishments."

Sybal pressed her lips out to one side. "You'd never parted from them. Maybe the first time comes more quickly." She cleared her throat and pulled up alongside him. "I had a long talk with the Di-Huan," she offered.

She had this military way of wanting to discuss events every time they came back together. He wanted to hunt for now, get the most pressing matter taken care of first. In truth, he wasn't sure where to start, but the lowlands seemed like a good place.

"You wouldn't have liked it, though," she went on, ignoring his silence. "He spoke about how much better Xia was than other continents."

At this, he grunted in agreement.

Because of the runes and the sensations they'd been tormenting him with, the meeting he and Wu-Zhiang had had was almost driven from his mind. He opened his mouth to say something but stopped. Would she panic? Want to veer off course?

"Tzarik?" she asked. "Have you ever been in love?"

This took him by surprise. His eyes going wide and his brow furrowing at the intrusive question, he almost wished she'd ask about the meeting instead.

He stumbled around his reply, not sure how to answer. "I don't know. Maybe." Had anyone been in love with him? That wasn't her question. "I thought I was once. After Azar, I went back to her. But I was young, stupid, and naive. And she was evil."

Sybal laughed. Surprised, he glared at her.

"Women aren't evil just because they don't want to be with you."

You have no idea what she's like, he thought bitterly. Sybal was so arrogant and ignorant sometimes.

"Jin and Yui are in love," she went on. Her eyes glassed over and she smiled softly. "Love is amazing. I miss that feeling. The desire to touch another person, so strong that I might die. Having to fight my lust. Wondering what their soft flesh feels like when I lie atop them. Wondering if their kiss is gentle or savage."

Every thought she spoke in detail passed through his mind in her soft, yearning voice. "You deserve love," he said quickly.

"I think everyone does." She turned to face him. "Even if two people think they are so different." She stopped and bit her bottom lip, thinking.

"What is it?" he asked.

She winced. She wanted to speak; she just had to be satisfied with the words. She wanted to be careful.

He assured her, "Just tell me."

She pulled up on her reins. He did likewise.

"I don't know what it was," she started, "and Yui doesn't, either. But seeing as I think I spotted Sharar the other day, I don't think I can be too careful."

"You did see him," Tzarik cut in. Feeling compelled by paranoia, he cast his glance over both shoulders, scanning the hills and trees. "That was the meeting the general had."

"You saw him?" she gasped. Her horse picked up on her shifting and put its ears back, starting to panic. "Did he hurt you? Threaten you? What's he want?"

Tzarik raised his hands to calm her. "He did nothing, like he always does. He asked questions and I am sure he learned more than he let on. I could see he was scheming. He's after something Wushito possesses. In exchange for a boon from them, he promised them victory over the Di-Huan."

Sybal's face paled as her white blood rushed. Her blue eyes darted from shadow to shadow behind Tzarik. Seeing her on alert put him at ease, even if just a little. At least she understood.

"So is it not a civil war?" she mused out loud. "Does Wushito want to overthrow the royal family? Of course!" She almost stood up in her stirrups. "The Di-Huan said as much. But I can't believe it."

Tzarik sighed inwardly, forcing himself to not roll his eyes. Why Sybal insisted on championing for Wushito was lost on him. Her insistence to pick sides blinded her to the evil of everyone involved. She chided him for his cynicism, but it had kept him alive this long.

"Yui," she breathed. "Tzarik, she's not human."

"What do you mean?"

His apprentice winced, suddenly avoiding eye contact. "I helped them meet for a tryst. It had to be secret. When I drew atan, there was something else inside her. Like a spirit, maybe."

She checked his face. *She wants to see if I'm going to interrupt her,* he realized. Reaching for an inner piece, he let her go on. He had to let her speak. If he constantly cut her off, disregarded her thoughts, she might learn to never speak. The line between trying to keep her safe from herself and letting her grow as a Runer was not an easy one for him to walk.

"Go on, Sybal," he said gently.

She spoke quickly. "Her mother was some kind of creature. She said her father mentioned that she could give a wish, but only one. Was she some kind of djinn? Djinn aren't always vicious. Are they? Her mother warned the Di-Huan not to invoke the wish because it would destroy Yui." She stopped, her thoughts over-taking her mind. She squinted and looked away.

He loved watching her think, solve a puzzle.

"There's no way Sharar knows about this kind of creature, is there?" she asked. "Is she a djinn?" she asked finally.

Pulling himself away from admiring her, he replied, "I don't even know what she would be if not a djinn. What did her spirit look like? Did she give her mother a name?"

"She was a great white snake," Sybal offered.

He didn't know. Djinn were demons, not from the mortal plain. He supposed there could be variations across the map. No matter the truth, wish-granting creatures were often hunted and sought out no matter how vile and destructive.

Sybal's mouth dropped, not in shock, but deeper thought. "We need to find out what she is," she said with finality. "What if the war breaks out and the Di-Huan uses the wish to take the victory? He'd regret it for the rest of his life. He loves her so much."

"What if Wushito does?" he added. He kicked his horse's sides, trotting quickly now. "What if they want her as well?"

"Where are we going?" she asked, hurrying to keep up with him. "I thought you didn't want to get involved."

Of course she had to poke at him... He gritted his teeth and bore her remark.

"Where monsters are involved, it's a Runer's duty," he quipped. "And anything that involves Sharar involves me. I had a chance to stop him and I didn't."

"We tried," she consoled him. "His powers are beyond us."

That wasn't entirely true. His fear had stopped him last time. Sharar was on his way to becoming a sorcerer. Tzarik didn't know how close he might be right now. He still searched for pieces, power—he was taking his time.

"Tzarik, where are we going?" she repeated.

"To the monks," he replied. "They know about monsters and are far more learned than I can ever hope to be. They can also point us in the direction of a hunt."

⌘

IT TOOK days to descend from the mountains and reach Hikomi. According to those they met on the road, the monks were docked there. They sailed back and forth from the island where they prayed against the north and The Frozen Nation. Sybal used her language skills to ask a few fishermen near the coast where the monks' boat was docked. A couple enquiries later, they were able to ask a young apprentice in orange robes to see TaoShin.

The Masahk, genial as ever, invited them into his quarters on the grand ship. Tzarik noticed the monk's round, usually bright eyes drooped with weariness.

"A pleasure to have you two together in my company again," TaoShin said softly, pouring green tea into square clay cups. "And armed to the teeth."

"We're on a hunt," Tzarik began. "I was hoping you might know where to find something that needs killing."

TaoShin blanched but smiled at the violent intent. When he sat down, long legs crossed, he squinted at them. "What's wrong? I assure you, I can help you find something to maim, but you look..." He scratched behind a round ear.

"Runer's illness," Sybal offered, brushing it off.

Tzarik caught a slight twitch in TaoShin's right eye.

"I understand," the monk offered. "I won't pry. The secrets of your trade guard your life, lady. I am afraid my home is not kind to you. I'm sorry. But tell me what's on your mind? I thought I'd never see this one again." He gestured to Tzarik. "So I am pleased you have sought me out."

"I have a concern." Sybal launched into what she'd discovered with less tact than a blacksmith disassembling badly made armor. "I saw something inside Princess Yui in my rune light. It reveals monsters in their true form. She told me about a gift she could bestow as a result of this...other thing inside her."

TaoShin's friendly, gray-furred face dropped into a melancholy smile. He set his cup down and fiddled with a set of jade beads on his braided belt. "The Great White Snake. Yes." A sadness—maybe longing—tainted his voice.

Relieved that what Sybal had said hadn't thrown any obvious suspicion on them or made the monk clam up, Tzarik watched him with interest, hoping he'd go on.

"Her mother was a mogwei. A demon."

Sybal and Tarik glanced at each other, unsure if he meant the same kind of demonic creatures that rarely surfaced on Al'Myrah.

"Mogwei?" Tzarik asked.

TaoShin took a quick sip, then licked his lips as if preparing for a long story. "I believe you call them djinn where you are from."

"Gods," Sybal breathed. "We knew it! That's what he wants."

Tzarik frowned, not sure. "Is it common knowledge that the Di-Huan..." He cleared his throat, trying not to see the scene that floated before his eyes when he blinked in the darkness of the ship's cabin.

"Yes," TaoShin offered kindly. "That is why our Di-Huan treats so strongly with Wushito; to keep them on his side despite..." The Masahk shrugged. "But when the princess was born, she had no discerning marks of being spirit-touched."

A jolt hit Tzarik hard in his gut. He knew that phrase: spirit-touched. "One who is spirit-touched falls into madness," he said. "They cannot contain the power of the being that has touched them."

The Masahk nodded. "Exactly. They also lose all color,

turning pale, and often going blind, committing horrible acts to try to save themselves." He shivered. "It is a terrible curse. We see it come from The Frozen Nation. But if she thinks she has a wish to give, she is what we call a gini. A mortal mogwei. If she granted her wish, she would perish."

Sybal nodded. "She said as much. But also mentioned that her father loves her too much to use that wish."

TaoShin closed his eyes and took a deep, slow breath. As he let it out, he sang a low note. "I suppose we never had confirmation that the princess was a gini. If we did, Wushito would have had to...remove her."

Sybal inclined her head to Tzarik. "They must have known. To everyone else, it was just a funny story about their king."

"Sharar did his research," Tzarik confirmed. "That snake general met with him. It sounded like the generals are moving behind ShanBao's back." He stopped talking out loud then before he sounded foolish. He'd suspected ShanBao and Wushito, but perhaps he'd been blinded by his own prejudice. So many moved in secret to hide their involvement in the brewing violence.

"Speak your mind, Runer," TaoShin encouraged. "We will not judge you."

He shook his head. "I don't know what I'm thinking. The air is so thin and full of moisture on this continent, I haven't had a clear thought since we docked. There is a man here, though, who wants something Wushito has."

TaoShin asked, "Does this man desire evil?"

Tzarik half-nodded with a shrug. "We've encountered him before. We think he has a djinn. I don't know if he's used a wish yet or not. He captured and tortured a necromancer into doing his bidding, pitting us against each other."

At the mention of a necromancer, TaoShin made a holy sign

over his forehead. "The *Xai'de Jing*," he said quickly in a strained breath, making another holy sign over his heart.

"The what?" Tzarik asked.

"The book given to the first Di-Huan by the White Dragon. It told how to kill all thirteen thousand evil beasts and monsters of the continents. It also told how to overcome death. Or at least, cheapen death. I believe you might call it the *Mahit'onomicon*."

"Yes!" Sybal cried. "The book of liches. But in our mythology, it was written on Al'Myrah."

"I don't doubt it," TaoShin offered. "It may have been. On Alika, they call it the *Heiro'Alkitab,* and the story goes that it's buried deep under the pyramid of a great pharaoh who took his life and his nation's to lock away the secrets, terrors, and plagues inside." He smiled. "We live on a wonderful world, so many stories and versions of history."

"It doesn't matter which one is true," Tzarik interjected. "Sharar believes it's here and that Wushito has it. That's why he went after Tarkan; a djinn cannot bring back the dead."

"What would he want with the book?" Sybal asked.

"If it has all the knowledge in it that they claim, he could read it and learn how to kill every kind of monster, how to bring them back, any other dark magic we could dream of. Once he made himself a sorcerer, he could..." He tried to imagine what that much power looked like.

"He could open Diyu if he desired," TaoShin acknowledged. "Bring hell to the surface. Consume souls for their power. The options would quite literally be endless, lady Runer. How a man of that ambition has slipped past a magi's notice baffles me."

Tzarik scoffed. "He's patient. Gets others to do his work for him. Goes unnoticed. And the magi are not as holy as you'd think."

What TaoShin had said about hell on hearth reminded him of

something else: something they called the crypt. The more he tried to form the words, the more his head spun.

"Ha!" Sybal exclaimed. "Ala'Nar was destroyed because of him."

Tzarik shook his head. "Tarkan did that. It almost cost Zeva her life. Sharar is subtle. Sly."

"And he's here?" TaoShin asked.

Tzarik nodded again. "Somewhere. He hides so well. But he's been meeting with Wushito. They will no doubt protect him." He frowned, a thought occurring to him. "This book must have told them how to kill monsters without taking up the runes."

"They're why there are no Runers here," Sybal affirmed thoughtfully. "But how?"

A strong, slow bolt of pain shot down Tzarik's left side. He grunted. "Doesn't matter. We need to hunt. Monk, where can we find monsters not snuffed out by Wushito?"

Downing the last of his tea, TaoShin slapped his knees and stood up. "I am sorry to say Wushito has already been dispatched to the area. The island to the north, where we pray to keep The Frozen Nation at bay, has been attacked by the dark creatures. Just a few, but enough that we monks could not handle them. Jiangshi and shui-gui, mostly. I will call a sloop for you. If you hurry, you may get there before Wushito vanquishes them all."

Tzarik stood up and Sybal followed him. "Thank you, TaoShin. Your kindness has aided me more than you know."

The Masahk smiled warmly. "I know, Runer. I know."

CHAPTER 17

THE RUINERS AND THE REAVER

SYBAL SHOOK SO HARD, TINY RIPPLES RHYTHMICALLY wobbled out from under the circular boat the monks had lent them. Tzarik tried to hide the shiver the icy fog injected under his skin, but couldn't anymore. The closer they drew to the nameless island facing The Frozen Nation, the denser that white icy mist became. He judged that in a few minutes, they'd not be able to see a yard before their eyes.

"I can't stop shaking," Sybal grunted through chattering teeth. "It's not just the cold."

Steadying his voice enough to speak, Tzarik said, "A gate to Sheol resides on the northern continent. Think of it like a source. The closer you are to the fire, the more sparks spit and the hotter it gets."

Sybal made a face, only mildly curious in the darkening cold. "I thought Sheol would be fire and brimstone."

"That's the western hell," Tzarik corrected, eyes trained on a dark shape before them.

She smiled. "Makes me think back to the conversation I had with the Di-Huan about different histories. We live in a hot realm and the westerners live in a cold one. Our hells our each other's realms."

"Makes sense," Tzarik agreed. "Sybal." He patted her shoulder and pointed ahead. The shore loomed into view, a black shadow behind the white mist.

"Reminds me of Porsh," she offered, standing up carefully and taking a coil of rope.

"This island doesn't normally look like this." Tzarik leapt out into the freezing water, taking the rope from her and pulling the round boat to shore so she wouldn't have to get her boots wet. He almost regretted his decision out of habit, his toes instantly beginning to numb. "TaoShin said the creatures bring it with them."

"Cold spots!" she said jubilantly.

"Exactly." Tzarik smiled at her. A hot sensation warmed his chest.

He tied the boat to a post sticking up out of the sand. "Look." He kicked the ground with his black boot. A soft wave of pink sand leapt up from the kick, almost tinkling like tiny bells when it landed.

"Oh!" Sybal breathed in delight. "It's beautiful." She knelt down and ran her hand through it. "It's as soft as ashes."

Watching her run her hands gently over the sand almost distracted him from realizing something was missing. "Where are the Wushito?"

Halting, Sybal's yellow head snapped back and forth. "No prints. No boat. At least not here. Maybe they landed somewhere else?"

Crouching together, they ran low, in step with each other, to the rocky expanse of the beach that led up into the island they could not see.

Tzarik stopped suddenly.

"What?" Sybal whispered. The wind picked up but eerily did not dispel the fog.

Pointing ahead, the last of Tzarik's blood drained away. Before them, the horizon spread out white and smooth. Snow covered all they could see.

"It's not too cold, though," Sybal said encouragingly. "I am still shivering, but it's not biting."

She was right, of course, but that didn't help his disdain for the frosty hills. Still, he followed her deeper into the island, looking for any sign of the creatures that had driven the monks away. The jiangshi would leave footprints, whether on the ground or on any vertical surface they chose to walk on.

"What's a shui-gui?" Sybal asked about an hour later, their eyes growing weary from sweeping the dense fog. "I don't even know what to look for."

"I'm not sure," Tzarik confessed, pulling his hood over his head finally. "It doesn't translate?"

Sybal shrugged. "Not that I know of."

They came to the first outpost. As TaoShin had said, it lay empty and dark. Not even a torch signaled where it stood. They were upon it before they knew it, since they couldn't see far. The outpost was a mass of sharply peaked buildings standing on elevated legs for when storms pushed the ocean farther inland.

"Let's split up," Sybal said, sighing, tired of not finding anything. "But not too far."

Tzarik knew splitting up was always a bad idea, but he, too, grew restless and wanted to find something before the Wushito did. Not sure how the warriors would take to others hunting their prey, he hoped to find it, kill it, and get out without ever running into them.

They scaled the rope ladders and then split off from one another. The different areas of the outpost were connected by swinging bridges weaved from ropes and driftwood. Every wall, rail, and gable creaked. Tzarik investigated a few rooms, drawing atan for light. Open tomes, bowls of half-eaten food, and other indicators told him the monks had left quickly. He knew TaoShin could fight. He'd seen him defend against pirates. But when it came to otherworldly monsters, the monks must have been just as helpless as anyone else. Even an immortal Masahk.

Not finding anything, Tzarik went down the back side of the outpost and knelt into the pink sand and drifting snow, looking for tracks. Nothing. He'd never suspected the Wushito were so good as to not leave even a mark. Had the warriors not fought yet? No signs of struggle or tracking could be seen anywhere.

Behind him, soft footsteps made his ears perk up. Whoever it was didn't want to be heard; their steps fell slow, gentle. He waited until it was just a foot behind him. He tensed his legs to leap up when they spoke.

"Find anything?" Sybal's voice whispered softly in a heavily accented tone.

Before he could stand, her hand touched the top of his head. Confused, he froze, legs bent. She trailed her hand down his neck, pulling his hood off. Atan dwindled and faded while he crouched.

Her hand slipped around his neck, fingers gently caressing his collarbone.

"What are you do—?" he started, but stopped when she spun him around.

Her dark brown eyes dropped in sensual beckoning. She pressed her hand against his chest and took his hand in her other. "Follow me."

Shaken, his legs disobeyed him and followed her as she pulled him back towards the beach. "Wait," he gasped. "Did you find anything?"

Sybal giggled. Her laughed echoed hauntingly in her throat. Again in a Xian accent, she replied, "I found you."

"Stop!" a woman's voice screamed from behind him. "Duck!"

Without hesitating, Tzarik dropped to the cold ground. A black-shafted arrow with an orichalcum tip zipped over his head and thudded into Sybal's forehead. Her head jerked back and she cried in pain.

Panic flipped his stomach and jolted his legs into action. Whipping his head back, he saw another Sybal running towards him, nocking a second arrow to her string. Shuffling backwards on all fours, Tzarik locked his wide eyes on the creature before him. No longer Sybal, the thing turned into a shadowy, drowned corpse. Its long black hair fell over its entire face, with a gap for one round, glowering eye to peek out. The thing's skin was white and bloated—like it had been left in water for years.

Behind, Sybal gripped him under his arm and hauled him to his feet. He drew atan quickly while she fired again into the ghostly monster. The arrow, with its special tip, lodged into its chest.

Together, they put space between it and them. Tzarik drew his scimitar. The monster's eye swirled to Sybal just as atan once again went out. In a panic, Tzarik fumbled to draw it again, trying to go slower. He looked up to draw the rune and caught a frightening sight.

The ghost transformed into him. The thing looked at him, then back to Sybal. In his voice, it said, "Let's go to the ocean. Come with me. I want to be with you." It held out its hand. It was exactly his: black gloves with the tips of its fingers exposed. The thing had frightening powers, stronger than even the way a crocotta mimicked voices.

"Let me love you," it begged, its face simpering.

Wincing at the pleading look on his own face, Tzarik slashed at it with his scimitar. It made contact with the ghost and black ectoplasm spurted out. The thing screamed and stumbled back.

Its cries alerted the other monsters on the island. Spinning around, atan bright, Tzarik caught sight of two humanoid creatures. One perched on the sloping rooftop and the other ran down the long legs of the outpost, horizontal with the ground. They moved fast, bodies lithe, black hair waving down their backs.

"Jiangshi," Sybal informed him. "I've seen one before."

"Time to fight, then," he shouted, putting his back to Sybal's.

The running jiangshi flickered and blinked, appearing only a yard away from him. In the light of atan, he saw the soul-hungry monster inside the corpse it inhabited. It carried a long spear in its hand with a blue tassel on the end. It had a much longer reach than he did.

Spinning away from Sybal, he drew its attention. Snuffing atan, he gripped his scimitar with one hand high, near the hilt, and the other on the round butt: this gave him more mobility. The jiangshi bared its pointed teeth at him, snapping like a wild dog.

"You have bad blood," it hissed in grave disappointment.

That wasn't all a jiangshi or edimmu wanted: they could take your soul with them, sucking it out from their bite.

Keeping his eye on the other one, he entered combat, spinning the spear off his curved blade. He tried to keep his eye on Sybal as well. She kept up with the fleeing shui-gui, trapping it in halat just enough to stop its retreat. His attention divided, the jiangshi easily overpowered him, knocking his sword out of his hand with a powerful blow that shot the wind out of him. He fell hard onto his back, dropping the runes that had been wrapped around his wrist.

"What is this?" the jiangshi asked, red eyes going wide at the foreign magic.

With him down, the second blood-sucking monster rushed him. He heard its steps before he saw it and then scrambled for the runes. The first jiangshi grabbed his ankle and pulled him through the sand away from the leather string. He screamed, kicking at it, but it caught his other foot easily.

"Fire!" Sybal screamed from near the water's edge.

He couldn't see her, but this reminded him of how she'd killed the edimmu during the battle in Ala'Nar. Oil, fire, and halat to trap it. But he had no fire and no way of making any in the midst of a battle.

Thrashing as hard as he could, he could not release his legs from the strong grip of the jiangshi. The second appeared, seizing his throat in its cold death grip. Cackling a deep, rotting chortle, the second popped its jaw, opening its mouth wide. All of its teeth turned to vicious points.

Pulling a regular knife from his belt, Tzarik thrust it up into the yawning jaws. The jiangshi didn't reel away, but the weapon propped its mouth open. Dropping the Runer, the monster clawed at its face. Free of one grasp, Tzarik spun his torso and found his scimitar. He managed to slice the jiangshi that held him, lopping one of its hands off at the wrist. Enraged, it reared up to strike.

A burst of flames behind him scorched the back of his neck, pushing him forward. Holding the scimitar up, the curved blade sunk into the jiangshi's head enough to make it drop him. Leaping to his feet, he spun around to see the other monster engulfed in flames. A narrow knife with a round handle stuck out between its shoulder blades. The fire came from there. Wrapped around the blade's handle was a piece of yellow paper covered in red Xian lettering.

Behind the flaming jiangshi, another form appeared that made Tzarik's sulfates freeze: a tall, white-hooded figure in mottled robes that made him impossible to see.

"Reaver!" Tzarik cried to Sybal. When he shouted, the Reaver ducked into an all-out sprint, headed straight for them.

Pulling his scimitar out of the monster, he continued to defend himself against it, trying to push it away from the Reaver. The other man would use the monster to aid in his own attack on the Runer. But Reavers could also kill from a great distance, making often impossible shots. He'd taken an arrow from one before.

Shoving the jiangshi away, he turned to pick up his runes, but the Reaver was upon him. Kicking the runes away, the Reaver drew his long, single-edge sword. Tzarik faced the white-clad killer, expecting to fight him, but the Reaver instead turned his blade onto the monster. His face was covered in a white mask over his nose and chin.

"Help Sybal," the Reaver ordered, taking another yellow- and red-inscribed parchment from his belt.

Shaken that the Reaver knew their names, Tzarik didn't waste any time in finding her. He was concerned she might be locked in eternal combat with the watery ghost. They'd drifted out of his vision after the second jiangshi attacked. He looked quickly for his runes, but couldn't see them. The damn Reaver had kicked them into the darkness.

"Sybal!" he shouted into the fog.

A burst of light, like rounded lightning, flicked then vanished into the darkness. Knowing she was signaling him with a quick drawing of atan, he rushed in that direction. As he ran, he took up the burning femur of the dead jiangshi. The fire dwindled even as he hurried, but it would be enough.

"Trap it," he shouted to her when he saw her dark shadow fending off the shui-gui. "I have fire."

"I don't know if that will work!" she cried.

The fear and tears in her voice spurred him on with dangerous speed. He almost slipped several times on the smooth sand— making tinkling trickles echo through the mist—before he finally saw her solidly before him. She held one hand out with a golden circle around her: halat.

"Help me!" she begged, sobbing.

Not knowing what had driven her to tears, he rushed to her side and sliced at the ghost. "Just hold the barrier," he instructed.

Seeing the fire, which turned a deadly green, the shui-gui recoiled towards the water.

"Stop her!" he ordered Sybal.

Fighting to regain control of herself, Sybal re-drew atan around the cowering ghost, walking to keep up with it. It ran into the back of the barrier, stopping. Swinging her own orichalcum blade, Sybal cut the ghost in two. Tzarik stabbed it with the flaming femur. The monster's eye lit up with green flames and its skin cracked. With a harrowing scream, it burst, shooting out burning ectoplasm onto the magical barrier.

Tzarik grabbed Sybal's hand and pulled her to a clump of bushes with sharp barbs to hide. The Reaver sauntered down to the beach, his head snapping back and forth, looking for them.

"Where are your runes?" Sybal sniffed, savagely wiping her tears.

"He kicked them away from me," Tzarik growled quietly. "He also knew your name."

The Reaver stopped, surveying the dead ghost.

"What happened?" Tzarik asked gently.

Sybal shook her head. "Nothing. I let my guard down. It got to me. Stupid."

He allowed himself to grip her shoulder firmly. "You did so well." A genuine smile relaxed his face. "You've come a long way."

Meeting his eyes in the dim light, which came through as the mist dissipated with the vanquished monsters, she smiled back. "Thank you."

"Tzarik? Sybal?" the Reaver shouted.

Both Runers froze in their hiding spot.

"Don't!" Tzarik hissed as Sybal stood up.

"Jin?" she gasped.

The Reaver's hooded head tracked to her voice. "Are you all right?" he called, walking towards them.

The mist rolled out, back north, and the sun was able to shine down now that the creatures had been dispatched. The pink sand and blue ocean quickly turned the dark mist into a memory. In the late day light, Tzarik clearly saw Jin under the Reaver's robes, pulling the white mask off. Around his hips and shoulders were the myriad of tools of the Reavers' trade: scrolls, a bottle of red ink swinging from a cord, the sharp stars, two swords, and more on his back.

"You?" Tzarik roared as Sybal ran to Jin.

"Why? How?" she gasped, taking the boy's face in her hands. She pushed his hood off, exposing his long white hair. "Is this...?" She choked, fresh tears filling her blue eyes. "Is this what Wushito does?"

The boy's face turned hard, guarding the secrets. "I'm sorry I didn't tell you," he began.

"Are you the one who attacked us before, when we docked?" Tzarik asked, re-gripping his scimitar.

Jin shook his head then looked back to Sybal. "Wushito trains the Reavers. Anyone can be admitted to the Hallow City. A few foreigners come to train."

Now Tzarik understood. The only foreigners he'd seen had been taken to the Hallow City. Xia had a strange desire to keep its cities and provinces clear of foreigners. No doubt once they trained with Wushito, they were either sent out into the world or...

"How do you train to do this?" he asked, still glaring at the youth. He indicated the dead monsters.

"I'm sorry, Tzarik," Jin said strongly, "but Wushito's secrets are mine to keep. We are not permitted to even write them down as that would be heresy and diminish the first book." Jin grabbed the knife wrapped in the scripted talisman and tucked it away in a black cylindrical box on his belt.

Sybal clung to Jin, desperate to understand. "But why? You hunt Runers. Us!"

"I am a Reaver, but I am not your enemy," Jin tried to reason. "I have never killed a Runer. I was curious when I first met you. You were different than the Runers we'd been warned about."

Tzarik scoffed.

"It's true," Jin countered. "I trust you, Tzarik. You know I do. You even took it upon yourself to give me aid."

Sybal smiled cautiously. "Oh?"

Jin nodded. "I want to make sure Xia stays loyal to the White Dragon. A touched heir should rule us. Even if it's not me, many in my city are also dragon-touched. We deserve a chance to over-throw Wushito."

Sybal blinked and finally dropped her hands from Jin's shoulders. She took a step back. "But that's your life. ShanBao took you in, trained you, taught you to kill monsters." She swallowed. "Without taking up the runes."

"But Wushito wants to rule Xia," Jin interjected passionately. "My father fought and crusaded to bring about a revolution to stop Wushito. None on our shores would listen."

Tzarik's heart stopped beating when he saw a light flicker on behind Sybal's eyes. In two quick strides he came to stand beside her. He opened his mouth, but Sybal raised her hand to him, silencing him.

"Who was your father?" Her voice came out flat, even.

"This isn't the time or place," Tzarik cut in.

Seeing the odd tension rise, Jin held his head higher. "He was a great man. He fought all who tried to take him down, and came from a long line of dragon-touched. But he was the first in genera-tions to not bear the mark as I do. He tried to admit himself to the Hallow City, knowing that balance must be kept between the Di-Huan and Wushito, as the Dragon instructed. He was denied because ShanBao knew what he truly wanted. But it was his right! All outside Wu-Tang resisted him, so he did what he had to: he crusaded for twelve years and no one told me who he was until he left Xia."

Sybal's breathing turned to soft panting. Tzarik saw a vein in her forehead pulse and her jaw clench. "But he abandoned you. ShanBao raised you."

Jin nodded. "Took me for his own when word came out that the son of the butcher of Wu-Tang was dragon-touched. Stole me in the night. I didn't know until I was fourteen. By then, I was nearly a Wushito master, and I kept what I'd learned from Shan-Bao, knowing I had to be patient. To wait."

"And Yui?" Sybal's voice started to crack. "Does she know?"

The Reaver nodded. "We are balance. We are what the Dragon wanted. I should be Di-Huan."

Covering her mouth and closing her eyes, Sybal took a weak step back from the boy she respected so much. Tzarik didn't know how to prepare for the fallout that was about to erupt.

Jin's face lost a little of its luster when Sybal crumpled. "It's how it should be," he reasoned gently. "Xia needs to be in balance. Who better to bring that balance than a dragon-touched Wushito?"

"I don't know!" she gasped, turning away. "I don't understand this place anymore." She caught her breath. "What was his name? Your father?"

Tzarik gripped her elbow. She frowned down at him.

"Whoang Xiaoh, general of Wu-Tang and descendent of the greatest dynasty of Di-Huans," Jin said proudly.

To Tzarik's surprise, Sybal didn't do anything impulsive. She nodded stiffly.

"The butcher of Wu-Tang is right," she said in a low tone. "He slaughtered villages. Overtook towns. When my father did business in Singad, Xiaoh put thirteen hundred stakes in the earth and impaled every child under the age of three upon them, taking away an entire generation and devastating the province. My father fled for his life when Xiaoh attacked that day. He prayed to never meet the man. But Xiaoh worked his way across Al'Myrah." She closed her eyes, remembering something dark that made her shiver. "I remember his hands on me," she whispered. "And now you want to continue his legacy."

The boy's face didn't pale or contort in horror. A mask of bravery and forced understanding darkened his brow instead. "He did what he had to do to those who stood against him," he said sternly.

With an animal-like cry, Sybal cursed and turned back to the shore, marching to the boat. Tzarik strode after her.

"Sybal, we cannot answer for the sins of our fathers," Jin called after her. "His methods may have been wrong, but the ends justified the means."

Sybal stopped and spun on her heel. She stopped so quickly Tzarik almost ran into her.

"Jin," she moaned, fresh, hot tears in her eyes. "I love you. But whatever you think your father was, he was not."

"I can't believe that," Jin shot back. "His memory is all I have. What do you know about—"

"I killed him!" she shouted over his words.

Jin went stiff.

"Murdering him is what led to this." She brandished her runes. "They were going to burn me for his murder and, for taking the life of the witness I accidentally killed." Her voice rose to a shrill shriek. "I killed the butcher of Wu-Tang and *this* misery, this lonely, blood-soaked life is what I got for it! My entire family killed, wiped out."

"*Xai-lay*," Jin swore in his native tongue.

"He threatened me," she went on. "He was going to destroy Ala'Nar if I didn't..." She choked on the last few words. "I did it to save my family and my city. But it didn't matter in the end. He still destroyed everything I had."

Gathering all his courage, Jin replied, his own voice cracking, "Then you understand. Sybal, don't be angry with me. I have more reason to—"

"No!" she shot, cutting him off. "Don't say that. That day—with the pandas—you said we were allies. Did you think I would help you overthrow the Di-Huan? What did you imagine I would say if you asked me to help slaughter Xians just to be king?" Venom rose in her throat. "You are no different than him. A butcher. A tyrant. And..." her voice broke, "...you *used* me!" She turned, sprinting back to the boat, done with the confrontation.

Tzarik looked back at the boy, clothed in killer's robes. He had no words.

"She can hate me," Jin whispered softly. "But I cannot stop."

"Sybal is governed by impulse and emotions," Tzarik offered. "She feels all things greatly. I know she thought highly of you from the moment she met you. You filled a void in her life for a time."

"She's a special woman."

His left brow twitching slightly, Tzarik nodded. "She is." His eyes traced the pointed hood he'd come to fear. "Are all Wushito Reavers?"

Jin shook his head lightly. "There are many paths for Wushito. We—Reavers—are the elite."

"You didn't come to kill us?"

"The Hallow City sent me out," he said, "to deal with the monsters."

Once again, his defenses went up. Running from Al'Myrah hadn't solved his problems or brought them safety.

"Stay wary, Tzarik," Jin warned. "ShanBao may be the leader of Wushito, but I fear his generals far more. I'm so close. Please, don't give anything away to him or them."

The Runer forced himself to look into the youth's eyes. "You're betraying your creed. You're not attacking the Di-Huan or Xia outright." Even as he spoke, he wasn't sure what to do. It wasn't his place to interfere again. Based on all he knew, Jin only wanted peace for Xia—even though that meant an unavoidable slaughter. "You're taking on everyone outside House Xiaoh," he finally said. "You have enough to bear for now."

Jin pulled his hood further over his head, almost vanishing into the background. He nodded in thanks. "Will you leave now?"

The Runer shook his head. "There is a man on Xia who wishes you more harm than perhaps even your civil war. He's my responsibility. I need to find him, stop him before he pours salt on the wound. You may be right about the generals."

But he couldn't take Sybal. She needed time alone, off the hunt, resting, recovering. He'd have to track Sharar alone. Immediately.

Jin turned and walked back towards the outpost, bending and snatching something out of the sand. Tossing the runes to Tzarik, he vanished almost entirely into the mottled horizon. "Good luck, Runer. I hope that when we meet again, we are friends."

CHAPTER 18
WUSHITO RISES

EVEN WARY OF SHANBAO, TZARIK LED SYBAL BACK TO THEIR base in his estate. Vanishing now might bring suspicion on them they didn't need to deal with. Still, he said he had to leave and find Sharar, or at least get an eye on him.

Tzarik barely had time to see Sybal settled in once they returned. She put up a little bit of a fight when he said he was going to leave alone. She just wanted him to stay, to rest together, gather their senses, but Tzarik always had to be on the move. Once he left, she found she didn't care that much. Exhaustion made her joints creek, and her brain fogged over like the island they'd just liberated. The relief from the hunt came like a cold drink of water after days of wondering the desert, preparing her body to rejuvenate. Tzarik hadn't let them rest much after the hunt, pushing through the days-long journey back up the continent to Shiuki. Summer was in full swing, and the heat and humidity finally got to her.

How long has it been? she wondered as a servant ran to take the reins of her horse. She'd lost track of time now for well over a year. The days blurred together.

"Sybal?" ShanBao's voice came to her muffled, far away. "Careful!"

The world tipped. She fell sideways off her white horse, knowing she could save herself if her body would just adhere to her brain. But it didn't. The ground flew up to meet her and her temple hit hard after a crunch told her she'd dislocated her shoulder. All her breath left and she let her mind go into the darkness.

ᔓᖿ

WAKING, she lay on her mattress in the room ShanBao had given her. The old master sat on his knees beside her, eyes closed, mumbling something in ancient Xian. Her head split and her shoulder moaned in agony when she tried to move.

"I am glad you are awake," ShanBao said kindly, opening his eyes. "I need you conscious to put your shoulder back."

Rubbing her face with her right hand, Sybal moaned in embarrassment. "I feel so weak and stupid."

"You are stronger than you think." ShanBao put his hand behind her back and helped her sit up. "I will let you regale me with all your woes if you will but give me a minute to set things right."

Grabbing ShanBao's proffered hand, she stood up. He led her to the vanity in her room and sat her down.

"Brace yourself, Runer," he cautioned.

Sybal had seen the miners who worked her land dislocate their shoulders and had witnessed a healer putting them back in place. She'd never understood why they'd screamed so. It should feel good, going back into place, right? She looked at ShanBao in the mirror, skeptically raising one brow.

"Won't it just slide back in?" she asked.

ShanBao winced but smiled. "Something like that. Ready?"

Still in doubt, she tensed her back and braced herself against the vanity with her good arm, ready for the pain to go away. ShanBao gripped her shoulder with one hand and her upper arm with the other. He inhaled sharply and quickly snapped his hand. Sybal wasn't sure if he pulled, pushed, twisted, or some combination of all three.

With a pop, a wave of hot pain rushed from her joint down her arm to her fingertips. She couldn't stop the scream that followed. Just as quickly, the pain eased, replaced by a soreness she could tolerate.

"I understand now," she said, sighing and flexing her arm.

"I will have a hot bath drawn, with salts and some oils to ease the pain," ShanBao offered.

With the distraction of her shoulder gone, Sybal saw Shan-Bao's gray brows furrow, a line between them creased in constant worry. His eyes, while alert, looked distant.

"What's wrong?" she asked, turning to watch him walk away.

The old master stopped and hid his hands inside his sleeves. "I have many worries, Sybal-kim. I'd not wish to burden you."

ShanBao had never shown emotion to his guests before. "I'll confide in you if you confide in me," she offered. "I could use someone to talk to right now."

He turned, smiling warmly. "Where is Tzarik? In Wushito, the apprentice may approach the master with any question and the master must hear it without judgment."

When he said this, Sybal's sulfates rushed, icy under her skin. "Master ShanBao..." she started, not sure if she should go on. "Wushito trains Reavers."

"Ah." ShanBao dropped his hands. "I did not keep this from you and your master for any nefarious reasons, Sybal-kim. When I found you, you were dying. Hurt. Your master... Well, I've never seen a more desperate or lost man. There was no reason to speak of it, especially since I wish you no harm. Like Runers, we Reavers go after marks. I have had no pay for your head on Xia. And..." His eyes drifted out the wide, round window. "I have more pressing matters on my mind. Let's have a chat once you are clean and fed, with your wits about you."

He left swiftly. Sybal's brain slowed down and the fog came over her. Without waiting to be summoned by one of the house staff, she made her way down the hall to the bath and slid into the hot water without checking to make sure she was alone. Like ShanBao had said, the salts and oils almost instantly soothed her muscles. The aroma cleared her mind and her stomach rumbled.

When clarity returned, she remembered Tzarik saying he had to go. He had to find Sharar.

"Let me go with you," she had begged. "I swear, I won't do anything you don't tell me to do." She knew he hated her impulsiveness. That was why he was so cautious about everything.

"I trust you," he'd said. "That's why I need you to go back and keep an eye on ShanBao. I don't know if he is aware who Sharar is or what he wants, or if his generals are going behind his back. I could have read him wrong. He might be reasoned with."

He had left then. She'd watched his black form until it had vanished into the arching trees. The colorful blossoms had all fallen off, covering the ground where his horse's hooves had kicked them up.

Reaching behind her, she grabbed a handful of petals from a basket. She crushed them then dropped them into the water. Realizing they were lotus petals, her heart swelled painfully in her chest.

Why had Jin had to tell her all that? Why had she responded the way she had? *I felt betrayed,* she reasoned. *Like he'd known what I'd done, and he could help who his father was.* She sank into the pink water until just her nose stood above the hot ripples.

Once again, she'd lost someone she'd thought she could trust. *I have to stop being so willing to give my affection,* she thought.

She dried off, dressed in some of the soft garments ShanBao had provided, and went down to meet him in the dining hall. He'd had his kitchen make a pile of fruit, fried vegetables, rice, and a variety of sea meat. All the smells mingled into a sweet, tangy aroma that made her mouth water.

"I wasn't sure what you would want," ShanBao said, smiling more genuinely than he had before, "so I had a little of everything brought up."

"Thank you," Sybal said earnestly.

ShanBao allowed her to sit, eat, and drink before he opened up the conversation. "What is weighing on your mind, Sybal-kim. How can I put you at ease?"

Feeling better than she had in a long time, she took a long drink of the rice wine and let it settle in her stomach before answering. "I'm sorry if I seemed to accuse you before. Reavers are the one thing I have seen Tzarik fear, and I suppose that fear rubbed off on me. In my defense, we were being hunted on Al'Myrah. The devil even followed us to Porsh."

"You've been to Porsh?" ShanBao asked, picking through the vegetables in his bowl expertly with his utensils. "I have only heard horror stories about it."

"It's very empty right now," she said. "The lich king is dead, and I don't think any Porshains live there. They left, forced into a nomadic life when the first lich rose up."

"Not long ago," ShanBao interjected.

"Probably a hundred or more years," Sybal said quickly, ready to defend her country again. "I don't actually know. My education is in business."

ShanBao smiled and laughed for her benefit. His face turned serious. "You feel alone, don't you? Your master pulled you from your home, took you across the world to hide—you are not the kind to hide. I see that in you. That's the spirit of a warrior."

A little surprised that ShanBao hit the mark so well, she asked her own question. "Are Reavers like Runers?"

"Very direct," ShanBao mused. "Tzarik must like that about you."

She scoffed, rolling her eyes.

"But no," he answered her question simply. "We in Wushito are not criminals. We have not taken an oath to black magic or tied ourselves to runes." He gingerly wiped at the corner of his mouth with a cloth. "I have been curious about the runes for some time. They are an old magic."

"How do you kill the monsters, then?" she cut in. "If you don't have to undergo a runing—which was horrifying and painful and often kills—then how?"

At this, ShanBao gave her a playful smile. "Sybal-kim, Wushito has been around since the dawn of time. I cannot impart our oldest and most sacred secrets to you. I can tell you this: we draw from the same fount: magic. Our means are simply different."

"Why does everyone think only a Reaver can kill a Runer?" she pressed on.

Seeing she wouldn't let up, ShanBao frowned in mock thought. "Most likely because it is hard to get close enough to one to kill them; you Runers are hyper-alert, so it must be difficult to assassinate you. You have so many defenses and cannot bleed to death. I've seen Runers replace their sulfates as easily as catching a fish."

"It's not easy," she added under her breath. With that statement, she realized Tzarik had never shown her the ingredients for the sulfates that kept her alive and in-tune with the paranormal. If she ever bled out, and he wasn't around, she'd be dead. He carried the extra he had in his saddle.

"I suppose it takes a hunter to turn a hunter into prey," ShanBao said finally, pouring himself some of the rice wine. "Our methods may be different, but it is not an easy life. The foreign Reavers are often pitiful when compared to those born and raised in Wushito. But we take them in and return them to their homelands."

Realizing how open and honest ShanBao was about the Reavers put Sybal at ease. He still wouldn't divulge every secret, but the honesty was refreshing. She owed him something in return. The warm food and wine turned her skull to a soft mass.

"You're right," she started, changing the subject. Too much weighed on her. "I am alone. I reach out to people so easily, desperate for attention."

"I wouldn't call it that." ShanBao kindly took her hand. "Sentient creatures are meant to have a pack, Sybal-kim. The bond between those who share affection is strong, as is the bond between those who share hate. We want reasons to be drawn together. There is nothing wrong with that."

She opened her mouth, but something inside stopped her, warned her. Pushing it to the back of her mind, she said, "Wu-ShanBao, if someone you cared about betrayed you, would you show them mercy?"

The old man raised his head, folding his hands and looking out a wide-open window. "Wushito tells us to find times of mercy, but to not play a fool." His eyes drifted back to her. A forced calm flowed just under the surface of his skin. "One has to weigh the outcomes of such a betrayal."

She swallowed hard. "I fear many may die if I keep silent. But fewer will if I speak."

And then there was the personal touch: House Xiaoh had

tormented thousands, killed innocents. Just thinking about it reminded her of the feel of Whoang's hand on her face, the threat of imprisoning her and forcing her to bear his children while he overtook Ala'Nar. Jin didn't know. He was innocent. Young and impetuous. Perhaps he wasn't aware of the chaos he caused by chasing the throne and his father's ambition. He was good and reminded her of Abdul. She couldn't let him go down this path. ShanBao had raised the boy; he'd understand.

"I tell you this to help someone I care for," she started over, staidness bending her brow. "To stop him from doing something foolish."

ShanBao tilted his head, his fine, long hair slithering off his shoulder.

The words almost died in her throat, contracted. She shoved past it. "Jin is creating civil unrest. He told us he believes he should sit upon the throne—as a dragon-touched. Tzarik and I needed to hunt; it's something Runers have to do. But he was there. Naturally, we confronted him. He's been to Wu-Tang." She met his eyes, almost shaking. "Did you know who his father was?"

The old man's eyes snapped up to hers from his plate. Sybal had learned to read people and quite forgotten what it felt like when someone's eyes weighed and measured every crease of her lids, the way her chest rose and fell. The sulfates in her veins cooled, on alert. Was she doing the right thing in telling him? He couldn't be trusted, either, but with no one to confide in, she'd go mad.

Finally, taking a drink and satisfied with his prying gaze, ShanBao answered, "When Xiaoh left, I went to his home and took the child, hoping it would stop the hate from spreading over the city. It did for a time. But the blood of Xiaoh is strong and runs thick in Jin's veins. I had hoped Jin Xiaoh would not return and finish what Whoang started." ShanBao sighed sadly. "Oh, Jin, why?" His shoulders slumped and he hung his head, shaking it slowly.

His manner almost convinced her, but the slight coldness in her veins told her to watch out. She only cared about keeping everyone safe. Safe from themselves if she had to.

"I wanted to meet the Di-Huan halfway," he said. "Come to some diplomatic agreement. Now I must decide what to tell him." He stroked his long mustache.

"Was I wrong to tell you?" Sybal asked carefully. "This is that impulse Tzarik hates so much. I do and say things without thinking. I say it in the hopes that Xia need not go to war. Even the smallest battles in one or two provinces can have lasting effects on the entire continent."

"No, Sybal. It took great strength to tell me this." ShanBao sat up and took her hands in his. "This is treachery. Treason, even." He drew himself up higher. "We must move quickly."

Suddenly, the sulfates inside Sybal rushed, making her pale. They tried to tell her something. Tzarik had never told her much about them and what this meant. It was not unlike sensing eyes on her. She used her instincts to check around her: nothing. No danger presented itself. It was just her and ShanBao.

"I could use you and your master in our fight," ShanBao finally said, gaining some strength back.

"Oh, uh..." Sybal stumbled over reminding him she could not kill.

"I'd be grateful," ShanBao said. He locked eyes with her. "It would do me well to know that I, a Reaver, did the right thing in saving the Runer in the woods that day. As you said, you are strong. You have abilities we do not."

He was right. She owed him her life.

He offered, "I could take you to the Hallow City, show you

how Reavers fight without needing to die or take an oath to unknown magics. It might be able to help you."

She'd tried to cheat the runes once before. She'd never found out if it would have worked, but what had happened after had devastated her. "I cannot go back on the runes," she said sternly.

"There might be something in Wushito that says otherwise," ShanBao whispered. "We could find out."

She bit her bottom lip and looked away. She couldn't. But she could repay her debt. "I owe you my life," she said steadily. "That cannot change. I cannot kill and I will not harm Jin above all."

"Of course!" ShanBao burst out, elated. "I want him home. I will instruct the generals to take him alive. I want the Di-Huan to have time to decide who may ascend the throne before Jin comes forward with his attack." He sighed again. "I failed Jin if he thinks he needs bloodshed to take the throne."

"The generals?" Sybal's heart fell a little. Wu-Zhiang still made her skin crawl.

"We must go to Wu-Tang." ShanBao stood up and rang a gong for the servants to come and clean up. "If we can snuff the flame before it spreads, we can protect all Xia and the Royal City before the Di-Huan is in danger. If Jin is as ambitious as I know him to be, he will not wait. We must hurry."

Sybal followed him out to the dojo. There, ShanBao sent out messengers and courier birds to the generals before asking for his armor and weaponry to be cleaned and prepared. Sybal felt helpless as everything around her started to move quickly.

"Have no fear, Runer," ShanBao said. "It will take at least a day to prepare. I will send word to the Hallow City and have the army meet us on the southeast side. Your master should surely be back by then." He gripped her shoulder. "Your powers will come in handy. I need you."

Rather than fighting against the whirlwind of movement and

preparations, she gathered her own armor and mended every hole, tightened every strap, and oiled her sword. The rush from the hunt on the island had fueled her. Tzarik wasn't here to stop her. Finally taking action soothed the incensed sulfates, but a tingling still buzzed just below the surface.

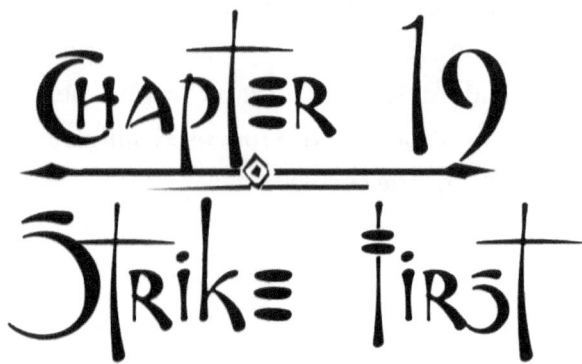

CHAPTER 19
Strike First

"You've been back and forth for days." TaoShin pulled Tzarik off the street and into a small eatery, where he pushed him down before a heaping pile of salted fish and a jug of cold spring water. "I've seen you while I've been out giving blessings, even the time you were running across the rooftops like a lunatic. Where is Sybal?"

Ignoring his own rule about drinking steadily when thirsty, Tzarik guzzled down half the water straight from the jug. It was the first cold thing he'd felt since leaving the ship that had brought them there; he thought he might weep for joy if the monk weren't there watching him. The summer came quick and hot on Xia. The humidity didn't relent, and he found himself almost pining for Al'Myrah and its dry desert heat.

"I'm looking for someone," he said, gasping and setting down the jug to get some air.

"Yes, I thought so. I hope you were not trying to be covert." TaoShin scratched behind his round ear. "That man whom you believe carries a djinn?"

Tzarik was tired and the doubt of his knowledge annoyed him. "I know he has it. Tarkan told me." He never had found the vessel, though. Sharar kept all his secrets so closely guarded, Tzarik couldn't even guess at what item the scholar might carry that housed the demon.

TaoShin's monkey tail twitched excitedly above his head. "I was hoping you were sure. I saw him, Runer. I spoke to him."

Tzarik almost dropped the precious cold water. "When? Where?"

"I tried to find you," TaoShin said, his eyes widening as he shared Tzarik's energy. "He spoke to the head of my order while we were in communion together, preparing to go back out to the island. Oh, on that topic..." He reached into a silken satchel and pulled out a red drawstring bag and handed it to Tzarik. "For your hunt. We wanted to thank you, but we were not on the docks when you and your lady returned."

Taking the coin with a nod, Tzarik waved his other hand. "What did Sharar say?"

"As you can guess, he asked about the Wushito and spoke very demeaningly of my order when we knew little about it. 'No one knows about it,' I tried to tell him. I think we disappointed him. I didn't let on that I'd heard of him and asked him why he was here.

" 'To study, my benevolent monk,' he replied. 'I have an unquenchable thirst for knowledge and it has led me here, where I seek answers to the riddle of the *Mahit'onomicon*.' He's very brazen and open about what he wants. And a bit of a pompous ass."

Tzarik swallowed. "He knows no one can stop him. He's saving his djinn, but if he so desired, he could ascend to sorcerer now."

TaoShin pressed his large lips together. "Why won't he do it now?"

A shiver crawled up Tzarik's arms. "Because he has something worse in mind. There have been sorcerers, a djinn in a sentient body. It usually takes over when the last wish is gone. He'll be something else. He's searching for something to elevate himself above those who have bound a djinn before."

"Correct me if I'm wrong," TaoShin said as an aside, "but haven't many possessed djinns before?"

He wasn't sure, but it was a common tale. "Could be. Most men wish for power, wealth, happiness...love. But if they're not cleverer than a djinn, the wish can easily be tainted, riddled with misfortunes." A strange calm erased the bolt of energy he'd just had. "That's why I'm not sure what to do. I'm not clever enough to stand up to something like that."

"Ah, no," TaoShin said, sighing and slumping into his seat. "Runer, you don't have to outsmart this devil. Something tells me you believe yourself inferior to him despite his evil desires."

"I'm a Runer, a criminal," he reminded the monk darkly. "I'm not better than him."

When TaoShin didn't reply right away, Tzarik looked up to see why he didn't speak. The monk's brow had fallen, his lips downturned. What Tzarik read as sorrow lingered on the lines of his face. But that couldn't be right.

"Oh, Runer," TaoShin said, sighing and shaking his head. "I wish I had years to speak to you about the value of a man. But I don't. We've gotten side-tracked. Your man Sharar has gone to Wu-ShanBao. A day ago, he departed up into the mountains."

Tzarik leapt up. "A day?" He racked his brain: could Sharar travel fast? "Did he have transportation? Was he carrying anything?" How strong could a desk-bound scholar's lungs be?

"He had a horse," TaoShin said quickly, wrapping some fish in a silk cloth he pulled from his pocket. "He carried a leather bag, some bound scrolls... I am sorry, Runer, I do not have your ability to notice things. But chances are he can travel fast. He's on a mission, after all."

"Damn!" Tzarik took the fish TaoShin shoved at him.

"If he's as wise as you say," TaoShin shouted, chasing after him, "he won't do anything yet. He's plotting, probing to find what he's looking for. You'll kill yourself if you don't sleep!"

Flinging himself up onto his horse, Tzarik grabbed the reins. "It's not him I'm worried about. Sybal might try to attack him. She'll be overcome. He'll kill her!"

He kicked his horse, TaoShin shouting after him.

"Give her some credit. Trust her!"

THE BIG BLACK horse screamed as it gasped for air when Tzarik kicked it once more to urge it over another incline. He'd pressed it hard for a day and a half and he felt its patience waning thin. White froth gathered around the martingale and the large saddle slipped with every beat of its hooves. He knew he might kill the beast, but he could not stop imagining what might happen if Sybal encountered Sharar without him.

He imagined her attacking him. She moved clumsily and out of pure rage, all her revenge and sorrow pouring from every cloddish move she made. In his mind, Sharar was an expert swordsman and easily overpowered her. He wounded her. She cried in pain. Then he took her to some lair where he cut her open—alive—and pulled her entrails out while she sobbed in pain.

The scenes took a darker turn, but he couldn't dwell on them. His horse gave a cry and reared up, unseating him. Flung from its back, he hit the ground hard and rolled down the rocky path. At first, he flailed for something to stop his fall, but hit his elbow so hard that sparks flew into his vision. Then he tucked in his arms and dug his heels in, finally coming to a stop.

Blood trickled down from his scalp, but he didn't stop. He ran back up to find his horse gasping and lying on its side.

"I'm sorry, boy," he murmured. "I have to keep going." He pulled his sword and a few other items off, swinging them over his shoulders, and marched the last leg of the journey on foot. He strode through the night, only stopping to sleep for a few hours. He rose as the moon set, ate the fish TaoShin had wrapped for him, and came upon Shiuki just as the sun peeked over the high mountains on what must have been the fifth day.

He took his brass glass out and pointed it towards ShanBao's towering home. He could just see over the high, gabled red walls, but it was enough to show him movement in the garden and front gate. With no sign of ShanBao, Sybal, or Sharar, he slammed the glass shut and ran closer. Climbing up onto an outcropping, he had a much clearer view of the front. Checking again, his heart leapt into his throat, beating wildly.

ShanBao stood outside the gate, speaking quickly with Wu-Yasuke and Wu-Zhiang, gesturing out and down towards the south. Tzarik swiveled across the small group of servants and horses until he spotted a tall, black-clad figure. Sybal stood with her hands clasped behind her back, nodding as she listened to someone speak. Her face was as stiff as marble, and he could just make out the shadow of her clenched jaw. The one speaking to her had his back to Tzarik, but he knew it was Sharar from the scrolls on his back and the long, wide sleeves of an Al'Myrahn scholar. He'd almost missed him because Sharar wore the conical straw hat of the fisherman near the Xian coast.

He panned back to Sybal's face. Her blue eyes stuck out in her dark face like sapphires, stern and emotionless. A swell of pride lapped up over his heart like a warm ocean wave. She was cool, calm, and by the looks of it, had given nothing away. She also showed no fear in the presence of the evil man. In this way, she was far stronger than Tzarik.

"You're amazing, Sybal," he whispered to himself.

Feeling more confident than he had in six months, he stowed his glass and walked far more at ease to the estate.

"Runer!" Sharar cried when he came to the walls. "Where is your horse?"

"Tzarik!" Sybal pushed past their enemy and ran to him. She stopped and put her arms down, falling in step with him.

Seeing her harness her emotions, Tzarik almost initiated the canceled embrace. But he kept his eyes on the scholar.

"Sharar appeared early last night," Sybal said casually.

"Good thing, too," Wu-Zhiang hissed pointedly.

"Why? What's happened?" Tzarik asked.

Sybal answered for the group at large. "ShanBao has decided to preemptively strike House Xiaoh once and for all. This will quell any civil war before it is started, protecting Xia."

Tzarik couldn't stop himself. He asked, "Where's Jin?"

"Dispatched to deal with monsters," ShanBao answered quickly. "Correct, Yasuke?"

"Indeed," the foxlike Masahk answered stoically.

Wu-Zhiang rose high up onto her snake body, arching her back in an energizing stretch. "No matter. We will have victory today and I will be the one to bring it."

Sharar smiled darkly. "Well said, General Zhiang."

Tzarik asked the scholar, "What part have you to play in all this, Sharar?"

The scholar's face tensed in joyous anticipation, but ShanBao answered for him.

"He is studying the battles of the east, Runer. He will stand aloft with me as I command my army."

"And if I remember," Sharar said, smiling and stroking his

oiled black beard, "we still have a contract. You will defend me, right, Runer? No matter the necrotic dead you almost allowed to consume me back on Al'Myrah."

"Hazard of the job," Tzarik offered casually.

"So I hear." Sharar's hand stopped stroking his chin. "How goes your little hunt? I can only assume you are here on business? Strange place for a Runer to be."

"We mean them no harm," ShanBao cut in. "Runers, will you come with me?"

Tzarik's impulse was to say no. Sybal couldn't kill and he didn't want to fight like this. He wasn't a soldier.

But Sybal nodded. "As promised, ShanBao. My runes are at your service."

◦◦◦

ONCE THEY WERE on the road, Sharar leaned closer to Tzarik. "I am glad to see you are still on my side, Runer."

Nearly offended, but keeping his cool, Tzarik asked softly, "What do you mean?"

Sharar jabbed with his chin towards ShanBao. "You haven't mentioned to the old man that I met with his generals behind his back. That much is obvious."

Nodding, he took in the confirmation. "He doesn't know you're double dealing? Wu-Zhiang didn't tell him about the meeting?"

"Exactly," Sharar said. "After you passed out, I told General Zhiang to say I didn't show up for the meeting. I find the general's far easier to control than the old man." He reached onto his belt and took out a few coins, handing them to Tzarik. "I can count on you, correct? This may turn ugly, and I might need your services."

Behind him, Sybal sighed heavily.

"Of course, scholar," he mumbled half-heartedly, pocketing the coin.

Tzarik burned to get Sybal on her own to speak. He didn't know what he'd say or why; he just wanted to get away from the tangled web he'd helped weave and decide what to do. ShanBao had given him a horse from his stables and he rode alongside Sybal, but they could not speak in the company of Sharar and ShanBao. Even when they made camp, Sharar never seemed to be far away. Once Tzarik thought they were alone only to have the scholar appear just behind him. When they joined with the Wushito army the next day, it was even harder to try to separate himself. After so many attempts, he had to come up with a different plan as Sharar's dark eyes roved to him more and more.

"Master ShanBao," Tzarik called on the third day of their travel. "Let us go ahead and find a vantage point. Runers do not fight like your warriors and we will need to prepare."

"Careful, Runers," ShanBao offered, waving them away. "We cannot know Wu-Tang has not laid traps for us."

Sybal guided him off the path and over a rocky drop to a lane of elegant trees. Tzarik might have thought the clearing pretty except for the dozen or so corpses hanging from the trees, more than half-rotted and partly chewed on by birds. Beneath them, small stone shrines had been erected from river rocks. Melted wax showed where candles had been lit, and gifts of gold coins, flowers, and small food items littered the ground.

"Wu-Zhiang did this," Sybal said. Her voice sounded hollow. "I suppose now I will be part of whatever they do next."

Once they were among the dead, the smell of the humid, rotting corpses almost made Tzarik gag. "You told ShanBao you would defend him?" he asked.

Her face twisted in confusion. "He was open about the Reavers. He was..." Her horse stopped as she dropped the reins and put her face her in her hands. "I am never sure if I have done the right thing. But in the moment, I always think I am."

She was berating herself for not knowing when she might be led into a trap, for not being able to look past possible manipulation. With her confession, Tzarik knew almost instinctively that he'd been right about ShanBao from the start. She'd guessed it, too, but had shoved the warnings out of her head.

"Sybal," he said, knowing she liked it when he used her name directly.

She looked up, sad and despondent.

"You did well when Sharar came. When I couldn't find him, I assumed the worst. I thought you'd try to take his life the moment you saw him. By not striking out, you showed you can control yourself. I know how hard it must have been."

Her eyes lit up like the fireworks they'd witnessed the night of the festival. She said, "When he touched his palms together and bowed to ShanBao, I couldn't take my eyes off them. The hands that took my brother's life, my mother's... But I thought of you, how you can hide those emotions. You control your urges. It came easier than I thought. Perhaps I am learning after all."

"You are," he added.

Gathering up the reins, she said, "I shouldn't have parted like that with Jin. I gave up on him too easily. I can't help but think if I had stayed around him more, I could have helped him. I have to make it up to him and make sure he's all right."

A voice from behind said, "Maybe you still can."

Both Runers wheeled their horses around, hands on their scimitar hilts. Jin, in the white camouflage of the Reavers, stood on a rock jutting out from the hillside. They relaxed when they recognized him.

"I come here to pray," he said, leaping down, not making a sound when he landed in a squat on the ground. "To remind myself what my men did for me and my house. You did inspire me, Sybal. I asked myself if it was worth my father leaving his home, writing his history in blood. But I cannot just give up, not when Wushito wants to take control from the Royal City. It's mine and others' birthright—not theirs. They wish to take it by force. Too many on Xia would not go quietly under Wushito law. But the Hallow City is stronger than even the bravest fisherman or farmer. So I cannot give up."

Sybal gazed at Jin with sad admiration. Then she turned to Tzarik, a question on her lips. He gave in. They couldn't run now. She'd never stop wondering what could have happened. Jin would be just another sorrow she had to bear. He couldn't do that to her. Not when they could at least try.

"We're here with a war party," he said to Jin. "ShanBao, his generals, and a very dangerous man named Sharar are on their way with an army of Wushito warriors. ShanBao wanted to stop Wu-Tang before you retaliated." His eyes roved over the trees and the hanged dead. "Quell the uprising before anyone else had a chance to get behind you, all under the guise of protecting the Di-Huan."

The Reaver looked away, his chest rising and falling in a melancholy sigh. "I didn't want to cross blades with Master Shan-Bao. No matter his intent when I was a child, he did save me. Train me. At times I thought he might even be fond of me." He shook his head and turned, marching out of the lane. "I have a war camp just down the next valley. I wanted to keep it out of the city to protect the people. ShanBao will no doubt march to the fields between the hills to do battle." He stopped and turned to face them. "You do not have to come with me."

Sybal glanced at Tzarik to check what she was about to say. Seeing him taking action, sitting in the midst of danger, guilt filled her. She'd trusted ShanBao before trusting Jin. He didn't say it, but she knew that would cause him pain. She had to make it up to him somehow.

"Of course we'll go with you," she said.

⸺

JUST AS THE camp and its many red and yellow tents came into view, so did the army marching down the rocky slope to their left. The Wushito warriors stopped, standing at attention. They were far enough away that they couldn't make out any of the commands being shouted. Jin galloped among his men on his horse, rallying them up quickly.

"Where is Kei Lu?" Jin shouted. "Where are the Vandauls?"

A few answers went up that Sybal translated for Tzarik. "They seem to be a wild tribe from the lowlands, but they're missing." She listened to a few more warriors before adding, "They must be wreaking havoc somewhere."

Sybal and Tzarik sat astride their mounts in the shadow of the trees, making a small attempt at hiding as Jin finished gathering his men. Sybal checked the ridge with her own brass glass.

"I don't see Wu-Yasuke or Wu-Zhiang," she relayed.

Tzarik scanned the tree-lined sides of the grassy ocean before them. He'd not seen such an open field like this on Xia yet. Glancing over his shoulder, he caught sight of the stone city of Wu-Tang in the distance. The sun was just setting over its pink rooftops.

"The generals might be preparing a flank," he thought out loud. "Or coming in from the sides."

"I didn't think till now," Sybal mused. "ShanBao did not bring any war machines. No siege equipment."

Tzarik scoffed. "Can you imagine trying to get a ballista over these hills?" What ingenuity the Xians had come up with to fight amongst their terrain intrigued him. He wouldn't know today. "Wushito doesn't need it anyway," he added. "They fight like ghosts and assassins. This will be a slaughter."

Sybal half-smirked with confidence. "Perhaps."

"Do not attack, Sybal," Tzarik warned her. "Just defend. Let me do the killing." He pulled the long string of runes out from under his armor and pinched jiun between his thumb and index finger.

"They're moving," Sybal said, gasping and taking her scimitar from its sheath.

"Wait," Tzarik advised. "They might not know we're here."

"They know we haven't come back."

"Wait."

The two masses of opposing armies slowly moved. Wushito stopped again, allowing the ragtag army of Wu-Tang to move closer to where the field turned into the rocky slope. They had an advantage, but Jin still led his men forward. Jin shouted up to his enemies, but they couldn't hear.

Even without knowing the language or hearing, Tzarik understood. His skin prickled and something in his head alerted him to the sides.

"Zhiang!" he shouted, pointing with his scimitar to the tree line on the right.

Just as he'd predicted, Wu-Zhiang and a small band of Wushito warriors charged out from the side, spooking Jin's army. Instant chaos erupted. Jin pulled back, his men fleeing behind him as Wushito descended from above. When the charge happened, Tzarik caught sight of the other general. Wu-Yasuke rushed down in a flurry of foxfire. With everyone accounted for, Tzarik kicked his horse to join the fray. Before he charged off, Sybal leapt behind him, grabbing his waist.

"Go for the snake!" he shouted at Sybal. "Protect me."

He slowly drew jiun as they rode out towards the hill where ShanBao, Sharar, and his small entourage of advisors stood, watching the battle begin. Sybal drew halat slow and wide around him. He registered it just before the sulfates boiled under his skin. His vision sharpened, and his sense of smell picked up the iron tang of hot blood, every clash of a sword a piercing scream in his ear. Then the rush came.

"Stay on the horse," he growled. He leapt from its back at Wu-Zhiang.

The viper general saw him coming and smiled, flicking her tongue as he approached. She tossed aside the man she'd just bitten. The body hit the ground hard and didn't flop, her venom stiffening every limb.

"I've wanted to tangle you in my coils for so long, little Runer," she growled in glee. Her slitted purple eyes bulged in anticipation.

The fury piqued and Tzarik struck out, quick and vicious. Wu-Zhiang stuttered backwards at the strength and ferocity of his attacks. His veins bulged, white like rivers of ice under his dark skin. He knew his eyes had turned pure white as well when she froze for just one second to look at his face in confusion.

She was slippery, crawling on her belly to avoid his strikes. He drew buhkar when she almost landed a blow, misting to the side.

"Diyu, Runer," she cursed. "Face me like a man."

Tzarik laughed darkly. "I would if you were a man, snake."

Insults, it turned out, infuriated General Zhiang. She spit, purple venom flying from her mouth. Snapping to the side then rearing up, she moved like lightning to strike. Tzarik drew buhkar, but he realized quickly it wouldn't be fast enough.

From the side, Sybal drew halat and thrust her hands out like she was pushing against a wall. To his surprise, the protective barrier flew across to his own halat rune. The serpent general hit the barrier, bloodying her own nose.

"I didn't know that would work!" Sybal called.

The one second Tzarik stood in amazement at her ingenuity, Wu-Zhiang turned to shoot across to Sybal. He charged at her, abandoning drawing buhkar.

"Don't!" Wu-Zhiang hissed. Her long dark coils shot out, wrapping around Tzarik's ankle like a vise. She raised her wrist and shot a hidden dart at Sybal, who dodged, reeling the horse in a wild circle. Then she jerked her tail so Tzarik dropped the sword he was about to cleave her with. The Runer fell hard, his head smacking against the unyielding dirt.

With the fury of jiun wearing off and the white light from the impact, he had to gasp in air to clear his mind. He felt himself be dragged on his back by his foot.

"You two are no match for me," Wu-Zhiang hissed, pulling him into her. She grabbed his wrist, holding him up with strength he hadn't known she possessed. Her tongue flicked out, lightly touching his face.

"Hey!" Sybal shouted, releasing an arrow at the exact same time.

Wu-Zhiang lurched to the side, but Sybal anticipated the snake's movement. Her black arrow lodged itself in Wu-Zhiang's left hip and the snake screamed, dropping Tzarik. Scrambling to his feet, the Runer charged away from her only to be greeted by Wu-Yasuke and ShanBao. In his armor, ShanBao looked like a demon: flat horns on the helmet arched up to the sky and a monstrous mask covered the lower half of his face.

"Runer whore!" Wu-Zhiang hissed, advancing on Sybal.

Vastly outnumbered since Sybal could not kill, Tzarik rushed to join her, grabbing his sword from the grass. Together, they stood side by side as the generals and ShanBao moved in.

"I wanted to let you live," ShanBao roared, unsheathing a long, straight blade. "It didn't have to be this way, Runers."

"You're right, it didn't," Jin said, appearing behind them.

ShanBao stopped, sighing in frustration. "You really have disappointed me, Jin." His eyes flicked to Tzarik and back, and then he rattled off something in Xian like he'd just made a discovery.

"No!" Sybal screeched, raising her sword.

With that, the two generals leapt at them, swords drawn. Wu-Zhiang was noticeably slower and gasped for air as she fought, clutching her wound with one hand. Tzarik defended against the beast-like Wu-Yasuke and ShanBao bore down on Jin.

"What are you doing?" Sharar's voice cut high and confused from where he perched.

Wu-Yasuke was perhaps the strongest man Tzarik had ever crossed blades with. His Wushito robes exposed his arms, knotted and angled with hard muscle. He bore down on Tzarik, using his strength purely to make Tzarik stumble or shove his sword out of a defensive block. Using his Masahk gift, Wu-Yasuke rushed in a fiery blaze past Tzarik, around him, making him dance. The demonic nine-tailed fox outline was enough to make those fighting nearby cringe in fear. It was almost impossible to keep up with the Masahk. Wu-Yasuke never attacked, merely kept Tzarik busy. But it worked. Sweat poured from Tzarik's brow as he fumbled to wrap his runes around his hand, back away, and get a few offensive attacks in. Even his most evasive and cunning attacks were easily pushed aside by the strong man, almost like the general was toying with him. Finally, the demon fox shape vanished and Wu-Yasuke parried away, catching his breath. Tzarik took the advantage and landed a skillful slash to the Masahk's muscled midsection. The fox glanced down, almost offended at the bloody wound before raining down a fresh onslaught of attacks.

Sybal advanced on Wu-Zhiang, misting quickly to avoid her coiling snake attacks. Wu-Zhiang's blood still ran down her face from where she'd bashed it against the barrier. She shrieked Xian curses. Tzarik was in awe of how flawlessly Sybal used the runes and fought against the giant serpent. But this admiration cost him.

Wu-Yasuke lunged with a powerful punch the second Tzarik let his eyes move to Sybal. The Wushito warrior then leaned back and kicked him so hard in his chest, Tzarik felt something pop as he flew backwards to meet the earth with a thud. Wu-Yasuke lunged, stomping on Tzarik's hand that clutched the runes so he couldn't draw. Pointing his long sword down at his throat, he ordered the Runer not to move.

"Jin!" Sybal screamed before the breath was knocked out of her, too.

Writhing under his captor, Tzarik turned to see the boy's hand fall and his weapon land softly in the grass. ShanBao stood behind him, growling with a monstrous grimace. His sword came through the front of Jin's chest. The boy's face was already pale, smattered with his own blood.

Sybal made a mad leap towards him, but Wu-Zhiang spit, snapping her fangs at her.

"Don't!" Sharar screamed, halfway to them, running across the battlefield. "If you kill them, ShanBao, the deal is off. That includes you, general!"

Wu-Zhiang had arched, her jaw popping open, but she stopped when Sharar shouted.

Tzarik made a weak attempt to dislodge Wu-Yasuke, but to no avail. The general looked down at him. Seeing caution scrawled over his face, Tzarik studied it. Ever so slightly, the general flicked his head to the left, then lifted the foot that trapped Tzarik's rune hand.

Wasting no time, Tzarik yanked himself free, rolled backwards, and pulled his single-hand crossbow off his hips, aiming it at Wu-Zhiang.

"Sybal!" he shouted.

Torn, panting to get her emotions back under her control, she backed away. Tzarik whistled for her horse.

"Where do you think you'll go, Runer?" ShanBao growled. He grunted, pulling his sword out of his young ward's chest. Jin moaned and fell backwards, hands scrambling at the bleeding wound. "This is my continent. We found you in Porsh. There is nowhere you can go that we will not follow. It is our duty and our privilege to hunt down the Runers who let the necromancer go, the devastation of your country just behind you. No one will give you sanctuary. You destroy everything you touch. Everywhere you go suffers."

Tzarik grabbed Sybal's arm, pulling her close to him. He felt the rapid hoof beats of her horse charging up behind them. Sharar stopped about twelve feet back, keeping his distance from the dying warrior and the other armed killers.

"What's happened?" he gasped, clutching his chest and panting.

"We're leaving," Tzarik growled.

"No, you're not," ShanBao hissed.

Tzarik pulled the trigger, releasing a short, thick arrow into Wu-Zhiang. She screamed and writhed like a stepped-on snake as another arrow pierced her flesh. Sybal's white horse circled them, allowing them to leap up before it took off, weaving between the battling hordes. A few arrows chased after them.

"Shit," Sybal grunted in pain when a bladed star hit her shoulder. She ripped it out and threw it aside. "I'm fine, go!" she urged when Tzarik opened his mouth to ask. Her voice cracked with sobs. "Jin. Is he...?" She couldn't say it.

"He will be," Tzarik confirmed. "I'm sorry, Sybal."

ShanBao was right, of course. Tzarik had no hope of hiding on the continent. Wushito not only knew every valley and mountain, but they were a ruling power and could turn anyone against them.

Almost anyone.

"Where are we going?" Sybal panted, tears cutting clean tracks down her cheeks.

"The Royal City," Tzarik called back.

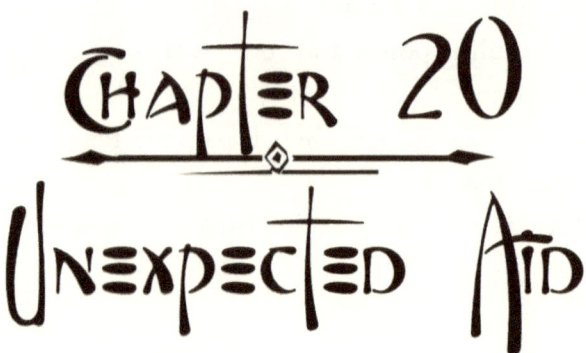

Chapter 20
Unexpected Aid

Sybal's arms wrapped tighter around Tzarik's middle once they broke from the battlefield. The horse, sensing the danger, obeyed Tzarik's every minor squeeze of his leg or movement of the reins. It cut sharp corners to dart behind angled hills and boulders, braying madly.

"He's coming!" Sybal cried after he felt her crane her neck round to look. She cringed, ducking her head tight into his shoulder. She completely covered him with her size; she'd be hit with anything their pursuer shot or threw at them.

"Which one is it?" Tzarik called. "Get my crossbow."

"Wu-Yasuke, that beast general," she replied, taking the bow. She struggled to pull the string back and lock it in place. With him in front of her, there wasn't much room.

At least it wasn't Wu-Zhiang.

Sybal gave a raging, guttural cry. "I can't load the bow and I can't aim my recurve bow like this." Her voice cracked with emotion. She took a deep breath. "We have to stop running."

More meaning to her words came out in her tone than perhaps she meant, and Tzarik heard it.

"We have to lose him," he said. Turning sharply, the horse

panting from running uphill, he cut hard south and galloped down the rocky paths.

Sybal clutched him tightly as they picked up speed and dove into a dark underbrush. Thick trees with dark purple leaves cut off the sun quickly. The ground leveled out around them as they went deeper into the forest. Tzarik pushed the horse until he felt it might collapse. He ordered Sybal to get rope and a few other things out of her saddlebag before they abandoned the horse. Satisfied they had a good enough lead on Wu-Yasuke, he told Sybal to jump.

Together they tumbled off the horse, rolling to hide. Sybal watched her white mare charge into the darkness across a white, low rushing river. They didn't have much time. Tzarik took the rope and tied a quick loop on one end that could slide up and down to tighten. He gave it to Sybal then scaled a tree to drop onto their prey. Half-hoping it wouldn't work and half-expecting Wu-Yasuke to not follow them, Tzarik breathed deeply to soften his gasping.

His hopes were soon dashed as the general appeared, eyes trained on their horse's deep hoof prints. Tzarik prepared to leap down but Wu-Yasuke stopped, eyes darting among the foliage below. Knowing the cunning Wushito warrior would quickly discern the trap, Tzarik leapt soundlessly. The general was vastly larger than Tzarik; one of Wu-Yasuke's biceps was roughly the circumference of Tzarik's thigh. But with surprise, he landed hard on the Wushito warrior. Wrapping his legs around the general's neck, Tzarik spun down to the ground, taking Wu-Yasuke with him. A short tussle followed.

"Sybal!" Tzarik shouted as the warrior landed a hard punch to the right side of his face.

Sybal leapt out, grappling with his legs. Much taller and with more leverage, she managed to harness them. The two of them pulled Wu-Yasuke's arms back and lashed them to his legs, pulling the rope tight but not before he managed to brutally make contact with Tzarik's face twice more. Like his beastly half, he hissed and spat, his soft red fur standing on end as he barred his teeth.

Tzarik stood up and spat blood out. "Take him to the river," he ordered.

They each hauled him up by an arm, straining under his weight and the mild struggle he put up. When they dropped him hard on the riverbank, he spoke.

"You don't have to half-drown me, Runers," he growled. "You think you could actually overpower me?"

Annoyed at the jab at their inferiority, Tzarik gripped a handful of the general's red hair and shoved his face under the water. He expected Sybal to stop him, but she stood by, glaring down at them. Wu-Yasuke didn't struggle at first. In fact, Tzarik marveled at how long the warrior stayed under before trying to twist his shoulders and throw Tzarik off. He waited until the general's attempts became more panicked, genuine.

With a grunt, Tzarik pulled the general's head out of the cool water. Wu-Yasuke coughed and sputtered.

"Runer!" he shouted, trying to shake the water from his thick hair. "I will not harm you."

"ShanBao killed Jin," Sybal said. She lunged to the pair and stomped on the back of the general's head, forcing him back under. "We can get him to tell us what they're doing," she grunted, pressing hard onto her boot.

"My thoughts exactly," Tzarik mused.

When the general's legs struggled against his bonds, Sybal stepped back and let him up. Tzarik tossed him onto the rocky shore, stood up, and drew his scimitar, hovering the bladed curve just above the Masahk general.

The general panted and coughed, struggling to roll onto his side to relieve the pain of the rocks digging into his arms. "I let you capture me," he started. "I didn't think you'd do that." He glared up at them with his foxlike yellow eyes.

"Why?" Tzarik asked, his pride stinging again at the remark.

Behind him, Sybal pulled back the crossbow and loaded an arrow onto it. Her breath shuddered. "Start talking, Wu-Yasuke," she mumbled dangerously.

"Yasuke," he offered. "I am not a Wushito master right now."

"What do you want to tell us?" Tzarik barked, thrusting the blade closer to his face.

Yasuke licked his lips and wiggled away from the scimitar to sit up as best he could. "Zhiang has gone behind ShanBao's back with that scholar from Al'Myrah."

"How so?" Sybal asked darkly.

"ShanBao wants to usurp the Di-Huan. When he decided Jin would not be molded to his ways, he thought the next best thing would be to sit on the throne himself. He already has such a hold over the highlands, I suppose he thought no one would stand up to him."

"What about Sharar?" Tzarik cut in.

Yasuke nodded. "Zhiang has rebelled against ShanBao before. When I was promoted over her, she slaughtered a whole village. The people fear her. But ShanBao could not cast her out of the Hallow City."

"Why not?" Sybal scoffed. "She's a monster."

The Wushito didn't answer this. He locked eyes with her but pressed his lips closed. Sybal took one angry step toward him, but Tzarik grabbed her arm. That didn't matter right now.

"She made a deal with Sharar?" Tzarik asked.

Yasuke nodded. "But ShanBao did as well. Sharar wanted the *Xai de'jing* in exchange for his services. But ShanBao won't allow that. He can't. So Sharar bargained for ShanBao to deliver the gini to him instead and for Zhiang to deliver the *Xai de'jing*. She doesn't believe in its divinity as much."

"She'd give it to him?" Tzarik asked. He hardly believed a Wushito would give up the ancient artifact, especially with so much sacred and hidden knowledge in it.

The general didn't answer that, either. He raised his head and closed his mouth.

"Put him back in the river," Sybal growled. "That'll get the truth out."

Tzarik hesitated, though. "ShanBao wants to be Di-Huan? He already has so much power and control over the continent."

"Not the lowlands," Yasuke offered simply. "And that man—Sharar—has a power ShanBao wants."

"The djinn?" Sybal asked.

Yasuke's face closed off. He didn't shake his head or give any other indication at her guess.

"He cannot give up the djinn until he uses the wishes," Tzarik said. Then he remembered. He'd seen Sharar's powers before. "Sharar can control monsters and beasts," he mused aloud. "With that, ShanBao would have no need for Wushito."

Sybal's brows raised in shock. "He can?" Her eyes unfocused, looking back over the last year. "He could have killed us. But ShanBao wouldn't disband Wushito. He just wouldn't have need to fear them like the Di-Huan."

Tzarik nodded. "If he ever got to the Royal City, he'd know that overthrowing the current dynasty is possible and would take every measure to make sure that didn't happen to him."

"Jin was just a tool to him." Sybal dropped her arms, her shoulders falling. She quickly turned away, covering her face with her hands.

"You." Tzarik tugged at Yasuke's bonds, making the Masahk

wince. "What good does Sharar's power do for ShanBao? He won't stay here and do the Wushito master's bidding. If he said as much, trust me, he's lying."

Yasuke shifted again, flexing his muscled arms. "I will be killed for what I have told you," he said to Tzarik. "I have betrayed my oath to the Hallow City."

Tzarik took out his small hidden blade.

"The crypt," the Masahk said quickly. "But that is all I will say. Runer, you are man of oaths. Please, do not make me betray mine more than I have."

It would be easy to slide the knife into the fox-demon's neck, killing him. Yasuke might turn again and tell ShanBao or Wu-Zhiang. Could he trust the Masahk?

"Why come after us?" Tzarik asked. "Why tell us this?"

"I could not stand by and watch that which I gave my life to destroy my home," Yasuke replied. "But I am loyal to Wushito."

Reaching down, Tzarik began to untie the knots. "I will let you flee with your life in return." With a pull, he untied the Masahk and stepped back.

Yasuke stood up, rolling his great shoulders. "Next time I see you, I will have to kill you." He put his fingers in his mouth and whistled for his horse. Keeping his yellow eyes on Tzarik, he mounted, turned, and pounded back out towards the light of day.

A sense of wary calm permeated Tzarik as he watched the general disappear. Yasuke would report back that he'd found the Runers and would reveal the direction they were headed. The easiest thing would be to turn and run again. He knew Sybal would fight that. He sensed her waiting for whatever he intended to say.

"We have to get to the Royal City," he said at last. "Warn the Di-Huan and...tell Yui what has happened."

She faced him. The lines between her brows relaxed and her

eyes rounded from the worried slits they had been. "Really?" she breathed, emotion catching her voice in her chest.

He nodded. "There may be no ghosts or ghouls here, but there are monsters. It's our job to stop them."

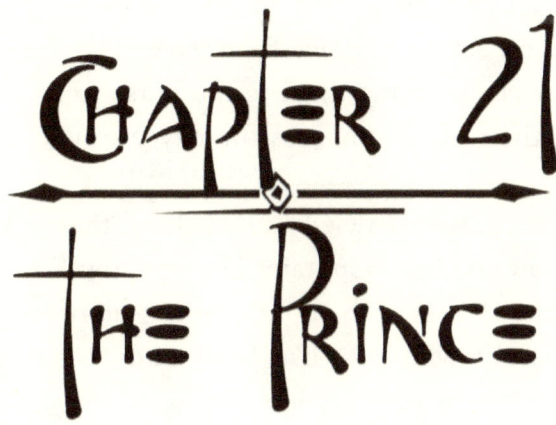

CHAPTER 21
THE PRINCE

WITH ONLY SYBAL'S HORSE AT THEIR DISPOSAL, THE WINDING road up to the Royal City took days to climb. They rarely slept, always watching over their shoulders. Every snapping twig or owl cry made them jump. They contented themselves with foraging fruit from the flora around them every night, since neither were great hunters. They happened upon some hilltop temples, small villages tucked away, and other signs of simple pastoral life on their way up the mountains. They passed traveling fortune tellers, hard-working farmers, and occasionally a pair of monks humming softly.

Tzarik tried to keep them off the roads, but the rough terrain exhausted them too quickly. With the rising and falling grassy hills and rocky peaks, if they did not stay on the main road, it was nearly impossible to see where they were going. One night, simply too worn out and knowing he wouldn't be able to stay awake, Tzarik broke into a barn and he and Sybal slept in the loft above a stable of braying mules and tiny goats. The air changed that night from hot and humid to cool. The seasons turned. The animals kept them warm, but the change put him on alert.

After an actual night of sleep and stealing cheese from the

farmer's pantry in the barn, they made it to the very top of the highlands. Their boots wore down from the rocky terrain and they discarded their cloaks, tying them to the horse to let any breeze blow through their black tunics as the day warmed, despite the cool change.

The Royal City sprawled out before them, a circular metropolis below the last mountain. Up here, the Runers gasped and panted. The sun set to the right, painting all of the highlands gold. Huge statues with boar-like faces under sharply pointed helmets greeted them first outside the round city. The statues stood on one leg, brandishing a spear towards any who came near.

"I forgot how beautiful it was," Sybal said softly, wiping sweat from her brow. "I've only been to Hatal a few times. This reminds me of the domes on the sultana's palace. The grandeur and splendor."

Tzarik joined her looking over the elevated city. Above them, the clouds hung near, thick and pink in the setting sun. He understood in this moment why Xia believed in their White Dragon, and that they had been chosen as one of the first civilizations. It was easy to believe this close to the heavens. But as he took it in, he couldn't understand how a people this old and this rich could want war with each other. Perhaps ShanBao had spoken the truth all those months ago: sentient kind was born evil and had to be taught to be good. He often found himself making the simple decisions, avoiding anything that took effort he didn't see worth in.

Sybal gently pushed his shoulder. "Are you all right? I've never seen you so contemplative."

Nodding, he headed towards the palace at the center of the city.

NOT KNOWING how to get in to see the Di-Huan, they approached the palace gate after winding their way through the maze-like city. The stoic guards—gilded in red and gold with elaborate, curved pauldrons and pointed helmets—refused to let in two dark-skinned, blue-eyed foreigners. Sybal tried in her best Xian to explain, but they wouldn't relent. Walls and gates of varying sizes surrounded the palace.

"How much coin do we have left?" Sybal asked.

The skin around her eyes had blackened to a dark purple and her lips were cracked. As they turned to walk away, he caught her scent as well. He didn't mention it to her, knowing if she stank so badly, he did, too.

He pulled open his black leather draw-string bag and checked. "Not much. And even less in Xian coin." He took out the odd eastern coin with a hole in the middle. "Perhaps enough for one night in a public house. And water. I don't know if they'll take Al'Myrahn coin for food."

Watching her sigh sadly and glance around hopelessly made him feel like a failure. Had he been even slightly educated, he might have known Xia was low on monsters and hated Runers more than any other civilization. There had to be a way to get money. She needed to rest. He had to find her shelter and water. The jade bracelet on her wrist caught the sunlight and he remembered his own. They might fetch a price. Perhaps not much, but maybe enough to supplement the coin they did have and get them some food. Or a cool bath while they looked for a way into the palace.

As if some higher power sensed how close he'd come to giving up the one thing he'd given Sybal out of affection, the unmistakable rattle of dice caught his ear. Spinning around, he saw a gaggle of men sitting on crates and barrels with cups, dice, and a familiar deck of cards.

"No!" Sybal hissed, following his eyes. "Men lose more money gambling than you could ever make."

For some reason, her panic made him smile. "I used to play Black Sheep's Dice all the time when I was on the street. Most players focus too much on the cards, but the real victory is the dice."

"Holy Rabast," she moaned, covering her face.

"Sybal," he growled, still smiling. She peeked at him through her long fingers. "Trust me. And I need you. These men have probably never heard Al'Myrahn."

Moaning and rolling her eyes, she grabbed his arm and they walked together to the gambling men. He instructed her on what to say. She translated to the men that they wanted to be delt in.

☙

SYBAL DUG her fingers into Tzarik's arm as he made himself comfortable on a barrel around the crate the other men played on. To her surprise, he didn't flinch or try to throw her off. He took it, knowing full well the risk and letting her express her distaste. When he sat down, she saw the top of his head better. His tangled hair was matted over his shoulders and smelled sour. She wondered if she stank as much as he did. If they did stay the night in a public house, she'd insist on a bath. Maybe he knew that. He'd want a room and food. She'd want a bath. She wondered if he was doing this to get her what she wanted. A warm appreciation for Tzarik washed over her and she reached down, tucking the white streak of hair behind his ear, the one that grew near his temple. He didn't look at her with this gesture, but she caught his left brow almost twitch.

The dealer was a man wrapped in cotton so only his brown eyes could be seen between the mask and wide, pointed straw hat he wore. He held his back straighter than the other men and his fingers were cleaner as he dealt the cards. Inspecting his purse on his belt, she saw it was nearly empty. The piles in front of the other men were stacked high and wide.

She met the dealer's eyes and a sense of familiarity washed over her. Leaning down, she opened her mouth to whisper to Tzarik.

The dealer cut in, speaking perfect Al'Myrahn. "No outside help. Let him play."

Tzarik and Sybal glanced up at him.

"Only Xian," he said, tossing out the cards. In Xian, he said, "Cups down."

She relayed this to Tzarik, who understood the game just as well as he'd said he did and didn't need her prompting, slamming his cup upside down in time with the others.

Not understanding the game, she watched as Tzarik flicked his fingers up and down in different counts. Apparently language wasn't needed for the game, only numbers. He'd ask for a card, discard one, flip one over, then they'd start showing fingers and tapping the underside of their upside-down dice cup. After a round or two of this, they started to glare into each other's eyes. She assumed the betting now commenced.

The bets started low. One small copper coin. Two coppers. Tzarik's stone face gave nothing away. Standing behind him, she knew what his dice read under the cup, but didn't know how to feel one way or another. These street games had never made sense to her. There were so many finite rules, tricks, and techniques.

A moan went up from the three other men and Tzarik pulled the stack of copper and silver Xian coins towards him. He didn't smirk in his victory or show any signs of struggle. This had to be part of it. She'd heard of men who were good at gambling and lying. Tzarik's ability to show no emotion on his face had finally come in handy.

After three more rounds—Tzarik winning two and the pot getting bigger—the dealer sighed, rubbing his last two coins between his fingers. One of the side gamblers smiled so hard his eyes almost squinted shut.

"He's going to lose again!" he taunted in a sing-song voice to his partner. "What should it be this time?" He faced the dealer. "A flogging?"

"How many times have you owed us?" the other said, spitting over his shoulder. He weighed a heavy purse in his hand. "We could give you more coin if you want to stay in the game."

The dealer's posture up until now had been formal, straight-backed, and almost what Sybal might call regal. Now he collapsed in on himself a little.

"Give me twenty," he mumbled through his cloth mask. He held out his hand.

"No," Sybal cut in.

Tzarik looked up, the conversation lost on him.

To the dealer she said, "Don't take their money. If you're out, you're out. Just leave. Is it worth a whipping?"

The dealer met her eyes, squinting curiously. "You don't have to stick up for me. I chose this."

"Don't choose to take his money." She shoved the other man's purse back towards him.

The man jumped up when Sybal's runes fell into view as she leaned over to push his purse away. "Foreign monsters," he said, gasping. Swiveling to the dealer, he shouted, accusing him of cheating. With that, a few other players stood up.

Sensing the danger, Tzarik jumped up, quickly taking his money. "What did you do?" he hissed at Sybal.

The others dived into action. The Runers lunged away from

the crate as one of the gamblers lurched towards the dealer, fist cocked. Sybal draw halat and shoved it towards the dealer. When the gambler's knuckles made contact with it, a crunching noise cracked over the rest of the ruckus. She flipped the crate over and pulled the dealer out of the ensuing tussle. Dragging him around a corner, she let go of him.

"You're welcome," she panted, checking to make sure the raging gamblers hadn't followed them. "Debt like that isn't worth it. I've seen workers fall in with men like that. It never ends well."

"Just as well," the dealer sighed in Al'Myrahn, leaning against the stone wall and closing his eyes. "It wouldn't matter if they drained me of blood and threw me in the gutter."

Tzarik winced almost empathetically at this remark.

Sybal asked, "I don't suppose you know a good public house near the palace, do you?"

The dealer looked down at her. "You wanting back in the palace?"

"Back?" Now she squinted at him. Suddenly it hit her. "Hiro?" she said, gasping. Her hand flashed up, tearing his cotton mask away. He didn't fight her; the cotton snapped away to reveal the stoic visage of the prince.

His placid face gazed out from under the straw hat. "Yes," he said, sighing and averting his eyes. "I come out, as you see, to be among the people."

Tzarik made a grunting hum in response to this. Sybal knew he understood the younger man's plight. She'd seen her mentor's struggle firsthand.

Gently placing her hand on his shoulder, she said, "We need to see your father and Yui."

"Of course you do." Hiro pushed himself up, re-wrapping his disguise.

"For everyone's sake," Sybal said quickly. "For all of Xia. We're trying to protect you. We need to speak to the Di-Huan. Can you get us inside?"

The prince considered the Runers before him for a long time before shaking his head in defeat. "Yes. Follow me."

WITH HIRO LEADING THE WAY, the gates opened to them and he took them straight to the throne room almost without any fuss. A few guards ran to flank them as they walked down the long, now empty courtyard to the Di-Huan's royal receiving hall. They had both been there before, but something about its emptiness made it feel darker—ominous rather than welcoming. In the dark with very few torches lit, it didn't have the same wonder and grandeur Sybal had experienced during the celebration of the princess's birthday.

"I have to tell Yui alone," Sybal said softly to Tzarik as they approached the hall doors. "I don't think her father knows about them."

"He knows," Hiro cut in. "It's hard to miss, these days. Like father like daughter." The contempt in his voice cut through Sybal's heart like a new dagger.

She understood his meaning when they went inside and found a few dignitaries in conversation with the Di-Huan. To his right sat Yui, hands clasped over her middle. When the princess saw the Runers, she stood up expectantly.

Sybals's mouth went dry, taking in the princess. The girl stood, hands cradling her slightly bulging belly. Mouth agape, Sybal turned to Tzarik, who looked just as shocked to her trained eye.

The Di-Huan rose and hit a gong beside him, and all the dignitaries filed out, bowing as they walked backwards away from the throne. The ruler waved his hands for the Runers to come closer with Hiro. Then he trotted down the steps to meet them, throwing his silk-clad arms around Hiro's neck.

"Where have you been, my boy?" he breathed. "We've had such devastating reports. I was so worried." He held his son out at arm's length and met the Runers' eyes. He looked them up and down and wilted just a little more. Then he embraced Hiro once more before leading them and his children to a side room where there was a golden table with cushions around it. Closing the doors to the more private chamber, he asked them if they had any news.

"Much," Tzarik offered first. He glanced at Sybal, then Yui. He couldn't help but try to examine her midsection. He was staring rudely, but didn't stop.

The Di-Huan nodded, following his gaze. "My first grandchild."

Sybal stammered. "How? When? You know?"

Yui smiled sadly, rubbing her belly. "It's been a while, I suppose. I only started to show recently. I can hide nothing from my father."

To their surprise, the Di-Huan beamed.

"This makes what I'm about to say so much worse." Sybal's eyes immediately burned with tears and her lip trembled.

Yui paled, her entire body freezing. The smile she'd shared with her father slipped down her round face.

"There is a war now," Tzarik said. "ShanBao and Wushito attacked Wu-Tang. A member of House Xiaoh was planning a revolt against their authority. ShanBao struck first."

"Jin Xioah," Hiro said.

Sybal started at the name. "You knew?"

"Guessed, more like," the Di-Huan said softly, aghast. His face fell. He reached out to his daughter.

Yui shook, gulping air to stop herself from crying out. Her

hands clutched at her belly, where Jin's child grew. "Is he all right?" she gasped. "Where is Jin?"

Without speaking, Sybal engulfed the princess in a sisterly embrace. She caught Yui just in time. The princess wailed, collapsing into Sybal's arms. They both went down onto the golden floor. Sybal stroked Yui's hair as the girl released chest-rattling sobs into her shoulder.

Unable to stand seeing his daughter in such pain, tears trickled down the Di-Huan's face as he fought to hold in his emotions. Even Hiro lowered his head in solidarity with his sister's loss. Sybal did not miss his furrowed, contemplative expression, though. Wondering what he might be thinking, she asked the first thing that came to mind.

"Majesty?"

The Di-Huan looked up, gently wiping his eyes.

"Jin was dragon-touched." She stopped. How could she ask without devaluing Hiro even more than he already felt, without sounding ignorant of their customs? "There is a lot of turmoil amongst your people." She tried to weigh her words cautiously. "If Yui bore his child—being your daughter—could that child be a good leader?"

Drawing himself up and clasping his hands inside his wide sleeves, the Di-Huan replied, "This child could be the balance we are supposed to have, the teachings of Wushito and the touch of the Dragon. I have no doubt it would be blessed by the Dragon, considering—"

"Damn Wushito!" Yui growled through gnashed teeth. "Power hungry brigands. Traitors."

Her head snapped up so quickly, Sybal almost got a bloody nose. She jerked out of the way just in time.

"Father!" Yui said, gasping. "The *Xai de'Jing*. Inside there are passages about how to bring back..." She choked, a fresh wave of emotion almost muting her. "How to bring back the dead."

Tzarik stiffened in alert and Sybal looked at him, wondering. "Would it work?" she asked her mentor.

"If what TaoShin said is true, it is the *Mahit'Onomicon*," Tzarik confirmed. "The book of liches. It would have such things written inside. But, princess, it's not the kind of undead life you think." Tzarik made sure the Di-Huan listened too before he went on. "We've seen it. Unless Wushito knows more than a necromancer, it's not the kind of revitalized spirit you want. It wouldn't be Jin."

"Most likely," the Di-Huan agreed. "Still..." He rubbed his chin, eyes unfocused. "It is their only claim to power. If it were to vanish, Wushito would be weaned from their source in perhaps just one generation. I tried for years to ignore the subtle threats from Master ShanBao."

"He wants Wushito to rule," Hiro cut in.

Tzarik shook his head. "He wants to rule as Di-Huan, start his own dynasty, with a sorcerer by his side who can control beasts and monsters, the one thing Wushito is supposed to protect Xia from."

This didn't come as news to the Di-Huan. He raised his brows and nodded. "ShanBao has fought his entire life to elevate himself. House Shikirumi has never been a powerful one. His ancestors were content in their place, never seeking to climb, to gain power. When ShanBao became the Wushito master, it was a great honor for his house."

"Why he's doing this doesn't matter," Sybal cut in. "The man he's aligned himself with—Abigor Sharar—has far darker ambitions, and ShanBao has no idea who he's dealing with. And his generals are going behind his back with Sharar as well. They are going to help him get him that book as payment for his aid."

She left out the part about Yui and her wish. For once, she restrained herself. No need to worry them with that. Yet.

A moment of silence followed as they all considered their place and what the others had said.

"I may have had some part to play in this," Tzarik murmured. He caught Sybal's eye. "I can't leave Xia now. I should see this through."

Proud, a warm smile eased the tension on her face. She let him see it.

"And I cannot cower any longer," the Di-Huan added. He dropped his hands. "Wushito won't stop. Neither will Master ShanBao nor his generals. They will come here, to the Royal City."

"Father—" Hiro started, but the older man cut him off with a wave of his hand.

"I will martial the army. Get General Zhen." The Di-Huan's face changed in the rising moonlight. He glared out a window that looked down onto a foggy mountain side, as if his enemies lurked just there. "Runers, I ask for your aid even though you offer it."

Sybal stood up, her hand still on Yui's shoulder. "Of course. What can we do?"

"When the time is right, I will send you into the belly of the beast," the Di-Huan said.

CHAPTER 22
WAR WAKING

TZARIK TOOK HIS NEW QUARTERS ADJOINING THE PALACE without complaint or wounded pride. Over the months, he'd slept on the traditional floor mattress of Xia and had come to appreciate it. The first few nights he'd had to sleep on the hard floor beside it, unused to the softness. Now, he almost enjoyed laying his head on something comfortable. The Di-Huan guessed at the Runer's privacy and pride and gave them a wing meant for foreign dignitaries. It joined the palace by a long hallway, but had the privacy of distance and two sets of sliding doors.

His horse long gone, the Di-Huan let him have his pick of the royal stables after several days' rest and force-feeding from Sybal. His apprentice spent most of her days with the pregnant princess out in the gardens, going for walks, doing things he assumed women liked to do for comfort. Hiro accompanied him out to the stables.

"I think you might find this one to your liking," the prince said solemnly. He showed Tzarik to a couple stalls near the back.

Inside, he was shocked to find Porshain horses. "Akhelatek." He couldn't keep the wonder out of his voice.

The stallions inside glowed with a metallic sheen, golden hues under their black coats. The white one shone like a diamond, reminding him of the glint from his orichalcum blade. The hair of the Akhelatek gave off the effect due to the opaque core of their hair being slimmer than the rest. This caused the light to refract and split into its glimmering colors. Even the black one glittered gold.

"How did you get these?" Tzarik asked, drawn to the black stallion. It easily stood over seventeen hands high, its shoulders several inches above Tzarik's head. "The Porshains used to breed them. Most people thought they died out when the island blighted."

Hiro also indulged in petting the soft, magical hair. "Xia traded with most continents for years. There is a breeder in Alika who keeps up the Akhelatek traditions and sells them at great cost. They are strong and can go days on little water and rest. They are desert mounts, but do well on our terrain. I thought it would suit you."

A sense of honor guided Tzarik's hand as he stroked the long, silky mane of the black stallion. "I've never been given such a gift," he said. "A horse reserved for kings, surely. It would make me stand out in a crowd. Not exactly the low profile I like."

Hiro nodded. "A gift for friends of Xia. But I understand if you don't want it." The prince turned away, pacing and forming his next words. "I cannot hide my conflict from you Runers. I know you see through my hesitation."

"I don't blame you," Tzarik offered, opening the stall gate to get closer to the horse. It nickered and tossed its head when he removed the barrier. "But I cannot help the judgment I feel. Your country is crumbling, and all your people can think about is the way things used to be. You should be Di-Huan after your father. Living in uncertainty like Xia does is chaos."

"It's not that simple," Hiro said. "The balance must be maintained. I don't expect you to understand or believe us."

A part of Tzarik did understand. He just couldn't help the doubt he felt at the way the Xians clung to tradition and their metaphysical beliefs. He'd survived by abandoning all such things.

"I am grateful for the horse," he offered. "Thank you."

Seeing the attempt at peace, the prince bowed, thanking the Runer for accepting the gift. "In the tradition of his breed, you have to name him."

"I've never named my horses," Tzarik said, at a loss. "They come and go so quickly."

"Pity," Hiro mused. "Perhaps if you name this one, it will stick around? It might mean more to you and you might take better care of it."

Tzarik suddenly missed the prince's quiet stoicism. "What does one call a horse?"

Tapping his chin, the prince suggested, "Something special to you."

Looking around and down at himself, the only special things Tzarik had were his blade and the runes. He couldn't fathom shouting "orichalcum" as a name. The black coat offered little inspiration, despite its beauty. "I don't know. I'd just as soon call it 'dog' or 'dusk' as anything else."

Hiro pressed his lips together and looked at the horse with sympathy. "Might I suggest Dusk, then?"

◆

THE PALACE REMAINED FAIRLY EMPTY, just as it had been when the Runers arrived. Something about the grand expansive grounds didn't seem right with hardly anyone inside. A few servants moved around, keeping plants alive, cleaning outdoor debris away, and guards still patrolled, but visitors and other people of the court trickled away. It didn't help that rain had been coming down in torrents ever since that first day. Rivers rose and many gardens flooded.

Tzarik, arms crossed, leaned against the side of their quarters on the balcony and looked over the stone yard where he had once seen dozens of men and women moving together through poses and moves. A safe distance from the edge, he listened for the clop of hooves. Every hour or so, a new party of royal messengers went out to deliver news about the gathering army. They put posters up on boards in the centers of the surrounding villages and some of the larger cities. It would take days, if not weeks, to gather a volunteer army.

"The Di-Huan thinks the army he has is not big enough," Sybal said, appearing behind him. She joined him, looking out into the rain. She sighed and her breath appeared in fog before her. The air grew colder with every day.

"Winter is on the way," Tzarik said. "A war in winter in this terrain would be futile. If he ever lost the advantage, he'd lose the country for sure. Or drag out the slaughter. Wushito might turn on the people, weakening the cities and settlements that support the Di-Huan. Most likely, he wants to end it quickly, before the snow falls. But that hope may be in vain."

Taking this in, Sybal looked out over all they could see. From the highlands, all of Xia could be seen. The wall of the Royal City circled the whole top of the continent so that one could walk around, taking in the land.

"How long would it take to walk the length of the wall?" she asked.

Tzarik ran his eyes over the part of it he could see. "Eight hours on horseback?" He understood her and quickly shut down the idea. "It's raining. And cold. You could catch the rain sickness."

"Or we could walk around the crown of Xia," she said, smiling.

"And see the people below us shake with fear, panicking over a war they know will take its toll on them. Unwilling sacrifices." He turned and went into the main room of their quarters where he sat on a wide, circular set of cushioned seats. His scimitar lay before him, half-oiled. He'd also disassembled his small crossbow for cleaning and a new string.

Sybal sat next to him, unbelting her own blade and joining him. "I'd only seen small battles—family feuds, mostly—in Ala'-Nar. An uprising of slaves or workers. Until Tarkan."

He handed her an extra rag for her own sword. "I see this war going on for months, if not years. An entire country at war with itself is ugly and needless. Devastating. It may never recover."

"Have you seen a large-scale war before?" she asked.

He nodded. "I was on Bahratt when they fought Alika, before the peace treaty, just over twenty-one years ago."

She smiled coyly. "Maharaja Saksham headed that treaty. He saved his entire country."

"Who?" Tzarik asked, curious about her grin.

It took her a moment to overcome a sudden wave of melancholy. Her voice lowered in her throat as she struggled to speak. "Rahul's father. He negotiated peace with the pharaohs over his entire life. The Tashid temples in Bahratt and the Alikan priests clashed over religious order and power. Alika is still very religious, their high priests and magi often sitting in court with the pharaohs. But I never saw the war. Rahul told me about it once." She took a deep breath and shook her head, passing her hands over her eyes.

Tzarik didn't think much of this motion. He understood Sybal was emotional over her losses still. But she kept looking at him. He glanced up from his scimitar. "What?"

Her eyes weren't expectant, prying, or investigative. She just looked, almost like an artist gazing over a fine work. He quickly became aware of how, while she beheld him, she relaxed. Her eyes roved over his long, ever-whitening hair, his chest and arms. His heart rate picked up and his palms grew hot.

"What were you doing in Bahratt then?" she asked. "How old were you?"

Unsure what she was hunting for, he went back to his weapons. Her calmness was contagious, forcing his nerves to relax. Her voice soothed him.

"My family did not live atop a diamond mine," he started. He fought to keep his tone even and not offend her. She didn't take her eyes off him, so he went on. "When I was newly thirteen, they sold me to a lord on Bahratt. I was his slave for nine months before I couldn't take it anymore. I'd stolen before, lived on the streets. I'd often run away from my father, so I knew I could do it again. One day, I was starving after being sick for weeks. The merchants in central villages knew we street rats liked to take easy targets. This one always laced certain baskets with poison to thin us runaways out."

"How cruel!" Sybal whispered.

Tzarik shrugged. "But he was on the outside of the village market, easiest to steal from. So I was ready to get sick again just to have bread. He caught me and called the guards. They prepared to sever my hand right there in the middle of the market."

She tilted her head and repositioned herself to look him square on. "But?"

The mixed, tangled feelings he had about this part of his life swelled, making him reconsider the story.

"Please go on," Sybal begged, touching his arm. "You never tell me about your childhood."

"Because it's not like yours," he said. "You wouldn't understand."

She bit her tongue, biting back a remark. Instead, she placed her hand on his knee. "Go on."

The warmth of her palm seeped through his pants to his skin. Sighing, he kept going.

"Azar found me just then. Weak, crying like a scolded child and vomiting into the street from the illness." The sunny streets of Bahratt flashed before his mind's eye. He could smell the dirt. The spices. Women in gold and red. "When he stepped out of the crowd and I saw him, I remember thinking, 'What's he done wrong?' "

Sybal frowned, keeping her hand steady where it lay. "Why?"

"Azar was not like other men. His skin was so light—almost white. He had crystalline blue eyes, and hair as pale as the moon. His hands were always cold. But when he rescued me and pulled me up onto his horse, I thought, 'I wouldn't mind him. Anything but this.' " He stopped.

"Your mentor?" Sybal asked. "The one who later abandoned you?"

He nodded. "Azar had many demons. But I was used to being on my own."

This prompted another thought. He set down his now glowing scimitar and went to work on his small crossbow.

"You could leave any time, Sybal," he said. He held his hand out, signaling her to hand him a set of wound strings on the table next to her.

She handed them to him then picked up a small square of wax for the strings. "I don't see that happening. When I think about us, I see us together for years."

"Why?"

She started to wax another bowstring. He noticed how she did it without purpose, trying to distract herself.

"As you are so fond of reminding me, I am not like you, Tzarik. I don't like being alone."

"It might be better than spending years with me." His finger slipped while pulling hard on the latch, jamming it into the bow. The instant rage that often accompanied such gaffs roiled up instantly.

Sensing the tension, Sybal took the bow from his hands, placed it aside, and then massaged his throbbing thumb and palm. "Careful," she said.

He didn't take his hand away. Something akin to the adrenaline that surged through his body while battling monsters suddenly rushed through him when he said, "I don't know what I'd do if you left, though." The admittance stopped his breath and his head spun. Why was this happening?

She handed him back his bow, satisfied he wouldn't throw it in rage now. "You must have been in a very dark place before me, or you wouldn't have admitted that."

She smiled, but her words were true. He couldn't deny it.

"I was. You know that. I didn't know what I wanted. And you made things more complicated." He met her gaze to gauge her reaction. Only attention and openness shone in her blue eyes.

"How?" she pressed.

He couldn't swallow. He became hyper aware of her hand returning to his knee. Strands of her yellow hair drifted around her face. She had a scar on her chin he'd never noticed before. Just a small one.

"I suppose I wanted to use you as a reason to stay alive," he said. "Other Runers are killed every day in battle against simple monsters. But not me. I thought if I left you, the runes might take me. But you hunted me down. They knew you were not far behind. Maybe they took pity on me for your sake."

Her eyes warmed into a slow, deep smile. Before he could move, she wrapped her long arms around him in a tight embrace. She pulled him into her, her golden hair obscuring his vision. Her heart beat against his chest until his matched hers beat for beat.

She pulled back, beaming at him like a ray of midday Al'Myrahn sun.

"I am a determined woman," she said.

The warmth vanished as he read the intent in her eyes. His body told him to flee. She leaned just a fraction of an inch in towards him, her eyes becoming heavy. He froze.

She sensed him go rigid and stopped. Her face flushed pale, the sulfates rushing to color her cheeks in embarrassment. Licking her lips, she swallowed hard and dropped her head. He'd shamed her by not reciprocating her intent. She stood up suddenly, ducking her head into her shoulders and walking quickly with hard, long strides out of the room. He heard her breath shudder as she turned into the hall outside the doorway and then broke into a run.

Once she was gone, the mental abuse bombarded his brain. "Idiot," he chided himself out loud. "Coward."

☙

"Tzarik, with me," Hiro ordered, taking the Runer away from where he gazed out onto the Di-Huan's royal gardens.

Behind the prince, a rush of royal guards followed. Sybal brought up the rear, tossing her deep black hood over her yellow hair.

"What's happened?" Tzarik asked, quickly falling in step with the prince.

"Riots," he replied, ramming a golden helmet onto his head and catching a long narrow sword tossed to him by Commander Zhen. "Those living in the royal city are destroying the city in fear and have turned on the Wushito who supplement our royal guard. Most are advisors, not even active warriors. I will not tolerate this violence in this city."

More than once, Tzarik had watched as a mass of people turned into animals in fear. Often, they didn't even understand that the place they attacked and destroyed was their own home.

"Are you going to fight them?" he asked.

"I am going to do my duty," the prince quipped.

Together, the prince, the Runers, Commander Zhen, and his small entourage marched out the front gates of the palace. Taking a slopping, rain-soaked path down into the city astride their horses, Tzarik smelled burning thatch even before his eyes caught the gray smoke against the stormy sky.

Cries and shouts from people looting and clashing with makeshift weapons greeted them as they rounded a wall into a small square where a large statue of a past Di-Huan overlooked them, glaring down in the likeness of a demon with tusks and a boar's nose. A home of a wealthy silk trader crumbled in flames. Before the large front doors, a shouting crowd pulled a man in Wushito robes out by his long black braid. The Wushito's feet kicked out and he screamed in fright, blood already staining his silk tunic. He had no sword, only scrolls on his belt and back.

The man who dragged the Wushito raised a small-handled scythe like one might use in the fields and shouted to the people. They replied in a cheer, raising their fists. Behind Tzarik and Sybal, someone gurgled in blood as a vicious strike cut their throat. Tzarik spun and clashed swords with an attacker. The mob had come with intentions of violence. Hiro kicked his horse into the square, shouting and waving the royal banner. The trader wanting to kill the Wushito scholar shouted back at Hiro, pleading violently as he gestured towards the Wushito. When the silk trader did not stop, raising the sword to cut the Wushito's braid, Hiro roared and thrust the end of the banner at the man. It glinted in sharp gold, pointed to easily be plunged into the ground—and the man's thigh.

Taken aback by the prince's savage nature and swift judgment, boldness allowed Tzarik to shove his own attacker off more harshly and kick him in the face to keep him down. Sybal joined him, already gasping, strands of her golden hair plastered to her face from either sweat or rain.

"Are you all right?" she said, gasping and hauling him up from his lunge.

"Fine," he grunted back. "You?"

She nodded, wiping blood from her lip. "These people are wild with fear." She nodded towards Hiro, who leapt from his horse and brandished his sword at his people, defending the Wushito scholar.

She translated for Tzarik. "He says, 'Not here, not now! Not within our city. This man is innocent. The Wushito are our brothers—only those who fight against us are the enemy.' "

She stopped and frowned, a wrinkle of worry creasing her brow.

"What is it?" Tzarik prompted, eyes still trained on the prince. He circled the defenseless Wushito, who was on his knees, his hands covering his face, sobbing in thanks to his prince.

Sybal licked her lips. "He says that he will never be their king, so he does not fear using violence to quell their uprising. That they will be taken care of." She sighed. " 'I am not your king, but you will not spill your brother's blood on our continent.' He's promising to save them."

Hiro savagely ripped the banner out of the man's leg, shouting at his healers to tend to him. Extending a gloved and armor-clasped hand down to the Wushito, he hauled him to his feet and clasped his shoulder, then shoved him towards his guards for protection. After a quick warning glare at the rest of those gathered, he marched back to the Runers.

"Well done, Hiro," Sybal breathed.

"For now," he shot back. "There are more riots springing up all across the continent. I do not wish to spend my time stopping my people from thinning themselves out, but I must. It is my duty."

Commander Zhen fell in step with the three of them as they led the horses out. "That was very brave and right, my prince. But we cannot spread ourselves too thin."

"Your place is with my father and wherever he needs you," Hiro answered, head tilted in determination. "My place is where Xia needs me."

Suddenly worried the young man might throw himself away, Tzarik cut in, "Be wary, Hiro. Do not give your worth up callously. They need you."

He felt Sybal's eyes bore into him from the left. Her hand gently squeezed his upper arm.

Hiro nodded stiffly. "You inspired me, Tzarik. I do not charge into battle seeking my own end. If all I can do is stop riots in the streets of the royal city, so be it."

"Let me go with you for a day or two," Zhen countered, stepping in front of the prince to stop his determined gait. "We cannot defend the entire country if our borders are not taken care of first. One cannot pull water from a dried well for a village," he said, quoting what must have been an old Xian proverb.

Studying the older man only a moment, Hiro nodded. "Let's go."

"We will go with you!" Sybal offered quickly.

"No." Hiro put his hand on her shoulder, stopping her. "Go back to my father. Watch him. He needs protection."

Smiling proudly, Sybal nodded. "Watch your back, Hiro."

Chapter 23
The Messenger

"The rain won't stop!" Commander Zhen said, kneeling before the Di-Huan. Mud caked his long mustache and the ends of his trailing salt and pepper braid. Blood trickled down from beneath his shingled helmet. Behind him panted two lower-level military men Sybal didn't know the ranks for. Their faces twisted with pleading.

The Di-Huan looked to the Runers on his left, sympathy turning the corners of his lips down. "We have never suffered a rain like this during autumn." He turned back to the commander. "I understand, Zhen. But I cannot stop the rain."

"The lowlands are flooding," one of the others piped up. He immediately bowed his head when his commander gasped at his forwardness before the Di-Huan. "The people are fleeing the floods, climbing higher," he continued. "The ocean comes ever closer. The monks have left the island; the north is unguarded." He looked up now, urgency pushing decorum aside. "We must strike the heart of the beast. If the Hallow City falls, they may retreat."

Sybal quickly relayed this to Tzarik, adding that now might be the time to enter the city, if they could.

"That might only drive them into a frenzy," Tzarik said,

thinking carefully. "And we don't know how involved Sharar might be. The soldier may be right. The people are going to be the ones you fall back on, sira."

"I've already emptied them of every able-bodied man and woman," the Di-Huan said sadly. "The death count rises every day. I want to see my people, give them hope."

Commander Zhen shook his head. "There is a large camp of vacating refugees in the river valley to the west. Our army marches in their direction and Wushito will clash with us there. Hundreds of innocents will be killed."

When Sybal relayed this to Tzarik, a jolt of energy lit up his face. "That's part of the Hikomi region?" he asked.

Zhen nodded.

"We can move them," he said quickly, leaping down the stairs from the throne to the long table set before them for maps and planning. "Your people's faith may yet save them." He scanned the map. Not sure what he was looking for, he beckoned Sybal down. "Where is it?" he asked.

She smiled inwardly at his ignorance and pointed out the lines that outlined the Hikomi region in the west, down to where it met Wu-Tang's borders.

"Remember the story about the white qilin?" he asked. "When it's spotted, everyone who is able will flock to see it to be blessed. What if we spread word that one has been spotted..." He scanned the map. "...anywhere? Somewhere Wushito would believe they might travel."

Zhen's face brightened and he almost grinned. "They would divide their army. They would want to devastate such a large gathering, knowing the impact so many deaths would have on those loyal to the Di-Huan. They might commit more resources to it than we think. Spread word that the qilin is in Hikomi."

Hiro held up his hand at this. "But they would expect the Di-Huan to go. It's tradition that he go and meet the beast. They might attack the palace, the royal family, if they think he's gone."

"I agree with Master Runer," the Di-Huan said after a moment. "We will move them to Wu-Tang."

"What?" Sybal cut in. She knew the bias she felt against House Xiaoh was petty at this point. Whoang Xiaoh was not his people. She needed to redirect her rage. Instead, she brought Wu-Zhiang and ShanBao to the front of her mind. The people of Wu-Tang were innocent. "I'm sorry," she apologized quickly. "The stone city would be a good defense. They will attack, though. We cannot leave them defenseless."

Commander Zhen nodded, his wary eyes finally taking on a brighter light. "We won't. Wushito will be divided: some will come here, others will head to Wu-Tang, and the rest will continue their march to the other settlements. This may work."

Seeing everyone agree, the Di-Huan allowed himself a cautious nod. "We have to assume they will come here once they think the people are flocking to Hikomi. Their forces will be spread thin. Runers?"

Tzarik nodded. "Once we have word they are moving towards Hikomi, Sybal and I will go to the Hallow City. Until then, we need to be seen in other places. Sira, allow Lady Sybal and me to go to the refugee camp."

"And do what?" Hiro snapped aggressively.

Sybal shrugged, joining in on her mentor's idea. "Provisions from the royal stores? Clothes? A word from their ruler? Help them move to Wu-Tang?"

She matched the snap Hiro's tone with her own, narrowing her eyes at his unwillingness to help his people.

The Di-Huan did smile then. "Ah, Sybal, you are sharp. A

good plan. Do me a favor and speak to them. Look into their eyes. Make sure to spread hope."

"I will give you a map," Zhen offered. "We were driven farther back than is defensible, but you should be able to get there with a few wagons. We will get messengers out after you to spread the false news. Set the refugees on a path to Wu-Tang and I will meet them on the way."

"Won't we escort them there?" Tzarik asked.

"No." The Di-Huan shook his head. "I'd like you by my side after it is known you are among the travelers."

Sybal noted a new slump to his shoulders. He leaned back against his throne for support. Something weighed on him that had not just a moment ago. Looking sideways at Tzarik, she caught his left brow twitch into a frown. She glanced around, wondering if she'd missed something. With her senses on alert, she caught a high, tinkling sound. Chancing a glance over her shoulder into the courtyard, she caught what the Di-Huan saw for a moment.

Beneath the pavilion where the children used to play, amidst the cold fog, she thought she saw two glowing eyes. The things almost looked lion shaped. It stood upon a cloud, looking directly at the man on the throne.

She shook her head, blinked, and looked again. It was gone.

"Go with the speed of the Dragon," the ruler said solemnly. His eyes locked onto the area she'd just been investigating. "Bring my people good news. Remind them they, too, are dragons, and we will stand up to those who seek to put us under their boot."

Sybal bowed in sync with Tzarik and together they turned, leaving the hall to prepare to face not just the weather, but also the threat of an army of warriors trained specifically to hunt them.

SYBAL STOOD LEANING against one of the golden lion-dragon creatures that decorated the many halls and altars of the Di-Huan's palace. Before her, near the edge of the open pavilion leading out from part of the palace, the Di-Huan stood with his hands clasped behind his back, watching the rain. He'd removed his golden shoes and the tasseled and beaded crown he usually wore. Without it, he looked shorter. His back arched under the burden he bore.

"Gloriousness?" Sybal asked softly, approaching him. "Tzarik and I are readying to leave."

He didn't move. His lips were frozen in a permanent, forced small smile. His brown eyes slowly drifted over his domain. "We believe deliberately intervening in someone's natural death stops their soul from going to Tiang," he said sadly.

She came abreast of him, looking out at the steep drop below. "Yes. We experienced that. Tzarik took me utterly by surprise and tried to save a drowning woman."

The old man took a shaking breath. "I have found it hard to breathe these last few days. But I did not call for a healer."

"Are you ill?" Sybal asked gently. She almost reached out to touch his shoulder but held herself back.

"Not ill." He winced. "Just...dying, I believe."

"Are you sure?"

His cavalier attitude made her head spin.

When he didn't reply, she asked, "What is the point of your healers, then? If they cannot save the dying?"

"Natural death," he repeated. "Or if one wishes for their life spark to blow away in the wind. You see, we do not die when we die."

She tilted her head.

"Xians believe in reincarnation, Sybal. Woe befalls those who are trapped on this earth, the ghosts and spirits who die without peace." A tear trickled down his wrinkled face. "Woe to those who cannot see Tiang and return to earth in a shape they deserve. But," he raised his brows, "blessed are those who set the souls free."

A thumbing in her heart ached for the old man. Unsure what else to say, she whispered, "You will come back as a great creature. Perhaps even a dragon."

Suddenly, his eyes snapped to something in the shadow of a bush Sybal could not see. "What an honor it would be to live in the image of the White Dragon." His eyes brightened at whatever invisible thing he beheld. "Perhaps I was a good Di-Huan."

Sybal glanced over once again but saw nothing. "The magic runs deep in Xia," she mused.

The Di-Huan nodded, straightening up. "So it does. I think I will go for a walk. Find Yui. I haven't seen her in days."

"In the rain?" Sybal asked, taking two quick steps after him.

"Take my blessing, lady Runer," he called back. He stood up perfectly straight now and trotted down the path to a pavilion deep in the garden.

Concerned and baffled, Sybal shook her head.

☙

SYBAL EXPECTED Tzarik to groan during at least part of the journey down to the Hikomi province, but her mentor held his tongue. The days and nights spent in the rain drove even her to the edge of giving up. At night, the wind picked up and slashed through their tents, which had been provided by their Xian guides. They spent hours setting them up behind boulders or between sturdy trees. The sylvan canopy hardly provided cover, often dripping fat, cold droplets onto them while they slept. Tzarik and Sybal took turns going out farther to look for signs of Wushito, with little luck.

Once they reached the refugee camp, the reality of the war below the Royal City came into view. Sybal's heart went out to the mass of muddy, tired, cold, and starving people.

"Oh, Krishvu, Tzarik," she breathed when they looked down on them.

Mothers with babies, old men on crutches, and young girls wrapped for warmth slowly trudged up from the lowlands. Most pulled rickshaws filled with familial items or older relatives. Some towed their own wagons, empty bridles of deceased mules thrown over their shoulders. Only a few glanced up at them as they drew near.

For the first time since she'd known him, Sybal saw Tzarik affected by the sight before them. His lips parted in shock and a small bend in his back told her this weighed heavily on him.

"It was inevitable," she said quickly, knowing he was about to blame himself. "Xia wanted this. We couldn't stop it."

"I didn't have to start it," he murmured.

"You might have saved hundreds by warning Wu-Tang." She reached over and gripped his shoulder. "Let's distribute the gifts."

She let him remain behind, whistling loudly for the Di-Huan's men to follow her. She rode into the mass, shouting in Xian that they'd brought supplies from the Di-Huan himself.

"He knows you are suffering," she called. "He wants to show appreciation for your loyalty."

She thought they might spit on her, demand more, cry that they were dying. But they didn't. The younger refugees moved in to touch her, thanking her. One girl gripped her ankle and pressed her forehead to it, praying loudly.

"You are to march to Wu-Tang," she said after a moment. A small gasp rose up. "The royal army will meet you there, having already made a pact with the city. But you must hurry!" Urgency shot through her, encouraged by their good reception. "The stone city is fortifiable. Leave behind anything you don't need for the journey. We will escort you a good distance to start you on your path and protect you."

An anguished cry rose up, breaking the joyous mood. The woman screamed and pointed behind them, eyes wide. The Runers spun around, hands on their scimitars, ready for anything.

Tzarik, near the edge of the crowd, saw the man who'd torn the scream from the woman. His horse, limping madly, veered sideways and slipped. Tzarik leapt down from his horse to see if the man was alive. Blood soaked his face and poured from his mouth; he was missing both his hands at the wrists. Sybal jogged up behind him.

The man stammered, crying in Xian.

"What's he saying?" Tzarik barked. "These wounds are fresh."

Sybal homed in on the man's babbling. She could hardly make out his words through the gasping and panicked constriction in his throat. The harder she looked, the more she recognized him.

"This is the man from the river," she whispered to Tzarik. "The one who berated you for saving his mother."

Tzarik gently reached down and lifted the man into the crook of his arm to better hear his fading voice. The man hardy whispered now.

"Has he seen Wushito?" Tzarik asked. He gently pressed his hand to the bleeding wound on the man's head.

Sybal asked him softly, speaking slowly so the man could understand. "Did Wushito do this to you?"

"Yes," the man gasped, the bloody stumps of his arms shaking so much he flecked blood onto Tzarik's face. "Chased us into the water. Killed everyone. They told me to find a messenger for the Di-Huan. Wu-Zhiang killed her!" he wailed, showing his missing teeth. "My love, my flower!"

"It was Wushito," Sybal relayed to Tzarik. "They sent him as a warning."

The man opened his eyes, tears streaming down his wrinkled cheeks. "Father?"

Sybal stopped. The man's eyes locked onto Tzarik.

"I'm sorry, father," the man bawled. "I let mother die. Your grandchildren wept. I had to let her go. It was the will of the river, just like you taught me."

"What's he saying?" Tzarik asked softly, keeping a steady gaze on the man. He didn't know what the man said, but he knew a death stare.

Sybal's heart warmed at his sudden giving nature. "He thinks you're his father. He's apologizing for letting his mother die in the river."

Gently, Tzarik laid his hand against the side of the man's face. He asked Sybal for the words and repeated after her in Xian.

"I forgive you," he whispered.

The man's eyes widened and his near-toothless smiled relaxed. He leaned into Tzarik's arm, the energy leaving his limbs.

"Thank you, father," the man sighed. "I'll find her. Keep her company for you."

With a final breath, the man closed his eyes, a grin frozen on his face.

Sybal sniffed, running her arm under her nose to stop the sudden emotion leaking from her. Never in a thousand and one years would she have thought Tzarik capable of what she'd just witnessed.

"That was a good thing you did," she said through a sob. She knelt and folded the man's arms over his chest.

"But we can't stay. He needs to be seen on the road." Tzarik's voice came thick and he didn't let Sybal see his face. "Let's move these people out."

LIGHTNING ARCHED over the palace when Sybal and Tzarik reached it on their return journey. Frozen to the bone, Sybal shook from the cold and audibly roared in gladness when they saw the palace. Hoping for word once they were inside, she clicked her tongue to move her horse along, but it stopped, whining and tossing its head.

"What is it?" she asked. Beside her, Tzarik froze. She looked up.

Standing between the two open doors of the palace, flapping in the violent wind, was a beast gazing directly at them. The thing appeared to be horned, with antlers arching up majestically out of a lion-like mane. Tzarik noted its distinctly cloven hooves. Fangs protruded from its grimacing lips.

"Is that...?" Sybal breathed, her breath coming out in a thick cloud before her.

The monster walked towards them slowly. When it passed through the one torch standing lit outside the palace, its eyes came into view. They were not slitted monster eyes, but round. Sybal almost felt as if the thing would open its mouth and speak to them. When its hoof stepped off the stones, a cloud appeared under it. It stepped onto this cloud rather than crush the grass beneath its feet.

Tzarik picked up his small crossbow.

You need not fear me, Tzarik, a voice said from the very rain around them. *Sybal, your guilt is just behind you. Though you be rightly judged, I take your fear upon myself.*

Without warning, a wave of warmth pulsed once through Sybal. Her heart slowed its beating and her breathing came easier. "What are you?" she asked softly, knowing the thing would hear her anyway.

I am a messenger. It tilted its head, pointing its horns towards them. *I only come when a great ruler has ascended to Tiang. I am here on his behalf.*

"The Di-Huan?" Tzarik asked. He scanned the empty front courtyard. "I knew it looked too empty. What's happened?"

The creature turned and walked to the wide doors, opening the way for them. The clouds continued to appear under his hooves over the grass. *Hiro needs strong arms to hold him up,* the creature said gently. *He cannot take the throne.*

"Is it true?" Sybal asked. She turned her head to face Tzarik. "The balance."

Her mentor winced, shaking his head.

You face me, and yet you do not believe the White Dragon will put this country asunder if his rules are not upheld? Do you not slay ghosts, Runer? Have you not killed the undead? Why do you put aside Xia's safety so easily?

Sybal felt the rebuke on Tzarik's behalf as if the creature had said it to her. She opened her mouth.

You cannot always speak for him, Sybal, the creature interrupted. *Tzarik lives in a world he denies. He fights against it as if it, too, may be slain.*

"I don't deny anything," Tzarik said defiantly.

Then undo what has been done. That is the message I bring. It turned, walking up into the air over invisible stairs towards the palace doors. *I have faith in you, Runer. Accept it before it's too late.*

Just as mysteriously as it appeared, the creature vanished inside the palace's swinging door. Sybal jerked her horse around, looking for it. "Do you think it told the truth? Do you think the Di-Huan is dead?"

When Tzarik didn't reply, she turned to face him again. The look from before, when he'd held the dying man, returned to his face, but darker. His eyes looked far away, and an uncommon weakness weighed on his shoulders.

"I'm here," she said, not able to think what else to say. "We have to go in. We cannot let ShanBao and his generals hurt them anymore."

CHAPTER 24
THE HALLOW CITY

THEY FOLLOWED THE FAINT, EVER VANISHING GLOW OF THE creature into the palace. Its hooves did not clack against the hard floor. They lost sight of it after a few twists and turns only to be greeted by a guard.

"Runers!" she gasped upon seeing them. "We were hoping you'd come back." Her eyes were red and large, dark circles spreading from them. "Hiro is destroyed. His father has..." she gasped, trying to stop a sob. "And Yui!"

Sybal approached the guard. "Just speak plainly. What has happened? Where is the Di-Huan?"

She pointed to a hallway that led to a wing of the palace and some stairs they had not been up. "His chambers. Both are inside."

The last of the glowing light vanished into a circular doorway with sliding canvas doors on the other side of a bridge. A tall square tower waited in the darkness.

Tzarik hesitated when he got to the edge of the balcony where it turned into the bridge. Up here, the wind whistled between the monster-themed gutters. Below, the movement of people came distant and far away. He looked down and caught torchlight, the glint of rising sunlight off spears and swords. If the talking beast at the gate hadn't eaten the last of his courage, crossing this high bridge did.

Without a word of shame, Sybal gently put her hand at the

small of his back and pushed him forward. She walked in sync with him. Together, they crossed over into the Di-Huan's wing of the palace. Just as they reached the other side of the bridge, energetic shouts rose up below.

Inside, only one standing torch lit the vast bedchamber. It stood over a low lounge where the Di-Huan lay, his eyes closed. Beside it, kneeling with his head touching the floor, was Hiro. He mumbled rapidly, his voice cracking every other word.

"What's he saying?" Tzarik whispered to Sybal.

She sniffled, wiping a tear away. "I'm not sure. It's ancient Xian. Probably a prayer for his soul."

In the presence of a dead man, Tzarik became emboldened. This was his business. He walked behind Hiro and looked down at the Di-Huan. His flesh looked like wax, the skin around his eyes dark purple. Even from a glance, he saw the limbs would be stiff if he moved them. A weight settled onto his rib cage and he allowed it. Emotion pricked at the corners of his eyes. The ruler of Xia had been a good man.

"Hiro," he said, forcing himself to be gentle with the weeping prince. "How did this happen? We've not been gone a week."

He expected Sybal to kneel next to the prince to comfort him, but she stood her ground behind him, letting him take the lead.

After one more low bow to the ground, he sat up, closing his eyes so he couldn't see his dead father. "He went out looking for Yui after you left. I told him not to. The servants—even the guards —could do that."

"She's missing?" Tzarik asked.

Hiro nodded. "Soon after you brought the news of Jin. She fled in sorrow." He glared down at the golden floor. "I should have comforted her! But I abandoned her for duty."

"You couldn't have known." Sybal's voice came from behind,

thick with anguish. "You had to save the people closest to the palace."

Grief twisted Hiro's face. "Father knew this rain was her doing. He understood the obstacles it would create for warfare. She had to be stopped."

"How is this rain her doing?" Tzarik asked, guarding his tone to not show the urgency building up.

The prince's face twisted in a kind of jealous, hateful grimace. "Her mother's blood. She'll flood all of Xia in her sorrow. Father loved her, but she killed him." He sobbed and gripped his father's pale hand.

"Rain fever," Sybal offered softly.

"Yes." He raised his head, tears glinting in the torchlight. "The healer tried his best, but father spent too long exposed." He choked. "But he didn't know she was gone."

Tzarik caught the hidden meaning in the prince's inflection. "Where did she go?"

"Most likely to their meeting spot to mourn."

Hiro reached into his robes and produced a clay cylinder. Unscrewing one end, he tipped out a small scroll and handed it to the Runer. Tzarik took it and passed it to Sybal. Her eyes zipped down and up the parchment, her glare deepening the more she read.

"Wu-Zhiang," she growled. "You were right. Yui went to that desolate temple to weep. The general came upon her and took her to the Hallow City." She cleared her throat and steeled herself. "Says they are not bargaining. It's not a ransom. They know what she is and are trading her to Sharar—for his promise of taking the Royal City. It's a very bold threat. They're not afraid."

Hiro shifted to sitting onto the ground, moving his knees off to the side. He still held his father's hand. "I have to save her. You don't understand what she can do."

"We do," Tzarik cut in, saving the prince from having to try to explain, or worse, come up with a lie to tell them. "It was our promise to go. You have to stay here. You cannot leave this city without its ruler. That's you now."

Despondent, Hiro let out another sigh. "It's not. I am not dragon-touched."

Before he replied, Tzarik remembered the creature that had greeted them. There were higher powers at work that he didn't understand. Even if he doubted it, the Xians did not.

"I think if you take the authority as a way of saving Xia, the Dragon will understand," he said hopefully. "Intent is often known to these kinds of beings." He grimaced inwardly at reasoning so foolishly. "You believe you have the right and the responsibility to rule and care for Xia. So do it."

Only partly convinced, the prince stood up with difficulty. He teetered on his bruised and unfeeling legs. "I'm trapped. I can't argue now."

"Not trapped. Given an opportunity," Sybal said from the darkness behind them. "We will get Yui back."

The struggle inside Hiro's mind appeared on his face. He glared down at his hands as he came to terms with whatever raged in his head. "Very well. Rest before you go. Finding a way into the Hallow City won't be hard, I suspect. It's made to be entered. Getting out once you're inside is another matter."

⌘

SYBAL WANTED to jump into action right away, as always, but Tzarik insisted on resting. He'd spent himself more than once racing over the mountainous continent and knew they could not attempt to go behind enemy lines in any state less than perfect. He made her eat, sleep, and even train before preparing to leave. In that time, the Royal City turned from a golden jewel to the hub for the armies gathering against Wushito. Raids on roads happened every day, on both sides, as each tried to disrupt the other's supplies. Reports of battles came almost every day. Couriers near the stormy shores were intercepted, their goods stolen. Small bands of resistance sprouted up in smaller settlements. Travel quickly turned dangerous.

The Runers packed their saddlebags and were walking their laden horses out of the stables when a savage call and reply chorus rose up from the training yard. As the chanting came closer, the army of warriors present stopped their simulated combat to look towards the ruckus. The gates swung open to admit a black-clad horde. Some wore fur-lined helmets with sharp metal points and primitive garments of animal skins. Others carried banners from farther provinces. The largest group donned black armor and terrifying home-made masks, the House Xiaoh symbol worked onto their breastplates.

Sybal stopped to take in the ragtag army. The front mass, from Wu-Tang, shouted a phrase and those behind called it back. They marched in time to their calls, raising their spears and other cruel-looking weapons in beat. To the side rode Zhen.

"What is this?" Tzarik asked, tightening the last belt around his new horse's middle.

"The militia," the commander replied. "Or as they call themselves: the Vandauls. No army is complete without a terrifying, well-mixed army of rogues."

"They are regular citizens?" Sybal asked in awe. "They look so fierce."

Zhen nodded. "The Vandauls do not adhere to the codes of the assembled army. They are...wild. For lack of a better word."

"Where do they come from?"

"Everywhere!" a man leading the army answered. He pulled

his monstrous mask-shaped helmet off his head and grinned mani-cally down at the Runers. A scar ran from his hairline, over his left eye, and down to his chin. Other parts of his face were covered in black war paint. "Kei Lu Xiaoh," he said, offering a bow. "At your service, Runers."

Sybal's face fell and she turned away.

"Any relation to the warlord Whoang Xiaoh?" Tzarik asked, knowing full well anyone from Wu-Tang most likely bore the name.

The Vandaul man arched his brow and smiled curiously. "My older cousin by a decade. I wear our family name proudly, no matter the sins of my kin. You can bear that, eh, Runer? My Vandauls will be the fiercest in our history. We will take back what Wushito has stolen from Xia. A dragon-touched will rule us once more." He turned and called back to his irregular horde.

They shouted a bloodcurdling reply.

He turned back to the Runers and smiled. "I am Xiaoh, and I will defend Xia." He pulled the terrifying helmet back over his face and kicked his horse into a run.

Zhen shrugged when he caught the grimace on Sybal's face. "House Xioah is powerful. They are bread for war. This militia is not bound by honor since they believe their fight is just and true no matter what violence they commit. We need them."

"I suppose," Sybal said, nodding.

"At least they have a chance," Tzarik mused. He pulled himself up onto his horse. "If we're not back in five days, attack with full force. You'll have nothing to lose if Sybal and I don't return, and you may as well throw everything you have into stop-ping ShanBao."

Zhen nodded.

Leading Sybal out of the Royal City, Tzarik followed the map Zhen had given him to find the safest route up to the Hallow City.

It would take them at least a day if they hurried. Unsure what they were up against, they began to prepare for whatever lay in wait from Wushito.

⁂

When they came to the place Zhen had marked, they didn't need to check to see if they'd found the right place. This area of Xia, though high up on the continent, sprawled out in flat, marshy prairies. Mountains, like pieces on a game board, stood up as if dropped by accident into the marsh. Tall, they looked impossible to climb, going almost as straight as pillars with an ocean-like wave at their tips. In the middle of this prairie stood a single mountain taller than the rest. Long and thin, it was almost a perfect triangle, with a great hole in the center making a gateway hundreds of feet high. No city or even a village presented itself. They marched around the ominous but beautiful area for some time, looking for what they must be missing.

"I don't see anything," Sybal growled from where they crouched under thick leathery foliage. "We've circled the area Zhen marked twice."

Tzarik shared her frustration. The day grew colder, and the rain did not cease. The reed hats they had been given kept the rain mostly off and helped them blend in, but still the rain soaked through their cloaks and filled their boots. Tzarik pulled out the map again and looked. It showed the impossibly curved mountains of the flat lands they'd ascended to and one that stood alone.

Forgoing their cover, Tzarik guided his horse close to the looming gateway of stone. Lightning arched over it, vanishing behind it. As it did, he saw it dip below the opening, then vanish behind something not there.

"Sybal!" he shouted. "Come here." She had good eyes. He

narrowed his own, blinking. He thought maybe he had something in his eye, blurring what they saw through the opening. "Stand beside me and look directly through," he said, pointing.

Joining him by his side, she squinted. "Oh, it's like a smudge on a window." She gasped as lightning arched over them again, came down partway through their line of vision through the opening, then disappeared just like before. Her eyes widened and her breath caught.

"You saw it, then?" Tzarik asked. "It's there. We just can't see it." Even as he spoke, the sound of a distant, thick brass bell rang out. He'd heard it before while looking out from the balcony of ShanBao's towering estate. "It's there. I hear it."

"How...?" Sybal mumbled, kicking her horse gently to move closer.

"Careful!" Tzarik warned.

"Trust me, I am," she called back. She stopped just outside the cave-like entrance, looking to the fields beyond the mountain gate. "I hear wind in eves," she called back. "Can they hear me?" Without waiting, she reached her hand out as if to push a door open. "Ah!"

Rushing to her side, Tzarik witnessed her hand vanish. She pulled it back, examining it. He followed her lead. As his hand passed under the mountain, it disappeared into a faint blur. He felt nothing.

"We go in?" Sybal asked.

"We go in," Tzarik confirmed.

Clicking his tongue, Tzarik urged his horse under the mountain arch. It pushed its ears back and snorted deep in its barrel-like chest, but moved at its rider's bidding. Sybal's horse responded similarly. Tzarik expected a jolt, a buzzing sensation—something to indicate they'd passed under some sort of metaphysical barrier, but nothing happened besides the sudden appearance of what they had been searching for.

Just as they passed through, the city appeared. A sloping, basin-like hill half encompassed a magnificent turreted city atop a rocky rise. It looked as if the White Dragon himself had placed the city there after forming the defensive earthen structures. Thick blue waterfalls cascaded from underneath it, washing down into the marshy prairies below. Smaller than the Royal City, it still glittered like a golden spear, imposing and resplendent despite the rain.

"It's beautiful," Sybal breathed. "But we came in the front door." She jerked the reins, forcing her horse to move. She trotted to a grove of spire-like boulders and small trees to hide from the eyes of the Reavers above them.

"We have to cover at least a third of a mile of open marsh to get there," Tzarik mused, stowing the map and pulling his cloak tight around his shoulder.

"Could we make our way around the back?" she asked.

Her mentor rubbed his stubbly chin, eyes tracing every eve and wall of the city before them. "We don't know what that looks like. It could be a solid wall of earth."

Without warning, Sybal slid of her horse and crouched. "Damn, I think he saw me!"

Her instincts were sharp, alert. He didn't feel the pricking in his veins until she moved. His white blood rushed and he dove down as well, taking his small recurve bow off the saddle and nocking an arrow to it. Without speaking, he asked with his eyes where the one who'd spotted them had gone.

Jerking her head slightly, she pointed left. He peered through the branches of their minuscule cover. The monstrous helmets of two Wushito generals were easily discernible from the white cloaks of three Reavers. But these Reavers were bound to stakes surrounded by pyres upon wooden wagons. One was Xian and the other two were pale white men from the west. Tzarik recognized the generals as Yasuke and Zhiang.

"They're not on the front lines?" Sybal asked.

She was right, that was strange. Whatever was happening here must be more important to ShanBao and Wushito.

"Stop!" Zhiang ordered. "No more burnings outside. If the lowlands catch a whiff of us executing our own, we lose the upper hand."

Sybal translated quickly for Tzarik. She stopped when the Xian Reaver screamed and spat at Yasuke as he came closer.

"They're defectors!" she said, gasping. "Reavers who have turned against Wushito." She turned to Tzarik. "Why would they kill their own?"

On the surface it made little sense. "It's better to have fewer numbers you can trust entirely then an army that can turn against you. That's what ShanBao would think, no matter the Wushito lives lost."

Her shoulders fell. "I thought they were all evil."

Tzarik scoffed with a smirk. "That sounds like something I would say. Remember, some of them didn't have a choice about being drafted into Wushito. And perhaps they all don't hate as ShanBao does. Or crave the power he does."

Sybal smiled down at her mentor. "I never thought I'd hear you speak like that."

"Did I say something wrong?" he asked.

Still smiling warmly, she shook her head. The moment was cut short as the cries of the Reavers suddenly erupted in flames. Zhiang slithered back, torch in hand.

"There is no leaving Wushito!" she shouted at them. Spitting on the charring corpses, she tossed the torch onto them. "Take them to the tower." She lurched forward and slithered to the city.

Alone, Yasuke stood back and watched his fellow warriors burn. Sybal elbowed Tzarik hard in his side. He met her eyes and saw they had the same idea. He nodded. They drew their scimitars and softly made their way out of their cover. The roaring and snapping of the pyres covered their footfalls. Tzarik stepped out before Yasuke just as Sybal placed the wide curve of her blade against his throat, looming over him from behind.

"Unnecessary," Yasuke said, sighing before Tzarik could threaten him. "I've already given up my right to live as Wushito by aiding you. What's the harm in once more?" His red fur didn't stand on end, his ears didn't go back. He showed no fear or concern.

"We're here for Yui," Tzarik said, still not letting his guard down. The Reavers knew tricks to soothe their prey into a false sense of security. This could be one of those tactics. "Where is she?"

"In the tower," he said. His emotionless eyes zoned out to nothing in the direction of the city. "I'll take you there."

"Why?" Sybal hissed, pressing her sword down onto his neck.

The general's eyes fell. "Because I don't believe in slaughtering my kin over a dispute of ancient law. Unlike ShanBao, I don't care to bring Xia into the modern world. There was nothing wrong with our system."

"You're giving up?" Tzarik asked.

"No." Yasuke took Sybal's hand in his and removed her blade, walking back towards the now smoldering carts. "If I do, I lose my honor and cannot enter the afterlife. In your world, you'd be called in to slaughter my spirit—left behind. In this world, Zhiang or some other desperate Reaver would take my immortal soul, banishing it to the darkness where all killed spirits go. So I must die with honor away from those who would take my soul to the crypt, keeping me from being born again."

Sybal touched Tzarik's arm. Her other hand went to the back of her neck, pulling her thick braid over her shoulder. "The brand," she whispered.

"What brand?"

She took his hand, pulled his glove off, and laid his hand on the back of her neck. His fingers traced the mark left from their first hunt on Xia, when the monster had possessed Sybal. Jin had pressed something to the back of her neck, removing the spirit.

Sybal went on, "Remember the talisman he used on the northern isle?"

He nodded, not removing her hand from where his palm lay against her neck. Gently, he turned her and inspected the mark. Sharp Xian letters stood out from her soft skin in a perfectly burned script.

"This had to be something like that," she mused.

Yasuke winced in sympathy. "It must have hurt to have the spirit ripped from you in that way. I am sorry." He reached onto his belt and pulled out a thick canvas talisman with a red border and black lettering inside it. He didn't speak, unwilling to voice the secrets of Wushito.

"They're not vanquished, are they?" she asked, putting her hand over Tzarik's. "The monsters. You don't kill any of them. They're just trapped." A shiver took her entire body. "The crypt."

"Sharar's power to control monsters." Tzarik glared into Yasuke's eyes. "You'll help us enter?" he asked.

"No," Yasuke repeated. "*You* will help *me* enter."

CHAPTER 25

The Serpent's Kiss

MAKING A TEMPORARY HITCH OUT OF THE ROPE THEY carried in their saddlebags, the Runers used their horses to pull the charred wagons towards the city. Yasuke instructed them on where to take them.

"There is a low circular tower just below the city," he said, leading them under his protection. "That is where we dump the bodies. Take them there and do the job in case anyone sees you. There are two entrances to the tower: one is strictly for entering, the other for exiting. Leave your horses at the bottom of the entrance and walk the wagons up yourselves. This way your horses will be outside for you to escape. Follow the clean path off the tower and into the city. Keep your heads down; your eyes give you away. Normally a Reaver would spot you, but today they will not. We are...spread thin. Ascend the city roads to the tower. You cannot mistake which path will lead you there. When you arrive, the guard will be waiting for you to take Yui to another level. He'll know what it means."

"But we won't?" Sybal asked.

Yasuke shook his head. "Leave. I cannot promise you will get out, but you can run."

"We need one more thing," Tzarik put in, knowing he pushed his luck. "The book."

At this, the general almost laughed. "Don't play the fool, Runer. Take what you can and be gone. Put the gini on the throne and let Xia fight for its peace."

So the general still held on to his loyalty.

"The Di-Huan will not rest until Wushito is under control," Tzarik warned. "This war could go on for years."

"I do not doubt that's what they want," Yasuke agreed. "But you know what they say about snakes, Runer?"

They didn't reply. He waited for the general to go on.

"Cut off the head." Yasuke met Tzarik's icy gaze.

He sensed right away the general had a hidden meaning in his words, but he didn't elaborate. Yasuke pulled away.

"Follow this path. It will take you to the tower." With a swift kick to his horse's sides, the Masahk general vanished up the road into the city.

"Do we trust him?" Sybal asked cautiously. "Or do we try to find the book?"

Unsure, he scanned the city, spotted the tallest tower, then looked back to Sybal. "I'm not sure. Our armies seem to be getting the upper hand. We have the militia now and reserves. We've rescued refugees from the lowlands."

He hummed in thought.

"Wushito could be weaker than we think," she offered, leading the way to the area to dump the bodies. "They like to deal in facades, it seems."

"Or they could not care right now," Tzarik thought out loud.

"They could be putting too much trust in Sharar and whatever he's told them he'd do."

"If he's so powerful, why doesn't he just use a wish to take the book?"

"He wouldn't waste a wish."

When they crested the stone ramp into the low round tower, the smell overtook them. Bodies upon bodies piled around the expansive stone floor. Open to the sun—should it stop raining—the bodies lay in various stages of decomposition. Crows and other flesh-eating birds plucked at the eyes and soft belly flesh of the dead.

They didn't wait or halt to take in the horrific scene. They quickly dumped the dead and were ready to follow the second path out when Sybal stopped, bent down, and pulled two cloaks off two non-burnt bodies. These ones had tiny puncture marks on their necks and were stiff as boards.

"This might help us," she said, handing a cloak to Tzarik and swinging the other over her shoulder. As she clasped the Reaver cloak, she studied the corpses she'd taken them off. The bite marks were bigger than snake fangs. Or as big as a man-sized snake. "Wu-Zhiang," she mumbled.

In-step, they marched out and up the path that Tzarik deduced would lead to the tower. Yasuke was right: the tower looked crueler than the others. Sharper, perhaps.

"Walk with purpose," Sybal whispered to him. "Abdul and I used to avoid work when we walked like this." She picked up her pace and set her face in a passive, stony glare. "Made father think we were already on a task and he wouldn't call to us to check the ledger or some other menial task we hated."

Tzarik took one and a half steps for every one of hers to keep up, but followed her lead. The city lay quiet, for the most part. Most of the warriors must have been dispatched over the continent to fight or take provinces under their control. While they crept through the Hallow City, below them, hundreds of Xians were being slaughtered on one another's blades. The flood waters from the storms at sea and the rain drove the masses farther up, ever shrinking the hiding places and good battlegrounds.

The Runers didn't speak, afraid their tongue and accents might alert any who passed. Inside the city, there were very few guards. The warriors they did see trained, or ran to deliver messages. Only once did an older Wushito warrior track them with his eyes. When they rounded a corner, Tzarik dared to glance over his shoulder and was relieved when they were not followed.

Finally, they reached the top of the city to enter the prison.

"No guards?" Sybal asked softly.

Tzarik scanned the area. "They don't expect an attack from the inside. It's hard enough to get into the city; anyone inside is an ally. They don't need guards. They have complete trust in one another."

"Even in the traitors?" Sybal asked.

"It's a good system." Tzarik took the lead, poking his head around corners to find the places of holding. "They will turn on each other for the trust of the ones they think are loyal. No doubt they turn each other in for suspicion. Who needs guards when every person inside the city is one?"

Sybal smiled. "I'm glad you said that. I was starting to think this was too easy."

"Getting out will be the true test." Tzarik stopped. One of the first guards they'd seen all day appeared at the end of a long hall of cells. "We might just have to run if we're spotted."

"Wait." Sybal grabbed him by the hood of the Reaver cloak and pulled him back, out of the hall of cells. She gently pushed him up against the wall, hands tight on his shoulders. "I have to tell you something."

"Now?" he hissed, brows contracting in anxious fervor.

Her simple nod prompted him to control himself. He'd let her speak, but she'd better do it fast.

She sighed and smiled. Something in her smile was off, melancholy. "What you did, warning Wu-Tang all those months ago, was good. You did a good thing. I'm sorry I was angry and lashed out. I'm sorry I've been difficult to control and teach. But it's only because I've been trying to figure you out, and you haven't made it easy for me. You've changed so much since we met. I've loved watching you struggle to make decisions you wouldn't have before. I know you hate every country that's not Al'Myrah, but you've risked your life for Xia, and I'm..." Her voice caught. "I'm proud of you."

Like when danger appeared behind him, his sulfates twinged. What was she saying? Something wasn't right. He sensed danger.

"Sybal, what—" he started, but she pressed her hand over his mouth.

She closed her eyes, shaking her head before pressing her forehead against his. "When we get back to safety in the palace, with Yui, rest. Come to my room the night after." Her eyes flew open, bright. Her face glowed with a grin.

Releasing him, she marched around the corner. Tzarik's head spun, filled with everything she'd said. He still felt her hands on his arms. Despite the pleasant wave rising inside, the danger didn't relax. Grappling his mind back to the present, he joined her. Striding down the hall of cells, they passed the one with Yui inside. Fortunately, she looked fine. She sat straight, cradling her belly, glaring defiantly out through the bars. Tzarik figured Sharar had given instructions that she should go untouched. He needed her strong, alive. Willing.

Sybal spoke Xian with commanding resonance to the sentry. "The general says we are to take Princess Yui to another level."

"You?" the sentry breathed, coming out of his stiff pose.

Both Runers flexed their fingers as their guards went up.

Bowing, the sentry said, "I have waited for this day." He drew his sharp single-edged sword.

Tzarik took a step back, preparing to lunge into combat.

Gripping it with the point towards his chest, the sentry's face went slack. He backed up to the wide-open round window and stood tall.

"May the Dragon smile upon you. And may my soul find its way to his golden halls."

"Wait!" Sybal reached out.

Faster than she could move, the sentry shoved his own sword through the center of his chest. With it protruding out his back, he dropped the cell keys from his silken belt. Then, with a lightning-fast slice, he cut his throat. His blood shot out in a spray, misting the walls. He tipped backwards and fell through the circular opening.

"Shit," Tzarik growled. "They'll see his body."

"Why?" Sybal said. "Why would he do that?"

Tzarik snatched up the keys. "I can't say." The guard had done what he'd thought was right: helped to save his country and died by his own blade for honor, or so Tzarik assumed. He would never understand...

They ran to Yui's cell. The princess raised her dark brows defiantly.

"I will not come with you. You'll have to kill me before I subject my gift to that Al'Myrahn cu—"

"It's us!" Sybal cut in, flinging the door wide.

Tzarik pricked his ears but didn't hear any commotion yet. Yasuke was right: getting out would be the hard part.

"Sybal!" Yui shrieked, jumping to hug the lady Runer. "You came for me?" she sobbed.

"Later," Tzarik snapped, prying the two women apart. "We have to—"

The hollow, ominous brass gong of a bell sounded.

"Run," he finished.

THE TRIO GALLOPED BACK down the stone pathways, slipping and tumbling as they came to sudden halts to hide or leap down onto the sloping roofs to cut across a street. Yui panted, sweat dripping down her brow and mixing with the still pouring rain.

"She can't run like this," Sybal whispered as they scanned the streets below for a way out. "Take her. Use the walking paths and go out through the carrion tower."

"We'll be spotted!" Tzarik argued. He trained his eyes on Sybal. Her eyes focused on something far away. He snapped his head to try to see whatever had caught her attention, but it vanished before he could. The sulfates warned him again of danger, though he couldn't see it.

"I'll go one way," she said. "They'll chase me. I'm easier to see, bigger. I can distract them in their own tongue."

"Split up?" Yui said, choking.

"Tzarik." Sybal grabbed him roughly by the front of his leather armor. "Get her to the palace. She can end this before more people die."

Between the princess's frightened and understanding sobs, Tzarik gathered the sensations pulsating under his flesh. "Sybal," he asked gravely, "what are you planning to do?"

She glared down at him. "Trust me."

When he decided to heed her plan, every muscle in his body clenched. "I'll be back for you once Yui is outside the stone portal. If I don't see you there, I'm coming in."

She nodded. "That's fair. I know you like to leave me behind."

Clasping his shoulder in camaraderie, she nodded fiercely and took off.

"Will she be safe?" Yui said, weeping.

He didn't know. The soldier taking his own life played over in his head as he watched the straw hat covering a thick blonde braid disappear into the city.

"Let's move."

The effects of Sybal's plan moved into action right away. Splitting his disguise, he gave Yui the Reaver cloak and kept the reed hat for himself. With the few inside moving quickly to investigate the dead soldier and others rushing to search the streets, they slipped into the carrion tower almost easily and were outside the round portal within minutes.

"Yui," Tzarik ordered, heaving her up onto his glimmering horse. "Ride to the palace. Your brother is there and is waiting for you."

"No, I want to wait for Sybal!" she begged, choking on her own sobs again. "I have to see her to safety. I owe her everything!" Her hysterics almost made her incomprehensible.

"Go!" he shouted. "We'll be right behind you. She's on her way out."

The princess shook her head, her sheets of smooth black hair dancing. "She wanted to fight General Zhiang, I know it. She hates her."

Would Sybal chase a personal vendetta at this moment? Did her temper and impulsivity still overpower her rational thinking? Tzarik heard her words in his head again about how proud she was of him. How sad she'd said those words. Almost like she wished she had grown and changed as much as he had. Almost like she'd said goodbye. As if she'd known she'd fail.

With a scream, Tzarik smacked his horse's backside and it

bolted of into the marsh towards the rising center. Steeling himself, he went back through the portal. If she'd stuck to her word, Sybal would be running to him.

"Runer."

His head snapped to the voice addressing him. ShanBao stood with Yasuke and a few other warriors at his side, arms crossed. The Wushito master looked oddly disappointed.

He drew his scimitar and flew into a flurry of defensive maneuvers against the general and the warriors while ShanBao stood back and watched. Despite helping them not long ago, Yasuke mercilessly brought his long thin sword down around the Runer in a hail of blades. The other warriors jabbed and kicked at him, causing minor distractions.

Using the terrain, Tzarik managed to get away from the onslaught, if only just a moment. Expanding energy to leap up and scale a few rocky ledges, he put distance between himself and the attackers. But when he scaled another few yards, he turned to see ShanBao behind him. The shock rocked him to his core and he lost his footing. ShanBao flicked a wooden cylinder from his belt and it shot out, expanding into a staff. He twirled it once to grip it, then spun in a spurt of movements to drive Tzarik back. Something, like a ghostly version of ShanBao, shot out to the side.

Tzarik let his eyes move from his target just a second to follow the thing. He'd seen something like it before; running in a large arch around him, the shadow version of ShanBao dashed to the side. If he hadn't seen the clone shoot out from the original, he would have been fooled into following it. This shadow tactic seemed to be common among Wushito. Tzarik ignored it but fell behind ShanBao's strikes.

Before he could gather his strength and bearings to jump, ShanBao had him at the edge of the ledge. The shadow's purpose wasn't for him to chase it: it was just a distraction. He fended off a few quick blows, shocked his scimitar didn't cut through the staff, before ShanBao faked to his left then cracked his head hard. He kicked Tzarik square in the chest, sending him tumbling down into the circle of warriors below.

Landing hard on his back, all the wind exploded from his chest in a white light of pain. A trident-like spear pinned his sword hand down into the wet ground. Yasuke stomped his booted foot down hard onto the Runer's other hand.

Arms splayed, trapped, Tzarik panted up into the rain, looking for any weakness in his enemies. His eyes also darted around, looking for Sybal, listening for any sign.

ShanBao leapt down and landed softly, hardly making a splash. His dark shadow followed him. It mirrored his every move perfectly "I have someone looking for you, Runer," he said, retracting the staff and replacing it on his belt. "In our negotiations, he has asked a heavy price, but *you* cost me nothing."

Motioning to Yasuke and the others, they hauled him to his feet, quickly binding his hands behind his back. ShanBao ripped the reed hat from his head.

"You made this your war," he said calmly. "And now you will suffer for it."

⟲⟳

SHARAR HAD to be close to the Hallow City. They'd made it this far. Wu-Zhiang was accounted for—Sybal could see her snake-like body from her perch on a turret. ShanBao was on the move; he'd vanished farther down the city just a moment ago. Yasuke wouldn't stop her. This was her chance. She had an open window to find Sharar and put an end to him and his plan. And the viper general.

The rain pattered loudly, making it almost impossible to hear steps below underneath her reed hat. She skittered over the rooftops towards the city square where she'd seen Wu-Zhiang. Tzarik might be waiting for her, but she could do one last good thing. The general wouldn't be looking for danger right now, she'd be looking to the perimeter for fleeing intruders. With a few more careful leaps and slinking through some shadowy alleys, she finally peeked into the square.

Her heart stopped. The square was filled with X-shaped crosses stabbed into the ground. Blood mingled with the rain, running down the posts and onto the white stone, staining it dark red. Another place for public executions of dissenters. Scaling a wall, she climbed up to get a better view of Wu-Zhiang. The general slithered to a set of six warriors who spoke in soft, rapid Xian. As she received their news, the end of her white tail twitched in rage. This was Sybal's chance.

Taking her bow, Sybal nocked an arrow to it and aimed. The general's elaborately decorated hair covered most of her neck, but if Sybal judged the shot right, she could cut through it, killing her swiftly.

Sybal took a breath and held it. Then she released the arrow.

Just as she did, Wu-Zhiang dodged aside like a viper. The arrow lodged itself into the eye socket of one of the warriors standing behind her. Seeing this, the general spit venom and turned around, shocked at the attack. Apparently she hadn't dodged the arrow, she'd moved for some other reason and the black shaft had taken her by surprise.

Seeing Sybal scramble on the rooftop, Wu-Zhiang called for more warriors. Sybal had expected this and waited for them to disperse in the search before confronting Wu-Zhiang herself. She slid down, stowed her bow, drew her scimitar, and walked quietly into the square.

The general's back faced her when she emerged. "Face me, Zhiang," she said in a monotone.

The viper turned, still shaken. Her slitted purple eyes narrowed at the Runer. "Have I offended you, Runer?" she whispered, licking her lips. "What is this vendetta you have against me?"

They circled each other.

"You think I'm weak," Sybal hissed. "You threatened Tzarik. You helped ShanBao kill Jin."

The Masahk's tongue flicked out and in between her fangs. "I think you are placing more blame on me than there is, Runer woman."

Somewhere in the last few seconds, Wu-Zhiang had drawn two blades. Gently, taking her time, she placed one handle inside the other and twisted them together, making a double-bladed weapon. Sybal noted the purple sheen to the blades and cruel-looking sigils dancing down the edge of one. For a moment, she wondered if they were made of a special metal like the glimmering orichalcum she and Tzarik used. From the way it sat on the metal, it looked more like a coating. It matched the purple of her eyes.

Taking a breath, Sybal slid her back foot out to balance herself and launched into a tight-knit dance around the towering Masahk. Zhiang spun her two blades like a staff, deflecting every blow. Using her long tail, she lashed at Sybal and hit her hard across her back.

Sybal fell forward only to have to redirect herself to avoid the blade. This landed her in a pile of snake coils. The Masahk slithered around Sybal, entangling her in her snake body. With the ruckus from the fight, a few warriors appeared, ready to defend their general.

"No fear," Wu-Zhiang called to them. She grinned wickedly.

"Sybal?" She squeezed the Runer hard. "I have a proposition for you."

With a flick of her wrist, Sybal quickly drew buhkar. Her body turned to black mist and slipped through the snake's coils. Wu-Zhiang shrieked in rage and slithered a good distance away to gather herself. Landing, Sybal looked up and smiled.

"Proposition, you say?" She rolled to the left to avoid a swipe from the tail and fired with her one-handed cross bow.

The general dodged it and struck quickly, her mouth gaping open to bit. "Yes, a deal. One two warriors should be able to agree on." She waved her hand in some kind of signal and a rain of arrows clattered around the Runer.

Gasping, Sybal ducked and drew halat, creating a quick barrier to block the arrows. "Fight me with honor!" she shouted. "One on one."

"Come at me, then," the general replied.

Misting to the left and right, drawing halat to block a blow the closer she got, Sybal leapt, misted, then came down with a savage cry. Wu-Zhiang, unable to keep her eyes on the vanishing Runer, cried out when the scimitar came down and cut her skin from her shoulder to her navel. Lashing out with her claws and tail, she drove Sybal back. She clutched her wound.

"I didn't think you'd try to strike me," the general mused.

"Foolish of you." Sybal repositioned herself.

"Same to you." The general smiled. "I know your crime."

Sybal gulped. Her throat was so tight from the horror of giving her crime away so easily that a small sound of fear choked her. Weakness overtook her and her stance went ever so slightly lax.

Seeing the Runer distracted, the viper struck, wrapping her body around Sybal's. With a squeeze, she was able to reach down and tear the leather necklace of runes from her victim's neck.

"No!" Sybal cried, twitching madly to try to catch them.

"Are you trying to die with honor?" General Zhiang reflected. "Kill me and let the runes take you? Oh, how our ways have permeated you." She seized Sybal's neck, her claws digging into her. Below, a Wushito warrior ran and grabbed up the string of runes. Uncoiling from Sybal's body, Wu-Zhiang held her by her neck only.

Feet kicking above the ground, immediate pressure built up in Sybal's face and head. She couldn't breathe. A cough rose up but was squeezed away by the Masahk.

"This is why you never let your crime be known, Runer," Wu-Zhing whispered. She smiled. "I love struggling victims. The fear makes their blood so sweet."

With her other hand she raised her sword, placed it against Sybal's ribs, and drew back quickly.

A strangled cry ripped from Sybal's lips and she kicked. Within a second, the hot sulfates trickled down her side and soaked through her pants, already cold from the rain. Wu-Zhiang threw her to the ground and called the warriors in.

"Give her the punishment your dead brethren deserve!" she ordered.

Panic surged through Sybal as she rolled over onto her knees, searching for her scimitar. She spotted it and reached for it, but stopped when a blow to her wound made light flash before her eyes. Someone kicked her. Hands reached down and tore her armor off. Then a whip lashed over her back. Then again. Four, five, ten times before she collapsed onto the stones. Choking and sobbing in agony, she rolled onto her back when the abuse stopped.

Wu-Zhiang towered over her. She smirked and reached down, grabbing Sybal by her thick braid.

"This is how we treat foreigners who would stand against us!" she shouted. Dragging Sybal by her hair, she slithered across the square, leaving a white trail of sulfates behind. When she reached the base of the cross, she stretched out, raised Sybal onto one of the X-shaped crosses, and fastened her wrists first. "They are no different than those within our own land who would see us fail."

Hanging from her wrists tore agony through Sybal's body. Her feet skirted against the other posts, trying to relieve the pain, but she slipped against the wood in the rain. Gasping, she fell, her head leaning against her arm. Wu-Zhiang took her ankles in her blood-soaked hands and strapped them to either beam.

The rain soaked her aching body. She tried weakly to pull herself free but couldn't. Wu-Zhiang rose up and looked her right in the eye.

"You will not die. But you will wish you could." She struck, fangs clamping down over Sybal's throat.

With the viper's teeth digging into her neck, Sybal's veins slowed the flow of sulfates. Feeling tingled away from her toes and fingers. Her chest grew heavy, stopping her breath. Scanning the highlands, the mountains and hills, she looked for a black form rushing amongst them. He'd come for her. He'd save her.

Wu-Zhiang pulled away, smiling and licking at the white blood. "You taste like the plague," she mused. Her eyes followed Sybal's. Her Runer eyes darted, dancing from unconsciousness, across the horizon.

"He's not coming, Sybal," Zhiang hissed, leaning in and licking the outer rim of her ear, slowly running her hands over Sybal's sides, and digging into her wound on the way down.

Unable to move, Sybal stiffened, falling. The pain in her wrists lessened and the scars on her back stopped screaming. A dense, senseless fog clouded her brain. She felt nothing. Listening, her vision went black.

He wasn't coming. He wouldn't save her.

Chapter 26

Prisoner

Tzarik paced the tiny cell so fast his head swam. It took two large steps or three smaller steps to cover each side, including the one with the door. A perfect square. His heels came to hurt after so many hours; they'd taken his boots. They'd taken everything but his pants and shirt. For some reason, they'd allowed him to keep his runes. He'd thought of misting through the bars, but the long hall of cells was too long and too many sentries patrolled for him to get far. This pacing went on until long after the sunset. He took a break to try to peek out the window above him, but it was too high. It rested against a pathway above at ground level. Water trickled in, making the cell cold and the rocks too wet to lean or sit on.

Before he knew it, a guard brought him water and a bowl of flavorless rice. He tried to check outside, but couldn't see the sky, and the rainclouds made it impossible to gauge where the sun hung. So he paced.

Outside the cell was just a long hallway of stone and more cells. This wasn't the same place Yui had been held. This was darker. Underground. More hidden. Two more guards came and went with water and rice and he assumed two more full days had passed. On the third day, he made up his mind to scream and rattle the bars just to get someone else to come in. But he didn't have to.

The door at the end of the long hall of cells opened and Shan-Bao's slender, silk-clad figure glided down the hall to him.

"Sharar is coming, Runer." The old master clasped his hands behind his back, taking in the Runer's situation. "He told me in detail what he wants to do to you." He took a step closer. "If you speak to me, I may be able to save you great hurt. I cannot stop him, but I could ease the moments."

Tzarik slipped his arms through the bars and leaned against them. "You're supposed to be an educated man, Wu-ShanBao. A master Reaver. How can you not see how Sharar and even your own generals are playing you?"

"I am aware." He tilted his head up in order to look down his nose at Tzarik. "I knew Wu-Zhiang's lust for my position would drive her to seek a deal with the desert man before she even met him. In fact, when I ran into him on a boat—just days before you washed ashore—I knew she'd find him. Go behind my back."

Was he bluffing? Tzarik shifted his bare feet and homed in on ShanBao's face, hunting for any line or crease that would give away his facade.

"And you let her? You even sent her to speak to him alone, before you met." He couldn't keep the curious criticism out of his tone.

ShanBao nodded. "She's ambitious. A loyalist, though. And Yasuke." He closed his eyes and shook his head, his shoulders falling. "I chose my generals badly all those years ago."

"Especially since they'll outlive you," Tzarik added. "Why choose Masahk? Wouldn't one of them take your place when you died? Soon, by the looks of it."

"Juvenile boy." ShanBao slid his hands into his wide sleeves as he so often did. "The Masahk have many valuable properties. Each tribe has its gifts. How old do I look?" He held his arms wide here, the fabric slithering away from his hands.

Genuinely considering the Wushito master, Tzarik tagged tell-tale signs of age with his blue eyes. Creases around his lips, the loose skin on his neck. A droop to his eyelids. But ShanBao stood tall: no slump to his shoulders or back. He didn't favor a certain leg. In fact, he was a beast in combat. As spry as a jaguar. Checking the old man's eyes, he saw age there, but not wariness.

ShanBao smiled. "I see you thinking, Runer. It's wonderful to behold. Did you know your pupils narrow, almost like a cat's, when you look deeper? Must be your sulfates. These are the things Sharar wants to discover in you."

He didn't know. He'd never exactly held a mirror to his own face.

"Fifty?" he threw out casually.

A deep, gentle laugh churned in ShanBao's throat. "Fifty has been and gone, Runer. I remember it fondly. But it just goes to show, you need to know who you surround yourself with. As I said, the Masahk have many uses. But enough about me."

He stepped closer to the cell, his eyes going to the runes under Tzarik's black shirt.

"Why did you come to Xia?"

The question took Tzarik by surprise so much he dropped his arms from where they leaned. "You know. Especially if you've been in discourse with Sharar. He's the reason we ran."

"Only recently has Sharar learned you were not under his pay any longer, Runer," ShanBao said. "Up until not long ago, actually. You had him fooled with that display with the necromancer. He told me," he added when Tzarik twitched in surprise.

"Then why is he here?" Tzarik growled.

The master shook his head. "Let's focus on you. Why did you come to Xia?"

Unsure what ShanBao wanted to hear, Tzarik pushed away

from the bars that separated them and paced back to the stone wall. There, he leaned against it and crossed his arms.

"We have methods of centuries past that can make even the hardest man speak," ShanBao offered in a businesslike manner. "You are not special. You will break under our torture."

Tzarik spit aggressively to the side. "What makes you think I have something to tell you? You can hang me over bamboo, break my thumbs, hold hot iron to my flesh, but I cannot tell you secrets that do not exist."

The old master gently brushed the hairs of his long mustache. "I am no fool, Runer. You must be here for nefarious reasons. Foreigners know not to come to our shores. Only an idiot Runer would willingly walk into a Reaver's nest."

At this, Tzarik smirked. "I think you've answered your own question, Wushito master. Ask anyone. I'm frightfully ignorant."

For just a fleeting second, a shadow of doubt passed over Shan-Bao's face. That brought some comfort. The Wushito master thought two Runers had appeared on his shore for a reason. What could that reason be? Taking what he now knew of Xia, of course it seemed suspicious. They'd come from Al'Myrah; could that mean anything to someone like ShanBao? Was just the fact that two Runers walked unconsciously into the Reaver's web puzzling the old man? It had been an honest mistake. Tzarik hadn't known the Reavers even had a formal place of education. Of course, neither had Sybal.

Sybal! Where was she? Safe? Had she gotten Yui back to the palace? His heart picked up the pace, pulsing under his chest.

"What troubles you, Tzarik?" ShanBao asked. "I can hear your heart."

"Liar," he accused darkly. No way could ShanBao hear that. He must have given it away another way: a twitch of his eyelid, his hand gripping his arm tighter.

Sighing dolefully, ShanBao turned back to the guards at the end of the hall and signaled them forward. Tzarik's heart rate doubled. Positioning his feet wide apart, he prepared for whatever might be coming. ShanBao unlocked the door and the two guards entered. Springing into action, Tzarik took this moment to fight for his freedom. He kicked at one guard and dodged the grip of the other. Rising up from his evasive maneuver, he lunged toward the cell door just to receive a crack on his forehead from ShanBao's staff.

The sunlessness and lack of food hindered his sharp abilities. Moaning and clutching his face, he didn't move as a hand reached down under his shirt and pulled on the leather string of runes. His vision blurred but he fought weakly against the hand. It pulled him by his neck only to drop him against the stone as the cord was cut. The two guards grabbed his ankles and pulled him back into the cell.

"Your interrogation begins now," ShanBao said, slamming the cell door. "I hear Runers are incapacitated without their runes. Let's see how long you can go."

"Forever," Tzarik chuckled, pushing himself up and shaking his head. "We still got away, ShanBao. Yui is free, probably back at the palace already. You've lost."

"Incorrect." ShanBao's tone warbled ever so slightly. "Those damned Vandauls may have the upper hand for now—"

A lightning bolt of relief and joy struck through Tzarik's center at hearing this.

"—but that doesn't spell defeat. The waters are rising. The Shezai Ocean and the Caravan Sea are a raging maelstrom. No help can come from outside. None would anyway."

He faced Tzarik again and the Runer couldn't stop the small flick of his left brow showing his delight at the look on ShanBao's face: doubt.

"There is still a way Wushito ascends," he finished.

"Don't you care about the balance?" Tzarik asked. "What happens when you take over?"

"Ah," ShanBao said, sighing. A smile with sadistic intent gently lifted his lips. "I thought Runers were all cold-hearted criminals. But not you, Tzarik. You care about people and things. Entire countries. I don't." He shook his head. "If what I do sinks this continent, I will not suffer guilt. In fact, thinking about it brings me inexorable delight. To think that I did that, toppled the world's oldest and most revered civilization. I will write the history of Xia; the ink will be the blood of its people." His eyes glassed over and a tear leaked down the side of his cheek. "What enormous calamity one man can bring."

"I never considered myself a good man," Tzarik said. "In fact, I thought I wasn't worthy of life. But up until recently, I had nothing to compare myself to."

ShanBao clicked his tongue, wiping away the lone tear. "Never compare, Runer. It makes fools out of wisemen and monks out of sinners." He glanced toward the window in the cell. "I'll send word for Sharar. He's been busy with your little woman."

As though fire of hell itself sprang up under Tzarik, he flew up from the stone floor and gripped the bars, shaking them in asperity. "Sybal?" he shouted, grinding his teeth so hard it hurt. "Where is she?"

ShanBao jumped back, frightened of the sudden outburst. He pressed his hand to his heart. "Gods, Runer, calm down!" He took a few steady breaths. "She's gone." He stopped, observing the devastating effect those two words had on the man. "I'm sorry I had to be the one to tell you."

The strength in Tzarik's knees left, buckling. He couldn't feel his cold feet. But he couldn't collapse in on himself either. He stood there, eyes wild with rage. "Where is she?" His voice broke as he shouted. "ShanBao! What did he do to her?"

The master took this opportunity to leave, inflicting the psychological damage he couldn't do with threats of torture. Maddened with not knowing if ShanBao had told the truth, Tzarik ripped at the bars, tearing his shoulder joints. With a wild roar, he kicked at the cell door and tore at the hinges. He punched the stone wall until his knuckles bled. He carried on until exhaustion forced him to the ground.

Overcome by the spontaneous outrage, he huffed hard, his back on the floor. Every pulse of his heart cut out his hearing. He'd acted weak and ShanBao had seen it.

I've given up any strength I held in his eyes, he thought. *Now I'm a broken man to him. One to be molded and brought to confess whatever he thinks I'm hiding.*

Gathering his senses, he pulled his knees to his chest and sat up, leaning against the wall. ShanBao could've been lying. He clearly hadn't expected that outburst from him. What did it matter now?

⌒◦⌒

Worry for Sybal stole his sleep for the fourth night in a row. He couldn't pace this time. He needed to keep his heart rate low with the runes gone. He theorized that perhaps his heart could pump the sulfates only so many times before they turned against him. It wasn't a sure thing, but it let him focus on something else besides the helplessness. Hours passed with no sound from the window or the hallway. Perhaps the Hallow City—if he in fact was trapped there—had emptied out over the last few days. ShanBao had lied about having the upper hand. Did that mean he knew things tilted in Xia's favor?

Somewhere, the war raged on. He didn't know how long, or if leaders like Zhen and Hiro were alive. How many had died? How many villages burned, crops destroyed, cities taken under Wushito control? A new kind of helplessness blackened his heart.

The fact that ShanBao didn't care for his country also brought another factor into the equation. Once again, Tzarik cursed sentient kind. One single person could destroy nations. No other monster had that kind of power. Even a djinn needed a human vessel to inflict real harm.

⌇

TZARIK COUNTED two bowls of rice—two days—before his limbs signaled him to the Runer's death setting in. The painful tingles started in his left fingers and quickly spread to his chest over the second day of being without the runes. His legs lost all feeling, but he got a little back by walking slowly around the tiny parameter of his cell.

The next day, his fingernails turned white, as did his feet. A permanent lump choked him whenever he tried to swallow. On the fourth day, he lay down and couldn't get back up. The guard called for ShanBao when this happened and his runes were returned to him. The hateful pricks of feeling slowly came back over a twenty-four-hour period. He breathed easily and eventually paced his cell again. Seeing this, his runes were once again taken. It took four guards to hold him and pry them from him—he refused to give anything away without a fight, but they always won.

This cycle went on for so long he lost count. They'd take the runes, he'd collapse, feeling like death stood just outside the cell door, waiting for him. Once he tried to feign how much pain he was in in order to get them back sooner, but someone counted the days and knew he'd gone longer before. The runes were returned to him after the fourth or fifth day.

Finally, while he lay paralyzed and in agony at the same time, he expected the door to swing open and have the runes placed around his neck. But nothing came. No footsteps, no creaking cell door. Using all his remaining strength, he turned his head to look down the hall.

Nothing.

That was when he noticed a white fog creeping in on his eyesight. The utter agony his body was in didn't compare to the realization that his vision had started to fade. Blinking rapidly, he tried to focus on the door. No amount of fluttering his eyelids produced a clearer image. Breathing hard, he tried to control his fear.

He couldn't hear his labored breathing and gasped deeper.

No sound.

Try as he might, his body refused to listen to his brain's orders and he couldn't lift his hand to his head. Every effort shot through him like white fire. He still faced the door and caught the shadow of the world beyond when it opened.

Despite his waning vision, he knew the black and gold robes that floated down towards him.

"Runer, you look awful," Sharar sang loudly. His voice rang in Tzarik's deaf ears somehow.

He tried to reply, but nothing he said came out from behind his stone-cold lips.

"That was pathetic," Sharar replied. He held up his hands, the runes draped and entwined around his long fingers. "Time for our agreement, my little bug. I've waited so long to have this chat with you."

CHAPTER 27
Scholarly
Studies

ARMS CLASPED BETWEEN TWO GUARDS, THEY DRAGGED Tzarik—toes scraping along the cobblestones, head lolling to the sides violently—up from the underground cell. In his delirium and fading eyesight, he caught the familiar shapes of ShanBao's garden and even the dojo out back where Jin and Sybal had first bonded. His brain reeled as he tried to regain his bearings and realized he was no longer in the Hallow City. Sometime either before or after he was captured, they'd moved him down to ShanBao's own estate. Surely the city of Wushito would be safer?

They shackled him just high enough so his numb toes danced on the floor below, arms held high overhead. It wasn't until Sharar leaned close and tied the runes around his neck that the prison came into better view. Deep breaths and several blinks later, everything focused. The pain of feeling returning to his limbs was almost as bad as the initial numbing. The only other person in the dark, torch-lined square room was Sharar. The scholar smiled when Tzarik's eyes finally landed on him and focused.

"I said I'd get your body one day," Sharar said simply, as if a class of eager naturalists waited to see what would happen. "But I'm more interested in what's inside."

Tzarik stretched his legs down to try to find a better standing position, but couldn't. Pain in his wrists made him stop. "Cut me open and you'll find I'm full of bullshit." He smirked defiantly at the scholar.

Sharar granted him the satisfaction of a smile and a light laugh. "You've changed a lot since I last saw you, Tzarik. I should have known you'd turn into the kind of man who jokes in the face of danger."

He pulled his satchel off and laid it on a rickety table beside him. Digging inside, he found a leather roll with various silver handles sticking out and pulled one out, dipping it in a pot of ink. Laying out a parchment beside the roll, he wrote in quick looping letters. Tzarik saw it was Al'Myrahn script, but he couldn't read it.

"What have you done with Sybal?" he asked.

"She's fine," Sharar replied quickly, shoving the roll of instruments open. They glistened with a rainbow sheen: orichalcum.

"That metal will kill you, scholar. It's toxic to red blood."

The scholar nodded, lifting his brows. "The things I do for science. I purify my blood regularly. It's unpleasant, but allows me some time."

"Doesn't matter," Tzarik cut in. "No amount of purification will save you."

Sharar chewed the inside of his left cheek and stopped his hands for a moment. "I know," he said quickly. "But it does the job on monsters like you."

He lifted a tiny razor-sharp scalpel and in one smooth motion strode to Tzarik, slashed his wrist, and retrieved a triangular glass vial from his bag to catch the white blood.

The blade was so sharp, Tzarik hadn't felt it tear his skin at first. The sensation of his hot white blood flowing down his arm came first. Then the fiery pain from the wound registered and he growled.

"You won't bleed out. Calm down," Sharar mumbled, holding

the sulfates up to the window to catch the gray sunlight. He swirled it around like Tzarik saw barmen do with coffee back on Al'Myrah. Sharar squinted. "It's almost like oil," he mused.

Going to the table, he retrieved a dropper from his bag and filled it. Carefully, with the steady hand of a naturalist, he plopped it onto a tiny rectangle of glass before pressing another on top. He made a few humming sounds before rubbing his chin.

"This won't do."

He pulled a long curved dagger from his bag, then turned on his heel and marched back, arching his hand over his head.

"Wait!" Tzarik cried. His voice was cut off as the dagger sank up to the hilt into almost the center of his chest. It hurt, but to his surprise, his breath didn't catch. His heart fluttered, though, and sent a shock through his system.

"Like a tap in a tree," Sharar said in his most annoying scholarly tone. "Now, deep breath and hold on." He gripped the handle and pulled it out. A spurt of white blood followed it. He held up the dagger.

Along the blade, a tiny channel ran over the length of it, white and full of his blood. Sharar held the tip over another triangular vial. When he pressed a red jewel on the end of the handle the blood released, flowing into the glass. Tzarik had never seen anything like it.

"From the mori of Altevine," Sharar explained. "Aristocratic monsters. Far more civilized bloodsuckers than the jiangshi or even the blood cult of Masahk on Alika. Leaves no bite marks and often doesn't kill the victim. But for me, it works for collecting. Blood has always fascinated me and was my area of study at the institution. But as you know, Runers are hard to find, let alone convince to give blood."

Looking down, the flow didn't stop. His white blood soaked his black shirt and the top of his pants. Sharar probably knew what he'd done. Runer's bodies did not replace their sulfates. In fact, Tzarik usually carried a few vials of it on his horse for emergencies. Rarely had he had to replace his own blood, but he still prepared sulfates just in case. Perhaps this preparation was what Sharar was after.

"I'm not going to show you how to make the poison, Sharar," he managed to say. "You can't do it. It takes a Runer." His throat went dry. A slow *plop* told him that his clothes were saturated with enough of his blood to now drip to the stones below. Dizziness made the room swim before his eyes. With every pulse of his heart —desperate for blood—the room darkened.

"Well, damn it, Runer." Sharar dripped more of his blood onto the glass pieces to examine it. "You just may die, then."

Tzarik smirked, letting his head tip backwards. It fell, heavy, straining his neck. "Too bad."

"Runer?" Sharar looked up.

Tzarik heard him drop the glass.

"Tzarik?"

The scholar tapped his chest, then pulled his head forward by a handful of his hair. Tzarik didn't speak. Lying somewhere between wakefulness and sleep comforted him. The feeling went down from his arms and his body stopped hurting. Slipping away, like into sleep after a long hunt.

He wanted to hunt. He missed the simple Runer life he'd had, the one he'd so desperately desired to throw away. Now he'd give anything to be paid to dispatch even something as meager as a ghoul hiding in a graveyard, only to be spit on and cursed on his way out of town. Yes, a good old-fashioned Runer hunt.

Sharar cursed and dropped his head. The door opened and soft steps announced ShanBao's entrance.

"Ah, Wushito Master ShanBao." Sharar used his pompous

voice, but Tzarik heard the mild disdain. "Come to give me the book, I assume."

"The impatience of your country never ceases to amaze me," ShanBao cut back.

"Hmm." Sharar scribbled some notes down. "I am a man of great patience, Master ShanBao. Also a giving man. I didn't have to stop the mong sho from killing you during the spring."

"The Runers fought it off," ShanBao countered. "I should be grateful they stepped in when they did."

Tzarik felt eyes on him. He tried to pull his head up, but the weight restrained him. "I know, Sharar," he said.

He couldn't see the scholar, but felt him waiting.

"You used a wish to take dominion over the beasts and monsters."

Sharar hummed a high, staccato note of mild surprise. "Of course you know, you clever boy." He dropped his pen and angled himself halfway to ShanBao again. "Why would it be bad if a mong sho ripped apart one of the most influential and powerful Wushito masters to ever grace this continent? Oh, of course!" He feigned an epiphany and tapped his temple. "Mong sho only go after guilty men, often drawn by their dark spirit, and try to drag them to hell. That would never do."

ShanBao scoffed and mumbled something in Xian before answering Sharar in his own tongue again. "You are bold for a weak man unable to lift a sword."

"Ah-ah!" He tapped his satchel. "You know what I carry. On that note, master, have you located the little gini? I'd hate to think you reneged on *all* our deals."

ShanBao's eyes settled onto Tzarik and his heavy chest as he fought to stay conscious. "You speak boldly in front of your foe."

The scholar ignored this remark. "Wu-ShanBao." His tone darkened, using the warrior's noble title. "Perhaps I have not shown you enough to convince you of my assuredness. Get me the princess as requested."

"If you force her to grant you the one wish she possesses," ShanBao said measuredly, "it will kill her. That is the riddle of the gini. The story goes that one who loves her would never harm her, even for a celestial gift."

Something about this interested Sharar. He bit the end of his metal pen between his straight teeth. "Speaking of stories, won't putting you on the throne upset your precious balance?"

At this Tzarik forced the air out of his lungs to make words. "He doesn't care, Sharar. He told me so. He'll raze the continent to the bottom of the ocean."

"And I thought you didn't care," ShanBao offered gently. He stepped into Tzarik's line of vision.

The Runer groaned, forcing his head up. He almost blurted out that Yui was with child and that they had a chance to stop the civil war, but he knew better. ShanBao had no love for his country. "I'm not sure I believe it, is all," he mumbled.

"Ah, Runer, you above all should know there is magic all around us," Sharar said. His eyes flitted to ShanBao, thinking. "Is this worth the risk of disbelief?"

Tzarik noticed his eyes darken, the gears in his head turning. Sharar calculated now. If he used Yui's wish however he planned, ShanBao would take the throne. The scholar knew if the stories were true then they'd all parish in a flood they could not escape. An act of a literal god. Tzarik hardly believed it for himself, but he did trust Sharar's grandiose knowledge. It was the only thing about Abigor Sharar that he could trust.

With a gasping moan, Tzarik's head fell forward and the sounds around him came muffled.

"Sulfates!" Sharar proclaimed suddenly. "Tell me the ingredients, Runer, or this is your final sunset."

Fighting to raise his head, Tzarik snarled a slurred reply. "Too late, Sharar." He wanted to sleep. Sybal was gone. What was the point anymore? "You can't get the ingredients."

The scholar walked up to his prisoner. With a swift flick of his wrist, he cracked Tzarik over the head with his metal pen. "Stay awake. Tell me what's in them." He lifted the plate of glass up so Tzarik could see it and squinted. "There is something in here I cannot place."

Pressing the plates between his fingers, he rubbed them together. A high scraping sound, like the voices of ghostly fairies, scratched the surface.

"Even without my microscope, I know that element must come from a metaphysical beast." He slapped Tzarik's chin when the Runer nodded off again. "The rest can be deduced. But not this one. Runer!" He raised his hand to strike him again.

"Lost too much already," Tzarik replied, wincing away from the raised hand.

Sharar took in his victim. Sense must have hit him hard and suddenly because he gave a shout of annoyance and immediately started to wrap the wounds he'd inflicted. "Damn it, Runer! Don't you have sulfates?"

"On...my horse." But that horse must be long gone. A white cloud infringed on his eyesight again. His body seared in pain from the lack of life-giving white blood and his mind went blank. Shan-Bao's voice cut through just before the room disappeared in a white haze.

⚜

A SHARP PAIN in the crook of his right arm brought Tzarik to. His neck was almost too stiff to move, but he managed it. Bars surrounded him again. He took in the cell with his strengthening eyes. The pain in his shoulders and lower back told him he had been lying on this wooden plank, chained by his feet, for hours.

"Thank the gods," Sharar's voice said from his left.

Tzarik turned his head, sending a strike of lightning through his body. The scholar leaned against the table next to the hanging chains. Beneath them, a burst of white sulfates was splattered out over the stones. ShanBao was gone.

"Your horse apparently wandered back to the master's estate when you abandoned it. ShanBao let me act the fool, thinking I'd killed you," Sharar explained, pointing with his pen to a glass vial hanging upside down. The familiar needle and intestinal tube snaked down from it and into his arm. "I saved you, Runer. You almost killed yourself."

"Wasn't the first time," Tzarik said, sighing and re-inflating his lungs with the cold air. A sensation not unlike gasping for air after nearly drowning consumed him.

Sharar opened the cell door, leaning against the frame. "I hope we can pick up where we left off. We're running out of time."

Tzarik's brows knit slightly. Did he mean he wanted to kill Tzarik, or were the sands of time running out in some other way, beyond his control? Reading his posture, Sharar tried to put on a relaxed air, but he had a habit of spinning the pen between all five of his fingers and back again. The fidgeting signaled to Tzarik that something else pressed in on his enemy. Perhaps there was no harm in keeping him here, talking.

"The ingredients cannot be gathered, Sharar. The most common death for Runers is bleeding out. We don't live long lives."

"While you were sleeping, I've deduced seven of the ingredients." He held up his leatherbound scroll. "There are two I cannot. I even looked at it under my microscope. When seen under the lens, do you know what I saw?"

"Looked at it under what?" Tzarik asked honestly.

"Something like ectoplasm swims among the other ingredients," the scholar went on, rolling his eyes at his prey's ignorance. "But it's not regular ectoplasm. It's almost crystalline. When I tried to extract it, it liquified. Or something akin to liquefaction. It exists in a gaseous and solid state all at once."

At this, Tzarik smirked crookedly, understanding the ingredient Sharar couldn't figure out.

"That's it, isn't it!" Sharar spat, running to his side and kneeling down to be on eye level. "What is it, Runer?" He gripped Tzarik's shoulders and shook him violently.

"A monk here would know," Tzarik offered, wincing.

"A monk?" Sharar frowned, his eyes dancing between the Runer's. "Ah." His eyes went wide. "Something from the North?"

"Well done," Tzarik said, shifting his body but not finding a better position.

"There are many monsters from The Frozen Nation. The fell land." Sharar's eyes glassed over as he imagined the wonders waiting in that place. "But it would have to be one Runers all across the map run into."

Tzarik waited but the scholar seemed genuinely lost. Relinquishing any drama about revealing the monster Sharar could not think of, Tzarik spat, "It's called a Mahar'nolreith, scholar." He did allow himself to use the title as an insult.

Sharar's brows knit into the first genuine curiosity Tzarik had ever seen.

"There are over a thousand myths surrounding it, how to kill it, trap it, even find it." He closed his eyes. "They're too dangerous for even a Runer to hunt, but we must for its marrow."

"Marrow!" the scholar proclaimed, throwing his hands up. "This is not like any marrow I have ever seen."

"Clearly."

Leaving his prisoner alone in the cell, Sharar bounded to his table and began scribbling madly, muttering half-formed sentences to himself. He spun on the spot, halting in his pacing to stoke his trimmed black beard before grunting and turning again to march in the opposite direction.

"I suppose I could..." he mumbled. "Damn." He sighed. "You know, the generals betrayed ShanBao to offer me that damned book and I've not seen it yet. That old man is more willing to sink his country than to wait for a better opportunity." He pressed his lips together.

"He's losing," Tzarik offered. "That has to be it. He wouldn't throw caution to the wind otherwise. I think he knows he's lost."

"Astute observation, Tzarik. I do hope you're wrong. But alas..." In a whirl of motion, Sharar gathered up most of his things and stowed them in his satchel. "I don't suppose you're going anywhere. I'm sure the warden will see to you. I must head to the crypt before that old fool opens the gates of hell on Xia. If you're still alive when I get back, you can join me in Al'Myrah with your precious Sybal."

The reminder ignited a rage in his belly. Sharar took no notice, turned, and left the garrison.

CHAPTER 28
INNOCENT

TZARIK COUNTED HOW LONG HE COULD INHALE THEN SLOWLY exhale, lengthening each breath every time. His heart slowed down, his mind unclogged, and his body relaxed as he did this. Sharar had force-fed him something stale and tasteless before nearly drowning him with a jug of water. Then the scholar had left, taking everything with him. Tzarik assumed he'd be alone for some time. Perhaps the next time someone appeared, they'd lead him away to his execution.

Outside, the rain still fell, and every once in a while the sound of footsteps marched past the ground-level window above him. Sharar had left him with his runes around his neck, but he couldn't reach them, his hands bound by his sides. He tried to toss and twist, seeing how he could move them. All he needed was to grasp buhkar. He only had to draw it enough to slip one hand out of the restraints. After several hours, his wrists bled again, ripping the careful wrapping Sharar had put there. His legs ached from tearing muscles. Eventually, exhaustion overtook him and he lay still.

"Sybal," he whispered, closing his eyes against the darkness after the sun set. "Where are you?"

Despite his eyes being closed, something painful pricked at the back of them. Wincing, he opened them. When he did, hot tears rolled down his temples. Growling, he shook his head. The rings around his wrist stuck in his blood, clinking against the jade dragon bracelet. Hearing the tinkling sound from the jade, he glanced down at it. It remained intact, unbroken. Dare he believe in the superstition of the Masahk monk and hope Sybal still breathed?

Behind his watering eyes, a glow appeared at the end of the long hall of empty cells. Straining against his bonds, he sat up and craned his neck to look. At the end of the hall, surrounded in white light, stood the beast he and Sybal had fought away from ShanBao's home. The scholar had called it a mong sho. A low, lion-like growl emitted from its throat and it shook its mane when Tzarik met its fiery eyes. Taking careful steps, it approached him, its two-pronged antlers bobbing with its steps. Every hoof fall echoed with a celestial resonance. Stopping just outside the cell, it watched him with one good eye. The other—though obviously slashed savagely—had healed over with a scar, closing it.

"You again," he said, knowing the beast wouldn't answer.

It made a deep purring sound, tilted its head to his hand, and waited.

Tzarik looked down, his white blood shining against his dark skin. Making a fist, he ran his finger over his palm, cutting a clean line through his blood. Rubbing all four of his fingers over it, he erased the line, making a white canvas of his palm.

He stopped, opening his hand to stare. "Would that really work?" he mumbled to himself.

The mong sho, raising its antlered head, made a kind of nickering sound.

"Sybal asked if that was possible," he said to himself. "She's clever."

Holding his breath, he sloppily drew buhkar on his palm. With the rune dripping in his own blood, he drew the rune in the air as best he could despite the restraints. The sensation of turning to black mist prickled through him and his body vanished into the black smoke for just one second before materializing again.

"Krishvu save you, Sybal!" he crowed, hysterics almost making him cackle in joy. He smeared his blood over his palm to try again. It dried and stuck to his fingers. He needed more.

Without hesitating, he used the rusty ring to saw at both his wrists; he wanted to use both. He couldn't draw slowly enough so perhaps two runes would prolong the effect. The pain jittered through his arms, but he pushed past it. He'd lost track of time, but was sure he'd spent days in these cells. He didn't know how the war fared, if Sybal was alive, or if the royal family remained safe. There was no time to lose.

Finally, his skin broke, releasing more blood. He let it drip onto the wooden slab and dipped his finger in it like an ink pot. Using his ring finger, he drew buhkar on each palm. Instantly, his body changed. Grunting, he flipped himself over and landed on the floor just as he rematerialized.

"Ha!" he shouted victoriously. His own jovial exclamation took him by surprise and he pressed his lips together, looking to the mong sho.

The creature shook its mane and turned to walk back down the hall.

"You came to me," Tzarik called after it. "Why? They said you only approach innocent sentients."

In reply, the mong sho flicked its bifurcated tail and walked through the unguarded door at the end, vanishing. He knew he couldn't lie to something like that creature. It knew. No other living creature knew.

Pushing himself up, Tzarik pulled the string of runes around to his chest and clutched buhkar, drawing it slowly. Once he metamorphosed into the black mist again, he passed through the bars and set about to find his missing gear. If anything, he needed his scimitar. He passed through a few doors but didn't find it. Judging from what he knew of ShanBao, the old warrior had probably taken them somewhere himself. Most likely kept them near himself, if not on his own person.

With nothing but his shirt and pants, Tzarik left the garrison. He ran up tightly wound stone steps to two doors above him. Pushing with all his strength, they flipped open, flopping onto the grass with a splash. Lightning cracked across the sky as he emerged. He came out near the edge of what he recognized as ShanBao's estate. The towering house loomed a good distance away in front of him over the rolling gardens and other structures. Scanning the grounds, his guard went up upon not finding a single worker, sentry, or house servant. Even the ever-lit lantern in the arching gateway surrounding the main house was out.

Keeping low to the ground, he crawled out of the hole and slinked towards the dojo. He knew there were some weapons there, and even the long awkward spear of the Xians would be better than nothing. Still, once out in the cold rain, he felt the simmering of his white blood: it yearned to be near the magical metal of his scimitar. As he approached the dojo, he saw the sliding canvas doors hanging off limply. Inside, the weapons racks, suits of armor, and practice dummies lay everywhere, almost like the place had been sacked. He turned to the only rack that still contained spears and saw, scrawled in black paint over the entire wall, the symbol for House Xiaoh. The script was sharp and jagged. It reminded him of the ragtag militia he'd seen just before embarking on this long journey. They must have been here for a raid. He guessed they'd hit fast and left, trying to cultivate fear more than do damage. Perhaps ShanBao hadn't even remained in his house.

With this realization, Tzarik went for the stables. Sharar had said his former horse had wandered back after he'd left it out in the wilds of Xia. Rubbing the jade bracelet for luck, he found his way to the stables. They, too, had been partly destroyed. The far side was charred black and part of the wall had collapsed in from the fire. A few horses stood in the remaining stalls. The Xian horses were typically bay-colored or a dark, vibrant red. Tied to a post out behind the stable, visible through the destroyed wall, stood a tall black Al'Myrahn stallion.

Warm familiarity filled Tzarik as he approached his horse, hand out. He clicked his tongue and whispered to it. At first it tossed its head and put its ears back.

"I know, old friend," he murmured. "You have every right to be angry. I'm sorry I left you." He placed his palm on the horse's nose. "You know, Hiro made me name another horse. It got me thinking about you."

He went to work untying the knots that tethered it. The horse had pulled on it for days, most likely, making them almost impossible to undo.

"We've been together for..." He frowned. "Five years? I stole you off that pirate from Singad, remember? He wanted to sell you for meat to that man from Oceanya. 'He's too tough,' I said. 'He'll give you indigestion for weeks.'"

The horse made a satisfied whiney before sighing heavily.

"Exactly," Tzarik agreed, having no idea what his loyal mount meant. "You hated me and I thought 'What's the point of a horse I cannot ride?' But it just took time. Besides, I'd worn out too many boots walking the continent. There."

He pulled the leather out of the ring and slung it over his great head. Gripping his shoulder and lower mane, Tzarik jumped, flipping his leg over the great beast.

"We must be swift and silent," he whispered, and his horse nickered in reply. "Mamun," he decided suddenly. "That will be your name. Means loyal." He patted its neck and started a trot.

Not wanting to go out the front gate, he surveyed the back parameter and was surprised to find part of the wall destroyed. He guessed this was where the Vandauls had entered. It took a running jump and some persuading to get Mamun to leap over the rubble, but eventually he was free, outside the garrison and away from the torture.

"To the Royal City," he commanded, kicking the horse with his bare heels.

～♒︎

Tzarik took paths near rocky edges and steep cliffs so he could look out over parts of the country and try to get an idea of the situation. High up, his stomach flipped with anxiety with every peek over an edge. Below, the water rose and he could see where rivers grew, swallowing up villages and outlying farms. Fields of rice turned to lakes. A wind swept up from the ocean he couldn't see, cold and salty. A storm must be raging in the seas beyond Xia's borders.

He spotted a few columns of smoke here and there, but couldn't see where they came from. While he'd been imprisoned, the war had raged on. Road signs had been painted over with the black sign of the snake, showing where the Vandauls had attacked. He wondered if what Sharar had hinted at was true: was Wushito losing the battles? He thought they'd overrun Xia and the loyalists easily, but the people were putting up a fight. Perhaps Sharar had not upheld his end of the deal yet. From the sounds of it, Wushito had not, either, neither man wanting to give in first. Sharar hadn't said it out loud, but Tzarik had concluded from the scholar's mannerisms upon hearing ShanBao toss his beliefs to the wind that he feared what might happen if ShanBao did officially take the Xian throne.

Looking up the mountainous path, he wondered how close he was to the Hallow City. It would take days to get to the Royal City, and perhaps he could pass by Wushito to see if the state of the city of Reavers had changed. Perhaps find a clue as to where Sybal had gone.

His mind made up, he stayed near the cliff paths and changed course to pass by the Hallow City. On his way, he raided empty homes for any scrap of food, water, and warmer clothing knowing he'd need to keep up his strength. He went off the path to sleep in abandoned homes, stables, or other partly destroyed structures. Only a few times did he run into other people. They didn't speak his language, so their interactions were brief.

One happened to be a group of monks who recognized his jade bracelet. In their string of rapid Xian, Tzarik only understood TaoShin's name. Realizing he knew one of their own, they built a fire inside an abandoned family home and shared their food and drink with him. One monk, a female bird-type Masahk, made an excited cheeping sound and dug through her bag once they got a good look at him.

A fox-type asked her a question in Xian, confused. She replied, motioning to Tzarik as she did. He caught the word "Al'Myrah." Not finding what she was looking for, she upturned the large bag and dumped a colorful assortment of letters, small packages, and scrolls from the bag. It almost looked like she had robbed a messenger. She pulled out one particular scroll from the pile. He recognized the wrappings and the seals stamped all over it as being from a courier in Al'Myrah.

"This is a letter from Al'Myrah?" he said, taking it.

"Al'Myrah!" the monk repeated, clapping her hands. She spewed a story he didn't understand until she tried again, using exaggerated gestures. She stood up, flipped her hood on and crouched behind empty fishing barrels. She mimed taking something from the top of it. Then she circled her hand to indicate her brethren.

"You are intercepting outside communication?" he guessed. She smiled, blank-eyed. "Must be." He scanned the letter's encasement and his heart dropped. "I'm grateful," he told them, knowing they could not understand him. "But...I cannot read."

Confused as to why he didn't open the letter, the monk sighed and shook her head. With nothing else to say, the helpful monks whispered amongst themselves but included him with smiles and offerings of more food. The bird-like Masahk offered to let him share her blanket as the night grew colder, but he refused.

The next morning, they gave him a thick belt with a small hip satchel where he stowed the letter, shoes, a sack of food, and a skin of water before parting.

Several days and nights later, Tzarik saw the shadow of the city above him. He stood in a rocky clearing near a set of bluffs that plunged down into a cliff face, measuring his next march, when two sets of hooves approached from behind. He was about to turn and greet the travelers when one of them spoke.

"I've been looking for you, Runer. You've taken me away from my battle, but the scholar insists I bring you in personally." ShanBao's voice came low and unafraid. "You were simple to track."

Turning his horse, Tzarik faced his enemy. "I have other things on my mind besides hiding my whereabouts, ShanBao. You should have killed me when you had the chance."

The Wushito master smirked. "Your countryman stopped me. I would say he has an unhealthy obsession with you and your kind, but I'm beginning to understand. Perhaps I've spent too long around Reavers and not enough time studying our foe."

Reading ShanBao's tight grip on the reins, the way a vein in his neck throbbed, Tzarik realized the master had come to do what he couldn't with Sharar around. He had to fight. Resigning himself to combat, he swung his leg over the saddle, took up the spear, and readied himself.

"Runers are not your foe," Tzarik challenged him. "You took your Dragon gift—your vocation as protector—and turned it against us. I know about the crypt, ShanBao. I know Wushito has not slain a single monster. Because you can't. You were supposed to be guardians. Now you're going to turn that against your country."

ShanBao joined him on the ground, taking a long, curved, wrapped item from his saddle. His one warrior joined him, unsheathing his straight hilt-less sword.

"You miss Al'Myrah," ShanBao said. "You would never do this to her. I am not like you Runer. Not like the other Xians who sing songs about jade hearths and golden windows—in love with their home. Xia deserves what is coming."

"Why?" Tzarik asked, watching ShanBao shift his weight and unwrap the long mysterious item. "Your country is no more evil than mine or Rhostrana. Even the black temples of Bahratt seem viler than Xia. Why wipe the millennia of culture and civilization off the map? Not to mention all the lives that will be lost."

At this ShanBao almost nodded. "Being a hero does not suit you, Tzarik. You don't understand. You're too selfish to try the self-less savior role. I did. Tried over and over again to do the right thing. But none of that matters."

Tzarik had had enough. He raised the spear. "If I'm no savior, then I should be easily removed from the situation."

ShanBao grinned. He took a step back and bowed. With a

flourish, he tossed aside the wrappings he'd been handling to reveal a long curved sword. Etched over the blade were swooping Xian letters that spelled something he could not read. The letters crawled over the metal to create the shape of a long four-legged dragon like he'd seen all over the continent. He realized the blade must work as the talismans, locking the creatures away. As ShanBao paced closer, Tzarik swore he could hear the ghostly, demonic whispers of the spirits trapped in the blade.

Striking first, Tzarik spun the spear to put a little distance between him and ShanBao. The master lurched backward, easily dodging the onslaught. The other warrior circled around, and that was when Tzarik spotted it: on the warrior's back hung Tzarik's scabbard and scimitar. They must have been taking it to the Hallow City when they came across his tracks.

He ducked a swipe from the warrior's blade and rolled to avoid a wide-arcing slice from ShanBao's demon blade. As he came up, he drew halat to deflect the warrior's blows, then misted to avoid ShanBao. When he did this, the non-magic spear fell through his hand with a clatter. The orichalcum blades would stay clutched in a Runer's hand during buhkar, but not base weapons. Running to the rocky outcropping, he forced himself to not look down as he vaulted off the rocks, jumping over the warrior's head. Using the environment, he secluded himself and the warrior. He made a charge for his scimitar, but caught the warrior's straight edge on his forearm. With his armor gone, the blade bit his already raw wrist, smattering his blood onto his face.

Clambering up a boulder, he jumped back into the clearing where ShanBao waited. He shielded himself then drew atan quickly, shoving it towards ShanBao like he'd seen Sybal do. The thrust empowered the rune, sending a blinding light into the Wushito's face. ShanBao roared in rage, turning his face into the crook of his arm to block out the light. With that second of distraction, Tzarik scooped up the spear. He needed some weapon to fight with until he got his hands on the scimitar.

He spun the spear again when ShanBao blinked his blindness away, hearing it crack against something. The warrior had tried to sneak up behind him and it had smashed against his head. The man teetered on his feet, eyes wide with shock as his brain rattled. Tzarik drew halat and shoved it towards ShanBao. The old master staggered backwards, allowing Tzarik time to kick the warrior to the ground. He pressed his sandaled foot into the warrior's throat, giving him a chance to forfeit the scimitar. Then he thrust his hands out towards ShanBao again only to have the warrior stab him with a tiny throwing blade. Enraged at the pain. Tzarik lifted the spear above the man's chest.

"You can't!" ShanBao crowed, stopping now and waiting for the Runer to end himself by killing another man.

"I can."

With a grunt, Tzarik plunged the spear into the man's chest. Pressing his weight onto it, it went in deeper, cracking his sternum and spurting hot, red blood. Tzarik glared at ShanBao as he did this. The Wushito's visage paled, but then he tilted his head.

"He's not dead yet," he reasoned. "When he dies..." His voice trailed off as Tzarik stomped on the man's head, making his eyes go blank.

Reaching down, Tzarik unbuckled his belt from the dead man and took back his scimitar. "What were you saying?" he asked darkly. Loving the familiar weapon in his palm, he ran his hand over the round curve or the glimmering blade.

"How?" ShanBao gasped, stutter-stepping backwards. "Your crime—"

"Was not murder," Tzarik cut in. "Killing you will have no effect on me, just as crushing the life out of this man has done nothing." He slid his foot back, preparing a stance. "Come on, ShanBao."

"I see," the master Reaver sighed. He let go of his long demon sword and it hung in the air, suspended by nothing.

Tzarik tensed, eyes transfixed on the floating sword. ShanBao reached into a clay jar on his belt and pulled out one of the canvas talismans. It had writing on it; inside, a spirit waited.

"You have your tricks, Runer. I have mine." He pressed the talisman to his forehead, where it fluttered then lay flush against his skin. When ShanBao opened his eyes, they smoldered red like a dying fire.

"What the hell?" Tzarik mumbled.

Before he could take it in, ShanBao lunged at him so fast he could only tumble to the side to avoid the strike. As ShanBao moved—faster than a jaguar—a ghostly remnant hovered behind him, like smoke left behind. Only this remnant was black as soot, with brighter, redder eyes, protruding fang-like teeth coming from its sinister snarl, and wide, tall horns thrusting up from its head.

Drawing halat, Tzarik deflected an onslaught of rapid-fire slashes, then had to mist to the side to avoid another. ShanBao had taken the dark spirit into himself, gifting himself with its powers and abilities. At least, this was what Tzarik guessed. He hardly had time to wonder if this was something all Reavers did before he found himself only being able to defend. ShanBao assailed him mercilessly. The sandals gifted to him by the monks didn't work well to grip the ground and Tzarik quickly understood he could not fight this possessed warrior.

Instead, he tried to get in a few wounds. He landed several hits, but they didn't slow the monster. Deciding to match the fury, he put some distance between them to draw jiun. He scaled up a boulder and clutched the rune in his hand. Just as he raised his hand to draw it before him, ShanBao leapt up—almost flying—and caught the Runer's wrist. Twisting it hard, Tzarik was forced to drop the rune against his chest. ShanBao, letting go of his sword, which floated where he'd released it, seized Tzarik by his neck and squeezed. Kicking Tzarik behind his knees, he forced him down. Before Tzarik could clumsily slash with his scimitar, ShanBao punted the hilt. The sword spun from his hand and clattered on the sloping cliff below, clanging out of sight.

"I remember how much you like heights, Runer," ShanBao whispered in a low, gurgling demonic tone. His hot breath pushed Tzarik's hair with every word. "I can't kill you because of the deal with Sharar, but I can—as you say—remove you from the situation."

With a violent shove, ShanBao tossed Tzarik hard with his monstrous strength. Lungs convulsing as he tried to choke and scream at the same time, the Runer felt his body become weightless in the air before plunging down. He drew buhkar to avoid the branches of trees growing out of the cliff face and then halat to save himself from the impact, but he couldn't do it fast enough to make too much of a difference. The first impact rattled his entire body. He felt ribs break before he rolled down the next section. Hitting boulders on the way down, he managed to scream in agony as a branch punctured his side. He couldn't stop rolling down the steep cliff. His consciousness slipped in and out until finally, whether by the pain or blunt force, his mind went black.

Chapter 29
Siege

"THAT WAS QUITE A FALL."

Tzarik's eyes stuttered open with great effort. Turning his head to the left hurt; the rocks cut deeper and his skull throbbed. Taking in air, he felt his broken ribs grind. "Sybal?"

She lay beside him on the crags as if they were soft flowers and down. One arm crooked under her head, pillowing it as she gazed up into the sky. She wore a green dress with gold trim. Almost how she looked when he'd first laid eyes on her in the courthouse. A lady, wealthy and refined. Clean and pretty.

"I'll never forget seeing the Di-Huan's palace for the first time," she mused, raising her hand up to block the bright sun from her glittering blue eyes. "How it stood, gold and sharp amongst the mountains. Reflected in the bright green water. The water here is so clear and somehow still sparkly like emeralds, but brighter and more beautiful than the ones we mined."

She dropped her hand, touching his arm. Pain shot up to his neck. At least he could feel his limbs.

"What's the water like on Al'Myrah?" she asked, genuinely wondering. "Tzarik, do you remember?"

Swallowing to speak, he almost choked. "Gold. The water inland is gold. Like the sand. It's warm and clear."

"Mmm," Sybal hummed happily, closing her eyes and raising her chin. "Except on the shores of Singad. Have you ever seen the red shores, Tzarik? My family used to visit. We had land there. I used to think it was blood, but my father showed me how the plants made it that color. It used to turn my hair red." She giggled.

"Are you here?" he asked, doubting his wounded head.

Sybal sighed sadly. "No. Where I am is dark. Rocking back and forth. I see someone watching me sometimes. They're far away, but glow like a ghost. They catch a glimpse of me, then look away. I think they're watching over me."

Shifting his body, he turned onto his side to look at her more fully. Her chest rose and fell with gentle breaths.

"I must be dead, then, since I see you," he said.

She smiled. "I'm not dead. But I'm scared. I can't move."

"I'll come find you," he said, blinking against the sun.

She turned her head, her blue eyes beaming down on him. "Save Xia first. You can't leave: the continent is flooded, surrounded by hurricanes. Please, see this through. Besides, I'm not going anywhere."

Her laugh energized him. Grunting through the pain, he raised his left hand to stroke her face. "How are you here?"

Lightning cut across the sky, inking out the false image of the sun. Rain poured down so thick and fast, he thought he might drown. His reaching hand touched only cold stone.

I'm always with you. Your blood is my blood.

Fully awake, he screamed in agony where he lay. Above him, the cliff jutted out from where he'd fallen, hitting the sides on the way down. Bloodied and bruised, his body refused to move. A tinkling sound next to him alerted him to his scimitar and belt just beside him, rain pattering against the broad side. Forcing his arms to move, he gripped it. Slipping his hand under his shirt, he felt the runes still there. He lay like this for some time, taking stock of his injuries. To his surprise, his limbs didn't seem broken. Only his chest ached in that way. His head split with pain, but he didn't feel nauseated.

Forcing himself to sit up, he took in his surroundings. He'd been on his way to the Royal City when he'd run into ShanBao and his warrior. They must have been on their way to the Hallow City. If that were true, he didn't have time to waste. Clicking his tongue, he listened for his horse. Surely it couldn't have gotten far. It disliked the rocky cliffs just as much as him. Unless ShanBao had taken it. He whistled but heard nothing in reply.

Rolling to his side, he pushed himself up. Slowly, he drew artiah over his chest, then his head. It didn't completely heal him, but some of the pain vanished. Getting to his feet, his head spun and he teetered drastically. Looking up almost toppled him over again. He took a few steady breaths into his aching lungs and started the march back up the ascending paths. His steps came small and slow, hardly inching his way up. With no water or food, he judged he might make it three days. Unsure where he was, he couldn't calculate how long it would take to get to the Royal City. Once again wishing he had studied maps or anything useful during his life, he gritted his teeth and continued up.

～❦～

IT WOULD BE EASIER to give up. He knew that. But the jade bracelet around his wrist made him press on. She wasn't gone and the only way to find her was to set things right on Xia. Yui's storms trapped him here. And if he did leave, ShanBao would open a crypt filled with a millennium of monsters that Sharar would have complete control over. The continent would descend into a monstrosity not unlike the tales of The Frozen North, owned by spirits and monsters. Sharar may be one man, but his power was great enough to take the world, if Tzarik let it.

Over the next two and a half days, Tzarik's pace slowed. He drank from the rivers, but his hunger weakened him. He sat down atop a cliff face that overlooked a great portion of the Shiuki province. Fires of burning villages and no doubt piles of bodies rose up into the rain. He sighed, taking in the destruction. His breath rose in a white cloud before him. The drop beneath him was a sheer angle, not like the one ShanBao had tossed him over. If he fell from here, that'd be the end of it. It'd be so easy.

Movement below caught his eyes. Standing up, he inched as close as he dared to the edge and looked down. The white and blue robes of Wushito stood out against the black and green backdrop of Xia. The leaves of the trees had started to fall days ago, and he could see through the forest the paths the army took, winding its way up to the Royal City. Elephants pulled what looked like a watchtower on wheels where archers perched. Other structures on wheels glided along behind this, packed with warriors. Something that resembled a ballista wheeled behind these as well. Wushito planned to siege the palace. He took one step closer, making a mental list of everything he saw.

"Don't do it, Runer," a heavily accented voice said behind him.

Nearly jumping, Tzarik wheeled around, brandishing his scimitar. The sudden movement caused him to lose his footing and slip backwards.

The masked warrior who had appeared behind him reached out and seized him, pulling him away from the edge with a cry. Together, they tumbled backwards into a line of black fur-clad warriors and their war horses. They snorted and stamped their hooves. They were all black and smattered with white paint.

Removing his mask, the one who'd saved him revealed himself to be Kei Lu Xiaoh, the Vandaul chieftain. "I did warn you," he grinned maniacally through his scarred face. Behind him stood nearly two dozen of his ragtag team of fighters.

"You—" Tzarik breathed, hunching over in pain. "You almost killed me!"

Kei Lu rolled his eyes in his tattooed face. "I think I saved you, Runer. I thought you were going to jump."

The thought had crossed his mind, but he didn't have time to philosophize with the wild man. "Look." He pointed down into the forest. "Perhaps a day's march behind us."

Squinting, the commander peered into the trees. He turned to his men and called back something in Xian, to which a few nodded and others shuffled their feet, disturbed.

"We have been tracking them since the Muengo Yai border," Kei Lu informed Tzarik. "We lost them near the river."

"I'll take your word for it," Tzarik agreed, not knowing the Xian map nearly at all. "Where are they headed?"

"To the Royal City, no doubt," Kei Lu replied, stroking his long black beard and its many silver-clasped braids. He turned and shouted to his men, who agreed with a soft war cry. "We've kept them off as best we can. Perhaps it's time we met them there. We can bring you to the Royal City. You look in need of a healer. A few monks have joined us and can help."

Tzarik lightly jabbed at his broken ribs. "We don't have time. ShanBao is heading to the Hallow City to open the crypt. I fought him and lost."

"Survived like a warrior!" Kei Lu crowed, thumbing Tzarik on his back.

The Runer groaned, closing his eyes in agony.

"He's probably looking for you," the chieftain went on. "The Royal City is closer by a day and a half. You may have slowed him just enough to allow us to get to the city before he does."

"What makes you think ShanBao will not go to Wushito's crypt?"

Kei Lu signaled for a horse for Tzarik. "I have fought a few wars, Runer. I followed my cousin into battle, even went overseas for the holy wars on Caerwren almost two decades ago. I know men like ShanBao. He hates foreigners and wants to win this on his own. Yes, I know about your man Sharar. He is the one who lead ShanBao to our princess. ShanBao will want her gift for himself, to cut the Al'Myrahn scholar out." He stopped, waiting for Tzarik to agree.

Tzarik mulled it over in his head. Deducing from what he knew of ShanBao, the man would look for Tzarik to make sure he was incapacitated and take him prisoner again. Finding him gone, he'd search for him, not wanting him free. When he couldn't find the Runer, he'd convince Sharar to let him lay siege to the Royal City himself to prove Wushito's strength before the scholar knew his prey was gone. ShanBao was looking for a way to turn traitor on Sharar.

"If we push Wushito back from the Royal City," Tzarik said out loud, "he will flee, no doubt abandoning his men, and go to the city himself with Sharar, using him as a last resort. He will do his best to take Yui, even if Wushito is defeated. The siege will be a distraction. He'll try to get in himself."

"Now you are thinking like a Xian!" Kei Lu praised him. He stopped himself from smacking the Runer on the back again.

"Oh, I have something of yours." He gave a strange call back to his men. One pulled a terrified horse out from the many painted ones. "Your Al'Myrahn steed," he said, beaming at the horse. "Brave lad, this one. Found him wandering the paths, terrified."

Seeing its rider, the horse whinnied in relief and snorted harshly. Tzarik took the proffered reins gratefully. "How is it you never leave me?" he asked it softly.

The horse nickered in reply, tossing its head.

Kei Lu grinned at the bonded pair. "Let's get you back to the palace. We'll get you bound and healed and ready to fight in no time."

HIRO WAS PLEASED to see Tzarik again and embraced him like a brother upon his arrival, thanking him for saving his sister.

"She made it?" he asked. Sybal must have saved her after all. "Did Sybal return?" he asked.

The prince's face fell. "I'm sorry, Tzarik. She did not."

He'd expected that. Sharar had told him as much. Still, doubt and denial lingered in his heart.

Hiro explained how the monks had intercepted many pieces of correspondence for them, allowing their secret militia to head off many attacks. At this, he brought in the familiar Masahk monk.

"I knew you were still alive," TaoShin beamed, gently taking Tzarik into a soft hug before calling for healing instruments to be brought into the war room where Hiro showed Tzarik the battles.

"I didn't expect to see you," Tzarik confessed. "Isn't choosing a side in war against some religious rule?"

TaoShin let the snide remark pass. "When the Dragon has said something is to be done, it must be done. We are his servants," the monk replied simply, opening a bottle of shimmery purple ointment. "Now, take your damned runes out and help me heal you."

He drew artiah slowly over himself again while the monk murmured a prayer, clutching his jade beads in his hands. A wash of comfort flooded through Tzarik as both magics reached into his flesh, knitting him back together. Once the monk was satisfied they'd done all they could, he smeared some of the purple ointment onto him and wrapped his wounds tightly.

Tzarik wanted to ask TaoShin about the monks he'd met on his journey and the letter in his pack, but knew it would distract him from what needed to be done now.

Commander Zhen and Kei Lu joined them with a few other

high-ranking warriors as Hiro pointed out their victories on the map.

"Every time we push them back, more seem to spring up from the mountains and marshes," Hiro mused.

"But we have taken back many villages," Kei Lu boasted of his warriors. "Wu-Tang and all of Ze'oul is secured. We followed them around Muengo Yai and saw them taking able-bodied villagers for their army. They are no doubt forcing them to march with them, but they are not trained Wushito."

Hiro ran his hands through his hair. "I do not want to slaughter my own people."

Zhen nodded sympathetically. "What choice do we have right now?"

Tzarik interjected here. "Where is Yui?"

They all looked to Hiro, who replied, "She has locked herself away in her room. I fear she is unwell."

"Can't you put her on the throne and stop all this?" Tzarik asked.

"That will not stop Wushito," Hiro said. "We must quell them no matter what."

"But we cannot destroy them," TaoShin reminded them calmly. "Xia must produce the balance the Dragon calls upon us to have."

"And it's her child who might be the touched and chosen Di-Huan." Hiro's face turned dark. "That bastard who impregnated her was touched. That doesn't mean his child will be."

TaoShin lightly planted his hand on the prince's shoulder. "Still, the child is the son of the snake and dragon. I have faith it will restore the balance."

"We fight first," Kei Lu interjected. "Wushito is on their way no matter what ass sits on the throne."

A fondness for the wild Xian settled in Tzarik's chest at this proclamation. "Kei Lu is right. We have to fight, if only to keep ShanBao here and away from the crypt."

"I have men watching them," Kei Lu went on. "A messenger will hasten to us when they are close."

"Hasten?" Tzarik said.

"Was that the wrong word in your tongue?" Kei Lu asked.

The Runer shook his head. "It's just a little formal. But it's more words than I know in your tongue."

The chieftain smiled proudly. "So we fight. Hiro and Yui should barricade themselves in the palace."

"No," Hiro said. "I will lead this charge."

"My prince!" TaoShin exclaimed.

"It's the honorable thing to do," Hiro went on. "I am no Di-Huan. To try to pretend to be would put my country in jeopardy. This is all I can do."

Tzarik recognized the helplessness and uselessness the prince must be feeling. Still, what he chose to do was brave.

"I will stand with you," he offered.

Kei Lu gave a barbaric war cry, raising his arms in jubilation. "We fight!"

⤳

Tzarik slinked around the wide-open field before the Royal City, following closely behind Kei Lu. The rain hammered down in fat, cold drops, but even amidst the patter, he could hear the marching and rolling of ShanBao's army. Kei Lu stopped to speak to a few hidden archers and other militia who had armed traps farthest out from the city. As he spoke in rapid Xian, Tzarik instinctively looked to his left for Sybal to translate. The empty space at his side pierced his heart. The pain that came with it forced him to gather his strength to fight the fear that filled him.

He wanted to leave, to find her, to have someone he trusted completely read the letter the monks had intercepted—but there was no way off the continent. She had to be on Xia still. Reports from the lowlands told of the raging storms at sea. Yui's grief had locked them all in whether she knew it or not.

"They will be here within the hour," Kei Lu said to Tzarik in Al'Myrahn. "We must hurry back. Hiro must be ready."

"We should have gone out to meet them," Tzarik said, searching between the dark, rain-soaked shadows for any movement.

Kei Lu shook his head. "We will make them come to us. The royal family have been moved to Wu-Tang. Yui is ill, but protected, and we can keep her within our sights here. And we have the royal army." He gripped Tzarik's shoulder suddenly, beaming. "Trust me, Runer, my men have turned the inhabitants into a well-ordered militia. We have won most battles. This is just the final stand. Wushito is decimated, and while that may upset the monk, I care not at this time."

The ways of the Xians would forever be lost on Tzarik, and he didn't care to understand them now. "I'll go back," he said, sighing and standing up, clicking his tongue for his horse. "We will wait for your signal."

When he slung himself up into his saddle, a sudden emptiness filled him. Despite his feelings towards the woman, Sybal's absence crushed him. He'd grown accustomed to having her by his side, listening to her remarks and chirping commentary on every-thing. She'd grown into her life as a Runer faster than he had. He admired that in her, her bravery and selflessness, even though it often cost him.

"Perhaps I wish I had her courage," he said to Mamun, who gave a small noise in reply.

Hiro sat at the front of a line of mounted warriors before the Royal City gate. The horn-like ornaments on his helmet and the grimacing mask that protected his face made him almost look like a monster. Zhen sat next to him, a banner flapping in the cold breeze.

Far away from the city walls, a few servants ran back from tall pyres, having doused them in oil and black powder. Beside each pyre stood a lantern, ready to ignite to send a signal to their corresponding defenses.

"They are coming?" Hiro asked, his eyes never leaving the tree line Tzarik had just ridden from.

"Yes," he replied, coming abreast with the other two. "Kei Lu has accounted for every war machine I saw the other day. Perhaps twelve siege machines, six ballistas, and nearly two hundred warriors."

To the Runer's surprise, the prince smirked.

"The loyalists of Xia really have decimated the Wushito numbers. Even their recruits dwindle."

Tzarik nodded. That wasn't ShanBao's final move, though. A much greater—undefinable—danger lurked in the shadows of his next steps.

"I will find ShanBao. If he retreats, or disappears, I have to follow him. He'll go for the crypt, and if he opens it, there is nothing we will be able to do to save your continent."

The prince didn't give any indication that he'd heard this. Instead, he said, "The monk thinks Yui is contracting. She is two months early, but her illness and the power she pours into this storm has weakened her."

"Why won't she stop?" He couldn't keep the frustrated contempt out of his voice. He knew the girl had loved Jin and that sorrow often overcame its victims. He'd forced himself to give Sybal patience when her betrothed was killed. And her family.

"Have you ever lost someone, Runer?" Hiro asked, unsheathing his sword. His eyes suddenly darted over the horizon.

Tzarik mulled over his answer, trying to stay away from the harrowing memories that ghosted to the surface. "No. I've always been thrown away. Abandoned."

Hiro faintly turned his head to face Tzarik. "I understand. I'm sorry, Tzarik. I know the feeling of being…useless. Unnecessary."

That was when Tzarik heard it: the chanting of the Wu-Tang Vandauls went up around them. Suddenly, the Wushito army came into view before them as if appearing from mist. Kei Lu flanked them before they appeared. Tzarik drew his short black bow and nocked an arrow to it. His scimitar was not suited to slashing from horseback. The spears and long swords of the Wushito would easily outreach him.

"You have shown everyone you are not unnecessary, sira," Tzarik said. "If nothing else, you've inspired this Runer."

A call went up from behind the suddenly visible Wushito forces. A rain of black arrows rose up, pelting down as the Wushito raised their shields to stop the deadly missiles.

"Not wasting any time, is he?" Zhen said, sighing and raising his sword to command his men. "That barbarian is always ready for a fight."

"Charging head on?" Tzarik shouted over the sudden uproar of warriors.

"We cannot let those siege towers near the walls!" Hiro called back, kicking his horse.

Tzarik followed him quickly. He stood up in the stirrups to lessen the jostling from Mamun's gallop and aimed a shot at an advancing Wushito warrior. The man did not dodge the arrow, taking it between the eyes. As Tzarik wheeled around to nock another arrow, he made note of the warriors' colors and ornaments: not all Wushito were Reavers. A Reaver would have not taken the arrow to the face like that.

"Watch the back side!" Zhen shouted to Tzarik in Al'Myrahn.

Mamun's hooves splashed and slipped in the mud as he cut sharp turns to look. One of the siege towers, which he now saw was full to bursting with armed men and women, rolled to one of the outer turret's walls. Screaming to the horse, he galloped back, kicking a warrior away and ducking a thrown spear. He made it to the far east pyre and kicked the lantern in. The pyre exploded, making Mamun whine and rear up in fear. But the fire crackled up to the dark sky, signaling the bombers on the walls near the approaching tower.

He caught a few black powder bombs being launched towards the siege tower, catching it on fire and throwing a few warriors from its top, blasted out from the bombs. The western side of the city walls suddenly crawled with archers and other warriors tasked with defending. But the machine had already gotten too close.

Fighting his way over, Tzarik took a knife-cut to his forearm but otherwise approached the breached wall without harm. He stayed back, defending himself from the few warriors who leapt out or picked themselves up off the ground from the bomb blasts. Above him, some of the royal warriors shouted at him to get back. Already he saw the top of the siege tower opening, preparing to release a flood of Wushito warriors onto the western wall. They had to be stopped.

Fleeing on Mamun, he used his blood to draw halat onto his palms like before. Once he had them, he turned back around and charged at the tower. The Wushito above shouted and rained arrows at him amidst the onslaught of bombs. Clutching buhkar, he misted from the back of his horse, who took the opportunity to retreat. Sliding under the siege tower as black smoke, he solidified.

A Wushito screamed above him, seeing him under the floorboards of the tower.

Screaming, he drew halat with both hands and thrust it up. The floor exploded upwards, shattered by the magic shield. Inside, screams of pain and confusion went up as the splintered wood shot into the flesh of the warriors. Misting again, he slithered out to try his next plan. With the ten seconds of distracted pain, he slowly drew jiun.

Starting from his chest, the fury roiled. Hot, burning his veins, it spread out to the very tips of his fingers and toes. His mind spun and all his inhibitions vaporized. Leaping up, he gripped a beam of the siege tower and began to climb. Seeing him, the western defenders moved their aim to the side as they prepared to be greeted with the opening tower.

Tzarik scaled the tower easily, fueled by jiun. He couldn't stop to think, letting his pure animal instincts guide him. He stabbed a warrior who attempted to shove him off and cut the arms off another with his scimitar. After that, he tossed the blade over his shoulder. It whirled down, lodging into another Wushito's skull below. Once he got to the top, he shouted at the royal commander on the western wall to toss a barrel of the black powder to him.

Whether his wild, glowing white eyes and pulsating white veins or the heat of the moment moved the commander, Tzarik didn't know. Without question, the commander lit a thick fuse in a keg of powder and launched it towards the Runer. Just as a Wushito appeared to stab Tzarik, he kicked off the siege tower, flipping backwards in a graceful arch. As the tower reeled back into view, so did the keg. Drawing halat and fueled by jiun, he thrust his hands out, surrounding the keg with the shield.

As he fell, he shoved it against the top of the tower, smashing it hard and causing it to tilt. Halat fizzled away just as the keg detonated, snapping the top of the tower and shoving it even further left. With the explosion, the tower tilted and crashed to the earth. Tzarik drew the shield rune once more, breaking only part of his fall. With a crunch, he splashed deep into the wet earth, hitting the barrier before sinking almost completely into the mud. He cried out as he felt his arm break from the impact. His ribs also snapped again.

Rolling over with a groan, he drew artiah over his wounded side. The fury of jiun made the pain less, but that wouldn't allow him to move. The bones inside his left arm mended a little, causing a tingling sensation to run up to his shoulder.

"Runer?" the commander on the wall shouted down.

"Kill them!" he screamed back up.

Satisfied the insane Runer still lived, the commander went back to his onslaught on the now destroyed siege tower. A band of royal warriors arrived to finish off the Wushito from the fallen tower. Tzarik drew artiah again, knowing it wouldn't heal much more. It was enough to allow him to stand.

Pushing himself out of the mud, he limped over to his scimitar and pulled it from the skull of the warrior. Jiun dwindled and wore off just as he stepped onto his injured leg and collapsed in pain down into the cold mud again. Looking out into the battlefield, he spotted four other siege machines burning, not even close to the wall. Zhen's banner still fluttered from the back of the horse where the commander protected Hiro's side as they fought. Wushito hadn't gotten near the city yet.

Tzarik managed to stand again. As he came to his full height, the hairs on the back of his neck stood up. Spinning around, his eyes landed on a white-cloaked Reaver. The sharp, angled hood hid the woman's face except for her thin-lipped smirk. She drew a blade from her side nearly as long as she was. Something on the blade, like beveled lettering, caught Tzarik's eye before she ran her hand over it, smearing it with some kind of purple ointment.

She asked him something in Xian, her smile turning manic. When he didn't reply, she held her palm up to face him, which was covered in the purple stuff.

"Runer poison," she said in heavily accented Al'Myrahn.

"Shit," Tzarik said, gasping and dodging a quick and sudden stab from her long-reaching sword.

As they danced around each other, Tzarik staying as far away as he could and drawing halat and buhkar to stay safe, he noted the elements on her person that were becoming increasingly familiar: the scrolls, the talismans, and vials of liquids. He couldn't get a better look at the inscriptions on her sword, but every time it came close to his flesh, something in the sword pulled the sulfates in his veins towards it. Somehow, it reminded him of the first contact he'd had with the orichalcum scimitar.

The fall had winded him and artiah could only heal so much. He knew before the Reaver had him on his knees that he'd lose this fight. He concentrated on taking as little damage as possible. She kicked him and tried to slice his flesh with her poisoned sword, but he was able to keep away until she leapt up in a flurry of robes, spinning in a dizzying motion. A shadow flew out from her and landed first. It ran at him. Thinking it would pass through, he stood still, eyes on it. The thing knocked him hard in the chest, cutting his shoulder as it sprinted past. Baffled, he spun to the side only to be crushed by the Reaver. She landed on him, breaking him underneath. She raised her sword to pin him to the earth.

A monkeylike shriek made her jolt upright. She spun to face the new adversary, but a silver staff cracked her skull. As she stumbled, Tzarik unleashed his small crossbow and put a thick bolt between her eyes. As she fell, TaoShin came into view, retracting his silver staff into its small cylindrical container.

"I need you, Runer," he panted, his wide brown eyes full of fear. "Yui's child is coming." TaoShin pulled Tzarik to his feet. He held him fast, stopping him in his haste. "She will not make it. If we are to save the child, I need your healing. Do you understand?"

Unsure what TaoShin meant, his mind still spinning and his body throbbing, he shook his head.

Sybal would understand.

"We have no time." TaoShin's monkey ears twitched, listening to the battle, but his eyes remained fixed on Tzarik's. "Your work here is done. Help me save the future of Xia now."

Chapter 30
Son of the Snake
and Dragon

TaoShin pulled the Runer into the palace and up several flights of square stairs, into the upper layers of the sloping architecture. The palace halls and golden statues passed in a blur. Tzarik tried to wrap his head around how he could help with a pre-mature birth. He'd seen one infant creature birthed and it had given him no desire to see something similar again.

"Get your runes," TaoShin instructed, stopping outside two great golden sliding doors. "I have a nursemaid who knows some witchcraft, but that is all. The rest is up to you."

From inside the doors, a girl's panting scream rose up, cutting through the walls.

"I don't..." Tzarik stammered, trying to find a way to explain that he couldn't help Yui. "I'm not a healer." His body twinged in agony with every breath into his damaged lungs.

TaoShin whispered, gripping the doors and flinging them open, "We have to try."

Inside the royal bedchamber, Yui lay on a wide circular mattress covered in silks and surrounded by a gauzy net to keep out bugs. Dozens of colorful round pillows peppered the bed and she gripped two tightly in her hands. Her face was strained, red, and dripping sweat. The witch sat at her ankles, pushing her cotton gown up over her knees. Tzarik's immediate reaction was to turn away, but he stopped when his eyes caught all the blood under the princess. Her round belly heaved with every breath.

"It's bad luck to have a man present!" the witch cried, spotting Tzarik in his blood and mud-soaked state.

"And what am I?" TaoShin interjected, crouching next to the princess. He beckoned Tzarik down. "The child is coming whether we are ready or not. I need you to draw quickly over her here," he touched Yui's hips gently, "to ease the pain, if nothing else." To the witch he barked, "Get the poultice and place it under her back."

The witch, not unlike others of her trade, clinked with ornaments and bones as she stood up to run to her pied cloth bag and pull out a jar of blue-black paste. Kneeling back down, she ordered Tzarik to help her lift the princess enough to smear some onto her skin and place a rag there to ease the pain.

"Yui," TaoShin huffed after checking between her legs. "I know I've asked before, but you have to push harder."

"I can't!" she screamed, causing lightning to snap across the sky.

Seeing the weather still tightly under her control, Tzarik hovered his hands over her lower half and drew artiah quickly. The princess gasped and threw her head back. She cringed, then moaned with a guttural, animal-like roar.

Tzarik froze. She was a gini. He still was not entirely sure what kind of creature her mother was or how it affected those who shared half her ancestral powers, but the runes only harmed creatures of that sort.

"TaoShin, I can't," he said, jerking his hands away. "It might kill her."

Yui, eyes closed, breathed heavily but no longer screamed. "That helped," she whispered. Just as she spoke, a wave of anguish took her and her entire body contracted into a spasm. Her head slammed backwards and her throat closed.

"The fever!" the witch gasped, pulling a damp cloth out of another jar. Its fragrance immediately permeated the air: something akin to lavender and another scent Tzarik couldn't place. The witch pressed it to Yui's forehead and sprinkled cold water over it. Looking up to the monk, she whispered, "She's not going to make it, TaoShin. She is too weak. Her pulse is softer than the death throes of a butterfly's wing."

Tzarik saw it, too. He'd seen life leave even unconscious bodies. The signs were subtle but visible to his Runer eyes. Even now as she lay still, he saw Yui's spirit preparing to leave.

"If she dies now, she won't see her child," Tzarik said.

"At least then we can liberate the infant," the witch said sadly.

"No." Tzarik reached into his boot and took out a curved Al'Myrahn knife of plain steel.

"What are you doing, monster?" the witch shrieked, lunging over Yui's body to grab away the knife.

Tzarik dodged her sloppy attempt and signaled TaoShin to make sure Yui was fully unconscious. "She gets to see her child. Hold her."

"Uncivilized cretin!" The witch stood up, gripping her long tangled black hair.

"You can help," TaoShin offered while Tzarik sterilized his blade in a jar of the witch's clear cleaning solution. "Hold her legs and I'll hold her arms."

"But the child?" the witch tried again.

"He'll be fine," Tzarik barked. He tossed Yui's gown up to expose her belly. He wasn't actually sure what to do. He'd cut open men before, pulled cursed objects from guts, sewn up a leg. Never very well, but it was better than nothing.

Guessing where to cut, he placed the blade at the underside of

Yui's stomache and gently drew his knife across it. His hands went numb as he worked the wound, TaoShin calling instructions his mind numbly followed. For several minutes, he held his breath. His vision blurred until he could hardly see. Blood, fluids, and insides he didn't recognize swam before him in a haze.

"He's not breathing," the witch cried somewhere to his left.

Yui gasped, crying. Her hand shot out towards the baby. Thinking she'd fallen unconscious, this startled all three of them.

Realizing she was reaching for her child, Tzarik seized it— much to the witch's and TaoShin's protests—and tipped it onto her chest. Half-conscious, the princess stopped screaming and gasped as her cheek touched her child's. Pressed against her, the baby began to cough. For two seconds, the princess held her baby before she went limp again. Deep in Tzarik's heart, something clicked. This was what Sybal wanted. He didn't fully understand, but seeing the primal desire for the mother to hold her child moved a piece inside him. A mere fraction of the burden Sybal bore came into focus; she wanted this—this mystifying bond—and she would never know it.

"Well thought, Runer," TaoShin praised him.

A few seconds later, the unmistakable yowl of a baby cut through Tzarik's mind and brought him back to the present. Blue, bloody, and kicking, the baby opened its toothless mouth to shout his annoyance to the rafters above. TaoShin dipped the child into a golden bowl of warm water and padded off his head. An overabundance of shocking glossy white hair covered the baby boy's head.

"Here, hold him," TaoShin huffed, dropping the now swaddled baby into Tzarik's arms as he and the witch went to work on Yui's wound. "We have to stitch her up and bind the wound if we're going to give her any time with her child."

His hands, covered in the blood of the child's mother, stained the white blankets. Tzarik awkwardly clutched the bundle like a rotten melon, holding it away from his body at arm's length, inspecting it. The mewling child kicked its wrapped legs and its head lolled dangerously to the side.

"Really, Runer," TaoShin said, sighing. The monk hopped over in a crouching motion. Taking Tzarik's hands in his, he repositioned the baby into the crook of his arm and pushed it against his chest. He moved Tzarik's other hand to the side of the cradling arm. "Walk with him or rock him to sooth him."

The moment he held the baby closer to his chest, it calmed down. Still weeping piteously, it fought to free its arms. Tzarik swayed back and forth, unsure exactly how fast or how wide to swing his body. Eventually, the child relaxed more and his mouth opened in a huge yawn that made his eyes squint closed and his nose wrinkle. Deciding to walk the infant prince, he took slow steps around the bedchamber while the witch and the monk cared for Yui.

Taking up a clean cloth, he dabbed more at the child's head, drying his white locks. The hair was so fine, he thought he might rub it off if he cleaned it too much. The boy's face was round like his mother's, but bore the long thin nose of his father. After scrubbing a little more water and residue off its face, the babe looked up at the Runer.

The eye contact stopped Tzarik in his tracks. The prince looked up with mild curiosity and more awareness than he'd thought a newborn would possess. One of his tiny arms finally free, he reached up and grabbed hold of Tzarik's long, dirty black hair. He knew the grime and mud would be unhealthy for the baby, but he didn't fight it, letting it take hold.

"Sybal would have cooed over you," he told the nameless child. "She was drawn to your father, respected him. I don't understand her worldly view or her understanding and patience for the people in it. She enjoys liking people." He reached his hand up and gently laid his palm against the child's warm head. "They'll expect a lot from you. I hope you are surrounded by those who will love you and support you. Not use you. But there is little hope of that. Or..."

That could be false. The boy was a Xiaoh. If Wushito was repressed, there might be a chance for him to grow up surrounded by good advisors. But more than that, the boy needed someone to love him.

Tzarik turned to the forgotten, panicked nursemaid. "Go out onto the wall. Tell a warrior to bring Hiro in."

The maid stammered, eyes wide with panic. She didn't understand.

TaoShin, overhearing, shouted the translation to her. She bolted quickly, nodding and bowing on her way out.

Turning back to the other two, Tzarik saw they had Yui stitched, wrapped, and that she was coming around. Her head lifted gently to look around.

She moaned something so quietly Tzarik almost didn't hear her. TaoShin signaled to Tzarik to bring the baby.

"Oh, Runer," Yui sighed in Al'Myrahn. "I thought that was you. I couldn't see you clearly. You made it out of the Hallow City?"

He nodded, gently placing the baby in her weak arms. "Sybal helped save you," he said, giving his apprentice her due credit.

The princess gave a ghostly smile. "She'll want to see him. She was so kind to Jin and me. Where is she?"

Tzarik didn't have to choose to answer or not. She closed her eyes, too weak to keep them open. Knowing that telling Yui Sybal was gone might push her over the edge, he refrained.

"I have to go," she muttered, wincing.

"You don't need to do anything, princess," TaoShin cooed. "Just rest and hold the child."

Her arms tightened around the quiet bundle. With great effort, her eyes fluttered open. "I am giving myself to Wushito."

The monk, the witch, and the Runer all started in surprise.

"Has the fever taken her mind?" the witch gasped, pressing her hand to Yui's clammy forehead.

Yui shook her head.

"You cannot hand over your gift," Tzarik said quickly. "ShanBao has an alliance with a man named Sharar who wants to take your gift and use it to destroy Xia. If you give it up, it will kill you."

"Runer," Yui said, smiling. "Look at me. I'm dying anyway. I could use my wish to save myself. But to use it is to die. Let me go to him."

Behind them, a clatter of armor, boots, and weapons being dropped announced Hiro's entrance. A wave of relief washed over Tzarik at seeing Hiro unharmed. Alive. The prince rushed in—rain-soaked, dripping in blood—to his sister's side. He tossed his gloves away and stroked her forehead. His eyes landed on the baby and to Tzarik's surprise, he smiled.

"Is this him?" the older prince asked. "Yui, he's beautiful."

She smiled up at her brother. "I'm glad you think so. You have to raise him. Teach him to be good, to have courage, to be merciful and mindful of those around him." She strained, raising her head to kiss the babe's. "They will want to use him. Others will want his gift. Protect him, but teach him to protect himself."

Hiro nodded quickly, sniffling. "I will, Yui."

"Runer?" she asked, weakness overtaking her.

Understanding her request, Tzarik said to Hiro, "She wants to give herself up to ShanBao and Sharar."

"No!" the prince shouted immediately. "We will not hand her over."

"Yes," she interjected. "Take my body. Show him. With me

dead, they may give up. With a piece of their plan missing, Shan-Bao's deal will weaken."

"How goes the battle?" TaoShin asked quickly.

Hiro beamed dimly. "They are retreating even as we speak."

The witch fell to her knees, pressing her head to the floor and singing a quick prayer, thanking her god.

"Brother," Yui whispered, her voice trailing ever deeper into her dying chest. "Let me do this. So I may enter Tiang."

Hiro shook his head, taking her hand. "You will, Yui. You are the daughter of the Di-Huan."

She sniffled now, a tear tracking down her cheek. "I am the daughter of a demon. I cannot enter Tiang. I cannot see Jin again." She gasped a sob, wailing softly. "I must die with honor to see him again. Please, let me do this. Runer." Her watery eyes locked onto him. "Will you do it?"

Knowing he had the strength, Tzarik nodded to the dying girl.

"Yui," Hiro begged.

"She's right," Tzarik cut in. "She will not live even another hour. Give her soul the honor it needs to enter your afterlife."

TaoShin took the child from its mother. "Princess, give us a name," he asked. "Before these witnesses." He eyed the nursemaid and the witch.

Yui looked at her baby, brows furrowed. "Yoshitsune," she finally said. "After father. Yoshitsune Xiaoh. Son of the snake and dragon."

Hiro turned away, taking the child. Tzarik heard him weep as he knelt before the princess. TaoShin crossed his legs, clutching his jade beads before him, praying for her soul with his eyes closed.

"You will feel this," Tzarik whispered, placing his hand at the back of the princess's skull to raise her head. He took up the knife he'd used to cut Yoshitsune out just moments before.

"I know," she whispered. "Runer, thank you." She clasped his hand. Even more softly, she breathed, "I used my wish. It will take me sooner than this illness. I don't know how terrible that death would've been, so I thank you."

"You used your wish?" he whispered in reply, shaken.

She smiled. "Go on."

Knowing she would not be questioned, he braced himself. She clutched his arm behind her head, lifting herself a little more. Slipping the blade behind her skull, he forced himself to watch her eyes. She looked up at him. He knew from experience it was better to leave this life with someone watching you. Beside him, the monk continued to chant his prayers.

"You will see Jin," he promised her.

"I know."

With all his strength, he thrust half the blade up underneath the soft spot at the base of her skull. Her eyes almost instantly glassed over, then faded. He made himself watch her face for a long time. Her flesh paled and her body went limp. Sunlight splashed over her profile as he let her go.

"The sun..." the witch said, gasping softly.

Outside, visible through the wide-open windows, the clouds dissipated and the warm yellow light of the sun shone down on the earth. The curse of the white snake had finally lifted.

CHAPTER 31

YASUKE'S HONOR

"YOU CAN'T TAKE HER!" HIRO CRIED.

The Runer took up the body of the dead princess, wrapping her tightly in the gauzy and silken bedclothes. The monk helped him, making sure her face shone visibly from underneath the netlike fabric.

"I have to," Tzarik spat back, tying her arms and legs together like the mummies of Alika. "Proof is the only way Sharar will believe ShanBao has failed. And we must go now. If Wushito is retreating, ShanBao has already fled. TaoShin, what can you tell me about opening the crypt?"

The monk pressed his monkeylike lips together hard. He winced as he mulled over what he knew. "I can only guess, Runer. Until recently, we didn't know the vault of monsters existed. It came as a blow to all of us of faith."

With no help from the monk, Tzarik decided to speak what he knew aloud, hoping it might inspire some ideas from the Masahk. "They use talismans to lock the spirits away," he began. "Almost like ancient magic. Symbols and words are used to bind them."

Now TaoShin's ear's twitched excitedly. "It could be layered," he started. "Perhaps there are certain sigils that must be broken to open it. The talismans—do they burn?"

Tzarik nodded.

"Then they are like gateways." The monk went to a palm-like

plant in a pot near the open balcony. "Like this leaf. It is attached to the trunk by the stalk. Each talisman transports the spirit into the crypt through its sigils and symbols."

"What are you saying?" Tzarik interrupted, not following the monk's trail of thought.

"They will have to destroy every sigil to open the crypt," he said kindly, ignoring Tzarik's impatience.

"How many can there possibly be?" he asked.

The monk shrugged. "Could be one for every type of monster. I don't know how Wushito operates. I don't know what their sigils mean or how they work. The point is, it could take them a moment to open the crypt, which is good for us. But still, we must hurry."

Hiro's face fell. "Even if you do, ShanBao has had at least an hour's head start. It takes two days for the well-acquainted traveler to get to the Hallow City from here. It would take a miracle for you to get there before him."

Yui's body swam into Tzarik's view where she lay waiting.

"I think I have that miracle," he murmured thoughtfully. If his inkling was correct, he'd get to the Hallow City in time. Maybe even overtake ShanBao and his generals. Could he have that kind of faith in something he didn't understand?

"How do you know?" Hiro asked. "We've won here, but Xia will still be devastated."

Tzarik shook his head. "No, it won't. It's already saved. I just have to act."

"What are you talking about?" Hiro begged as the Runer picked up the princess's body.

"Get Kei Lu and any willing men to follow me in one hour." Tzarik marched to the doorway, taking the princess with him. "TaoShin, any monks willing to fight should follow them."

"It sounds like another battle," TaoShin said. "What are you planning, Runer?"

He wasn't sure. He just had to trust Yui. "It won't result in a battle. At least, I hope not. But there is no harm in being prepared."

〜〄〜

Tzarik raced over the hilly paths towards the Hallow City. Putting his faith in Yui's dying wish, he rested at night and pushed on harder and faster the next day. By sunset, he came upon the hollow mountain and its mysterious entrance. Lifting Yui in his arms, he passed underneath, ready to take the same way up he had before. As he stepped through the invisible rippling barrier, the scent of smoke filled his nostrils.

Above him, the Hallow City burned. One great column of fire sprouted up from what he guessed was the central structure inside the city. Placing her body on his horse, he led it inside the city, going through the now dilapidated front gate. The red and gold paint was chipped, battered by some foe. Inside, the city lay quiet and dead. Not a sign of a single Reaver or Wushito warrior remained. Still, he heard a ruckus from further in. He moved deeper into the quiet streets, thinking maybe the Vandauls or even another faction of fighters had ransacked the city. Or maybe the traitors inside Wushito had finally turned on their master.

Several minutes later, his body tense with being on full alert, he came upon a living being. Wu-Zhiang slithered over the rubble, giving orders to a few white-cloaked warriors. A quick glance told him she was alone with the warriors on this layer of the city. Boldly, he walked out into view, leading his horse with the corpse in the saddle.

"Don't," Wu-Zhiang hissed to her warriors when they drew their blades. "Take the crates and go out through the tower," she instructed, keeping her slitted eyes on Tzarik.

He let them leave. He didn't want *them*.

"What are you doing here, Runer?" she asked, slowly unsheathing her long, curved blade. The sigils on it rang in Tzarik's ears for the first time. "You won. The Royal City has taken hundreds of Wushito captive. We are devastated."

"Where's Sharar?" he asked sternly, unsheathing his scimitar.

"Doesn't matter," she spat back. "We're destroying everything. No evidence will be left. You may have won the war, but Xia will suffer with all our knowledge gone."

"Only if the crypt is opened." Tzarik pulled the runes to the outside of his leather armor. "Sharar won't let ShanBao release the monsters when he knows the deal is off. Yui is dead."

Wu-Zhiang's eyes went to the body on the horse. "Ah," she mused. "Then I guess there is no harm in helping you join her. And your precious Sybal."

Tzarik froze. His hand started to shake.

Wu-Zhiang's fangs glinted in the setting sun as she grinned. "We tortured her before I bit her. Tied her up just there." She pointed to two great crucifixes. "That's her blood right there, Tzarik."

Risking a look, he glanced over at the deadly beams. A faint white stain covered the center of one. Each end of the X-shaped monstrosity had a shackle on it.

"We beat her, flogged her, then tied her up there." Wu-Zhiang slithered closer to Tzarik, encircling him with the wide arch of her body. "I remember how my fangs punctured her flesh. So soft. Her neck was made for biting."

She was trying to enrage him, to get him to act rashly. Wrestling with the anger, he closed his eyes, trying to push the image out of his head. She slithered closer to him. He needed to move, to get out of her grasp, but his feet wouldn't budge. They rooted him to the spot.

"She looked for you," the Masahk general went on. "Her eyes scanned the horizon. I could almost hear her: 'Help me, save me, Tzarik.' But you never came."

With a savage cry, he sliced at her scaly coils. She dodged but only just, not expecting him to strike yet. With a hiss, she snapped her open jaw at his torso. Rolling to the side, he dodged her bite, but the end of her tail wrapped around his ankle, snaking up to his thigh and holding him fast. He made a slash at her with his scimitar, but she parried the blow with her own sword. When he reached for his runes, she lunged again to bite him. Sensing the attack, he raised the curve of his scimitar up and her jaws clamped over the edge tightly.

Shrieking, she arched backward. The blade cut through her lips into her cheeks, baring her teeth between the bloody slits. Tzarik went for his runes again to mist out of her clutching coils, but she jerked and flailed in pain, yanking his trapped leg out from under him. He fell onto his chest, dropping his sword from the impact. Wu-Zhiang lifted him by his entrapped limb, pulling him away from his deadly blade.

"Look what you've done to my face!" she screamed, running her claw-like fingers through the flapping wounds.

He went for his runes again and she jolted him to the side, making him fumble with the string. Having enough, she slammed him to the ground, cracking his head against the stones. With him rolling on the ground, winded, she slithered a good distance away, regaining her composure.

"I'll bite you, too. You know that Masahk venom is one of only three toxins that can do to your sulfates what regular toxins do to red bloods?"

Tzarik pushed himself up, feeling blood leak down the back of his neck from the point of impact on his skull. It wasn't too bad: scalps always bled a lot.

"One must take care of the doses, though," she went on, slurring through her maimed face. "Masahk venom will all but kill you, allowing you just enough life, suspended somewhere between living and dead."

This information was new to him. Of course, he'd had little occasion to be bitten by another sentient being.

"I see you don't understand," she said, sighing. "Sybal is alive, Runer."

"Don't say her name!" With a war cry, he lunged at the general. Free at last, he drew jiun quickly, spinning into a flurry of attacks.

She parried a few blows and bit down once on his runic barrier; the wound made her reel. She moved slower and her breathing heaved. Whenever her blade came close to Tzarik, his sulfates slowed, pulling towards the mysterious engravings. With her moving slower, he landed a dozen strikes on her until she finally collapsed in dark smears of blood, panting.

Tzarik came up from the final blow and looked down at his pathetic rival. She gurgled in her blood.

Reaching for something on her belt, she choked, "You will not have the pleasure."

Her hand went for a tiny vial of what he guessed to be poison. Taking her own life, she'd die on her terms and bestow the coveted honor on herself. Unwilling to let her pass that way, Tzarik kicked the vial from her hand.

"No!" Wu-Zhiang shrieked. "I will not die by your han—"

Ignoring her, Tzarik swooped his scimitar above his head and brought the curve down, severing her shrieking, disfigured head. The power from the swing spun it off to the side, where it rolled until it came to a rest at the bottom of the stained crucifix. Hurrying to it, he made sure the lids of her panicking eyes twitched. He'd witnessed beheadings where the victim remained alive for several moments. Masahk no doubt took longer to dwindle away.

Gripping her eyelid, he cut it off and tossed it aside. A guttural, drowning hiss told him she felt his final dishonor. Gritting his teeth and reveling in the pleasure, he severed her other lid.

"Look upon her cross," he snarled. Standing up, he spat onto her face where her tongue lolled out, eyes dancing madly over the sky.

Gathering his breath, Tzarik reached down and picked up her blade. Repulsed, his sulfates recoiled under his flesh. Still, he didn't want to leave the mysterious weapon behind. Stowing it on his horse, he seized the reins and led the animal up another layer of the city.

One down, two to go.

ﻋﺮ

Tzarik had to follow any clues he could find outside the innermost structure to figure out where to go next. Reading the buildings as best he could, he found one that must be the main palace. Similar to the royal palace, this one reached up in stacked layers, with arching roofs of red and gold. The stairs that led up to it were wide and made of stone. Before it sprawled a square tile with ornamental stones that illustrated a great dragon clutching golden orbs in its foreclaws. A wild mane crawled out from its whiskered face, spreading over most of the court. Standing atop the stairs, long hair released from its ritualistic braid and blowing in the breeze, swords drawn, stood Yasuke.

"I knew you'd come." His spoke at a regular volume, but his voice echoed off the empty square. His fox ears twitched, catching the reverberation.

"Are you going to let me pass?" Tzarik asked, drawing his scimitar and walking a few steps away from his horse and cargo.

The Masahk general shook his head. "I'm doomed no matter if ShanBao passes our secrets on to the Al'Myrahn scholar or not. Like other Wushito this day, I've betrayed my creed, aided a foreigner, and allowed spies to pass among our ranks, among other treacheries."

"I wouldn't call it that," Tzarik offered the turncoat. "You acted on what you believed to be right. There's no dishonor in that."

Yasuke's lips twitched in disgust. "Don't try to use our ways against me, Runer. This is how it has to be. You are right, but not because you are honorable. I know you want me to let you pass. You will tell me it is the good thing to do."

The warrior bounced his blades in his hands. One looked like a regular blade. The other, long and inscribed like the others, rang in Tzarik's ears. Before Tzarik could take in the sensation too much, voices from within the headquarters rang out. Two men in a heated debate. Yasuke turned, holding his hand out to stop them advancing towards him. Tzarik recognized Sharar and ShanBao.

ShanBao cursed in Xian. "What is this, Abigor?" he snapped, taking a step away from the top of the stairs.

"I was going to ask you the same thing," Sharar snapped, his hand going to his belt and satchel.

"I have your gini," Tzarik shouted up to them. "She is dead."

"What?" Sharar turned on ShanBao, his dark eyes going wild and wide. His head snapped between Tzarik, Yasuke, and the corpse, which the Runer laid at the end of the stairs. "Show me," he commanded.

Tzarik noticed how the scholar placed one foot behind him, toes turned out to flee. Keeping one eye on the trio, he knelt and took the cloth off Yui's pale face. Sharar looked long and hard at her. Slowly, the corners of his lips turned down. He raised his head, preparing a statement.

"We can still open the crypt," ShanBao interjected.

"The book," Sharar shot back. "You've been a disappointment, Master ShanBao. I'm leaving this gods-cursed continent. I've wasted enough time here. I'll see you soon, Tzarik. Enjoy getting out of this one."

The old warrior dropped his head, shaking it. "Foreigners," ShanBao said with a sigh.

Before the other three could move, ShanBao stepped towards Sharar quickly. Tzarik saw the glint of the tiny Xian blade and ran up two steps before the scholar gasped, clutching at his middle. Even Yasuke took a stuttering step forward, unsure what ShanBao had done.

"Stop the Runer," ShanBao order Yasuke. He reached down, seizing Sharar by the back of his robes and dragging him inside the palace, a trail of blood smearing out behind him. "I still need this fool."

Torn between running after ShanBao and Sharar and fighting Yasuke, Tzarik looked to the Wushito warrior.

"You don't want that crypt opened," Tzarik said.

"Don't talk, Runer," Yasuke mused, descending the steps two at a time. "It's not your way."

Before the Wushito general lunged into combat, Tzarik swore he saw the ghostly, fiery outline of a nine-tailed fox behind him. When Yasuke charged, the mystical beast charged with him—almost like it was part of him. Taken off guard, Tzarik could only quickly draw halat to deflect the blow. In the second Yasuke's Wushito blade hit it, Tzarik's heart leapt into his throat: the sigiled blade struck through it a fraction of an inch, cracking it like a pane of glass.

Shaken, Tzarik drew buhkar to put some ground between them. Yasuke's eyes burned yellow, slitted like a fox's.

"Our sigils are made to destroy you, Runer," he said, smiling darkly. "You made it past Zhiang? I'm shocked."

Realizing no amount of traitorous aid would stop Yasuke from battling now, Tzarik gave in to the fight. The fiery shadow of the fox wavered now and then, appearing brightly whenever Yasuke struck fiercely. He tried to ignore it, realizing it must be a kind of manifestation of Yasuke's Masahk blood.

"There's no reason for you to die here, Yasuke," Tzarik panted, entangling blades with the fierce warrior. "You're immortal. Why die here, your Masahk blood wasted?"

With a flurry of attacks from his two blades, Yasuke pushed Tzarik back, cracking another quickly drawn halat shield.

Walking a tight circle to catch his breath, Yasuke replied, "Because Xia is the god's chosen land. There's more than one crypt here, Runer. Millennia of monsters hide under the surface, and one day they will break free. The demons from The Frozen Nation will come and burst them open, plaguing the world with an apocalypse of monstrosities. Why would I want to live to see that?"

Tzarik shook his head. "Nothing a Runer couldn't fix, given a few weeks." He almost smirked.

Now Yasuke laughed. "Like Caerwren? So much black magic walks that continent that the gods walk amongst their people. Do you know what gods like best, Runer?"

Confused, Tzarik didn't reply.

"Blood." Yasuke spun his sigiled blade. "They like blood. And they don't discriminate on what kind. White, red, Masahk. You Runers attract things far worse than ghosts and jiangshi."

The warrior spun at him, raining blows down so quickly, he

had to make snap decisions on which ones he let land and which he blocked.

"That's a lie," he grunted, almost getting in a slash himself. "Monsters are few and far between." Abandoning his offensive strokes, he drew halat and shoved it towards Yasuke.

As they were blown apart, Tzarik felt a million tiny cuts all over his body open. The warrior had landed more thin cuts than he'd thought.

"You are becoming obsolete," Yasuke mused.

Above them, a loud crack—as if the mountain itself was splitting—drew their attention back up to where ShanBao ran with Sharar. While Yasuke looked up, Tzarik drew buhkar as slowly as he dared. He slithered out of sight so that when Yasuke looked back, he spun on the spot, trying to find his prey. Knowing he only had a second to surprise the Wushito, Tzarik zipped behind him just as he materialized again. He raised his scimitar and Yasuke thrust his sigiled blade behind him.

Tzarik groaned as the special blade slid between his ribs. His arms grew weak instantly and his veins rushed hot. Yasuke turned, letting go of the ornate handle.

Facing Tzarik, he said, "You are one man, Runer. What do you think—"

Blood spurt from Yasuke's throat and now exposed chest. The scimitar cut through his thin, silken Wushito robes, slicing his chest to his bones. The warrior's foxlike eyes went wide and he fell onto his back, hands scrambling at his chest. Around his middle, his belt held a scroll of the talismans the Wushito used to seal away monsters. Tzarik pulled it off. He knew all he had to do was press it against Yasuke's forehead and his soul would be trapped, unable to ascend to the good afterlife he craved so much.

Seeing his intent, the warrior's whitening lips fluttered in a desperate plea.

The talisman shook in Tzarik's hand. The sword still protruding from his chest, Tzarik considered. He wondered what had stopped him. Before, his callous nature would have pushed past such inhibitions. Despite what Yasuke had done for him, he would have sent his immortal soul into the darkness. Somewhere in the last year, he'd started to ask himself why he did these things. Feelings of regret and guilt held his hand now.

"You helped us," he moaned, unable to get a good breath. "For that, I will show you mercy. Your honor has saved you."

To his surprise, the general smiled. "Better to have my life taken by one such as you than to allow a man like ShanBao to steal my soul." His throat constricted with a gasping gulp of air. Closing his eyes in agony, the Masahk waited for the death blow.

Gripping the general's sword, his sulfates rushing away from the intruding metal, Tzarik pulled it out of his chest. It was so long he had to pull, grip the blade, then pull again. Feeling it slide over his insides, his stomach flipped and bile rose in his throat. He held it in until the blade left him, then pitched forward, vomiting onto the stone. After emptying his stomach, the rumbling from above came to him again. He glanced over at the wounded general. Shallow breaths shone through the glassy shine of his bloodied chest.

Tzarik wiped his mouth, drew artiah twice slowly to heal himself, and stood up. His blood wetting it, he picked up Yasuke's blade and lashed it to his horse next to Wu-Zhiang's. Taking the time to put Yui back onto his horse, he instructed it to stay and then ascended the steps to confront ShanBao.

CHAPTER 32
DESPERATE,
FEARLESS

HE COULDN'T TAKE THE STAIRS TWO AT A TIME. MOST ON XIA didn't stand taller than him, but his wound ached despite it not bleeding anymore and slowed his ascent up the steps into the heart of Wushito. He stumbled up one stair at a time, stopping at the top to catch his breath. He needed to make more sulfates. He'd lost a lot and had very little to replace them with. Begging the runes to give him just a little more strength, he drew artiah once more over his wounds.

Sharar's red blood faded to thin smatters farther in. Just inside the wide and bright red torii arch, an expansive temple-like foyer spanned the entire first floor. Golden statues of warriors and jade monsters decorated a floor-to-ceiling altar. Bowls of colored sand with incense sticks in them smoldered, spilled over the floor and altar top, thrown in the struggle. Behind this, two sets of wide stairs appeared. One led up into the higher layers of the temple-like structure. The other delved beneath the floor into darkness. Somehow, the stairwell looked blacker than it should if it simply led to a lower level. The darkness almost waved like the surface of a calm lake. Tzarik momentarily wondered if it led to the garrison where he'd been held. Beyond these steps, a round lattice-decorated doorway opened out to the back where the garden emptied into a great waterfall he could hear from inside.

Tzarik followed Sharar's blood outside. There, the waterfall drowned out most of the sound of the chirping birds and other animals moving for the night. From atop the continent, the sunset almost blinded him. His foot hit hard ground on his next step, prompting him to look down. Around where he stood, the grass had been stomped down and flattened. It looked like there had been a scuffle. Claw marks showed where a monster had leapt, attacking something.

"Sharar is gone," ShanBao said, drawing the Runer's attention to where he sat, cross-legged on a boulder overlooking a sheer drop. "I opened the first sigil and that bastard commanded the first ghost of a creature he saw to attack me."

No obvious wound showed on the old man.

"I gave him a wound he would not soon forget." A tiny, wicked smile graced ShanBao's cheek.

Tzarik took a cautious step towards the cunning master, his eyes taking in every detail and looking for a trick. The orange light glinted off an empty bottle next to the old man's knee. Tiny bits of white powder clung to the bottom corners. Across his lap rested his long sigiled blade. He waited with his eyes half-closed, hands lying over the blade.

"What have you done?" Tzarik asked, indicating the empty vial. "Where's the crypt?"

"Hidden, of course," ShanBao answered lazily.

Curious, Tzarik stepped closer. ShanBao didn't move. Still, he gripped his scimitar. "What game are you playing, ShanBao? Stand up and defend yourself."

The old man raised his head, closing his eyes against the warm sun and cool wind. "The Wushito believe the only way to die is against a worthy opponent. We pray for a man honorable enough to take our lives."

Tilting his head quickly to the vial, Tzarik said, "You didn't. You took your own life. Even your generals faced me in combat."

ShanBao smiled lazily. "I am the only man worthy to take my own life. You cannot. I have trained for seven decades to fight those such as you, Runer. I have trained men and women who have killed Runers that outnumber them. There are no worthy opponents for a true Wushito master. Especially me. And especially not you. You are a stupid barbarian of a man." He pressed his hands together before his chest. "All of Xia could not stand against me."

Tzarik had seen many great creatures fall. The way ShanBao sat, uncaring of the danger around him—denying his imminent death—reminded Tzarik of such monsters. During those times, he'd take advantage: cut their head off, bound them inside a circle, taken them so savagely and completely to revel in the easy kill. A desire to finish ShanBao the same way consumed him. But deeper still, he felt that such barbarism in this instance would not satisfy him. Despite what ShanBao had done to him and Sybal—the dishonesty and pain he'd brought them—he wanted to fight him. ShanBao was denying him the satisfaction.

Maybe he could provoke him to fight.

"Stand up, Wushito Master ShanBao," Tzarik growled, taking a step back. "Face me in combat. Die with your damned honor intact."

"You are no opponent," ShanBao repeated.

"You're a coward," Tzarik spat back.

ShanBao scoffed gently. "If you are so eager to draw my blood, do it."

"Do not tempt me. I am desperate."

"Desperation leads to fear."

Tzarik expected his anger to flare, for the barbarous nature ShanBao had pointed out to take over. Instead, only divine repose held him back. He shook his head. "I am desperate and fearless, ShanBao. And therefore unstoppable."

Neither man moved. The wind pushed through their hair and clothes lightly, making soft rustling sounds.

"But you won't." ShanBao opened his eyes finally. "Is it the honor you so despise that holds you back? Why won't you kill a defenseless old man?"

"And give you the satisfaction?" Tzarik, overcoming his fear of the deep cliff, stepped in front of ShanBao. His back to the fatal drop and the Reaver before him, a tingling buzzed through his legs. "I think you're a coward to not fight me."

"And I think you're a simpleton for not smiting me as I sit." ShanBao's brown eyes flicked to Tzarik's icy blue ones. "Or is it something else? Are you trying to be good? To not murder me?" The old man dropped his hands from their prayerful position onto his blade.

"What about Tiang?" Tzarik asked, losing his patience. "Suicide without honor denies you entry. The beasts of the afterlife will chase you down to Diyu."

"Fine," ShanBao said, sighing, his shoulders slumping. In his chest, his breath rattled. "All my greatest enemies are in Tiang. I'd rather endure eternal torture, have my entrails ripped from me, and be speared on a molten javelin than see some of them again, no matter the golden halls or meadows of eternal life."

Tzarik had not thought out his own philosophy on the afterlife, but what ShanBao described didn't make sense. Sentient kind often avoided pain. If ShanBao truly believed in eternal hell, he'd rather suffer forever than see some of the men and women he'd crossed in his mortal life. Tzarik didn't understand.

"I see your confusion," ShanBao said, moaning and swallowing hard. "I ask you, Tzarik, to think on some of the evil things you've done. Surely it would be simpler to endure that forever than to meet those you have wronged in a place of everlasting life?"

"If the ones I have wronged end up in the same afterlife as me, there's a reason," he spat. "If there is such a thing."

"Oh, of course." ShanBao closed his eyes again. "You think you have done something good, worthy of enduring glory. Have you ever done anything good, Runer?"

Tzarik didn't have to think long or dig deep to find a few answers to spit at ShanBao. He might not believe they made him good, but he didn't want the Wushito master to win the philosophical battle. "I saved Xia, even if just for a moment. I once stopped a world war from breaking out. I did it in passing one night in Hatal when our sultana thought the world was coming to an end. You people in power are drunk on your fear mongering."

"And you saved a murderer from her lawful fate," ShanBao added softly, his face now turning a malignant gray. "No matter how you justify that, Tzarik, Sybal is guilty. Every Runer is. That's why you are not good men." He turned his eyes to the horizon, narrowing them slightly. "Except you. Murder is most Runers' crime. No other sin allots for such a wicked punishment. What makes you so innocent? Why are you blackened by the runes if not for a life stolen?"

At the mention of Sybal, all other thoughts fled Tzarik's mind. Kneeling by the dying man, he growled, "Where is she?"

Something inside Tzarik snapped. Arching his scimitar out of its sheath, he sliced in a semicircle at the Wushito. As expected, the man rolled away from the deadly strike. In a fluid, almost elegant motion, ShanBao somersaulted away, flickered, and created a shadow version of himself. One stood still and the other gripped the sigiled blade and ran to Tzarik's left.

Grinning, teeth clenched, the Runer chased after the fleeing warrior. ShanBao ran to a patch of reeds and slipped inside, skirting behind a red quartz statue. He came out the other side, but the sulfates told Tzarik that was another shadow. Drawing halat above him, he deflected a blow from the sigiled blade, which appeared around the other side of the statue.

"You're cleverer than I anticipated," the old man mused, crossing blades and parrying a blow.

When their blades met, they ground against one another as if trying to shove together two opposing magics. Pushing away, ShanBao turned to the statue and ran up half of it only to flip over Tzarik's head before fleeing again.

"Coward!" Tzarik shouted after him, sliding his small crossbow off his belt. Quickly pulling the string back, he aimed hastily and fired the bolt.

To dodge it, ShanBao flickered again, running to the left. The shadow took the bolt, lurching forward and vanishing as it died. Re-holstering the bow, Tzarik pursued his prey. He drew halat again just in case he ran into an attack. Free of the reed field, he scanned the outcropping for the Wushito. His wound opened afresh from the battle, stinging under his armor. Growling, he unlaced it and tossed it aside, tunic and all. Before him, ShanBao's actual shadow appeared. The man was behind him.

Turning, Tzarik faced him. He stood atop a boulder, perched on a stave like he'd seen TaoShin do: one foot on either side to grip it.

"Foolish to lose your armor," the old man said, smirking. Gripping his own silken robes, he tore them from his torso.

Never in his life had Tzarik seen markings the likes of which covered ShanBao's skin. Where hundreds of scars, brands, and other disfigurements mapped and etched Tzarik's body, colorful tattoos depicting red and gold dragons, symbols he couldn't read—even a tiger with bloody claws—artistically composed the canvas that was his chest and arms. Under the ink, lithe, knotted muscles coiled and flexed like snakes struggling to be free.

"Every image a victory, Runer," ShanBao informed him when his eyes traced the ink. "The pain of such art is the reward for overcoming trials."

Tzarik prepared a venomous reply but held his tongue when ShanBao's eyes took in his own canvas. He waited, bouncing the hilt of his scimitar in his hand.

"I see you are no stranger to such pain," the Wushito mumbled. "Bite marks, claws, burns..." His eyes landed on one large mark left by a maw large enough to take Tzarik into its jaws. The scar circled his side and lower stomach, disappearing under his belt and around to his back. "How are you alive?"

Finally sensing a change in power in the fight, Tzarik allowed himself a dark grin. "Runers are resilient. Never leave us in one piece or we may just rise again."

Flicking halat towards ShanBao, Tzarik knocked the Wushito off his perch. Weakened from the poison, ShanBao tumbled backwards off the boulder. Knowing he would employ the use of his shadow again, Tzarik skirted to the left. ShanBao had been favoring that side. Drawing jiun and halat quickly, for a spurt of mad energy and a flash of protection, he met ShanBao emerging from the other side. His reflexes kicking in, the Wushito lashed out with the stave, cracking it against the sputtering magic shield.

"Those runes greatly annoy me!" ShanBao roared, tossing the broken stave aside. Putting some distance between himself and Tzarik, he took out his sigiled blade and a long regular one of white steel.

With the quick madness coursing through his sulfates, Tzarik defended himself and even landed a deep slash through the red dragon on ShanBao's chest. But the sigiled blade pulled at his sulfates uncomfortably, almost distracting him. He swore he heard the metal moan the closer it got to him.

The symbols had to be where Wushito drew their power from. Not unlike the runes, there had to be some combination of them that did the things he'd witnessed: the binding of the spirits, defending against the otherworldly mong sho. It wasn't as unlike his runes as he'd thought. Still, they did not agree with the sulfates in his veins.

Spinning his curved scimitar around the sigiled blade, he confused ShanBao's ever-slowing mind. Getting both blades pointed towards the ground, he vaulted over them, kicking ShanBao twice, once with each booted foot. His wounds bled again, encasing his brain in a dizzying fuzz. He drew artiah rapidly to stop the bleeding as he landed and faced his opponent. Seeing ShanBao winded, he lurched forward, headbutting him hard. The sigiled blade thumped to the ground. The old man cried out, but Tzarik didn't stop. Taking up the sigiled blade, he spun like he'd seen the Xian warriors do, holding both blades out around his body, turning himself into a deadly dervish. With every slice through the Wushito's inked skin, satisfaction roiled up inside him. Once, his scimitar hit bone. He could tell when it met resistance, but the curved blade slid out with just a bit of coaxing. Losing himself in the dissipation of jiun, he let it take him until the last of it vanished.

Coming back, he gazed down at his prey. ShanBao stood on his knees, teetering dangerously. Bits of his long hair scattered over the grass. Large flaps of sliced, inked flesh hung off his body. Taking the brief moment, Tzarik kicked him over onto his back with a shout. Kneeling on his shoulders, he pinned ShanBao down. Pulling the small dagger from his boot, he reached down to the man's eyelids.

"Don't, Runer!" ShanBao screeched. "It is not your place to dishonor me with my own customs."

Ignoring him, he pinched his lids and cut them with a single swipe. Disgusted, he tossed the thin skin aside and stood up. His entire body shook in exhaustion, pain, and delirium. The lidless eyes rolled in ShanBao's head, bleeding and blinding him.

"Was this necessary...Runer?" he gasped.

Not remorse. Not regret. Something akin to self-loathing roiled in his gut. Glaring down at the mess of a man who wanted to destroy his entire people, he couldn't believe the emotion that consumed him.

"Where is Sybal?" he repeated.

ShanBao scoffed. "She was right to have that bastardized Runer pride. It ended her, but she was right, I'll give you that, Tzarik. On Al'Myrah, the holy men call it fitrah, yes? The innate goodness. She has done evil but is good. She struggles to balance it."

"Where is she?" Tzarik roared.

The Wushito gulped hard. "Sharar took her. I cared not at all for her. Zhiang fixated on her, the fool. That was why she would never surpass Yasuke. Dispatched him, too, I assume?" He looked away from Tzarik, blinded by his own blood. "Waste of an immortal life."

Reaching over and easily taking the Wushito master's neck in his grip, he squeezed until something cracked under his fingers. Tzarik asked again, "Where is Sybal?"

Choking, his wobbling eyes rolling back into his head, ShanBao didn't fight back. "It would be nice to know."

Realizing the dying man would never give him the answers he wanted, he shoved him down to the ground and paced away, stomping in rage.

"Are you truly innocent?" ShanBao gagged, froth pooling up in his mouth now from the poison. He lay where Tzarik had tossed him, unmoving. "What was your crime?"

"It would be nice to know," Tzarik spat back.

The old Wushito master withered before him, collapsing onto the damp moss. ShanBao's veins ceased pulsing and his eyes turned hazy. Lying amidst the rubble, Wushito Master ShanBao died nothing more than a weak old man with a head full of unrealized plans.

Tzarik reached down and picked up the sigiled blade. This one rang deeper in his head than the others, as if he had struck it against the rocks. It hummed like metal forks used for tuning stringed instruments. Something about it made his flesh crawl. Still, he would take it back through the temple room to his waiting horse. He glanced around once, wondering if he could catch a glimpse of where Sharar might have run off to, but knew the attempt was futile. If Sharar had wanted to leave, Tzarik wouldn't be able to find him. And now, the scholar knew the Runers were not on his side. Their simple ruse had been destroyed.

CHAPTER 33
THE WISH

WITH THE SIGILED BLADE IN HIS HAND, TZARIK LOOKED OUT over the edge. The mist from the waterfall chilled his exposed skin. He'd grown so used to the wet coldness from the rain and didn't notice this. His body shook from the wintry drizzle, but his thoughts went elsewhere. The last several months weighed on his mind, filling him with doubt, dread, and loathing. At times like this, he would have wanted to speak out loud to Sybal. But he'd never allowed himself that. She'd lived mostly in silence with him. More than ever, he craved conversation.

He glanced sidelong at ShanBao's corpse. Dead men made for confidential conversation.

"I can't keep up with Sharar. Sybal's right: all I do is run. Hide. Try to escape my problems. You don't deserve to hear this."

Then why was he speaking to his enemy so openly?

"You could be lying," he went on. "She could be dead." He furrowed his brow, trying to think. "If she were dead, they'd make sure I knew. Sharar left empty-handed." A small, satisfied scoff left his throat. "He must be enraged. He came for that damned book, the gini, and an army of monsters..."

His voice caught. Perhaps not entirely empty-handed. "He must have Sybal."

Behind him, snorting and hurried hoofbeats alerted him to Mamun's presence. The horse finally found its way through the temple room, coming to its master's aid. Without bidding, it stood next to him, looking over the edge.

Even then Tzarik looked out and over the fatal drop. His veins vibrated with the uncontrollable reaction to the heights he hated so much. Still, throwing himself off wouldn't be so bad. What was the point anymore? Xia might be saved, but he was no match for Sharar. The would-be sorcerer was always a step ahead of him. He'd still failed and was alone once again.

Toeing the edge, he leaned over. Well over one hundred feet to the craggy waters below. Nothing to stop his descent. If he aimed, he might hit the rocks just right, shattering himself before he even felt it. Looking around, he scanned for anything that might stop him. Nothing appeared. He slipped his scimitar into its sheath and unlaced it from his thigh, letting it hang straight down. As he did, his hand hit his little belt satchel.

Touching it, he remembered the letter. That could be a place to start. ShanBao and Sharar had all but told him Sybal might be alive...or something akin to alive. The truth might lie in the letter written in Sharar's handwriting.

He clenched his eyes shut to decide. If he threw himself off the cliff here, he'd never know if she could be saved. He'd be abandoning her once again. This feeling was wrong: they'd won. Xia might be devastated, but victory had come. Why didn't it feel like it?

With a shout, he turned away from the edge, gripping his hair in agony. He wasn't finished yet.

With nowhere left to hide—alone once again—he started his

trek up to the Royal City to bury the princess and finish what he'd started on Xia.

⚜

During the days' long journey back to somewhere safe, Tzarik become lost in his weakened state. Then he happened upon a lion-shaped wayfinder. Remembering the first hunt, he followed them for half a day and came upon the old temple where Jin and Yui used to meet. The dark old rafters echoed with emptiness. The wet wood smelled with mold and death. Taking a chance, he wandered inside and cast about lazily for the spirit. He'd never followed up, too quickly taken in with Xia's plight and too eager to get ahead of Sybal's rash behavior.

His cold fingers clasped around atan. Holding it in his shaking palm, he drew it slowly, walking a wide circle around the temple to search for lingering spirits. Nothing appeared. She was gone.

⚜

Tzarik tried to avoid travelers and villages. When he realized how many extra hours of travel that started to load on, he resigned himself to the main roads. Xians stopped to watch him pass and a few whispered prayers and thanks as if they knew who he was. Mass graves burned every few miles, sending columns of black smoke up into the air. Tzarik had stood next to the first one he'd came across for warmth before realizing what the pile of cinders was.

When he reached the boundaries of the Royal City, a thick wall of warriors and a pale makeshift wall around the muddy battlefield stopped him. Fortunately, Kei Lu was patrolling when Tzarik arrived.

"They are waiting for you," the chieftain said as they passed each other in the rickety gate. "TaoShin said you would return. Our Hiro was not certain. He thought the continent would be swallowed up by beasts come tonight."

"I'm glad for his confidence in me," Tzarik mumbled. "Where are you off to now?"

Kei Lu adjusted his fur-lined cloak and scanned the horizon before him. "Wu-Tang. My home has been the hub of refugees and those hiding from the war. I don't know if they have been attacked or not as I've been confined to the highlands. This war may have been short, Runer, but it was swift in its execution. Many of our provinces may not even know why Wushito attacked the Di-Huan. They do not know who to look to in a crisis now. There is much healing to come for Xia. And I fear if we do not continue to act as swiftly, there may be more unrest. Perhaps even more battles."

Never one for politics or the finer details of how a country ran, Tzarik took the wild man's word for it.

"This just confirms my hate for how the few who rule an entire people can send them into destruction and turmoil," he said.

Kei Lu's face broke into a hideous smile. "I agree. Let us govern our own lives. Run wild in the streets. Perhaps we in Wu-tang will secede from the monarchy."

Tzarik snapped his head around to look at the warrior.

"Ha! The look on your face," Kei Lu crowed. "Even you want order for now, Runer. I may be of House Xiaoh, but I love my country. I will not tear it asunder. Yet. Not while a dragon-touched sits on the throne." He kicked his horse, raising his long spear as he and a handful of his fur-clad wild men road down the southern road. "House Xiaoh has risen again!"

Once inside the palace, a servant showed Tzarik where Hiro, TaoShin, and some of the commanders stood around the maps in the war room. They all stood with slumped shoulders, dark circles around their eyes. Most still wore armor caked with blood and mud. Not one of them had slept since he'd left, or even removed their boots.

With a monkeylike gasp, TaoShin leapt over the table and galloped to Tzarik. Throwing his arms around him, he embraced him tightly. The Masahk's furry body emanated warmth and comfort.

"I told you he'd come back!" TaoShin exclaimed to the others.

"What happened?" Hiro asked, almost begging. The young prince's tone could not hide his desperation. "Are we safe?"

"For now," Tzarik said quickly to dispel his immediate fear. "They quarreled—fought. ShanBao did not open all the seals of the crypt. I don't even know where it is. I felt one sigil break, but Sharar was driven off. ShanBao is dead. So are his generals. I didn't find the crypt."

TaoShin drew a holy circle over his heart and whispered a quick prayer.

"It worked just as you said," Hiro mused, collapsing forward onto the table, bracing himself with his arms locked. Tears of relief filled his eyes.

"I met Kei Lu on his way out," Tzarik went on. "He said Xia has a lot of healing to do, and I must agree. You must send out messengers to the provinces, tell them the fight is over."

"Tell them what Wushito did!" Commander Zhen cut in, slamming his fist onto the table.

"Tell them what ShanBao did," Tzarik corrected. "Don't incriminate the entire creed. There were some—even if they chose their ideology over their country—who wanted to do what they thought was right. Which brings up a more pressing matter."

"The crypt," TaoShin offered when Hiro shook his head in

confusion. "With Wushito weak and us not understanding their secret ways, everything they hid away could break loose."

Hiro's eyes went wide and his back bent under the weight of understanding. "What have we even won?" he said, running his hands through his long, frazzled braid.

"You've saved Xia," Tzarik assured him. "ShanBao had no love for the country or the people. He wanted to destroy it completely."

"But the crypt?" Hiro asked.

"The monks can pray against it," TaoShin offered. "We have kept our northern shores safe for centuries with our own faith magic."

"Will that be enough?" Hiro asked.

The monk ran his long fingers over his jade beads. "We have our magic. Our prayers are not just wishes, you know. And the sigils are not broken. It may not...leak?" he finished, not sure if he'd chosen the right word.

Tzarik admired the monk's ever-increasing courage. He'd severely underestimated the religious faiths of sentient kind.

"But Wushito was a fraud!" Hiro cried.

"No," Tzarik said. "They lied, but they kept Xia safe for its entire existence."

TaoShin interjected, "And the balance. Wushito and the Di-Huan must work together. It is the way. They exist to carry out what the Di-Huan cannot. Master ShanBao used the warriors wrongly."

Hiro, almost collapsing in on himself, asked, "So what do we do?"

"Find a leader," Tzarik offered. "You have many Wushito imprisoned. Find one who will return the creed to their rightful duties."

"Part of those duties is keeping Runers in check," Commander

Zhen reminded Tzarik. "Rogue Runers, especially. It is part of their oath."

Tzarik nodded. "I understand. I won't be here much longer. And as far as I can see, Wushito is on hold, so I have nothing to fear."

For once Hiro smiled weakly. The exhaustion shown dark against his face. "Perhaps we should allow the runic oath."

At this, every Xian in the room jumped. Many hissed to their neighbor in Xian, glaring in concern.

"I cannot recommend it," Tzarik offered to quell the disruption. "Xia is the one continent without Runers, and it should stay that way. More countries will follow your lead. Already Al'Myrah lacks a sufficient monster population. And Runers are despised for their crimes. They lean into the ones they can commit, tormenting the cities they inhabit. And most are horrible men anyway."

Hiro asked, "If monsters are becoming rare, that just means you've done your job."

Tzarik nodded weakly. "We die if we don't hunt. By ridding the world of these creatures, we kill ourselves. It's just a prolonged death sentence."

"What a way to live," TaoShin breathed sadly. "The season of the Runers will end someday and those left behind will suffer. Or the cruelty of sentient kind will create more monsters."

Half-heartedly nodding, Tzarik said, "Our existence relies on the evils of sentient kind."

Silence charged with the gentle singing of the night bugs drifted from one end of the war room to the next. Tzarik shifted uneasily, knowing everyone present was imagining his sad, miserable life. It became almost unbearable before Zhen finally broke the silence.

"But what are we to do?"

Hiro straightened up. "As we said. We will find a Wushito

warrior we can trust or keep under surveillance. Until then, the monks will be our best defense. I will raise Yoshitsune until he can take the throne. I will gather trustworthy advisors to help me rule until then."

TaoShin nodded in agreement. "We have lived in fear of Wushito for so long. This will take some getting used to."

"But we won," Hiro said, sighing. "We made it."

CHAPTER 34
ELDRITCH HUNT

OVERCOME WITH EXHAUSTION, TZARIK TOOK AN OFFERED room off the palace gardens to rest and recuperate. He anticipated setting out the next day, but something overcame his will. The night after he returned from the Hallow City, Hiro gave him his own servant to draw a bath and see to his every need. Once he submerged himself in the hot water, milky with salts, oils, and other soothing remedies, he couldn't make himself move. Despite the heat, he shivered. A desire to scream into the night almost destroyed him with the effort it took to keep his emotions in check. Even with no one to witness his weakness, he forced himself to remain quiet.

At night, he moved the flat mattress to an open part of the roof to look up at the stars, finally visible in the clear sky. The moons and constellations shone clearer now that the winter approached. In the silence, the thoughts and images in his head bellowed in hellish oration. His mind ran scenarios of what could be happening to Sybal right now. Doubt at her being alive resurfaced. Desperation to speak to someone almost drove him to sit up and seek out any ear willing to listen to his weeping and raving. The longer he let this mood ferment, the heavier it pressed on him.

The sun came up over the mountains before he could quiet his mind enough to sleep, so he lay all day in the palace room, hoping for unconsciousness. He tried to calm his mind by sitting near the flowing streams amidst the royal gardens. He even watched lines of refugees returning from the lowlands and others leaving in the opposite direction. Xia moved around him, trying to return to some semblance of normalcy. That night, after sitting all day on one stone bench in the garden, he caught a line of lanterns rising up from some mysterious location. Hundreds filled the sky, lighting up the garden. Finally, he stood up, curious what the display signaled.

"Yui has been laid to rest," TaoShin's soft voice said from behind Tzarik.

He didn't turn to watch the monk approach. The Masahk carried a few things with him and began setting them up: some lanterns, a few plates of incense, and a box.

TaoShin laid the items out around the bench, almost like a protective circle, before he sat next to Tzarik. He crossed his legs, drew a holy circle around his heart, pressed his palms together in prayer, then picked up the box. When he opened it, a spicy, savory-sweet aroma wafted out. Steam rose from a pile of rice topped with a variety of cooked vegetables, fruit, and some kind of dark red sauce. TaoShin picked up a pair of sticks and pushed the contents around before handing it to Tzarik.

"Don't brood at me," the monk warned him. "Take the damn food and eat."

The curse was enough to make Tzarik realize the monk meant it. Taking the box of fresh, hot food, he held it loosely in his hand, laying it against his thighs. Despondently, he took the sticks. He didn't eat. He'd never mastered the infuriating utensils.

Without a condescending sigh, TaoShin gently took Tzarik's hand in his and positioned the sticks. "The bottom one does not move. A steady base. Use these fingers to operate the top. Yes!" he cried jovially when Tzarik managed it on the first try.

To his surprise, the monk's praise lifted a tiny bit of the blackness in him. Using the sticks, he picked up a chunk of red meat, scooped some rice on it, and popped it into his mouth. Realizing he hadn't eaten in days, he chewed quickly and swallowed.

"Now that the storm has ceased, the war is over, and Hiro is in command, I want to leave Xia," he said before daring to try the sticks again.

"Why are you sitting alone?" TaoShin asked, ignoring the Runer's cold tone.

Tzarik didn't look at him. "I like to be alone."

"You shouldn't."

He dropped the sticks into the box. "Did you come here to chastise me?" His voice cracked.

"Absolutely not, Tzarik." His tail flicked behind them. "I know you are wounded right now. I just came to sit beside you. When one is this far from home, company is often agreeable."

"I've been this far before."

"But never this alone and this far."

Tzarik offered the monk a skeptical look. "Yes, I have. My mentor brought me here once. Then I got lost."

"That's different." TaoShin arched down and produced a teapot from nowhere, pouring a clay cup full before sipping it. "Before, you didn't know what it was like to have someone like Sybal so close to you. It's worse when something is taken that you didn't have before."

A lump rose in Tzarik's throat so hard he couldn't choke past it. What did TaoShin want him to say? Why torture him with these revelations?

"I don't want to hurt you," the monk said softly. "I want you to know that feelings are normal. And that you are strong enough to do something about them."

He couldn't eat now. His gut rolled over. Guilt at not leaving right away to find Sybal filled him. He set the box aside and pulled out the letter.

"Some monks intercepted this," he said dryly. "They seemed to know me and you. They gave this to me. I recognized Sharar's handwriting."

"Oh!" TaoShin breathed. "What does it say?"

Now embarrassment burned his face. The maelstrom of emotions fighting for dominance inside him made him look for a seaglass bottle of the rice wine to drink until everything went numb.

"I can't read," he mumbled.

"Hardly an issue," TaoShin said kindly. He held out his monkey paw. "May I? If you trust me, that is."

"Please." Tzarik handed over the letter and looked away to hide his shame. He expected the monk to tell him not to worry, lots of people couldn't read. He could justify his position: he'd been sold into slavery as a child, his father hadn't been able to read and had hardly known a trade. He had valid excuses—he just couldn't use them.

While TaoShin unrolled it, he explained, "The monks tried to intercept communication when the first battles started."

"Won't being a rogue monk bar you from your afterlife?" Tzarik asked.

"Ah." TaoShin sighed dismissively, squinting at the letter. He reached into his belt and took out a round pair of spectacles, placing them on his flat nose. Tapping them, he smiled. "Al'Myrahn make, you know? Wonderful continent. Makes glass like no other. And no, we will not be barred from Tiang, Runer. The guardians of the afterlife know a good man when they see one."

"These guardians wouldn't happen to be horned, have cloven hooves, and walk on clouds over grass, would they?"

TaoShin looked up over his spectacles. "Why, yes, they would, Runer." His eyes danced over Tzarik, making him squirm uncomfortably.

"Hmm." He smiled and went back to the letter, reading quickly. "Tzarik, she's not dead," he said. In an undertone, he added, "Masahk venom."

"Yes, from that whore Wu-Zhiang. They said she wasn't dead... I just didn't believe them." His heart flipped in his chest.

The monk nodded, almost smiling. "He sent her to Singad! Do you know what this means?" He gripped the front of Tzarik's black tunic.

"Singad?" he asked, his pulse quickening. "Home." But his joy quickly vanished. "How? How did he get her off this continent? We heard the maelstroms kept all ships landlocked."

The monk looked up over his spectacles. "I imagine he has his ways. If he's as powerful as you say. But There's more here." The monk's eyes flicked back over the parchment. "This contact in Singad has informed Sharar that his, and I quote, 'original mark' has appeared." He read more rapidly. "She's missing."

"Original mark?" Tzarik repeated.

"Yes, your scholar writes, 'In your last correspondence, you said the original mark appeared. I find it intriguing that you didn't see it necessary to mention that to me until the Runer went missing.' "

Tzarik at first thought nothing of this. What kinds of marks could Sharar have? It didn't matter. What mattered was that Sybal had gone missing. Someone had taken her. This lit a fire under him that scorched his fervor. He had to leave now, go to Singad and find clues as to who would want to take a—as far as they knew, dead body—of a Runer. It made no sense why someone might take a crate the size of a human coffin. Then it hit him.

"His first mark?" he asked, finally facing the monk. "Does it give a name?"

TaoShin shook his head. "He writes as if it's a monster to hunt."

Understanding dawned. Tzarik stood up. "It was. Tarkan."

"I am pleased at your discovery," TaoShin mused. "A friend of yours?"

"No. Yes." Tzarik paced but kept inside the circle of lanterns TaoShin had set up. "I don't know. A necromancer."

At this, TaoShin gasped and sat up straight. "*Xai'long*," he cursed. "You know a necromancer?"

Tzarik shrugged. "Runers know some unpleasant folk."

"Yes, but a necromancer." For the first time, the monk's face pursed in concern. "I didn't know they were so...in the public eye. A cult of what is assumed to be necromancers has grown on Alika and found its way into one of the pharaoh's inner circles. I hear from my fellow spiritual leaders that it has caused something of a stir among the pharaohs, to say the least."

"I can't speak for them," Tzarik confessed. "But Tarkan is different from his tribesmen. He's alone, except for his ward."

"An apprentice?" TaoShin gasped again, clutching at his heart. "And on Al'Myrah? The last lich king resided on Porsh. How do you know he's not seeking the title for himself?"

"I don't. He killed the lich king."

TaoShin closed his eyes, mumbled prayers in Xian, and circled his heart again. "What does your scholar want with such a creature?"

Tzarik's hackles rose at this. Yes, he'd called himself a monster, but even Tarkan cared for Zeva. He wasn't a monster. "Runers and necromancers are not creatures. He must have taken Sybal. I don't know how he found her. Perhaps he can save her..."

"Bring her back?" TaoShin asked, swallowing hard.

"You said yourself, she's not dead." The memory of their first week on the continent came back. She'd been poisoned then. This had to be the same thing. It had been Wushito then, it was Wushito now. "There was a draft ShanBao had," he said suddenly. "He said it would keep her alive."

TaoShin looked up sadly. "No doubt one of the mysteries of Wushito. I am sorry, Runer, but I do not know what it would have been."

"An antidote to Masahk venom," he offered, hopeful.

At this, the monk's lips parted and his eyes narrowed. "There is no antidote. One of the so-called gifts of the immortals. A way out."

Tzarik shook his head. "No, there was. He had it!"

"I'm so sorry, Tzarik." The Masahk's ears drooped. "I do not know of one. As we said, Xia knew very little of the Wushito and their ways. It is forbidden to speak of them to those outside the creed. It's part of the balance. We had to have faith. I do not know what ShanBao may have given your Sybal to slow the venom."

How could a people look up to a creed so old and powerful as the Wushito and not know anything about them? Tzarik roared, punching the air. "Fine. But you said she's not dead."

The monk nodded, scanning the letter again, brows raised. "She might be *now*. Masahk venom is no light matter. Kills red bloods quickly. I can't imagine she's lasted this long if she'd been bitten by Wu-Zhiang."

Looking for something to smash, Tzarik growled. "Don't hurt my hope, monk."

"I'm being serious, Runer." TaoShin grabbed Tzarik's arm, stopping his mad pacing. "If she is gone and you bring her back, she won't be your Sybal. Even a lich king cannot bring a blighted soul back from the afterlife."

He'd seen Tarkan's work. Yes, the undead were mindless

monsters. But Tarkan had his entire family's legacy and knowledge at his fingertips. He didn't know what a lich king might know, but Ishmael might have left a clue to his knowledge somewhere.

"I see what you're thinking, Runer, and I don't like it," TaoShin whispered.

"I wouldn't know where to start. I'd have to find Tarkan. And someone familiar with Runers' blood."

The monk pulled Tzarik back onto the bench and faced him, cross-legged still. "I see I cannot stop you. Your courage is unquenchable, Tzarik. So, I will advise you as I cannot let you leap into this darkness with ignorance."

Not even hurt by the monk's apt proposal, Tzarik gathered himself and looked TaoShin in the eyes.

TaoShin steeled himself. "There are Runers aplenty on Caerwren," he began. "The continent is dark, barbarous. The veil between our world and the other life is thin there. This is why there are so many Runers: while they do give runing as a punishment, it is a lawless and savage land, rife with spirits, ghouls, and monsters. The gods walk among the people."

Never one to believe in a god, Tzarik narrowed his eyes at this claim.

TaoShin nodded. "Giant beings, horned gods with a thirst for the blood of their people, nephilim. The magic permeating the crystalline mountains has made it the site for many rituals and damned pilgrimages. There is a ritual they believe in called the Eldritch Hunt."

A dark, ice cold shiver ran down Tzarik's spine. A memory of a black liturgy tried to crack through the barriers he hid it behind. The monk saw the change in his face.

"You know what this is?"

Tzarik shook his head. "Heard of it. My mentor, Azar, tried something akin to it on Bahratt."

"Did it work?"

The Runer shrugged his shaking shoulder. "He died."

Sensing the unpleasant memories, TaoShin didn't press the matter. "It is said that those who complete the Eldritch Hunt can bring back a stolen soul. I fear—combined with the knowledge of a continent of Runers and your necrotic friend—you may be able to bring her back if she is gone."

"But?" Tzarik asked.

The monk nodded. "There is a terrible price to pay, if you even survive the Hunt. And if you survive Caerwren. It will not be unlike going willingly into hell."

Finally feeling like he had somewhere to start, Tzarik devoured the still hot food. Glaring at the monk in the lantern light, he growled, "I'd have my skin flayed off my living body, exposing every muscle and nerve, and walk the fiery depths of hell a million times over if it meant saving Sybal."

ᠼᠠᠷ

LASHING his and Sybal's Al'Myrahn horses to his new Akhelatek steed, Tzarik prepared for the journey down the continent to the docks between Wu-Tang and Hikomi. He made sure their weapons were fastened down well and covered with his threadbare black cloak. Beside them hung the three sigiled blades of the Wushito masters. He glared at them for just a moment before covering them back up. Inside his saddlebag, a bundle of salted fish and dried vegetables from TaoShin squeezed in beside the other tools of his trade. Picking up the black box, he opened it. Inside waited the transfusion tools and a larger bottle sealed with wax. Half-full of glittering sulfates, it promised little should he take a large wound. He'd have to be careful. But on Caerwren, he would have the chance to hunt what he needed to make more.

"Why so few?"

Tzarik dropped the bottle back into the black box and snapped the lid closed. Hiro walked out from the golden arch of the palace and took the reins.

"What are you doing?" Tzarik asked, following, confused.

"Showing you to the boundaries," Hiro replied. "Why do you have so few sulfates left?"

Tossing his hood over his head and sinking into the safety of the cloak's shadows, Tzarik answered, "Not long ago, I sought death. Most Runers bleed out."

Hiro raised his head and waved his hand. Citizens bowed, foreheads to the ground, as they passed. A few didn't rise. "They wait for you, Runer," he said softly.

"Why?"

The prince smiled at Tzarik's ignorant honesty. "They know you had a hand in it. Stories of your valiance at the siege have flown from the highlands."

Biting down hard at the awkwardness, Tzarik mimicked Hiro's gesture and the remaining ones stood up, whispering prayers as he passed. One wore the blue robes of a Wushito. Tzarik stopped and faced the warrior. Hiro stiffened beside him.

Tzarik met the eyes of the warrior. Glaring, he let the blue flare in his eyes. The warrior didn't move. He didn't flinch. His face slackened in understanding, but no fear showed. Keeping his brown eyes locked onto Tzarik's, he folded his forearms over each other, before his chest, and slowly bowed from his hips. Tzarik tracked his motion with a glacial gaze. When he stood erect again, the Wushito nodded and turned on his heel to walk into the city square. As he passed a statue of the Dragon made of gold, a breeze blew across him, flaring the sky-blue robes.

"What was that?" Hiro asked.

Releasing the grip on the hilt of his scimitar, Tzarik realized he'd gripped it unknowingly. "He knows his place," he replied.

Hiro led Tzarik through the Royal City, past their shrines of fragrant incense, and over the bridge he'd shown him before when Sybal and Tzarik had caught him gambling in the street. Below, the water had risen from the storm and the lilies floated suspended underwater. Hiro stopped when they reached the highest point of the arching bridge.

"Dragon's wind be ever at your back, Tzarik," he said, handing the reins over to the Runer.

Catching the glint of melancholy in the prince's eye, Tzarik clasped his shoulder hard in his gloved hand. "I won't lie to you and say you have nothing to fear after this war. You will. Do as you know you should: rule this continent until Yoshitsune comes of age." He put his foot in the stirrup and hauled himself into the saddle.

"How will I know what to do?" Hiro blurted, hands out and palms empty at his sides.

Taken by surprise, Tzarik looked into the young man's pleading face. He was not one for advice. When it came to preserving himself, the blade and the runes were his way. Scared, desperate for guidance, Tzarik saw Sybal in Hiro's face. He knew what he'd say to her.

"Stick with those who prove their loyalty. Look for allies. Don't do this alone. You will make mistakes: forgive yourself, but remember the bastards who feign sovereignty. Above all: take heart, be strong. You have overcome evil."

Hiro's chest inflated with a calm breath and he stood tall. Reaching into his robes, he produced a round, jade piece hanging from a black cord. A long, eastern dragon coiled and entangled itself to make the pendant. He held it up to Tzarik, who took it gently. Around the pendant's edge danced Xian lettering.

"If you ever come back," Hiro said, "the country of the Dragon will welcome you. As long as you wear this off her shores, it will protect you."

Grateful, Tzarik slipped the talisman over his head and down his tunic with the runes. "Farewell, Hiro."

To Be Continued

Tzarik will return in *Season of the Runer Book III: Eldritch Hunt*

The Runes

Artiah: The rune of healing. Drawing artiah will mend minor abrasions and heal larger wounds enough to allow escape. Artiah will also take away a small amount of pain.

Atan: The rune of light. Drawing atan will create an orb of light for all eyes to see by. Atan also reveals hidden spirits and can show disguised monsters in their true form.

Buhkar: The rune of mist. When buhkar is drawn, the Runer dissolves into a black, smokey mist able to slip between tight spaces, evade a grip, and blend into shadows easily to be undetected.

Halat: The rune of protection. When halat is drawn, the caster is safe inside a circle of protection. Anything that wishes the caster harm cannot pass the boundaries of the protective circle.

Jiun: The fury rune. Jiun—the most dangerous of the runes—turns the Runer into a berserker. Cutting off all feeling to wounds and ailments, the rune pushes the caster beyond their inhibitions. Jiun also lends temporary strength and heightened senses.

THE FROZEN NATION

SHEZAI OCEAN

HIKOMI

SHIUKI

MUENGO
YAI

WU-TANG

XIA

SINGAD

ZE'OUL

THE CARAVAN
SEA

OCEAN SKY

GYPSU

ALIKA

MYSIR

LONG TILL

ZHIGO

LYBRIA

OCEANYA

Abi has been a gamer all her life, but is a teacher at heart. When she is not writing, you can find her slaying enemies online or hunting for the next bohemian adventure. She has published works of fiction, poetry, academia, and even won awards for her short stories in science fiction and horror.

Abi is also a proud mom of two...ferrets! She live streams on Twitch where you can enjoy her terrible gaming skills and join the live discussion. Recently, she founded her own micro-press: SummerStorm Press that specializes in supporting self-publishers and first-time authors. She currently resides in Kansas.

She is one of nine children--all who share the creative spark.

Find Abi online at: www.abigaillinhardt.com

Also by Abigail Linhardt

Season of the Runer Book I: The Trial of Two
Why They Killed: A Waksha Virus Novelette
Golmasiah: The Outerwinds
These Darker Streets (coming February 2022)

www.ingramcontent.com/pod-product-compliance
Lightning Source LLC
Chambersburg PA
CBHW030850030726
47495CB00005B/1467